www.connecti

THINK BIG

by

PAUL STUART

This edition first published in June 2020.

Paul Stuart asserts his right to be identified as the author of this work under the Copyright, Designs and Patents Act 1988.

This is entirely a work of fiction. The names, characters and incidents portrayed within it are the work of the author's imagination. Any resemblance to actual persons, living or dead, events or localities is purely coincidental.

ISBN: 978-1-71679-172-7

All rights reserved. This book is sold subject to the condition that it shall not be resold, lent, hired out or otherwise circulated without the express prior consent of the author and/or the publisher.

ALSO BY PAUL STUART

Connections 1 - Who Did You Sit Next to Today?
Connections 2 - Hell Has No Fury
Connections 3 - That's None of Your Business
Connections 4 - Which Room Did You Stay in?
Connections 5 - I Need a Word
Connections 6 - An Extraordinary Life
Connections 7 - Stones in My Jar
Connections 8 - The Gift of Time (Short Stories)

The Mobile and the Ring - The John Lomax Story
The Mobile and the Ring - The John Lomax Story (Hardcover)
Lomax and the Biker - The Complete Trilogy (Limited Edition Hardcover)
The Exmoor Trilogy – (Limited Edition Hardcover)

OTHER PROJECTS

The Treasurer's Challenge
Piran's Pantry
Vignettes, with Pauline Harris
Dunkin' Penguins

FOREWORD

Dedicated to my late wife, Jan, who remains in my heart always. It gets no easier, even with the passing of time.

With heartfelt thanks to my family and friends who have been pillars of support through thick and thin.

EMILY'S MOTIVATION

She had lost her way and a girl child rode upon her back.

"Take her away," she cried.

Through mirrors dark and blessed with cracks, she searched. She told herself to reach out, to touch, to find. She gazed at the shadow, her heart holding on as she told herself to stay free and seek.

"Go seek the one who will give and not take away."

On the edge of dawn, she stayed, naked with stillness. The night started to empty and her song began. She would take him in, make him happy, her swollen eyes were hard with echoes of laughter but the city's thighs hid the truth.

"What would it cost?" she asked, "to give a girl back her life? The girl who couldn't tremble because she came without a name, looking for meaning and something, somebody to hold her together."

Love caught these fragments, swirling through the winds of night and her journey began.

-1-

Boxall said, "but I don't understand. You remember that conversation we had right at the start when I told you about the case and the Visa card? Without that you would never have been involved."

Emily smiled a knowing smile. She knew that the conversation may have appeared fortunate to him, but she also knew it was nothing of the sort. She had known about the card before he had even introduced it to her.

She had been briefed by her father. Her initial entry interview had been a set up and, once inside, she needed an access point to the case and that was it. She was on her own from then on, of course, but her father had complete confidence that she could 'manage' the situation. That involved using the resources of the police to their advantage without them realizing it or having to be informed as to why. There are always more ways of getting what you need than the most immediately obvious. It had also helped her in the battle with her terrible affliction. She had come of age as part of the secret elite team dealing with national security and her career path was set. She was on the way to finding out just who were the stones in her jar. Would she also find love along the way? It would be a lovely bonus, she thought. And she certainly needed it.

Interview, October 2006

Beyond the window, she could see three kites hanging in the air over Boscawen Park. One blue, one yellow, one pink. Their shapes were precise, as though stenciled. From where she was she couldn't see the lines that tethered them, so when the kites moved, it was as though they were doing so of their own accord. An all-encompassing sunlight had swallowed depth and shadow.

Emily observed all this as she waited for DCI Matthews to finish rearranging the documents on his desk. He shuffled the last file from the stack before him to a chair in front of the window. The office was still messy, but at least they could see each other now.

"There," he said, and Emily smiled in response.

He held up a sheet of paper. The printed side was facing him, but against the light from the window she could see the shape of her name at the top. She smiled again, not because she felt like smiling, but because she couldn't think of anything sensible to say. This was an interview. Her interviewer had her CV. What did he want her to do? Applaud?

He put the CV down on the desk in the only empty patch available and started to read through it line by line, marking off each section with his forefinger as he made progress.

Education, 'A' levels. University. Interests. Referees.
His finger moved back to the centre of the page.
University.
"Philosophy."
She nodded.
"Why are we here? What's it all about? That sort of thing?"
"Not exactly. More like, what exists? What doesn't exist? How do we know whether it exists or not? Things like that?
"Useful for police work."
"Not really. I don't think it's useful for anything much, except maybe teaching us to think."
Matthews was a big man. Not gym big, but west country big, with the sort of comfortable muscularity that suggested a past involvement in farm work, rugby and beer. He had remarkably pale eyes and thick dark hair. Even his fingers had little dark hairs running all the way to the final joint. He was the opposite of Emily.
"Do you think you have a realistic idea of what police work involves?"
She shrugged. She didn't know. How was she meant to know if she hadn't done it? She said the sort of thing that she thought she was meant to say.
"I'm interested in law enforcement. I appreciate the value of a disciplined, methodical approach."

Blah, blah, blah. Good little girl in her dark grey interview outfit saying all the things she was meant to say.

"You don't think you might get bored?"

"Bored?" Emily laughed with relief. That was what he was probing at. "Maybe. I hope so. I quite like a little boredom." Then, worried he might feel she was being arrogant – prize-winning Cambridge philosopher sneers at stupid policeman – she backtracked. "I mean, I like things orderly. 'I's dotted, 't's crossed. If that involves some routine work, then fine. I like it."

His finger was still on the CV, but it had tracked up an inch or so. 'A' levels. He left his finger there, fixed those pale eyes on her and said, "Do you have any questions for me?"

Emily knew that was what he was meant to say at some stage, but they had forty-five minutes allocated for the interview and had only used ten at the outside, most of which she'd spent watching him shift stationery around his office. She was taken by surprise and gave the wrong answer.

"Questions? No." There was a short gap in which he registered surprise and Emily felt like an idiot. "I mean I want the job. I don't have any questions about that."

It was his turn to smile. A real one, not fake ones like Emily had been forcing out.

"You do. You really do."

He made that a statement not a question. For a DCI, he was not very good at asking questions. She nodded anyway.

"And you'd probably quite like it if I didn't ask you about a two-year gap in your CV, around the time of your 'A' levels."

Emily nodded, more slowly this time. Yes, she would quite like it if he didn't ask about that.

"Human Resources know what's going on there, do they?"

"Yes. I've already been into that with them. I was ill. Then I got better."

"Who in Human Resources?"

"Katie. Katie Andrews."

"And the illness?"

Emily shrugged, not for the first time that afternoon. "I'm fine now."

It was a non-answer. She hoped he didn't push it further, and he didn't. He checked who had interviewed her so far. The answer was, pretty much everyone. The session with Matthews was the final hurdle.

"Ok. Your father knows you're applying for this job?"

The question caught her by surprise. Surely, this man cannot know about her father, his position, his influence. What were the chances that Matthews knew who she really was and why she was there? She kept her response short.

"Yes."

"He must be pleased."

It was another statement in place of a question and she didn't give an answer. He examined her face intently. She thought it must be part of his interview technique. Maybe he didn't ask his suspects any questions, he just made statements and scrutinized their faces in the wide open light from the big west country sky.

"We're going to offer you a job, you know that?"

"You are?"

"Of course we are. Coppers aren't thick, but you've got more brains than anyone else in this building. You're fit. You don't have a record. You were ill for a time as a teenager, but you're fine now. You want to work for us. Why wouldn't we appoint you?"

She could think of a couple of answers to that, but she didn't volunteer them. She was suddenly aware of being intensely relieved, which scared her a little, because she wasn't aware of being anxious. She was standing up. Matthews had stood up and came towards her, shook her hand and said something. His big shoulders blocked her view of Boscawen Park and she lost sight of the kites. He was talking about formalities and she was blathering answers back at him, but her attention wasn't with any of that stuff. She was going to be a police-woman. And to think that just five years ago, she was dead.

May 2010

It was true, Emily liked routine work, but you can have too much of a good thing.

A copper with the Met in London had twenty-two unblemished years on the force but was forced to retire following an injury received in the line of duty. He took a job in the accounts department of a law firm and started nicking money. Didn't get caught. Nicked more. Didn't get caught. Went crazy and bought himself a golf club membership, two holidays, a conservatory, a share in a racehorse and much more along the way.

The law firm's accountant's were dopey but not actually brain dead. They came to the police with evidence of wrongdoing. An investigation ensued and a whole lot more evidence was found. Jon Johnston was arrested but denied everything at his interview. He then decided that it would be best if he just stopped talking, so that was what he did. He just sat there staring at the wall and looking ill. The recording picked up his asthmatic breathing as a thin nasal whine which sounded like a note of complaint between questions. He was charged on fifteen counts of theft, but in reality the figure was probably closer to fifty.

He was still luxuriating as a guest of her majesty, denying everything. It fell to Emily to prepare the case for court, which she recognized as her reward for stating at interview that she liked routine work. She knew that Johnston would change his plea at the last moment because he knew he was completely stuffed. She also knew it would make very little difference to the sentence he received, whether he pleaded guilty five minutes before court or weeks before that, but she had to go through every single detail of his bank accounts for the last six years, every single card payment, and identify each and every rogue transaction. She had to make sure that her paperwork was so precise that the most diligent and perceptive defence lawyer would not be able to pick trivial little holes in the case at court. She also knew she was wasting her time because it wouldn't get that far. He would plead guilty and the fruits of her labour would not be needed.

Her desk was covered with paper. At that moment she loathed all banks and card companies, every digit between zero and nine and every law firm in the land. If Johnston had been in front of her she would have force fed him her calculator, even though it was a rather large model.

"Having fun?"

She looked up. Danny Boxall, a detective sergeant, sandy-haired, thirty-two, a moderate case of freckles and a disposition so friendly and open that she sometimes found herself saying something obnoxious because too much of a good thing can be disconcerting.

"Sod off."

She didn't count that. It was just her version of friendly.

"Still working on Johnston?" He asked.

She looked up properly. "His correct title is bastard, thieving, wish-he'd go and drown himself Johnston."

Boxall nodded sagely, as though she had said something sensible. "I thought you had sophisticated views on moral responsibility," he said, holding up two mugs. Tea for him, peppermint tea for her. Sugar in his, none in hers.

Emily stood up. "I do, just not when I have to do this." She gestured at the desk, already hating it a bit less. They moved to a little seating area in the window. There were two chairs and a sofa, the sort you find in offices and airport lounges and nowhere else, with tubular chrome legs and stain-resistant grey upholstery. There was a lot of natural light there and a view of the park. Her bad mood was increasingly just for show.

"He'll plead guilty."

"I know that."

"Got to be done, though."

"Ah, yes, forgot it was State the Obvious Day. Sorry."

"I thought you might be interested in this," he said and passed her a clear plastic evidence bag that contained a Visa debit card. Lloyds Bank. Platinum Account. Expiry date last October. Name of Mr. Brendan T. Rattigan.

Card neither shinily new nor badly marked. It was a dead card.

"Rattigan. Brendan T."

The name meant nothing to her. Either her face said as much or she did. She sipped the tea, which was still too hot, rubbed her eyes and smiled an apology at Boxall for being a cow.

He wrinkled his face at her. Brendan Rattigan. Scrap-metal man, moved into steel. Mini-mills, whatever they are. Then shipping. Worth some ridiculous amount of money. A hundred million or something."

Emily nodded. She remembered now, but it wasn't his wealth that she remembered or cared about. Boxall was still talking. There was something in his voice that she hadn't yet identified.

"He died nine months ago. Light aircraft accident. No cause established. Co-pilot's body recovered, but his never was."

"But here's his card." She stretched out the clear plastic around the card, as though getting a clearer look at it would unlock its secrets.

"Here's his card all right."

"Which has not spent nine months in salt water."

"No."

"And you found it where exactly?" she asked.

Boxall's face hung for a moment. He was stuck between two alternatives. Part of him wanted to enjoy his little triumph over her, but the other part of him was sombre. A fifty-year-old head on younger shoulders, gazing inward at the dark.

The sombre part won.

"Not me, thank God. Devon and Cornwall police got a call. Anonymous caller. Female. Probably not elderly, but not too young either. She gave the address of a house here in Truro. Highertown. She said we needed to get over there. A couple of uniforms did just that. Locked door. Curtains over the windows. Neighbours either out or unhelpful. Uniforms went around the back. The back garden was" - he held his hands palm upward and she knew immediately what that meant – "rubble. Bin bags that the gulls had been at. Rubbish everywhere. Weeds. And shit. Human. The drains were blocked and you can imagine the rest. The uniforms had been hesitating about going inside, but they broke down a door. The house was worse than the garden."

There was another short pause. No theatre this time. Just the awful feeling that human beings have when they encounter horror. Emily nodded, to say that she knew what he felt, which wasn't true but was what he needed to hear.

"Two bodies. A woman, maybe twenties. Red-haired, dead. Evidence of Class-A drug use, but no cause of death established. Not yet. And a little girl. Cute. Five, maybe six. Thin as a rake and, this was the horrible bit, somebody had dropped a sink on her head. One of those big Belfast things. It didn't break, just crushed her. They hadn't even bothered to move it afterwards."

Boxall had emotion in his eyes, and his voice was crushed too, lying under that heavy stoneware sink in a house that reeked of death, even from the office.

Emily wasn't good at feelings at that stage of her life. Not then, anyway. Not the really ordinary human ones that arise from instinct like water bubbling up from a hillside spring, irrepressible and clear and as natural as singing. She could picture that house of death, because the last few years had taken her to some pretty bad places and she knew what they looked like, but she didn't have Boxall's reaction. She envied it but couldn't share it. But Boxall was in front of her, wanting something, so she reached for his forearm with her hand. He wasn't wearing a jacket and the exchange of warmth between his skin and hers was immediate. He breathed out through his mouth, noiselessly releasing something.

After a moment, he threw grateful eyes at her, pulled away and drained his tea. His face was still sombre, but he was one of those elastic sorts who would be fine. It might have been different if he had been one of the people finding the bodies.

Boxall indicated the Platinum card.

"In amongst it all, they found that," he managed.

Emily could imagine it. Dirty plates. Furniture too large for the room. Brown velour and old food stains. Clothes. Broken toys. A TV. Drug stuff: tobacco, needles, lighters. Plastic bags filled with useless things: car mats, clothes hangers, CD cases, nappies. She had been to those places. The poorer the house, the more the stuff. And somewhere amongst it, on a dresser under a pile of enforcement notices from utility companies, a single Platinum card. A single Platinum card and a little girl, a cute little girl, with her head smashed to nothing on the floor.

"I can imagine," she managed to say.

"Yeah," Boxall nodded, bringing himself back. He was a DS. This was his job. They were not in that house. They were in an office with low-energy ceiling lights and ergonomic desk chairs and high-output photocopiers and views out over Boscawen Park.

"Jackson's running the enquiry, but it's an all hands on deck affair," he said.

"And he wants my hand on his deck," Emily ventured.

"He does indeed," replied Boxall.

"This card, why was it there?" she asked.

"It's probably just some druggy card theft type thing, but we need to follow the lead. Any connections. I know it's a long shot," he said gloomily.

Emily was good at long shots. Always had been, but there was no need at that moment to let him know that. She wanted information from him. As much as possible to soak up, sponge-like, without giving anything herself. She also had the advantage of her background, the elite secret Anti-terrorist group run by her father and the resources it brought. Ray Quinn's legacy passed on to him and now available to her as she started her own trajectory.

Boxall began to tell her things about the investigation. It was being called Operation Lohan. Daily briefing at eight thirty sharp, and sharp meant sharp. Everyone was expected to show, even non-core team members like Emily. The press had a very brief statement, but all further details were kept quiet for the time being. Boxall told her all this and she only half heard him. It was called Lohan because there was an actress of that name, Lindsay Lohan, who was a red-head with drink and drug issues. Emily knew this because Boxall told her and he didn't think she'd have any idea otherwise. She was happy to allow him to believe in her ignorance. Being regarded as famous for her ignorance was not a bad persona to portray. It meant people explained things to her, things they would not otherwise have divulged.

"You got all that?" he asked.

She nodded in return, and he did the same, nodding and attempting a grin. Not a brilliant attempt, but more than passable, she thought. She took the card back to her desk, pulling the plastic bag tight around her finger and tracing the outline of the card with her thumb and forefinger of her free hand. Somebody had killed a young woman. Somebody had dropped a heavy sink onto a little girl's head. And the card, belonging to a dead billionaire, was there as it happened. Routine is fine. Secrets are better.

-4-

They assembled in the briefing room next morning, where sharp meant sharp. One side of the room was taken up with noticeboards in pale buff, which were already starting to swarm with names, roles, assignments, questions and lists. The bureaucracy of murder. The star of the show was a set of photos. Crime scene images, which were all about documentary accuracy not careful lighting. There was something about their bluntness that gave them an almost shocking truthfulness.

The woman lay on a mattress on the floor. She could have been sleeping or in some drug-induced coma. She didn't look happy or unhappy, peaceful or disturbed. She just looked like the dead look, or as anyone at all looks when they're sleeping.

The child was another matter. The top half of her was missing. The kitchen sink stretched right across the photo, out of focus on its upper edge, because the photographer had concentrated on the face, not the sink. Beneath it peeped the child's nose, mouth and chin. The force of the sink had ejected blood through her nose and sprayed it downwards, like some joke-shop trick gone wrong. Her mouth was stretched back. Emily imagined that the weight of the sink caused the skin or muscle to pull backwards. What she was looking at was simple mechanics, not an expression of feeling. Yet humans are humans and what looked like a smile was interpreted as a smile, even it was no such thing and this girl with the top of her head missing was smiling at her. Smiling out of death, at Emily.

The coffee-breathed speaker behind Emily was Jim Davis, a veteran who'd spent most of his service in uniform and was now a sturdily reliable Detective Sergeant.

"Yes, poor little girl."

The room was full now. Fourteen in all, only three of whom were women. At that stage of the investigation briefings had an odd, jumpy energy. There was anger and grittiness mixed with a kind of remorseless male heartiness. Everywhere people wanted to 'do something."

At eight twenty-eight DCI Dennis Jackson motored out of his office, jacket already removed and sleeves already rolled up. A DI Hughes, whom Emily didn't know very well, followed him, looking important.

Jackson stood at the front and the room fell silent. Emily was standing by the photo wall and felt the presence of that little girl on the side of her face as intensely as if it were a real person. More intensely, possibly.

The case was less than twenty-four hours old, but routine enquiries had already thrown up a good pile of facts and suppositions. Jackson went through them all, speaking without notes. He was possessed of the same jumpy energy that filled the room, snapping off his phrases and throwing them out at the assembled throng. Iron pellets of information.

"No one on the electoral roll registered at that address. Social Services appear to know the woman and child, however. Final identification is hoped for later in the day, but the woman is almost certain to turn out to be Jenna Mancini. Her daughter is April. Assuming those identifications are confirmed, then the backstory is this. Mancini was twenty-six at the time of death. The child was just six. Mancini's home background was lousy. Given up for adoption. Taken into care. A few foster families, some of which worked better than others. Started at adult education college. Not bright, but trying to do her best.

Drugs, pregnancy. The child moving in and out of care, according to whether Mancini or her demons were on top at the time. Social Services pretty sure that Mancini was chaotic but not a lunatic. Not a sink-dropper, anyway."

He gave a grin that was more of a grimace.

"The last contact with Social Services was six weeks ago. Mancini had apparently been drug free. Her flat – not the one where she was found, but one of the nicer areas around here – was reasonably clean and tidy. The child was properly dressed and fed, and was attending school. So, last contact, no problems. The next time Social Services come around to visit, Mancini is a no-show. Maybe at her mum's.

Maybe somewhere else. Social Services are concerned but not hitting the alarm buttons."

He paused to look at his audience, making sure they were listening properly.

"The house where they're found is a squat, obviously. No record of Mancini having any previous connection with it. We've got a statement from the neighbour on one side. Nothing helpful." He stabbed at the noticeboards. "It's all there on Watch. Look at it. If you're not up to speed already, then you should be." Watch was their project management and document sharing system. It worked well, but the noticeboards fluttering with paper made it feel like an authentic incident room.

Emily had noticed the constant fluctuation between past and present tense, but dismissed it as less important than the subject, even though it grated on her sense of order. She recalled her 'I's dotted and t's crossed' comment at her interview. Another time perhaps.

Jackson stood back to let Hughes rattle on through other known facts. The evidence from utility bills, police records, phone use. He mentioned Rattigan's debit card, without making a big thing of it. Then he finished and Jackson took over.

"Initial post mortem findings later today, maybe, but we won't have anything definitive for a while. I suggest, however, we proceed on the assumption that the girl was killed by a kitchen sink." Emily recognized his first attempt at humour, if you could call it that. "The mother, OD, possibly. Asphyxiation? Heart attack? Don't yet know.

Focus of the investigation at this stage is, continue to gather all possible information about the victims. Past. Background. Known associates. Query drug dealing. Query prostitution. House to house enquiries. I want to know about anyone who entered that house. I want to know about anyone Mancini met, saw, talked to, anything in those six weeks since Social Services last saw her. Key question: why did Mancini move to that squat? She was drug-free, looking after her kid, doing well. Why did she throw all that away? What made her move?

"Individual assignments here" – meaning the noticeboards – "and on Watch. Any questions to me. If you can't get hold of me, then to Ken. If you uncover anything important or anything that might be important, let me know straight away, no excuses."

He nodded, checking he hadn't left anything out. He hadn't. Briefings like that, early on in any serious crime investigation, are partly theatre. Any group of policemen will always treat murder as the most serious thing they ever have to deal with, but team dynamics demand a ritual. The Haka of the All Blacks. Celtic Woad. Battle music. Jackson put his weary but determined look to one side and put on his grim and resolute one instead. Emily mentally added terrorism to murder, but only she knew at that stage of any possible link.

"We don't know yet if Jenna Mancini's death was murder, but we're treating it that way for now. But the girl. She was six years old. Six. Just started at school. Friends. At their flat, the one she left six weeks ago, there were paintings of hers hanging up on the fridge. Clean clothes hanging in her bedroom. Then this." He pointed to the photo of her on the noticeboard, but none of them looked at it because it was already inside their heads. Where they really didn't want it to rest for long. Around the room the men were clamping their jaws and looking tough. DC Rowland, Bev Rowland, a good friend of Emily's, was crying openly.

"Six years old, then this. April Mancini. We're going to find the man who dropped that sink, and we're going to send him to jail for the rest of his life. That's our job. What we're here to do. Now let's get on with it."

He started to move away, but then turned around and added an afterthought. "Remember, although we need to examine in minute detail, we must also look more widely. Let your imagination run. Think big."

Emily was way ahead of him.

The meeting broke up. Chatter. A charge for the coffee machine. Too much noise. Emily grabbed Bev.

"Are you all right?"

Yes, I'm fine really. I knew today wasn't going to be a mascara kind of day."

Emily laughed. "What have they got you doing?"

"Door to door mostly. The woman's touch. How about you?"

There was a funny kind of assumption in her answer and her question. The assumption was that Emily didn't quite count as a woman and therefore didn't get the jobs that female officers were usually assigned. Emily didn't resent that assumption. Bev was the sort to cry when Jackson put on his gravel voiced tear jerker finale. Emily wasn't. Bev was the sort of comfortable soul that people happily open up to over a cup of tea. Emily wasn't. She could do the door to door stuff. Bev was a natural and they both knew Emily wasn't.

"I'm mostly on the Jon Johnston case. Bank statements and all that. In my spare time, if I stay sane, I'm meant to track down that debit card thing. Rattigan's card. Funny place for it to show up," Emily said.

"Stolen?" asked Bev.

Emily shook her head. She had called the bank manager after talking with Boxall and, once she'd managed to clamber through all the bureaucracy to someone who actually had the information, got the answers fairly easily.

"No. The card was reported lost. It was duly cancelled and a replacement issued. Life goes on. It could literally be just that. He dropped it. Mancini or whoever picked it up. Kept it as a souvenir." Emily replied.

Brendan Rattigan's Platinum card? I would've done."

"You wouldn't. You'd have handed it in."

"Well, I know, but if I wasn't the handing in type?"

Emily laughed at her. Trying to use the inner workings of Bev Rowland's mind as a model for guessing at the inner workings of Jenna Mancini's mind didn't feel to her like an obvious recipe for success. Bev made a face at her for laughing, but wanted to rush off to the Ladies' so she could sort out her face before hitting the road. Emily told her to have a good day.

As Bev left, Emily realised that what she'd said to her wasn't true. Jenna Mancini couldn't have picked up Rattigan's debit card from the pavement. It wasn't possible. Mancini and Rattigan didn't walk the same streets, didn't go to the same pubs, didn't inhabit the same worlds. The places where Rattigan might have dropped his card were all places that would, explicitly or otherwise, have forbidden Mancini entry.

As soon as that thought occurred to her, Emily understood its implication. The two of them knew each other. Not casually. Not by chance. But meaningfully, in some real way. If Emily were to place a bet at that moment she'd have pointed at the millionaire killing the drug addict. Not directly she assumed, as it's hard to kill someone when you're dead yourself, but indirect killing is still killing.

"I'm going to get you," she said out loud. A secretary looked at her, startled, as she walked by. "Not you," Emily said.

The secretary gave her a little smile. The sort that you offer park bench drunks arguing over cider, or odd people muttering swearwords in the street. Emily didn't mind. She was used to that kind of smile now. Water. Duck's back. Paddle on.

Emily headed back upstairs.

Her desk stared balefully at her, flaunting its cargo of numbers and sheets of paper. She headed for the little kitchen to make herself a peppermint tea. Only herself and one of the secretary's liked it. Back to her desk. Another sunny day. Big windows full of air and sunshine. She lowered her face over the mug of tea and let her face warm up in the perfumed steam. There were a thousand boring things to do and one interesting one. She reached for the phone at the same time as pulling her face away from its steam bath. It took a couple of calls to get Catherine Rattigan's number – widows of the super-rich are inevitably ex-directory – but she got it anyway and made the call.

A woman's voice answered, giving the name of the house. She sounded every inch the servant, the expensive sort, titanium plated.

"Hello. May I speak with Mrs. Rattigan please?" Emily gave her name and rank as well. Mention of the police caused a moment's hesitation, as it always does. Then the training kicked in.

"May I asked what it is regarding?"

"It's a police matter. I'd rather speak to Mrs. Rattigan directly."

"She isn't available right now. Perhaps if I could let her know the issue..."

Emily didn't really need to see Rattigan's widow in person. Talking to her on the phone would be just fine, but she didn't respond to titanium plated obstructiveness. It made her come over all police force like.

"That's quite all right. Will she available for an interview later on today?"

"Look, if you could just let me know the matter at hand..."

"I'm calling in connection with a murder inquiry. A routine matter, but it needs to be dealt with. If it's not convenient for me to come to the house, then perhaps we could arrange for Mrs. Rattigan to come down to the station and we can talk to her here."

Emily enjoyed these little power struggles, stupid as they were. She liked them because she won...always. Within two minutes Titanium Voice had given her an eleven – thirty appointment and directions to the house. Emily put the phone down and laughed at herself. The return journey would take her an hour and a half, and what could have been a three-minute phone call would end up wasting half her morning.

She spent the next hour and a bit working through Johnston's hateful bank statements, lost track of time and found herself bolting downstairs for her car. It was a two seat, soft top, sports car and she loved it. Totally inappropriate for her lowly position, but she reasoned it was her one and only indulgence. Besides, her elite secret team had cars paid for them, sponsored by the government. She didn't see why anybody should question it and didn't much care. It could be explained easily enough if push came to shove.

She threw her bag onto the passenger seat and nosed out of the car park, mentally checking that she'd remembered her notebook, pen, purse, phone, dark glasses, make-up, evidence bag, etc. Cornish holiday traffic, Radio Cornwall inside the car, pneumatic drills ripping up the main road. Normal holiday time planning, Emily thought. Carpet stores and discount places strung along the outward corridor, along with unnecessary numbers of traffic lights.

Emily got herself lost in the narrow lanes because she tried to use short cuts to avoid the traffic and roadworks. She was twenty minutes or so late when she managed to find the entrance to the house. Big pillars and fierce yew topiary. Posh and out of place.

Emily made the turn and, sunglasses on, sped up the drive in a stupid attempt to minimize her lateness. A late twist in the way caught her out and she emerged into the large graveled parking area in front of the house doing about thirty miles an hour. Under ten would have been more appropriate. She braked hard and was treated to a long, curving slide, sending a wide spray of ochre dust hanging in the air to mark her arrival. Quite an entrance.

She gave herself a few seconds to clear her head, concentrating on controlling her breathing until she began to settle. Her heart was beating too fast, but at least she could feel it. She wondered why that should matter so much to her. It shouldn't, but it did. There shouldn't be such a thing as poverty and starvation but there is, and she worried about that too.

She pulled herself together, jumped out of the car and slammed the door. Might as well continue to make an impressive entrance. She didn't lock the door. A lesson she had already learned. On the front steps of the house there was a woman watching her performance. Emily presumed she was Miss Titanium and she did not look suitably impressed.

"Sorry I'm late. Traffic," Emily began, making no effort to apologise for her rally driving.

The house was a modest affair. Ten or twelve bedrooms. Immaculate grounds. A leylandii hedge screening what Emily presumed was a tennis court. Further away she spied a couple of cottages and what she guessed was a stable block or a gym complex. Or both. A river flowed over rocks at the end of a long sweep of lawn.

Titanium took Emily through the front door. Inside, everything was as she expected. The interior was designed so completely that any trace of human personality vanished along with the Victorian subfloors. Their heels clicked across the hall, past vases of fresh flowers and photos of racehorses, and into the kitchen. This was a huge room, an addition to the main body of the house. Handmade kitchen furniture stood still as stone and there was a range cooker in Wedgewood blue. She spied more flowers. The blinds allowed a perfectly measured amount of sunlight to enter and illuminate sofas.

"Miss Rattigan has been called away on something else, just temporarily. We were expecting you at eleven thirty." Titanium spoke with acidic triumph.

"Sorry. My fault, I'm happy to wait," said Emily with sincerity.

She was genuinely sorry and happy to wait. Mature of her, she thought, because she was a nice person. The trouble was that she was only being nice because she'd scared herself a few moments ago and couldn't take any hassle. For the time being, just sitting in the kitchen listening to her heartbeat was enough for her.

Titanium, who had given Emily her name along with a limp but elegant hand at the front of the house, was doing things with the kettle. Emily tried to remember the name but failed. For a moment she couldn't even remember why she was there. Titanium put coffee down in front of her, as though it was some art object the family had just invested in.

Emily couldn't think of anything to say, so said nothing. She blinked instead.

"I'll go and see if Mrs. Rattigan is ready for you."

Emily nodded as Titanium clicked out of the kitchen, through the hall, to somewhere else. She was calming slowly. She could hear a clock ticking somewhere. The range cooker emitted a kind of gentle rushing sound from its flue, like a stream heard a long way away. A few minutes passed, lovely empty minutes, then a woman came into the kitchen. Titanium was in position on her wing.

Emily stood up.

"Mrs. Rattigan, I'm sorry to have been late."

"Oh, don't worry."

The Internet had already told Emily that Mrs. Charlotte Frances Rattigan was forty-four. She had two children who were now teenagers. She was a former model. Her appearance seemed to confirm that. A pale grey shirt worn above pale linen trousers and sandals. Shoulder length blonde hair. Nice skin, not much make-up. Tall, maybe five foot ten, and then an inch or so more from her heels.

She was, of course, pretty, but it wasn't the prettiness that struck Emily. There was something ethereal about the woman, as though it wasn't just the house missing its subfloors. Emily was immediately interested. She asked Titanium if she would mind giving them a few minutes of privacy, and, on a look from her boss, she left.

She fixed Mrs. Rattigan with her firm professional quality smile.

"Thank you so much for agreeing to see me, madam. I've just got a few questions. A routine matter, but an important one."

"That's all right. I understand."

"I'm afraid that I shall have to ask you some questions about your late husband. I apologise in advance for any distress that may cause. It's all perfectly routine and.."

She interrupted. "That's all right. I understand."

Her voice was soft, a peach without a stone. Emily hesitated. Nothing whatsoever in the situation called for her to come over all hard-edged, but she couldn't quite resist and she could feel her voice harden.

"Did your husband know a woman called Jenna Mancini?"

"My husband...?" She tapered off and shrugged.

"Is that a no, or an I don't know?"

Another shrug. "I mean, not that I know of. Mancini? Jenna Mancini?"

"Do either of these addresses mean anything to you?"

Emily showed her notebook. The first address was where Mancini was found. The second was where she'd been living previously.

"No, sorry."

"The second address is near here. Were you ever aware of your husband having any business in the area? Visiting people?"

A headshake.

Quantum physics tells you that the act of observation alters reality. The same is true of police interviews. Mrs. Rattigan knew Emily was a detective assigned to a murder inquiry. There was some absence in her answers that teased her, but that could just have been an effect of her job function and her assignment. Titanium's cafetiere of coffee was steaming beside them. Mrs. Rattigan hadn't offered, so Emily took control.

"Would you like coffee? Shall I pour?"

"Oh, yes please. Sorry."

She poured one coffee, not two.

"Won't you have any?" asked Mrs. Rattigan. It was the first positive action of any kind since Emily met her, and it hardly rated high on the positivity scale.

"I don't drink caffeine," said Emily.

Mrs. Rattigan pulled the cup towards her, but didn't drink. "Good for you, I know I shouldn't."

"I have a few further questions to ask, madam. Please understand that we want the truth. If your husband did things in the past that he might not want us to have known about, well, that's all in the past now. It's no longer our concern." Emily tried to reassure her to the point of communication.

She nodded. Light hazel eyes, fair eyebrows. Emily realised she was wrong about the house. She was sure it had been interior-designed to within an inch of its life, but the designers caught something real about the person commissioning the work. Pale linen, light hazel, a stoneless peach. That was this house and its owner.

"Did your husband take drugs?"

The question jolted her. She shook her head, looking down and to the left. Her coffee cup was in her right hand. If she was right handed, then the down and to the left look suggested some element of construction in her answer.

"Cocaine, maybe? A few lines with business associates?"

She looked at Emily with relief. "You know, sometimes I didn't know what he got up to when he was away."

Emily reassured her. "No, I'm sure you didn't. But loads of business types do, of course. You didn't want it in the house, though, I can see that."

"You know, there are the children."

That sounded to Emily like the comment she made to him when he was still around. Oh, don't do that. It's not me. It's the children. I'm only thinking of you.

Emily fished out the debit card and showed it to her.

"This is your husband's, I presume?"

She looked at it and then looked at Emily. The nod was not a full one. Halfway there, Emily thought.

"The card was reported lost. Do you remember when or where he lost it?"

"No, sorry."

"Did he ever mention losing it?"

"I don't think so. I mean..." she shrugged.

When millionaires lose cards, they have people who sort it out. That's what the shrug meant to Emily.

"The card was found at a crime scene. Does that make sense to you?"

"No. No, I'm sorry."

"You're not aware how this card could have come into the possession of Jenna Mancini?"

"Sorry. I'm really not."

"Does the name April Mancini mean anything to you?"

"You are aware that the card was found in a poor part of town? Quite run-down. Rough. Can you think of a reason why your husband might have had business there?"

"No."

Emily had come to the end of her questions. They were the same as she would have asked by phone, but Emily was sharper than that. She noticed an absence in the air, teasing her with its scent. It wasn't that Mrs. Rattigan was lying to her, she felt. She knew she wasn't, but there was something there. She went for it; thinking big.

"Just a few more questions."

"Certainly."

"Your sex life with your husband. Was it completely normal?"

-5-

The traffic was slow as she drove back. She fiddled with the radio trying to find something she wanted to listen to, but she settled for silence. To her left were green fields and lambs. To her right, the intricate folds of old mine-works. Long, black tunnels, leading down into the dark. She preferred the lambs.

She couldn't quite face going straight back to the office, so she turned off and parked. To think. She relaxed as much as her thoughts would allow and she gave them freedom to roam; freedom to think big. She liked to work that way sometimes as it seemed to give her insight. She also preferred crimes she could see and victims she could touch.

She became aware of a familiar feeling and recognized it as the creepy feeling she got when she was close to the dead. Tingly.

She stepped out of the car and took in her surroundings. Cheap 1960s council houses that looked like they'd been made of cardboard. Same colour, same blocky construction. Same thin walls, same resistance to damp. There was nobody around apart from a boy repetitively slamming a ball against a windowless wall. He looked at Emily briefly, assessing her purpose, and then continued.

Number 46 still had a few ribbons of crime scene tape around, but the forensics teams had mostly finished their work by then.

She picked her way through the tape and rang the doorbell.

There was silence at first, but she soon heard footsteps. A stocky scenes of crime officer with pink ears and short mousy hair appeared at the door.

"I was just passing," Emily lied, "and thought I'd look in."

She showed him her card.

"Five minutes," he said, and shrugged his shoulders. "Five minutes. I'm just resampling fibres and then I'm done."

With that he went upstairs. Emily stepped into the living room where April and Jenna had died. Red curtains hung over the front window, which Emily thought an appropriate colour as they would undoubtedly have been there on the day of the killing. It was not red for love. By way of contrast, yellow halogen lamps of the of the type builders use had been strung up in the kitchen. Their glare was too strong to be real and Emily felt she was on a film set rather than in a house.

Some of the items that had been in the house had already been removed as evidence. Other items had been sifted, catalogued and then destroyed. Emily pondered on the dubious logic of that.

She walked around, not really doing anything, just trying to see if she felt anything by being there, but she didn't. That was not quite accurate, she realised, because she felt a dislike for the place with its red swirly carpet, its ugly sofa, the dirt marks on the wall and the smell of discount store and blocked drains. She felt strange and disconnected. She remembered the crime scene photos that were on display back at the station and recognized where the two corpses were lying when they were found. Where April was lying a pool of dried blood had caked into the carpet. She thought it looked more like a curry stain.

Emily bent down and felt the floor where April had drawn her last breath, and then moved around until she was in the spot where Jenna had died. She wanted to feel things, such as a sense of the dead. A lingering presence, maybe. She didn't. All she got was nylon carpet and a faint smell. The halogen lamps made everything unreal. Under the front window there was a wooden storage unit, which had been given a back and arms so that it doubled up as a window seat.

The SOCO came downstairs two at a time, crashing his way into the living room.

"OK?" He said.

"Did that thing have seat cushions?" Emily asked, pointing at the window seat.

The SOCO pointed to a place, four feet away, where a dirty black checked cushion leaned against the wall. It clearly fitted the seat.

"And there were drawings on the property? Kids' drawings? The sort of thing that April would have done?"

"Loads of them over there," he said, pointing down the back of the window seat. "Flowers mostly."

Emily lifted the red curtain and stared out into the street. She had a good view of most of the street and a parking area beyond. She sat there, imagining she was April. The SOCO stood close to her, breathing audibly through his nose. He wanted Emily gone. She had no reason to be there so she obliged him by leaving.

She stepped from the too-bright living room out into the too-dark hall, then out into the hot sunshiny street. Everything felt more odd now. The boy had taken his red ball somewhere else. The house and street looked as normal as anything, but inside number 46, April Mancinci was definitely murdered and her mother probably as well. Her mobile phone had been turned off while she was in the house and, when she turned it on, there was a blizzard of incoming texts. She didn't consider any of them important enough to respond to.

She thought about going back in but she hadn't had lunch and needed something to confront the empty feeling in her stomach. The sensation was not all about hunger, though. She also felt unsatisfied. Itchy.

She wandered around hunting a corner shop. She was sure she'd seen one on her way but, typically, she made a hash of hunting it down. She wasn't always good at locating large, static, well-advertised objects in brightly lit locations. She found it eventually and went inside.

Newspapers and chocolates. A chiller cabinet with milk and yoghurt and the sort of cooked meats that will block your arteries in about the same time as it takes an intensively farmed piglet to bulk up, squeal and die. Some tinned foods, sliced bread, biscuits and some sad looking fruit.

She helped herself to orange juice and a cheese and tomato sandwich. The girl behind the counter, with a plastic name badge that said her name was "Ross" just stood there and looked at her. Emily looked at the badge and smiled.

"I know," said the girl, "I get in trouble for losing my badge all the time. I don't care though, 'cos if I make mistakes Ross gets the blame. He loves me really."

She reached for Emily's goods to put them through the till. A CCTV monitor above her head flicked between pictures of different viewpoints in the store. It was concentrating on an OAP bending over the chiller cabinet.

"I'm on the police inquiry," Emily told the girl. "You know, the mother and daughter who were murdered up the road."

'Ross' nodded and said something bland and pacifying, the sort of thing people say when they are trying to indicate a general willingness to be helpful but without the crucial ingredient of such an attitude – namely, actually being helpful.

"You must have known them, I suppose?"

"She came in here, I think. The mother."

"The redhead? Jenna?"

'Ross' nodded. "You people were here already. I already told them."

Emily didn't quite catch whether she said "you people" or "your people." The former sounded a bit edgy, a bit them and us. "Your people" sounded rather flattering, as if everyone in the police was part of Emily's tribe, worker bees buzzing around their queen. Emily wondered whether she was reading too much into her word choice. Her goods were rung through the till and Emily was confronted by a 'pay-and-get-out-of-here face."

"You didn't see the girl? Not even to buy, I don't know, choc ices?"

"No."

"Hmm. Girls don't really buy choc ices, do they?" Emily offered. "What do they like"

Emily was thinking out loud, genuinely uncertain. She knew she used to be a six-year old girl once, equipped with pocket money enough to buy sweets at the corner shop, but those days seemed unbelievably distant. She was always bewildered at other people's memories of their own pasts. She continued thrashing around trying to guess April's confectionery habits. Rolos? KitKat? Smarties?

The counter girl was insistent that she hadn't seen April. The OAP who had come in behind Emily had finished foraging in the chiller cabinet and was waiting to pay. Emily fished for some money and handed it over.

The front of the shop was adorned with handwritten adverts. People selling off their mountain bikes or offering garden clearance and handyman services. 'No job too small.' There was a police notice already up in the window too. Smartly laid out by one of the communications team, printed on glossy card in four-colour reprographics, with a free-phone number in red at the bottom. Emily knew it was a wasted attempt. An alien intruder. The sort of thing that people in those parts would simply blank from view. The kind of disappearing act that is performed on utility bills, planning notices, tax requests.

Emily waited until the OAP had paid and then asked whether she could put up a notice.

"Card or A5?" the girl asked.

"Card," Emily replied.

The girl gave Emily a card. When she had finished writing it read, 'Jenna and April Mancini. Killed on 21st May. Information wanted. Please contact Emily.' She put her own mobile number, rather than the usual freephone one. She paid for four weeks and the card was duly stuck in the window as Emily left.

Sunshine, secrets and silence.

Outside, she sat on a bollard in the sun, ate her sandwich and called Bev Rowland on her mobile. They chatted for a while about nothing in particular just to pass the time while Emily ate.

When she got back to the office she didn't get the expected "where the hell have you been?" Perhaps nobody had even noticed that she'd been on walkabout. She let it slide, e-mailed her report and put her notes on Watch, the office information system. Teamwork.

She then got back to the bank statements that she'd been avoiding. They didn't add up, or didn't seem to when she operated the calculator.

Emily's mood was beginning to take a turn for the worse when she got a call from Jackson, summoning her downstairs. He wanted to know more about what she had been doing and what had been said. She gave him the gist, keeping her language bland and professional, but he wasn't fooled.

"You said *what* ?"

"I asked if Mr. and Mrs. Rattigan had enjoyed normal sexual relations. I apologized for the intrusive nature of the enquiry."

"Cut the bullshit. What did she say?"

"Nothing directly, but I touched a nerve. She could hardly speak."

Emily's ears burned as she said the words and her eyes were full of injury. The absence that had been drowning her before was suddenly very, very full of matter.

"And you left it there? Please tell me you left it there."

"Yes. Almost. I mean, she'd already half told me that..."

"She hadn't told you anything. You said she could hardly speak."

There was a long beat and Jackson used it to glare at Emily.

"I did ask her if her husband might have enjoyed rough sex with prostitutes," Emily admitted.

"That's what you said? You actually used those words?" Jackson asked, incredulous.

"Yes, I did." Emily deliberately omitted to say "sir".

"And?" he asked.

"I interpreted her look as confirming my suspicion," replied Emily, adjusting her position.

"A *look?* You interpreted a *look.*"

"It was a legitimate question to ask. His bank card was found there." Emily stood her ground.

"It might have been a legitimate question coming from an experienced member of the team, after appropriate consultation with the operation commander. It was not an appropriate question asked by a lone detective operating without permission, with no supervising officer present and addressed to the grieving wife of a dead man."

Emily declined to respond. Jackson glared at her again, but his heart wasn't in it and he rocked forwards again to shuffle through some papers on his desk until he found the one he was after.

"Vice Unit records. A few contacts with Mancini. Never on the game full time, as far as is known, but was certainly open to it when she needed cash." His eyes moved rapidly down the printout. "We let her know the risks she was running. Helplines; that sort of thing. Probably didn't make a difference. Well, it didn't, did it? Look where she ended up."

"You never know. It might have helped a bit. Seems like she mostly tried to look after her kid," Emily offered.

"Mostly," Jackson said.

He put a lot of emphasis on the word. Emily knew he was correct. It isn't much use being mostly good enough when your occasional lapses include heroin, prostitution, your child being taken into care, she thought to herself.

She shrugged to acknowledge his point, but added, "for what it's worth, I'm pretty certain that she wasn't selling plain vanilla, at least not where Rattigan was involved. Mrs. Rattigan's reaction wasn't just the reaction of someone whose husband had cheated on her. It was more than that."

"Go on." Jackson's voice was still grim, but he wanted to hear what she had to say. She considered that a victory of sorts.

"Rattigan had his pretty model wife for social and domestic use. She ticked all the right boxes. But I think Rattigan liked women he could abuse. I don't know in what way. Slapping them around, maybe. Roughing them up. If you want me to speculate wildly, then I'd guess that the neighbours would have been part of the fun. The squat, I mean. The squalor." Emily stopped and waited for his verdict.

"Wild speculation is exactly what we expect from our officers. Remember, Think Big." He stopped as well, satisfied he'd got his point across.

He soon moved on. Vice Unit's records placed Mancini as an occasional prostitute servicing an on-off drug habit. Emily's jaunt had added nothing. Maybe Mancini sold her services to clients who liked it rough, but then most prostitutes will cater for most tastes. No big deal there. Jackson was about to let her go with a senior officer type caution not to let herself get carried away when interviewing millionaire widows, when his phone sang out. Emily moved to leave, but he raised his hand to stop her.

She was alert for the first few seconds of the call in case it was a complaint about her. It soon became clear that it wasn't and her attention dimmed. Jackson listened intently before setting the phone down with some force. Emily wondered whether it would function thereafter.

"That was the pathologist," he said. "They're not done, but almost and they're ready to brief us. You can come over and take notes. A reward for your little private enterprise." His look brooked no argument.

They took their own cars as neither intended to return to the office afterwards. The road was its normal bad-tempered rush hour crush. Stop-start all the way. She could see Jackson's shirt-sleeved arm hanging out of the window, thumping the car to the beat of some unheard music.

The car park at the hospital was packed and they floated around for what seemed ages before finding spaces, quite a way apart. Emily reached for her glovebox and retrieved the POLICE BUSINESS notice to put on the dashboard. She disagreed that anybody should pay to go the hospital, no matter the purpose of their visit. She deemed it a money making enterprise that had no place in a caring society. She shook her head when she spotted that even Blue Badge holders had to pay, and made a mental note to make a fuss about it. Jackson was ahead of her, hurrying over to the entrance, out of the wind, lighting up.

"Want one" He asked as she caught up. "I know I should give up, but..." He let the thought drift in blue smoke.

"No thanks. I don't smoke." She tried very hard not to smirk with superiority.

"Are you the one who doesn't drink?" Jackson tried to remember her from beery police piss-ups.

Emily was normally the one holding the orange juice and leaving early, but he really didn't care and carried on without waiting for her answer.

"Only time I smoke, pretty much. Bloody corpses." He said. He took three or four drags, managed a grimaced and that was that. A shoe heal did the rest, before they went in.

Emily wasn't good with hospitals. The endless buildings, trees dotted around like apologies and, inside, people with job functions nobody understands. It all added to the air of incomprehensible busyness. Curtained-off beds and death settling like falling snow.

But it wasn't the hospital itself that concerned them. They headed to the least signed building in the entire complex. Peregrine Walsh, the senior pathologist, met them at the mortuary door. He was tall and thin, with the fussy pedantry needed to do the job he did. As they arrived he was fussing over the time, shooing out support staff and checking keys. Emily smiled inwardly as she thought his name perfectly matched his appearance and manner.

Hospital mortuaries have two or three functions. Firstly, they are storage units. Larders. Any big hospital generates plenty of corpses and people get tetchy if the corpses are left on the wards for too long. Thus, they are whisked away, to be replaced with clean sheets and the smell of detergent. The bodies have to go somewhere, so they go to the mortuary, like aircraft in a holding pattern, before being sent onwards to the undertakers or the crematorium. Of course, the coroner sometimes interferes with the smooth functioning of the operation by insisting on a post mortem.

The second function follows on. If grieving relatives want to grieve over something, they need more than clean sheets and a smell of detergent to get their tears flowing. In any case, hospital PR wants the relatives off the public wards almost as badly as they want the corpses gone. Therefore, hospital mortuaries all have a place where next of kin can go to view the corpse. It's a functional space, snipped away at by architectural practicalities and budget restrictions. This particular version had a framed print of birch trees in spring and a view out over the roof of a catering facility downstairs.

The third function had brought them there. The hospital ran a large forensic and high-risk post mortem service. Two bodies each day were sliced and diced there. The coroner needs a cause of death. The public health authorities need to know whether the corpse had HIV, HEP b, HEP c, so toxicology panels are run, organs removed and weighed, the brain examined. The pathologist reports to the coroner, who delivers a verdict. A report is filed. A life ends.

They got changed and Walsh waited for them at the door of the post mortem suite. He was in a long-sleeved white coverall with a plastic apron, worn over surgical scrubs. Rubber boots, face mask, a white cotton hat. They had to put on similar gear before moving further.

Walsh closed the door behind them. There were two gurneys in use, both covered with a pale blue cloth, and Emily was also struck by the strong overhead lighting and the hum of ventilation. The air was sucked from clean areas to dirty, changing it at least once an hour, passing through a HEPA filter before releasing it. It filtered out germs and it filtered out the dead.

Walsh pulled the cloth away from the larger body. Jenna Mancini.

Photos showed that she was pretty. Delicate, fine-boned and sensitive. Emily thought she still was, even in death. She wanted to trace the line of her eyebrow with her finger, lay her hand against her coppery hair.

Walsh didn't like dead people and he didn't like drug-addicted prostitutes with their high risk infectious corpses. He also didn't like police officers. Emily got out her notebook and cleared a space down by Mancini's feet so she could write as he talked. She had small feet and slim ankles. Emily found herself arranging the gown around her feet as though wanting to show them to best advantage. She stopped as soon as she noticed Jackson staring at her.

Walsh stared to speak with fussy precision.

"Let's start with the easy bits. We've tested urine and blood for drug use. Urine tests were negative for marijuana, cocaine, opiates, amphetamines, PCP and various other substances. We detected low levels of alcohol and methamphetamine, but her bladder was full, so we can't be sure of the extent of her drug use, or how recent it may have been. A clearer positive result for heroin. I'd guess a more recent use there."

"That'd be consistent with what we found lying around the house," said Jackson.

"Quite," said Walsh, treating Jackson to a withering look as reward for the unwanted interruption. Walsh wasn't interested in crime scene details and it took him a moment or two to restart. "Blood tests offer a more reliable guide, because they're less affected by fluid intake. Immunoassays confirm heroin use. Either very heavy use some time before death or moderate to heavy use closer to death. It's not possible to distinguish the two. Moderate blood alcohol levels. She'd have been below the drink-driving limit, for example. Some methamphetamine use, but not heavy and recent."

He talked a bit more about drugs and general health and the size of her liver and the absence of various conditions. Emily took notes, but Jackson was impatient for Walsh to get to the point.

"Cause of death? I expect that's what you are waiting for." Walsh was milking his moment. "Uncertain. There are really very few ways a person can die. Heart or lungs. Drowning, fire, gunshot and so on. It all comes down to whether the heart or the lung stops working first. In this case, it could be either. Her heart is in the state of health consistent with her age and lifestyle. You wouldn't expect a twenty-something heart to stop beating, but if you bombard it with drugs, then of course you can't rule out an attack, even a lethal one. Methamphetamines are a known risk factor. Plus, as soon as you start mixing drugs, the interactions can become highly unpredictable."

Emily was writing as fast as she could and her handwriting started to space out and get messy the faster she went.

"All the same, I'd say that the lungs would be a more likely cause. Fatal respiratory depression. Slow breathing. Disorientation. The problem is still the build-up of carbon dioxide. Acidosis. Taken too far, that'll kill you."

Jackson nodded and looked at Emily to make sure she had got it.

Price was on a roll. "Do I understand that the user may have been in an unfamiliar environment?"

It took Jackson a moment to respond.

"Unfamiliar? We don't know. It wasn't her home environment. We don't know how long she'd been there."

"Or with unfamiliar people? Or in some way in a new situation?" Walsh pressed on.

"Yes, definitely possible. Probable, in fact." Jackson seemed pleased by own insight.

Walsh nodded. "A lot of heroin overdose isn't overdose at all. It's the same dose as normal, but taken in an unfamiliar setting, it overrides the body's homeostatic mechanisms."

That was a new one for Jackson and Emily. Walsh knew it would be and smiled at the chance to explain at great length. This was his territory and he loved it.

"Just the short version, please," Jackson jumped in.

"Oh. If you're sure. I hope nothing gets missed then." Walsh tutted at the end of his sentence. "The gist is this. When somebody starts taking heroin, the body does all it can to counteract the effect of the drug. When the drug is taken in a familiar environment, the body is prepared for the toxic assault and is already doing its best to counteract it. The result is that users come to tolerate very high levels of the drug. If you pull them away from their home environment, the body's defence mechanisms haven't been primed to respond. The result is that even an ordinary dose of the drug – the same dose as the user was tolerating in their home environment – can become lethal.

"So," Jackson said, "she leaves home. She's having a bad time. We don't yet know why. She takes heroin. Same dose as normal, but it's a big mistake. Her body's not ready for the drug. Next thing, bang! She's dead."

Walsh fussed over this summary. It was all too clear and sharp for him. He started qualifying every statement and then added riders to his qualifications. He preferred the fog of precision to the clarity of a decent hunch. On a look from Jackson Emily stopped taking notes while Walsh's pedantry burned itself out. She thought Jackson looked like an idiot in his white overalls and rubber boots, but then thought she did too. They exchanged smiles. When either of them moved they sounded like taffeta. Walsh was wearing more or less the same kit, but it suited him for some reason and he didn't rustle.

When Walsh finished with his pedantic overdrive, he went back to his briefing. Routine, necessary, boring. Emily took notes. Jackson prowled, while Walsh lectured. Emily thought he enjoyed boring them. They hadn't found HIV or anything like that, but the tests were not complete. No obvious sexual assault. No recent semen found in or by the body.

They were finished with Jenna. Emily wrapped up her feet again and covered her head. This time she couldn't resist and moved one of her coppery locks with her hand as she brought the gown down over her face. Her hair felt recently washed, clean and silky and Emily wanted to put her head down to smell it.

The second gurney held April Mancini. Somebody had taped a dressing over the top of her head so that the splatter of her skull and brains was hidden, but the dressing sagged where it should have been smooth, exposing a gap where the head should have been.

"Cause of death," said Walsh, coming dangerously close to a joke, "is fairly evident. No drug use. We haven't been able to find any evidence of sexual abuse. I think we can say there was no major violence, apart from the sink, I mean, but there's plenty of stuff that can happen without leaving marks. We haven't found any infection, although blood analysis is still being done. I'm not sure what else you want."

He stood at April's head and tweaked the dressing in an attempt to stop it sagging. Emily didn't know whether he was fidgeting, wanting to preserve the little girl's dignity, or if he was just a neatness freak. She mentally plumped for the last of the options.

Jackson wasn't looking at either body. He was in the corner where an anglepoise lamp hung over a workbench. He was swinging the lamp around, working the springs.

"Any sign of a struggle? Blood under the fingernails, that sort of thing?"

"We've looked, of course. Haven't yet completed DNA testing and we might find something there, but if there is anything, then it's certainly not a lot. No obvious signs of a struggle anyway."

Jackson was frustrated, but Walsh was just a pathologist, a reader of evidence. He couldn't look into the past any more than they could. Emily had filled thirteen pages of her notebook in the handwriting that she disliked so much. He first job in the morning would be to get it put onto the office system. There was, however, one big question remaining. If Jackson didn't ask it she would, but she allowed him the time. He was, after all, an old pro. He bent the lamp down until its springs groaned.

"Fatal respiratory depression," he said.

Walsh nodded, knowing where he was going.

"What about respiratory depression that isn't enough to be fatal. Presumably the symptoms are still there. Slow breathing. Weakness. Disorientation?"

"Correct. There's not enough air coming into the lungs to permit the necessary gas exchange. If that's taken too far, it will prove fatal. But even if it doesn't go that far, you've still got a person who's badly disorientated. Maybe conscious, maybe not. Weak and uncoordinated. Quite possibly not able to stand. Perhaps temporary problems with vision." Walsh finished.

"A near overdose, in other words," Jackson said. "If she's left alone she'll live. Lucky to be alive, possibly, but she'll recover."

Walsh nodded again. "And if she's not left alone...."

"Whoever it is has got themselves the perfect victim. If anyone wanted to kill her, they could just put their fingers over her nose, close her mouth and wait."

"A minute or two," said Walsh. "Easy."

-6-

Job done.

They stood outside the post mortem suite in a little reception area that boasted an empty desk, a row of empty chairs and one of those office plants that looks like it's made of plastic and never seems to grow, flower, form seed, die or any of the other things that normal plants do.

Jackson and Walsh were standing outside the men's changing area, talking about when the post mortem report might be finished, how long the DNA identification may take and the like. Emily labelled it man-talk in her head. She was not included. She stood next to them in her long, white gown and ridiculous boots feeling like an extra from a low budget horror film. Her thoughts were interrupted when she noticed that her heart was fluttering. Not a bad flutter, but something definite all the same. She paid attention to the signals because she often needed physiology to show her the way to her emotions. A jumpy heart meant something, but she didn't know what. She let her awareness expand and go wherever it wanted.

Almost instantly it found the answer.

She hadn't finished in the post mortem suite. She needed to go back there.

The answer, when she found it, clicked into place. It made sense. She had no idea why, but she didn't always bother with the 'whys'. She just did what she had to do.

"Oh, just a minute, I think I've left my spare pen in there," she mumbled.

The two men didn't break their conversation. Jackson just looked down at Emily and nodded. She taffeta-rustled back to the post mortem suite, letting the door swing shut behind her.

The peace of the room welcomed her and she relaxed almost instantly. She felt her heart rate slow and lose its jitteriness. She reached for the light, but thought better of it because she liked the violet twilight that was gradually possessing the room.

She took her only pen and shoved it under the cloth shrouding Jenna Mancini, so that she had something to 'find' if necessary. Apart from that she did nothing.

She had one hand on Jenna's enviably slim calf, the other on the gurney and the peace of the room sank into her bones. It was the most peaceful place in the world. She bent her face down so that it touched the blue hospital cloth over Jenna's feet. There was a faint medical smell, but the human smells were long gone.

She wanted to stay there for ages, quite still, just breathing the empty, medical air, but she didn't have long and forced herself to move. She uncovered the two bodies so that she could see their faces again. Jenna's expressionless one and April's smiling half of one. April's head bandage had fallen in again, so she smoothed it out for her.

Emily thought they looked like mother and daughter and stared at them. Jenna stared back, but was not saying anything to her yet. Emily thought she was still getting used to being dead. April couldn't look, of course, but she did smile at her. Emily didn't think being dead was going to be too hard for her. Life was tough and death should be a cinch in comparison.

They smiled at each other for a while, just enjoying each other's company. She bent down to Jenna's hair. Smelled it, touched it, combed it through with her fingers. The combing released both a smell of Antiseptic and shampoo. Apple, or something like it.

She stood there with her fingers in Jenna's hair, trying to trace the root of the impulse that had brought her there. Jenna's scalp felt surprisingly delicate under her fingertips and she could feel little April smiling beside her.

There was something in their interaction that seemed incomplete, but she didn't know what was needed to complete it.

"Goodnight, little April," she said. "Goodnight Jenna."

It was the right thing to say, but the incompleteness remained. She paused for a few seconds more, but to no avail. The thing that was left hanging a few moments before was still hanging and she didn't think she would find it by waiting.

She didn't want Jackson and Walsh thinking she was a freak, so she 'found' her pen, covered the girls and went rustling out of the suite, brandishing it with a dumb look of triumph.

She got changed slowly. Rubber boots in one bin; oversized gown in another. The door to the cleaning cupboard stood next to the entrance of the women's changing room. Emily thought that it was a nice touch not to frighten the men by letting them see mops and buckets. She stared at the innards of the cupboard for a while before moving out into the lobby beyond.

The men were still talking. She didn't see why she should wait for them.

"Thank you, Dr. Walsh," she yelled, as she pushed the door to leave. It wouldn't budge and refused to pull open either. She was trying to work out whether they were unusually heavy doors and she was just being weak when Walsh arrived to help.

"I've got to buzz you out," he explained. "It's a secure area."

Emily smiled her thanks whilst wondering whether they thought the corpses were likely to escape if it were not thus secured.

Emily was feeling a bit odd and managed to get herself lost. She ended up tramping up and down some of the endless hospital corridors, looking for the way out. Pale yellow tiles that squeaked underfoot and reflected too much fluorescent light. Her head was full of hospital words. Paediatrics. Orthopaedics. Radiotherapy. Phlebotomy. She ended up walking around at random, taking lifts up or down according to which way they happened to be going at the time. Getting off when everybody else did.

Haematology. Diagnostic Imaging. Gastroenterology.

At one point a nurse stopped her and asked if she was all right. Emily said, "yes. Quite all right," but she said it too loudly and then squeaked off along the yellow floored corridor to show how all right she was.

She eventually realised that it was the hospital that was making her feel weird and she needed to get out. She found herself at a junction in the corridor, wondering how to find the exit, before realizing she was staring directly at a large sign which said WAY OUT>. She treated it as a clue and pursued it all the way to the main exit, where she found fresh air. There was also a soft wind which carried car fumes, but even that was an improvement, she thought.

She stood in the entrance for a while, letting people push past while she felt herself return. Her phone nudged her into the present when it announced a text inviting her for a drink. It was Boxall and she was already late for the time suggested. She had forgotten she had agreed to meet and didn't really want to, but it was too late to withdraw. She saluted the mortuary as she moved to her car.

"Goodnight, April. Goodnight, Jenna."

She didn't get an answer, but she knew April was still smiling.

-7-

Sharp meant sharp, and nobody was sharper, smarter or more bushy-tailed than Emily. Not long into Jackson's morning briefing, she got her moment of glory.

He summarized the result of the meeting at the mortuary and added, "Emily will be getting her notes onto Watch as soon as she can. "Right, Emily?"

"Already done," she beamed. She avoided the 'sir' as well, which made her feel even better.

"You've done it?"

"All done. I didn't want to waste time." Emily was glowing inside, but managed a degree of nonchalance.

Jackson raised his eyebrows, which had turned shaggy before their time, so the gesture was a signature look. He was either impressed or, more likely she thought, didn't believe that Emily had done a decent job. But she had. She had come in early and whizzed through it. She learned to type as part of her early training with her father's elite and secret group and she was blitzkrieg fast.

"Ok. Good. That means you lot can read all about it." He tried hard not show he was impressed.

Jackson delivered a few other nuggets, the most important of which was that they now had the full case files from Social Services and other agencies on the Watch system. He then handed over to Ken Hughes who summarized the first batch of findings from the door-to-door work. The house had attracted a good deal of hostility from the neighbours, being variously described as a drug den, a squat, a place taken over by the homeless and much more.

"Putting aside more fanciful ideas," said Hughes in his depressive and slightly hostile monotone, "the general picture seems to be this."

He told the assembled gallery that the house had been let out for some years, then had fallen vacant around two years ago. The landlord had not yet been traced. For some time, it had just stood there, getting quietly more and more damp and growing old. Then the back door was forced, possibly by kids out to cause trouble, possibly by a drug dealer wanting a place to operate from, possibly by a homeless person wanting a roof for the night. In any case, once the back door was gone, the house began to attract trouble.

Emily was alert. She knew of another possible reason for the house attracting interest, but could only keep it to herself for the time being. It was part of the reason she had been embedded, secretly, in the local force. The murky world of terrorism and all its various far-reaching tentacles was never far from her thoughts. She concentrated again, hoping nobody had noticed her brief distraction.

From the visual evidence, the house had certainly been used as a squat for longer than the Mancinis' few weeks of residence. It was highly likely that drugs had been taken in the house for some considerable period. If drugs were used there, they were probably dealt there too. If drugs had been brought and sold there, then it was likely that there were women selling themselves for drugs, although the place wasn't remotely nice enough to have prospered as even the most basic of brothels.

So much for the background. Specifics. Jenna Manicini had definitely been seen around the place. The girl in the corner shop had told Emily as much. She had reported seeing Jenna several times. She had remembered her hair, but that meant nothing as it been widely reported in the press. However, she had also correctly remembered some clothing and an item of jewellery that had been found at the house. Neither had been publicized. She also, crucially, remembered selling Jenna a frozen Hawaiian pizza, whose wrapper featured in the long inventory of the rubbish that had been found at the house.

Emily couldn't resist it. She interrupted.

"Mancini clearly had April with her in the house, because the same source confirmed purchases of Cocoa Pops and chocolate milk shake."

She was treated to the hardest stare Hughes could muster.

"Quite," he said, through tightly clenched teeth, before ploughing on. "Sources, whom we take to be reliable, have confirmed Jenna Mancini's presence in the neighbourhood and all agree that they did not see April Mancini with her at the time. We are for the moment presuming that April was present in the house but not inclined or not permitted to go out."

He had another few pages of notes to get through, but the room had become fidgety and attention spans were wavering. Jackson stepped in to rescue things.

"Anything else is on Watch. Familiarise yourselves with it all. Short summary: we have no reports of anyone other than the two Mancinis at the house. No reports of April being seen outside at any time. No reports of any regular visitors, or irregular ones for that matter. Curtains always closed, lights off – no electricity, remember. No music. The place was quiet. So we have to look at other resources. CCTV. The nearest cameras, the nearest working cameras, were five hundred and seven hundred yards away. It's fairly likely that one of them picked up Jenna at some point. We need to see if she was with anyone at the time."

He pointed to an officer at the back of the room to allocate that responsibility. Emily felt herself to be on the fringes so, emboldened by her previous success, raised her hand.

"There's CCTV at the corner shop too. Maybe they'll have recordings."

There was a short exchange of conversation up at the front. Apparently someone had already noticed and getting access to those recordings was already on an action list somewhere. Emily smiled and left it at that, satisfied that she had made her point.

"OK. Meanwhile, Jenna. We need to dig into her past. There's a good chance she knew her killer, so we need to find the people she knew and how she knew them. If she was a working girl and was killed by a punter, then it's a fair bet he wasn't a first-timer. Also, let's not forget our anonymous female caller, the one who tipped us off about the house. The caller is still out there. There's been plenty of media so she knows we want to talk to her, but she's not come in yet. Anything that leads us to her is valuable."

He finished by allocating tasks for the day and the briefing room gradually emptied. No breakthroughs, no easy victory. There was a general assumption that the killer would be found and jailed, but Emily knew that, sooner or later, the optimism would demand fuel to keep it burning.

She headed downstairs to the print room, but was interrupted by a knot of officers gathered around the coffee machine. They were discussing the merits or otherwise of adding pineapple to a dish that is basically savoury. She squeezed around them. They didn't make way for her or seek to include her in their banter. She knew they considered her junior and her small physique added to that impression. She was also female, which confirmed their views.

Emily smiled to herself. If only they knew. She could drop any one, or several of them, whenever she chose She had been trained to within an inch of her life and that gave her a confidence, a steel, but they hadn't spotted it. Let them remain ignorant. What goes around, comes around.

She continued down to the print room, where the slightly Polish print manager, Tomasz Kowalczyk, was bustling around in charge of his papery domain.

"Dzien dobry, Tomasz," she said.

"Dzien dobry, Emily. How can I help you today?"

"You shouldn't say that. It makes you sound like you're about to offer me fries."

Tomasz liked her. She was there for some photos and she showed him those she wanted from the system, which boasted not only the crime-scene images but also some of those found among the Mancinis' possessions. Not so many of Jenna, probably, Emily surmised, because she never had a regular person to take pictures of her. But there were plenty of April. April in party dresses, April on Perranporth beach, April holding a huge toffee apple and laughing. She had wide blue eyes, like her mother, and when she laughed, everything in her face laughed too. April Mancini, the toffee apple kid.

Emily picked out about a dozen pictures in total. Some of Jenna and some of April. Tomasz made her fill out some forms, which annoyed her because she didn't like forms. They left a trail. She deliberately made a mess of them so he had to do them for her. She polished up one of her nicest smiles and treated him to it when he was ready. He told her to collect them in half an hour. He could have produced them immediately, but wanted another dose of Emily later. She knew it, but played along.

Back at her desk, apart from the boring routine work on her original case, she had been tasked with two jobs for the day. One was answering any Lohan-related phone calls from the general public that were being generated by media appeals. The other was to get stuck into Jenna's benefits records, Social Services history and anything else to do with contacts with officialdom. Jackson had asked for a grand sounding 'executive summary,' and Emily decided she would blow his socks off.

She took three calls. One was nuts and two were sane but probably useless. She got stuck into the paperwork. She was good at that sort of thing and read mounds of stuff quickly, extracting the useful parts rapidly and clearly. She would have preferred to have been doing other more active things, so she worked fast, accumulating brownie points.

She was hard at work when the phone rang. It was Jackson, using the speaker phone on his desk, telling her to come over. He gave no reason.

She entered his office, but hovered by the door. She knew he did open-door meetings and door-closed ones. The former was usually better, but she waited for a signal. From the way he looked she took a punt and closed the door.

"Good work on the post mortem. Fast, accurate. Good stuff."

"Thank you."

"You're doing the same on the paperwork, I expect?"

"That's the plan," she said. "Already started, actually."

He was being nice to her which she found worrying.

"Where did you learn?" He looked directly at her. "I've read your file, but there's more I bet. Things not there, I mean."

Emily said nothing. She couldn't. She restricted herself to what she hoped was her best enigmatic smile.

"Never mind," he said, with an exaggerated sigh. "A sudden burst of hyperactivity usually means you want something. Why don't you tell me what that is?

It threw her because she didn't know she was so obvious.

"I'd like to be full time on Lohan. I think I could contribute."

"Of course you could. Every officer could contribute."

"Yes," she continued," but at the moment there are only two women on the team. Obviously, they are both brilliant officers, but I think they might be stretched a bit thin. I mean, I know you can get men to some of the interviews, but it's not quite the same, is it? I mean, if prostitution is involved."

She had hardly explained herself brilliantly, but he knew what she meant. He was pondering the problem when she spoke again.

"It's all very well getting men to interview prostitutes, but there's a certain kind of interviewing they just can't do. There's always a shortage of women for those interviews, and uniformed officers are often brought in to try and address the shortfall. That's fine, except that having a female officer in full uniform, baton, handcuffs, radio, protective jacket and boots doesn't exactly get the girly juices flowing. Oh, and maybe taser as well."

Emily searched his face for reaction. There was none. She pressed on. In for a penny.

"You remember the old days when prostitutes were just bundled off down to the interview rooms to be shouted at by a bunch of blokey officers who exuded dislike, lust and distaste from every masculine pore? Those days weren't exactly bathed in an eternal glow of success. Other approaches have their merits too. Merits like actually working, for example.

"OK. It's not the same," he admitted.

She stayed in her chair, trying to read the runes.

"What else are you on? You're getting Johnston ready for court, aren't you?"

"Yes, but I could have that done by the end of the week."

It was an implausible target and he knew it and said so.

"I'm sure I can persuade the CPS that I'll be ready by the end of the week.

Jackson did his shaggy-eyebrowed thing at her. "And if you join Lohan full time, which Emily am I going to be getting?"

She didn't know what to say. She opted for silence.

"Look, Emily. Lohan would benefit from additional female staff. Of course it would. For all the reasons you've given and others as well. Upstairs has already asked me if I want you. I wanted to say yes."

Emily knew she should express gratitude, but waited for what was obviously on the way. His verdict.

"The good Emily, I'd have like a shot. But the other one? The one I ask to do something and that something never seems to get done. Or if it does, it gets done wrong. Or done slowly. Or done after fifteen reminders. Or done in a way that breaks the rules, causes complaints or pisses off your fellow officers. The Emily who decides that if something is boring her, she's going to make a mess of it until she's moved to something else."

Emily made a face, even though she knew what he was talking about.

"Am I," he continued," going to get the officer who makes Rattigan's widow break down over some bit of total speculation about her dead husband's sex life?"

Emily bit her lip and Jackson nodded.

"I got a call this morning. Now, I handled it. No official complaint. Nothing that's going any further, but I didn't want to have to take that call. I don't want to have to wonder all the time if you're going to use your mature, intelligent judgement or if you're going to say and do the very first thing that comes into your head."

Emily knew that Jackson was aware of something else, even though he hadn't brought it up. Another incident. He had heard about it on the grapevine, and like all whispers it had grown in the telling and retelling. He had heard that Emily was interviewing in a case when the suspect thought it would be a clever idea to put a hand on her breast. A few minutes later she was calling an ambulance because the poor misguided soul required treatment for a dislocated kneecap. They would later discover other injuries to some delicate areas of his anatomy that could be treated with ice to reduce the swelling and bruising. She later found herself on a course with eighteen male officers and she managed not to disable any of them. She thought it was probably because not one of them had found it necessary to put a hand on her breast.

There was a long pause. She was normally OK with pauses. She could pause with the best, but this one was unsettling because she didn't know what Jackson was doing with it.

"If I may," she ventured, "I think the reports about April Mancini are significant."

"We haven't had any," Jackson said.

"Exactly," Emily confirmed. "That's my point. We haven't had any reports of her at the location. One of the SOCOs told me that they found piles of April's pictures dropped down behind the back of the seat in the front window. She must have sat there for hours and hours, drawing. Hours and hours. In the front window.

"Yes, but there were curtains across the windows. Doesn't look like they were ever opened," Jackson observed.

"That's what I mean. What kid wouldn't open up those curtains when her mother went out. You get a good view from the front of the house. You see everything that's going on. Most kids, even if they weren't allowed out, would be sitting in that window staring out. April didn't. I think she was terrified, and I think she was because her mother was. It was fear that took them to that house, and whatever it was they were frightened of caught up with them and killed them. I mean, I know we can't be positive, but it seems like a theory for now." Emily stopped.

"Yes, it does," Jackson nodded.

They seemed to have tumbled into another pause, but she decided it was his turn to get them out of that one, so she just stayed sitting with her mouth shut, trying to look like a good, professional officer, a little half-smile on her face by way of defence.

"Emily, I don't want you on Lohan. Not properly. Not overtly. If you want to continue working on Lohan in a support capacity then that's fine with me, as long as I don't get any more calls like I've had recently. As long as you don't injure anyone and avoid making a mess of work you don't enjoy doing."

"Is that it?" she asked.

"Yes. You're very close to being a very good officer, but you're even closer to being a pain in the arse. You decide."

Another pause drifted into the room and Emily decided to let it end naturally.

"I think you could be right about April. Why nobody saw her. Poor little kid." Jackson said.

Emily thought about her. Little April, drawing flower pictures in a stinking room. Little April, told never, ever, to open those curtains. Little April, whom nobody saw. Little April, invisible to everyone except her killer.

Jackson nodded to indicate the meeting was over and Emily left to make her way downstairs and pick up her pictures from Tomasz.

-8-

Back at her desk, she ran into Boxall. Their drink together had confused Emily. When she'd received his text she had assumed it was a coppers' night out sort of affair. The kind of thing that happened at least once a week with a bunch of people drinking in the sort of bars that would make work for their uniformed colleagues later in the evening. Emily wasn't always invited to those things, but she had been to a few. Emily and her orange juice. Only later did she realise that Boxall had possibly meant his invitation as a date. Not a big flowers and candles date maybe, but a sort of toe in the water, a deniable date, a drink ready to morph either into a flowers and candles jobbie or a simple drink between work colleagues. Emily was not good at decoding such things.

She hadn't given the drink any great weight. She had turned up late and without letting Boxall know that she was on her way. The result was that when she finally arrived Boxall had joined up with a couple of office colleagues, and they had all had a faintly tedious but good hearted coppers' night out. She had never meant to send any kind of signal.

"Hey, Emily," he said.

"Hi." She grimaced at him. It was an attempted smile really, except she'd got her head full of Jackson's bollocking and her hands full of photos of dead people.

"All right?"

"Yes. Sorry about yesterday."

"That's OK."

"I was in a muddle. I didn't mean to. I wasn't trying to…"

"That's OK. Don't worry."

"Maybe we could do it again sometime. A drink. I'll try my honest best not to make a pig's ear of it," she promised.

He grinned. "Good. Half a pig's ear would do fine. Definitely. Sometime soon."

Emily didn't want him poking around her photo pile, so she put them face down on the desk and sat on them.

"Are you OK? You're not looking your normal relaxed and untroubled self."

"Jackson gave me a bollocking. About seven out of ten. No. Six out of ten." She was trying to calibrate the bollocking, benchmarking herself on the assumption that the whole kneecap thing was worth a ten.

"Oh, who's in hospital this time?"

"Very funny. No listen, could you do me a favour?" She shoved some of the Johnston papers at him. "If I get some teas, will you add up this list of figures and tell me what you get?"

She set him to work with a pencil and calculator, pushed the photos into a drawer and left to get tea. When she came back, Boxall had an answer, which was the same as hers. It was still about £40,000 higher than it should have been.

"Problem?" He asked.

"No. Not really. Just too much of a good thing."

"You know, if you get stuck with this, you should get the accountants in. No reason for you to do all the number crunching.

She nodded, too lost in her own world to tell him that they'd already got some accountants involved and they were coming in for a meeting the next morning. A shortage of accountants wasn't her problem.

"Who the hell steals from their employer to buy one-sixth of a racehorse?" she said out loud.

She didn't hear his answer because she was already reaching for the phone.

-9-

She worked like a bluebottle all that day. At half past twelve Bev passed her desk and invited her to lunch, but Emily politely refused. She had a mountain of work to climb if she was to have half a chance with Jackson. She had Feta cheese and grilled vegetables, with bottled water. Luxury consumed in a nice little hum of busyness. She didn't even let any chargrilled aubergine slip from the sandwich down into the keyboard, as she gave a faultless exhibition of desk lunching technique.

She discovered things she never knew. Things about thoroughbred registers, how racing works, where the money gets paid. She also found out things she didn't want to know. Things that disturbed her. Things that she wouldn't have bothered to look for if Jackson hadn't given her such a kicking. By the end of the day she had done nothing at all on Mancini's reports. Her desk was awash with printouts from Companies House and Weatherbys, the thoroughbred breed register.

The phone rang and she answered without being conscious of doing so.

It was a Lohan caller, one of only five that day. The case had been treated to plenty of publicity, but it was a sad fact that, despite April's death, the public weren't much moved by the killing. The death of a mother and child would normally have generated about a hundred calls a day, but because of Jenna's murky past it had generated almost nothing.

The caller identified herself as Amanda and she said she had known Jenna slightly. Her daughter had been friends with April; same age and same school.

"I didn't know whether to phone or not, then I thought I might as well. Hope that's all right."

"It is. Any information can make the difference." Emily ran through the questions she was meant to ask. Known associates and so on. Amanda was as helpful as she could be. The only "known associates" she knew were other school mums, none of whom sounded like sink-droppers.

"Did she have a reputation?" Emily asked. "You know, did other mothers talk about her as being a bad sort or a bit wild?"

Amanda paused. That was usually a good sign and so it proved. Her answer was reflective and considered.

"No, I wouldn't say so. I mean, the school was quite mixed. I don't mean race wise. I mean there were the yummie mummies, the dolled up chavs, the ordinary mums, everyone. Jenna wasn't well off. She was never going to get invited to the next yummy mummy coffee morning or whatever. But she was OK. She used to worry over things. Like she asked me how my six-year-old daughter was getting on with her reading. I think she felt she should be doing more to help April, but didn't quite know how. Tilly, that's my daughter, went over to April's for tea a couple of times and I wouldn't have let her if I'd had any worries."

"Amanda, do you know how they died?"

"Pardon?"

"How and where. They were in a squat. It was filthy. There was just one mattress upstairs, which they must have shared. No sheet. One not very clean duvet."

There was another long pause. Emily worried that she might have made a mess again. Said too much. Not been tactful. Upset someone who would call Jackson and cause a stir. She thought she heard Amanda crying on the other end of the line. She tried to put things right.

"Sorry, Amanda I didn't want to upset you."

"No, it's OK. I mean what happened."

"I was only telling you because..."

"I know why," Amanda interrupted, "you wanted to see if I said it just proves that Jenna Mancini was a waster after all."

"And?" Emily kept it short.

"She wasn't. You know, I mean, I didn't like her particularly. I'm not saying I disliked her. We just didn't have much in common. But she lived for April. I know she did. If she took April to a place like that, well, she must have been terrified of something. That or her whole life just fell apart for some reason. Even so, I'd have looked after April, if she'd asked. I can't believe it. Sorry."

By the end, Amanda was crying outright and apologizing. Emily listened to her and said the things that she was meant to say.

Emily had never cried once during her time with her father's elite group. Actually, that didn't cover it. She hadn't cried since she was seven or eight, and hardly ever even then. She remembered a car accident, a nasty one, where the only serious injury was a little boy who lost both legs and suffered significant facial injuries. All the time they were getting him out of the car and into the ambulance, he was crying and holding his little tiger toy against his neck. Not only did Emily not cry, it wasn't until a few days later that she realised she was meant to have cried, or at least felt something.

She reflected on all that as Amanda cried and said, "it's all right," like a mechanical toy, wishing to find some tears of her own.

Eventually, Amanda was done.

"Amanda, would you like to come to the funeral? We don't yet know when it'll be, but I could let you know."

That suggestion set off another round of crying, but Amanda eventually came good with a "yes, yes please. Someone ought to be there."

The call ended leaving Emily faintly dazed. She had committed herself to the funeral without any forethought, but just knew she wanted to go. She also had Jackson's comments buzzing in her ear from earlier. Was this the good Emily, the one with the great interview technique, or was it an example of the bad one, a fingernail's breadth away from triggering another complaining phone call to the boss? She didn't know and didn't care.

She had too many things in her head and didn't know where to put them all. The racehorse that Johnston co-owned had five other owners. Four of those were individuals. One was an offshore, privately held company, with no publicly available information about its ultimate ownership. It did, however, have two directors and a company secretary, who were also directors and company secretary at one of Rattigan's steel companies. A second man was godfather to one of Rattigan's children. Emily couldn't trace any links between the other two owners and Rattigan, but that didn't mean they did not exist.

Apart from all that, even the links she knew about seemed to imply something. A company, which almost certainly belonged to Rattigan, owned a chunk of a racehorse, as did one of his company executives and one of his oldest friends.

As did Jon Johnston.

Maybe it was just coincidence. Maybe he had nothing to do with Rattigan and he was just there to make up the numbers.

Or maybe not. Johnston had spent about forty grand more on his purchases than he had stolen or than could be accounted for from his salary. It was, she thought, just about possible that Johnston had found some way to cash in his police pension in order to fund his purchases, but who on earth would have done that? And why?

Wasn't it more likely that Johnston had a source of cash from elsewhere, and if he did, then wasn't it also possible that Rattigan was in some way the origin of that cash? And if so, and if Rattigan had some connection to Mancini, then didn't that imply that Johnston was in some way involved with the Mancini murders?

It was five o'clock and Emily had not made any progress on the Mancini's records, so she decided to take them home. They were confidential and were not meant to be taken out of the office on a laptop, but that rule was broken all the time and she felt the need to get home early. That night was meant to be a gym and tidying up sort of night, but she had the feeling it was going to be nothing of the kind.

Before she left she decided she needed some human contact. She went on the prowl and came across Jane Alexander, who had just returned from house to house. Emily found her a bit scary if she was honest because she was the sort of person who always managed to find outfits that were seasonal and professional yet at the same time called attention to her gym bunny physique. Her hair was always immaculately blow dried and she never got food stains on things. Finally, she didn't make perfectly helpful witnesses cry for no reason and certainly didn't kneecap suspects.

As it was, Jane seemed genuinely pleased to see Emily. She complained about the day she'd had and how she still had to get her interview notes onto Watch. Emily was a much faster typist and offered to help her in exchange for some tea.

At the end of Emily's typing stint, she said "It's pretty skinny stuff, isn't it?"

Jane thought she was criticizing her notes and tried to set her straight. It wasn't her notes Emily had an issue with, it was the lack of leads that bothered her.

"Oh, but the forensic stuff will give us a few names. Maybe CCTV. A few interviews. Something will start to come out. That's the way these things go."

Jane's attention was wandering. Jacket on, hair flicked in one blonde shampoo-ed movement out from the collar. A quick inspection to make sure that every fold of fabric was obeying orders. Handbag, mobile, purse? Check. Perfect lifestyle, all present and correct. Spaceship Alexander was ready for blast off.

"See you tomorrow," Emily said, and was treated to a nice big smile, which showed Jane's very orderly white teeth, nicely arranged against exactly the right shade of lipsticked lips.

"Yes, see you tomorrow. Thanks Emily. I'd have been stuck for ages."

"You're welcome."

Jane Alexander blasted off to wherever it was she berthed for the night. She had a husband and a young son. Emily had neither and went back to her desk to pick up her stuff. Her computer was still on and Rattigan's Platinum card was catching a last ray of evening light.

Jenna Mancini was so scared of something that she took her daughter to that house of death.

Rattigan liked rough sex with street prostitutes. His wife hadn't told Emily with words, but she'd said it in every other way she possibly could. Rattigan died in a plane crash, but his body had never been found. His card was reported lost, but Jenna Mancini had it.

Jon Johnston bought a horse with stolen money and Rattigan, it seemed, was one of its co-owners.

Five thoughts buzzed around her head like flies in a glass jar. Nobody except Emily appeared to care about these things, but that didn't make the flies go away.

She Googled and came up with the names of some racecourse photographers who did a lot of work at Chepstow and other places. She made some calls and left four messages on voicemail. She got through to one real person, named Al Bettinson, and made an appointment for the next day.

She didn't have a good feeling about any of it, but it would be at least one fly she could squash. She found an official report on the air accident, printed it and shoved it into her bag along with her laptop and a bundle of papers.

It had been a long day and it wasn't over yet.

-10-
Home. Blue sky and golden light.

She had been put into a newly built house, which was used by the elite team. It was a modern semi, built on an estate of modern semis. Every house had its own bit of paved driveway, its own garage, its own tiny patch of close-board-fenced garden behind. Human rabbit hutches.

A new member of her secret team had also been placed there. His name was Books and they had history. They had met when he was saved from a life of petty street crime by her father and she was assigned to teach the illiterate newcomer how to read. Many hours were spent together and it became inevitable that they were attracted to each other. He had made rapid progress and was now an integral part of the elite team. He had a certain assuredness, a quiet confidence, a steely determination. Qualities forged on the far from gold paved streets of the metropolis that made him a steadfast friend but an implacable and deadly enemy. He could move in the shadows when necessary. He was also only the third person alive that could scare her to her very core. The others were her father and Ray Quinn. Now Sir Ray Quinn who had founded the unit and passed it on to his successor, Frank. Her father.

Anybody paying any attention naturally assumed they were a young couple making their way in the world and in a way, they were. But Books was there to ensure Emily's safety and to feedback to the Team Leader, Frank, information about the case. It wasn't just a murder case. They were convinced there were links to terrorism and the safety of the nation.

Emily let herself in. He was out when she arrived and she found herself disappointed by his absence.

The garden faced west and light filled the back of the house. She wandered outside and sat on a metal garden chair with the sun full in her face. Thinking. When was the last time it rained? Why was she so sure she was going to the Mancinis' funeral?

She sat outside until the sun left her face, and then went to the shed to check her plants before locking up and going inside.

Emily headed straight for the fridge and found lettuce, some sushi which was a day past its sell by date and a bean salad, which was turning fizzy three days after its best consume by date. She decided that fizzy beans would probably not kill her, plonked everything onto a plate and ate.

She sat after finishing, just pondering. Eventually stirring herself, she found some Blu-Tack and rubbed it between her hands to warm it up. There was a mirror in the living room. Emily mentally questioned the point of mirrors because they only tell you what you already know.

She took it down and leaned it against the fireplace, which had never been used. She fished the Mancini photos out of her bag and spread them out across the floor and sofa. A dozen faces stared out at her. Faces she had last seen in the mortuary.

She arranged and re-arranged the pictures, trying to make sense of them.

Those of Jenna were good. One in particular had decent lighting, nice, clear, useful for identification. It didn't hold her attention though. She much preferred a shot of her taken at the crime scene. All expression gone. The contingencies of life wiped away. The person herself remaining. She could have looked at that photo for hours, she felt, and might well have done so, except that it was April who fascinated her. April Mancini, the sweet little dead girl. She had six pictures.

In a sudden burst of decisiveness, she thrust the pictures of Jenna back into her bag and stuck the pictures of April on the wall in two rows of three. She felt April's peaceful presence. No wonder she'd been a popular child. The toffee apple kid.

"What do you have to tell me, little April."

The child smiled at her, but told her nothing.

Emily worked hard for the rest of the evening. Official files, the air crash report, her Johnston case notes ready for the accountants. Names, numbers, dates, questions, connections. At a quarter to one in the morning she stopped, feeling done in and surprised at the time.

April's face was staring down at her in sextuple, but she still was not telling Emily anything, so she said goodnight and went to bed.

-11-
Emily thought that accountants appeared in pairs. Usually, a . middle aged man in a dark suit and a film of perspiration, plus his younger accomplice, a woman who looked like her hobbies were arranging things in rows and making right angles.

She couldn't help feeling that her session with Jackson was three quarters bollocking and one quarter encouragement. It was clear she wouldn't be allowed to work on Lohan properly until she got the Johnston case tidied away, and she couldn't do that until the lads and lasses of the CPS reported that they were as happy as pigs in muck. In turn, that wouldn't happen until the accountants produced a report that gave the CPS what they needed.

"We're missing about forty grand, yes? Known expenditures about forty grand greater than incomings, even taken into account the money we know he stole."

"Yes. £43,754. 67," said the more senior accountant, "of course, that's only an estimate. We don't have receipts for most of the spending."

Emily stared at him. *Don't have receipts?* The man's an embezzler, for God's sake. You expect him to keep receipts? But she didn't say so. Instead she said, "The question is, when can you get us your report?"

"I believe we're scheduled to deliver in the second week in June. Karen...?"

The younger accomplice had a name apparently. She also had a goal now. Find a precise date. Eliminate numerical uncertainty. She dived into her papers to give her the exact date.

Emily interrupted.

"Sorry, that won't work. We've got a gap of forty thousand pounds to make sense of. We'll need your report right away, even if it's only in draft form."

They squabbled a little but Emily stood her ground and, in order to make her arguments even more effective, and to annoy the female accomplice, she seized the moment to make a mess of the papers in front of her. No right angles anywhere then. No rows of anything.

Eventually, Emily won. They would deliver a draft report to the CPS by the end of the week, and a final version later in June. Emily was delighted but did her best not to show it. To celebrate, as she was showing the accountants out of the building, she shook hands with the female accomplice very earnestly and for three seconds longer than the woman was comfortable with.

"Thank you so much for your help," she said, looking into her eyes. "Thank you so much." As she was retrieving her hand, she gave her upper arm a quick squeeze and fired off a for your eyes only smile at her. The woman almost ran for the door.

Upstairs again, she arranged things for the day. She was wary of showing too much initiative for fear of the reaction from her colleagues and yet she needed to show Jackson she meant business. Also, Jackson had spent less time than her with the breed register, and a lead was a lead. She therefore arranged a meeting with the CPS. She told others where she was going and made sure someone else was on Lohan telephone duties.

She took her papers, got into her car and drove out of the car park. She called the CPS people and told them that something had come up and asked to postpone things. A new appointment was made for later in the day. That gave her six clear hours to use a she pleased.

Bettinson's house was a redbrick 1970's thing, all sliding doors and brown carpets. She didn't get to see it, though. His office was in his garage. No natural light, just a garage light overhead and a desk lamp. There were two desktops and one laptop, a printer and some camera gear and lighting equipment in a corner.

Emily recognized that look that all photographers have. Bettinson was like a teenage boy who'd been given stubble, a hangover and freedom from female interference. He was wearing a black T-shirt, cargo trousers and a much pocketed canvas waistcoat hung over the back of a chair. He was brown-haired and didn't use deodorant.

"Coffee?"

"No, I'm fine thanks. If you don't mind, I'd like to just get cracking."

Bettinson was surprisingly solicitous. He was going out on a job, but was happy to let Emily browse. He set her down at one of the two desktops and showed her how things were arranged. Photos from each day were filed in their own folder. The photos had numbers for filenames, and the folders were arranged by date, but nothing else. A spreadsheet logged which assignments were done, on which days and there was some cost and billing information. He showed her how to toggle between viewing the photos as thumbnails and full images.

"They're arranged by date, so if you don't have a date..."

"I know. And I don't."

"Do you want to say what you're looking for?" He asked.

Emily hesitated. "I'm trying to find a connection between two individuals. They both had an interest in racing, both lived locally. A photo of them together at the track could establish a connection." She didn't want to say more. She was paranoid about Jackson finding out that she was there.

"Well, you've got some dates, then."

Bettinson gave her a couple of old racecourse calendars with race dates marked, asked her again if she wanted coffee, then went off with his camera gear.

Judging by his accumulated images, Bettinson did all sorts. Weddings, schools, the races, a bit of news photography. His biggest gig by far was the racecourse as about forty percent of the images were from there. Most of those, inevitably, were of horses but twenty percent of his racing images dealt with shots of owners and punters. Social scenes down at the track.

Emily couldn't think of a better way of doing it, so she started the week before Rattigan's death and worked backwards. After forty minutes of solid work she had covered one month of the archive. Coloured shapes moved behind her eyelids when she closed them. Endless photos of men in tweed jackets, horses' noses, rosettes, silver trophies, award ceremonies with low stages and country themed adverts, horsey women in padded gilets and fashionable babes with big smiles and low tops. Nothing of Johnston. A few of Rattigan when one of his horses won something, but nothing that seemed to help much.

She wondered if she'd missed something.

She checked her voicemail, worried that there might have been a message from Jackson or Hughes. There wasn't.

She carried on working. More horses. More tweed. More rosettes. The more photos she looked at that weren't the ones she was after, the less optimistic she became. By the time Bettinson got back she hadn't found what she was looking for and she was very unsure if there was any such thing to be found. She needed to leave.

He asked if she'd got what she was after.

"Are they, like, specific individuals you're searching for?"

"Yes."

"Are you allowed to say who?"

"Well, don't shout it around, but yes, Brendan Rattigan is one of the two. I've ….."

"Rattigan? You should have said. I've got about a million Rattigans."

Bettinson tapped the other machine. The one she wasn't on. He started to jiggle it out of hibernation.

"I thought I was looking at the complete archive? I thought I was running through your archive?"

"The archive, yes, that's the archive. Actual projects and stuff are here. I'd never find the stuff otherwise." He clicked around on the other desktop and brought up a whole list of files. He clicked the first one and got up a shot of Rattigan grinning with a bay horse leaning over his shoulder. "I did a lot of stuff for the Rattster. Lost my best client when that plane went down."

"He asked Emily if she had a laptop and he attached a cable to it from the desktop. He copied across the entire collection. Five hundred and sixty-three megabytes of it. She arrived forty minutes early for her meeting with the CPS.

-12-

The CPS meeting went well and although she accomplished less than she wanted, it was more than she expected. There was some sort of plan in place anyway, and the CPS was happy with the stuff that the accountants were preparing.

Afterwards she went back to the office and couldn't resist looking at her laptop. Within five minutes she'd found what she was looking for. Johnston and Rattigan together at the racetrack. Champagne glasses in hand. Laughing hard at something off camera. Celebrating a winner, by the look of it. Friends, not just casual acquaintances. She flicked through the entire collection. Perhaps she was missing some shots, but she could at least log seven dates when the two were snapped together at Chepstow. Fifteen months. Seven dates. The millionaire and the embezzler.

One of the dates was in March 2008. That fact resonated with her for some reason, but she couldn't work out why. She stared at the list until she decided that staring wasn't a useful investigative technique. She realised that she hadn't done any of the things she had returned to the office to do, so she hurried up and finished them quickly.

She worked until eight and then went to her parents' for dinner. Her father, Frank, was out, no doubt keeping tabs on the secret elite unit he had inherited from Sir Ray Quinn upon his retirement. Emily and Books had become the latest members, and the current clandestine operation was now in full swing, with the two of them at its heart.

The huge mock Tudor house enveloped Emily with happy memories and she felt completely at home. Her younger sister, Ant, hugged her and Emily was struck by how tall and strong she'd grown, despite being only thirteen years old. They ate a hearty dinner and settled to watch a TV chef telling them how to bake sea bream in the Spanish way.

Her sister had homework that she wanted to get on with and Emily went with her. It took just fifteen minutes because Emily dictated the answers, while music played loudly and filled the bedroom.

Ant then told her an involved story about her friend's dog who had damaged its forelegs and now had a kind of trolley it pushes itself around on. She lay on her front, kicking her calves in the air. She was at that age when she was almost exactly half girl, half young woman. Emily wondered if she'd done that when she was that age, feeling ordinary, feeling safe. Three years before her life exploded.

"It hurts its legs?"

Her sister treated her to a quizzical look, asking why she could be so daft when she'd just been told.

"Yes, the front legs. She didn't lose them exactly, but there was some problem with the joints and she couldn't walk on them anymore." She finished with an exasperated sigh at Emily's stupidity.

Emily had switched off before her sister finished, so she didn't cotton on to the request for support in her quest to get a TV in her room.

"Don't ask Mum, ask Dad," Emily advised.

"I have, but he only says to ask Mum."

"I know. And she's never going to say yes, is she? It's Dad you need to work on."

"Kay has one," Ant moaned.

Kay was their other sister. The middle one. Eighteen. Smokily sexy with random teenage sulks, leaving a trail of broken hearts behind her.

"She didn't get one until she was sixteen. But you need to forget about Mum and work on Dad."

"But you can tell her, though. Will you? She listens to you." Ant was in full whining and facial contortion mode.

"Why bother?" Emily said. "You can get everything you want on iPlayer anyway."

Ant made a face at her. Emily thought betrayal of the sisterhood, teenage alienation and a certain existential suffering were the major themes of the look in question.

Emily went downstairs and settled onto the sofa.

"Ant seems to want a TV a lot," she ventured.

"Only because her friends do. She really doesn't like TV that much." Mother countered the approach.

"It would keep her off the computer, though, I suppose. God knows what kids find on those these days."

Mum made a face that said everything was better when people wore corsets.

"You can block things, you know," Mum said. "There are ways that stop the kids watching TV after a certain point in the evening or whatever."

"You're as bad as your father," Mum replied.

She smiled at her mother and thought that Ant was halfway to her TV.

"I should go. Thanks for supper." Emily was thinking about the prospect of spending time with Books and felt a flutter in her stomach and a warm, moist feeling further south.

"Don't be silly, love." She hesitated for a moment but stopped short of inviting her daughter to stay the night. "You coming over at the weekend? Your Dad would love to see you."

"Maybe."

"Oh, don't be like that, love. You know he would."

Emily laughed and explained as she put on her shoes that her 'maybe' meant possibly she might come over at the weekend, not maybe her Dad would love to see her. Her mother's misinterpretation was instructive. Her mother had never been comfortable with the career path Emily had chosen, possibly because of the sacrifices that would inevitably need to be made and the difficult times her daughter would have. Not to mention the mortal danger she feared would come her way.

"I'd love to come over if he's around," she said.

"He'll probably be at work on Saturday," her mother replied. "They seem to be very busy at the moment."

Emily smiled at her mother and was grateful that she didn't know the half of it. Or anywhere near that fraction.

"That's good, it's good to be busy."

Emily got a face from Mum for saying that. She was a good Methodist girl married to a man who had never been a good Methodist boy and she liked none of the business that claimed her husband's attention. She could have married a bank manager, but that wouldn't have been anywhere near as exciting.

Emily headed home.

She had forgotten the photos of April, so they took her by surprise. She didn't turn the living room lights on and instead stared at them in the half-light of the street lights outside and the ceiling light through the half open door.

Six little Aprils. No answers.

There was one answer she could find, though. She booted up her laptop and checked the notes she'd made on all those racing websites. In March 2008, Johnston's horse had some veterinary problem that stopped it racing for eight weeks. A problem with its leg. It was Ant's story about the trolley-dog that jogged her memory. Yet Johnston and Rattigan were still there, down at the track, all friendly over champagne and horse dung. Horseracing friends without the horse.

She was tired. She closed the laptop and grinned up at April. She got six little smiles in return.

"It's been a long day," she told her.

No answer to that, but it wasn't a clever thing to say. She'd only got night and it stretched forever.

"I know where you did your drawing," she said, changing tack.

No comment.

"I used to draw a lot as a kid. I probably did flowers like you."

No comment again six times over, which made for a lot of silence in one small living room.

She didn't know if she had drawn a lot as a child. Because of the illness in her teens, her childhood seemed like something viewed over the side of a hill. Little snippets came back to her. But she didn't know where they'd come from or if they were true. She had a story about her past more than actual functional memories of it, but for all she knew, everyone was in the same position. Perhaps childhoods are things we all live through once, she pondered, and then we reconstruct in fantasy. Maybe no one has the childhood they think they've had.

"You think too much," said April, or at least, that was what she'd probably have said if she hadn't got this 'omerta' thing going.

"Goodnight, sweetheart. I'll see you tomorrow."

She slept well and dreamt of Ant combing her hair in front of a mirror. In the dream she wanted her own hair to look like that, but she knew it never would.

-13-
She sat up in bed at five the next morning. She lived on a housing estate, with the increasingly important Books for company, but it was strange. The estate was crammed with humans and she could hear almost no human noise. There was a strange feeling in her body, a kind of prickle, but she couldn't put words to it and she didn't know why it was there. When she was coming out of her illness, her doctor had given her exercises to work on. They were mostly bullshit and had little to do with her recovery, but they were still a fallback for her and she started them again. She tried naming the feeling. Fear. Anger. Jealousy. Love. Happiness. Disgust. Yearning. Curiosity.

Her doctors had imaginations as narrow as their educations and they never came up with more than six or eight emotions in total. She had more imagination than was good for her and she had far too many words. A sense of excess. A desire for simplicity. Envy of her sister's hair. She had a hundred names for a hundred feelings and they all seemed clumsy and inappropriate, like wooden coins. Clothes fitted for a different body shape.

Her failure to get to grips with whatever she was feeling freaked her out a bit. She tried her breathing exercise, the way she'd been taught. Long slow breaths brought her pulse rate down. When her breathing and heart rate were both in good shape, she gave it another two minutes, then pulled a dressing gown over her pyjamas. She wandered out into the garden, drank some tea and eventually ate a bowl of muesli and half a grapefruit.

The morning became gradually noisier. More traffic. The sound of breakfast TV from next door. Kids kicked balls around outside. A delivery van. She liked it and wanted to go on sitting around in her dressing gown, thinking of nothing in particular. But duty called. The last couple of days had been good for her and she didn't want to lose their momentum. She didn't want to lose the security of doing something in a way that earned the respect of her peers. In an ideal world, she'd earn the respect of her superiors too, but that was a different matter entirely.

She showered and dressed reasonably hurriedly, because she'd inevitably let things get late and she was in danger of missing the sharp means sharp morning briefing. As she left the house, she noticed her clothes. Beige trousers, brown boots, white shirt, khaki jacket: the office version of combat wear. She didn't have time to change. She compromised by applying a neutral, almost self-coloured, lipstick using her rear view mirror. It didn't make much difference, but she thought her sister would have approved.

Up and at 'em. She drove, too fast, into the station, was in the briefing room by eight eighteen precisely, and was the fourth officer present. The prickle was still there, albeit fainter. She decided to treat it as a good thing, a positive energy. An energy she intended to put to work.

When she logged onto the Weatherbys website, she knew what she was looking for and was not surprised to find it. Johnston only owned a share in one racehorse, the one she already knew about. But he had an alter ego, Bryan P. Henry, who owned shares in a further four horses. Two of those had Rattigan as co-owner. One more had at least close Rattigan associates as co-owners. The last one had no obvious connection to Rattigan, but she was convinced there was one. One of Bryan P. Henry's horses was a winner at Chepstow the day that Johnston's horse was laid up and unable to race.

Five horses, not one.

The two men were friends, not acquaintances, and the £40,000 hole had just grown into something a whole lot deeper and ten shades darker. She wondered whose bodied were lying at the bottom.

She was standing up and reaching for her car keys before she'd even logged out of the site.

-14-

The Crescent, off Station Road. The ordinariness of the place was almost overwhelming. The street was not modern, but the houses were Victorian and mostly large. There was a mixture of terraced and semi-detached properties and a good number were in need of some tender loving care. There was also a care home, which had been created by merging two or three houses, and the odd bungalow stood, brave and defiant, breaking up the pattern.

She rang the bell of number 27. There was a car, an old Toyota Yaris, in the road outside. Emily spotted that it had the required parking permit for the residents' zone. She also noted that several others did not and wondered how quick on the draw the local authority officers were around there. The gardens were either totally unkempt or beautifully tidy and colourful. There didn't seem to be much in between. The neigbours had made an attempt at planting, but there was much need of watering, she thought.

The weather was warm, but had a kind of pressing closeness. Distances blurred into haze, while objects that were close at hand seemed preternaturally distinct. The whole world need a good rainstorm to wake it up, and Emily thought she did as well.

She was about to ring again when she caught noises from within. A shape glimpsed behind frosted glass and then the sound of the catch and the door swinging open.

"Mr. Johnston. We met six weeks ago, down at the station."

There was no need to give her name, she thought, as it would be a test to jog his memory. They had met when he was being interviewed, even though she was very much in the background that day.

He was a tough looking fifty. His hair was still dark and was worn longish and untidy. His face was mostly unlined, but the lines that were present were deep. He was the sort who would have fitted straight into a 1970's TV drama. All leather jackets and free-flying fists. He was wearing jeans, with no shoes or socks, and a ropy old T-shirt that advertised some sailing club or other. His feet were tough and brown, with nails like slices of old horn.

He didn't answer immediately, or open the door any further, or indeed do anything else other than look at her and smirk to himself.

"Well, it must be important if they've sent you."

"May I come in?"

It was a real question that, as Johnston well knew. If he refused there would be nothing she could do about it. The law of 'my home is my castle,' the law made sacred by Magna Carta and everything since, meant that 'no' had the strength of iron bars. Unless she had a properly signed warrant, which he surmised, accurately, that she did not because she would have mentioned it at the outset.

He paused a long time before answering. "Do you want coffee?"

His question sounded invitational, but his posture was anything but. He was still hanging on the door, scratching his chest inside his T-shirt, showing his abs and pecs and body hair.

Emily was not normally impressed by macho display, but she was being professional and, in any case, he knew every police trick in the book, so she stayed calm.

"I don't drink coffee, but if you've got herbal tea, then I'd like that."

"You'll need to wash up first. The mugs are in the sink."

"Well," she shrugged, "if you sort out the tea things, I'll wash the mugs."

That response got another second or two of posturing, before he swung the door open and walked through to the kitchen. Emily followed.

The house was messy. Not slum messy, just single man messy. Or, more accurately, single man who's not expecting to pull messy. He wasn't kidding about the mugs either. His kitchen sink was piled with dirty crockery, with a fatty scum on the surface of the water. The lid of his kitchen bin was missing, and the bin bag was full of beer cans, juice cartons and ready meal wrappers.

Johnston ostentatiously flicked the switch of the kettle and told Emily that his share of the chores was done. He stood behind her, too close, deliberately crowding her space. She didn't want to touch his mugs or crockery, let alone put her hand in the slick of the sink. She compromised by picking up the two least repulsive mugs, running the tap into the sink and doing a quick, crude decontamination job. She presented him with the mugs, washed her hands in the running water. She managed to turn off the tap just as the slick threatened to spill out over the draining board. Wherever the overflow pipe was, it wasn't doing its job.

Johnston put coffee granules in his cup and poured hot water on. No Milk. No sugar.

"I don't have any herbal tea."

He grinned, challenging her to respond.

"Good. Then I won't need this," she said, as she tossed the mug she was holding into the open bin. "Shall we talk?"

Johnston left the mug where it had landed. He seemed genuinely pleased by their interaction and barefooted his way into the living room, which was untidy rather than squalid. There was a view through to the back of the house, where Johnston's conservatory jutted out into the town as if nosing into Falmouth Week. She paused just long enough to take it in. It was empty, except for some plastic wrapping and some builder's debris, swept into a corner but not cleared. A pair of keys hung on a nail banged into the frame next to the door. The piano was there, but it was dusty from the building work and she couldn't see any music for it.

Johnston sat in what was obviously his armchair, as it had an unobstructed view of the TV. Emily took a seat on the sofa, from where she got a slightly angled view of his face.

"I thought you might like to know where our case stands. I have one or two more questions. And, of course, the more you co-operate, the more that will be taken into account when it comes to sentencing."

He stared at her and sipped his coffee. He said nothing. Emily recalled that it was a back injury that forced his retirement, and she noticed that his chair was one of those ugly orthopaedic numbers. There was a packet of Paracetamol on the table. People always suspect that when a police officer retires with a back injury, it's mostly a question of the job having taken its toll over the years. Too many years of hassle and retirement the easy option. The Paracetamol suggested otherwise.

She quickly summarized where they were in preparing the prosecution case, which was pretty much all systems go, following her meeting with the CPS and the accountants. She gave an estimate of the timeline.

He answered with a question.
"How old are you?"

She paused for long enough to demonstrate that she was answering because she chose to, not because she was stuck in one of his games.

"Twenty-six."

"You look younger. You look like a baby."

"Good skincare," she replied.

"Who are you working with?" He asked.

Emily didn't answer. She waited as she wanted to know whether he knew anything about the various aspects of her life and work.

"Matthews, I should think," he eventually said.

Emily was pleased that he was obviously only aware of her police role and not her undercover work.

"Yes, Matthews," she agreed.

Johnston acknowledged the answer with a slight grunt, but he had already sacrificed a little of his authority. He had managed to establish that she had the answers that he wanted, and he'd reminded himself that baby-faced Emily was representing grizzled DCI Matthews. It was the first tiny victory she had won. He must have known that because he reverted to silence. For the first time she heard the slightly asthmatic whine in his breath, the only thing that could be heard on the interview tapes.

She let the pause continue. It was her pause now. She owned it and rode that fact for all it was worth. When she did eventually speak she said, "the thing is, we're both coppers, so we both know the deal. You stole money. We found out. You're going to jail. The only question is, how long for? That's the only factor you can influence. And we both know that the less co-operative you are, the longer you go down for. In a way, your life is shot whatever, but you can choose just how shot to make it. Anywhere on a range from quite a bit to quite a lot.

With ordinary crooks, I don't expect too much. They don't co-operate, because they are not being rational, or they can't bear to help us out, or whatever else it is. You're not like that. You're a pro, so you'll be hard-headed about these things. And the fact that you're telling us nothing makes me curious about a few things. And if you care to know what I'm curious about, then I'll tell you."

The silence in the room had a frozen quality to it, as though it might have cracked if anybody tried you move against it. Johnston couldn't tell Emily that he was hungry for information, because that would have offended against his little power games. On the other hand, he couldn't say anything because he wanted to hear what she had to say. Once again, she let the silence do its work.

"Firstly, where did your money come from? You spent more money than you stole, or your friend Mr. Brian P. Henry did anyway. Now, I'm going to take a wild guess and say I know the answer to that. I think the money came from Rattigan. But that brings us to question number two: what services were rendered in exchange for that money? As far as I know, multimillionaires aren't in the habit of giving something for nothing. And number three, just how much precisely do you know about this?"

From her case she extracted the evidence bag with Rattigan's Platinum card inside it. Johnston reached for it, stared at it and handed it back. He was not even pretending to be uninterested now. His brown eyes had a complexity in them that was missing before.

"You might like to know where we found it. We found it at an address where we also found a woman dead and her daughter murdered. The mother may have been murdered too. We can't say for definite. So you see why I'm curious. If it were only the debit card and the fact that you happened to share an interest in racing with its owner, then I'd say it was all a coincidence. Something worth investigating maybe, but not the sort of thing that Matthews would start throwing resources at. As it is, though, your silence kind of connects you to that house, doesn't it? Any reasonable ex-policeman in your position would be co-operating with us to bring his sentence down. You haven't co-operated at all. And the more you don't tell us, the more you are telling us that we have to investigate as closely as we possibly can. Which turns an ordinary little bit of embezzlement into something altogether more interesting. Something that's maybe just a step or two away from murder."

She finished. She'd said nothing about her other suspicions concerning terrorism and a sinister international connection that may have been threatening the nation. Johnston also said nothing. As a way of gathering information, it had not precisely yielded a rich harvest, but not all harvests look the same or ripen quickly.

Emily stood up. From her case she dug out the INFORMATION WANTED notice that was appearing in the locality. She dropped it onto the coffee table, but it slithered from there to the floor. Neither of them stirred to pick it up.

"That's the murdered woman. That's her murdered child. That's the number you'd need to call with information."

She snapped her case shut and went to the front door to let herself out. Johnston didn't move.

"By the way, this house is a shit hole," she called through to the living room. "And you should see somebody about that asthma."

Outside on the too-bright street, she took stock. Johnston was probably watching from the living room, but if he was, she didn't care.

His car was dark blue. There was a rust spot above the offside wheel arch and the whole car could have benefitted from a wash. She wondered who owned shares in a clutch of expensive racehorses and drove a car that, if not quite a pile of rubbish, was not exactly a thing of beauty either.

She looked back into the living room. He was at the window scrutinizing her. She smiled and gave him a twinkling wave as she returned to her car.

On her way back into the office, her mobile bleeped the arrival of a text. Despite knowing she shouldn't, and being very aware of the consequences if caught, she picked it up. 'JENNAS NOT DEAD YOU LIARS IF SHE IS SHES LUCKYER THAN SOME.' Her first thought was that it was a wind-up from a colleague, but then she wondered whether it was an answer to the notice she'd put up in the shop window. She pulled over and jammed the car into the only available space on the side of the road. She texted back 'WHAT HAPPENED TO HER THEN?'

She waited. She was parked by a chip shop. A young mum, overweight, led two overweight kids of her own. One of the two, a boy with a taut red face, started eating from a bag of chips, holding them away from his brother, jamming them successively into his mouth with a savage intensity.

Obesity. Violence. Drugs. Prostitution. A million different ways to screw up your life. Johnston chose embezzlement, his own sweet route to self-destruction. What made him take that turning? What accounted for the beat up car and the expensive empty conservatory?

Then, just as she was thinking she wasn't going to get a reply, a text beeped its way into her consciousness. 'RICH PEOPLE DON'T HAVE POLICE SHIT ITS PEOPLE LIKE JENNA THAT GET IT.'

There were two ways to read these texts, she thought. The obvious one was the way her colleagues would read them. They're deranged. They had no evidential value. Also, there was a reason why requests for information should have been channeled through official 0800 numbers, not to officers' personal mobiles. But there was another way to read them. Firstly, anyone who knew Jenna Mancini was quite likely a poorly educated, drug addicted prostitute, so bad spelling and non-existent grammar might have been a sign that the texter was in a position to know something. Also, the second text was odd. It was making a connection between Jenna's death and 'rich people.' That would have meant nothing, except that Rattigan's card was found in Jenna's squat. And that in itself might have meant nothing, except for the knowledge that he liked it rough and nasty. And all of that might have meant nothing, except that the frozen silence she had experienced with Johnston told her that there were big things hovering close by, unsaid.

No other texts came through, so she sent one back. 'I WON'T MAKE ANY FURTHER ATTEMPT TO CONTACT YOU, BUT YOU SHOULD FEEL FREE TO CALL OR TEXT ME AT ANY TIME. I WANT TO HELP JENNA AS MUCH AS YOU DO.'

She pressed send.

To Emily nothing was making sense. She was part of a secret, elite group to fight threats to her country and she had been placed within the police force, undercover, to facilitate that role. Other people's puzzles were her puzzles. She was on a hiding to nothing though, but even that phrase intrigued her. An act of concealment in one half with nothing at all in the other. The phrase itself was a mystery wanting solution.

Her brain was too busy. She figured there was one way to lower the pressure and that was to make sure Rattigan was well and truly dead. She rooted around in the back of her car for the AAIB report. She found it and dialed the number.

With an extraordinary lack of bureaucracy, she was put through swiftly to the person she needed to speak to.

"Robin Keighley." English voice. The sort of voice that Americans love to mock. The sort they associate with effete, end-of-empire aristocracy. But it was friendly and competent, which was good enough for her.

She introduced herself and told him why she was calling. She asked him about the plane crash. He was open and easy with his answers, which roughly speaking followed the gist of the report. The plane had taken off and headed for Rattigan's holiday home in southern Spain. They had run into bad weather, and the pilot reported an unidentified problem with an engine. He had asked Bristol airport for permission to make an emergency landing, which was given. His course was duly altered. Then there was silence, a short radio burst that basically consisted of two short expletives from the pilot, then nothing.

She spoke to Keighley for about twenty minutes. The plane was a Learjet, a good plane, properly maintained. Until the very end of the flight proper procedures had been followed. Emily noticed, however, a slight hesitation in his voice when he mentioned the pilot. When she pressed this, he said, "Well, nothing really. The pilot was experienced enough, but he had no background in either the RAF or any of the big commercial airlines."

"Any significance in that?"

"Not really. RAF pilots are obviously trained to operate in extreme conditions. Equally, any pilot for a big commercial airline like BA will be put into a flight simulator every six months and have every kind of disaster thrown at them. Those guys have to take it all and pass their tests or they're grounded until they do."

"So maybe a pilot a bit less experienced than you'd like?"

"Less experienced than I'd like, yes. But then flight safety is my business. Rattigan's pilot was fully qualified to be flying the plane he was flying."

"Any evidence of foul play at all in the wreckage? Anything at all? Even a whisper of a hint that you couldn't put in your report because there wasn't enough to go on?"

"No, nothing, but most of the plane is at the bottom of the sea. I couldn't rule out foul play, but have no reason to suspect it."

"Was this an aircraft type known to have problems? Does the accident fit any kind of known pattern?"

"Yes and no, I suppose you'd say. No in the sense that this was a perfectly decent plane and all the rest of it..."

"But?" Emily felt she was onto something.

"But then again, if you do get human or maintenance error, you're most likely to get it with smaller aircraft owned by outfits that don't have the depth of technical and safety culture that you're going to find at BA, say, or any of its peers. That's why most accidents are, and have always been, in the general aviation sector."

"So putting aside any official report, your gut feeling would be that someone cocked up. If the plane wasn't sitting many fathoms down, you might have a chance of identifying the culprit. As it is, you're obliged to shrug your shoulders and chalk it up as one of those things."

"Putting any official report a long way to one side, then yes."

"Can I ask one last question? Off the record, non- official, wild speculation?"

"Fire away."

"OK. Do you attach any significance to the fact that Rattigan's body was never found?"

Emily heard an intake of breath down the line. Keighley was taken aback by the sudden turn in the conversation and he answered cautiously. "Significance, such as what, for example?"

"Let's just suppose there was a theory that Rattigan in some way arranged the plane crash. That he escaped, his pilot died. Or perhaps the accident was perfectly genuine, but Rattigan seized the opportunity to disappear because he happened to want to for some reason. Is there anything at all in the circumstances of the crash that would make better sense in the light of such a theory?"

Keighley was silent for a long ten seconds. Then he said, "sorry, got to think about that," and was silent for another fifteen.

"OK, then, I've got to say probably no. Nothing comes to mind, except maybe...well, Rattigan's body was never recovered. The pilot wore a lifejacket and was quickly identified and his body retrieved. If Rattigan had been wearing a lifejacket, then his body should certainly have been recovered too. And there was no sign of it at all. That is odd. Contrary to the rulebook, if you like. Yet even for that, there are a million innocent explanations, all of which might be more likely than your theory. If, for example, he panicked and simply failed to release his seat belt, then he'd have been dragged under by the wreckage. Or if he refused to put his lifejacket on, even if the pilot told him to, then that would account for it too. Stranger things have happened."

They talked on, and Keighley remained helpful, but she got nothing definite. She was further ahead than she had been, but it felt like no progress at all.

She hung up.

The prickle of energy that had woken her that morning was still there and it occurred to her seriously for the first time that it might have been fear. She wasn't sure. There was not the clicking into place sense when the word really matched the feeling. She knew she didn't yet have enough clues.

She drove slowly back to the station, breathing properly as she went.

-15-

There was a briefing later that same day. All hands on deck. The DNA results were back from the lab and the word was that some came with names.

There was a frisson in the room, a stirring of the waters, a raised energy level that came from people assuming that the investigation was about to start coming up with real results. It would be the first time they could actually place named individuals in the house of death. All the report filing, statement taking, pavement pounding and phone answering done so far hadn't, in truth, yielded a single solid meaningful clue.

At nearly ten to four the incident room was already busy. Emily arrived armed with her peppermint tea and one of those energy bars. Jim Davis was at the coffee machine, as driven as a piglet at a teat.

"Hey Jim," she said a little warily. She knew he was not her greatest fan but those who could be counted as members of that club formed a fairly select body.

He acknowledged her with a nod even though he was in the middle of a moaning session with some of his colleagues.

"More work, less pay. Always the same, isn't it?" He declared to anybody who was listening.

Emily couldn't see that a lack of DI slots was going to affect Davis's life chances all that much, but she didn't say so. He had his coffee and was about to plunge his yellow teeth in for another caffeine bath. She didn't want to watch that and managed to squeeze by him.

By that time the room was full. Hughes and Jackson did their processional thing to the front of the room and silence took over. Jackson ran through the DNA findings. The lab had examined over a hundred samples taken from the house and of those, DNA was successfully extracted from a total of thirty-two samples, yielding seven different profiles. Of those seven, two were Jenna and April.

Jackson paused, enjoying the moment of suspense, before releasing his news.

"Of the five remaining profiles, we've got names on the database for four. That means we can place those four people at the house. We don't know when they were there and we don't know why they were there. Those are questions we need to get answered."

The briefing continued. The four names were Tony Leonard. Drug user. Small time dealer, which is how his DNA was on the database. No known involvement in prostitution. His sample was a single hair, found on the dirty velour floor in the living room.

Karol Sikorsky. Forty-four. Prosecuted three years earlier for a replica firearms offence, but the prosecution failed due to 'official error.' He was prosecuted and convicted instead for a minor charge of affray. Born Russian, but he possessed a Polish passport. Thus, he had not been deported. Sikorsky was suspected by Vice of involvement in drugs, prostitution and, perhaps, extortion as well. His was a poor quality saliva sample found on a glass in the kitchen. A much better sample, courtroom quality no less, was found on the tip of a nail that projected from the living room doorframe. He must have caught himself on it as he leaned against the door.

"A brilliant bit of forensic investigation," Jackson commented," to notice the nail, to investigate it, to successfully, extract a sample. Brilliant." The room burst into spontaneous applause for the SOCO concerned.

Conway Lloyd. Thirty-one. Arrested for a public order offence in his early twenties. Never prosecuted, but his DNA had remained on the database ever since. Big Brother had his uses. "Who needs civil liberties?" Emily pondered to herself. Big splatter of semen on the mattress upstairs and hairs as well. Further semen stains found on the carpet downstairs. He was not a tidy boy, wasn't Conway. Careless.

Rhys Vaughan. Twenty-one. Might have been Lloyd's twin. Semen found in four different locations, including, to Emily's amusement, a knotted condom that sat in a little china ashtray by the upstairs mattress. There was also hair and saliva in his case. Just as careless as Conway.

"And," said Jackson, holding up his hand to command silence, "we've got one extra name from fingerprints. Stacey Edwards. Thirty-three. Convicted of a couple of soliciting offences in her twenties. Five contacts with Vice over the years. She is still assumed to be active. Her fingerprints were scattered all over the downstairs of the house including the one place we didn't expect to find anything. The washing up brush."

This elicited laughter and sycophantic applause.

"Now," he continued, "strategy."

Jackson was a smart officer. The bullheaded approach would have been to go in hot and heavy on the names that had been identified, to try and force a confession. The problem was that anyone who had gone to the house to commit murder would have taken basic precautions. Even if the murder wasn't premeditated any vaguely competent killer would have attempted to protect themselves against crime scene investigation. Indeed, the killer had taken such precautions, since there were no prints at all found on the sink, which would have collected them perfectly.

Vaughan and Lloyd, on the other hand, had taken no precautions at all. Neither had Stacey Edwards. Maybe Leonard had tried to clean up after himself, but Emily guessed that Jackson didn't believe him to be the killer.

Sikorsky appeared to be the favourite contender, the prime suspect.

Jackson concluded by saying that they should treat at least four of the five names with a little delicacy, not as suspects but as witnesses. People who could provide information. That may involve a little bullying, but nothing too heavy. Jackson handed out assignments and Hughes updated the whiteboard.

The meeting broke up. Emily charged across the room to grab Jackson. She didn't get to him first, but she was persistent as she tagged alongside him and entered his office in his wake. She had a banter-rich opening lined up, but his face was tired and the way he said, "yes?" wasn't precisely designed to encourage. She decided to alter her approach.

"Stacey Edwards. If I can be of help there...."

"We've got that assigned already," he replied. "Jane Alexander and Davis. Between them they've got a million years of this sort of thing. And she is a woman, as you may have noticed, so we've got the feminine tact angle covered."

Emily didn't have a counter argument, just an urgency that she didn't herself understand. She used what she had.

"If you were a prostitute, maybe a friend of Mancini's, probably scared of the police maybe in possession or crucial evidence, would you rather talk to Jane and Davis or Jane and me? These girls are..."

"Women. They're not girls."

"I don't know why but this case really matters to me. I think I can contribute. I really want to contribute."

"You are contributing. You continue by doing what you're told to do. That's your job."

"I know. I..."

She didn't know what to say, so stopped and just stood there. It seemed to have the desired effect.

"Where have you got on the Johnston thing?" he asked.

She briefed him quickly. He then half listened and used the rest of his attention to check out her notes on the office system. She had got much further than he had any right to expect and she could see he was impressed. She didn't say anything about Johnston's extra horses, the strange texts or her other things. She kept it clean and simple.

He pulled his attention away from the computer and shoved the keyboard from him with an annoyed flip of his fingers. Going to the door he yelled for Davis and Alexander.

Returning to his seat, he told her, "you mess, you mess up at all, and you'll never work on a delicate assignment for me again."

Emily thought seriously about bringing him to heel with a simple phone call. It would have been easy, but what purpose would it serve? She swallowed her pride and nodded. He hadn't earned a 'Sir', though.

"I'm going to ask Jane Alexander to give me detailed feedback on how you comport yourself in your dealings with Stacey Edwards. Alexander makes the running. You make the notes. She makes the decisions. You make the tea."

She repeated the nod and he gave her a few seconds of shaggy-eyed scrutiny in return.

"You must have worked late to do this lot." He gestured at the computer.

She nodded again. The repeated nodding was beginning to strain her subordination muscles and she let them pause for a rest. Their conversation was brought to a close by Davis and Alexander appearing at the door.

"Come in. I've decided we need an all female team for Edwards. Jane, I wAnt you to lead. You'll have Emily for support. Jim, go to Ken Hughes and get an alternative assignment. Everybody clear? Ok then get on with it. Out of here."

As they left, Davis gave Emily one of the blackest looks she had ever witnessed. He was also muttering obvious profanities under his breath. Jane looked at his retreating back. It was pretty clear that she was taken aback by the strength of his reaction. As she turned to Emily she adjusted her face until it showed nothing but friendly competence. But Emily had caught something else on her face. A micro-expression that hadn't lasted long enough for her to capture and understand it.

They moved to Jane's desk and Emily said, "I suppose you'll want me to prepare an interview briefing? See what we can rustle up on Edwards before we go to see her?"

It was clearly a new thought for her. Not the way Jim Davis had been going at it.

"Briefing? You think there's enough material for that?"

"She's had five contacts with Vice over the years. We've almost certainly got people who have a reasonable idea of what she's like. She's probably had contact with the Street-Safe people. You know, the prostitution outreach charity. I'm sure they'd be willing to chat with us, as long as we made it clear that Edwards isn't a suspect."

"Ok, but look, it's Friday afternoon now. We need to get on with it. Jackson is going to…"

"I'll get straight onto Vice now. Then go and talk to the Street-Safe people this evening. They work nights, obviously. I can get some notes typed up overnight. Then I'll run those past whichever one of the vice boys I can lay my hands on tomorrow morning. We should be prepared enough to see Edwards by midday. It doesn't make any sense to call on her before that anyway."

Alexander raised her eyebrows at Emily. "Why?"

"Because she works at night. Midday might even be a bit early."

Alexander listened with a combination of surprise and amusement.

"Are you always like this?" she asked.

"Like what?" Emily wondered whether she had already messed up.

"Like a one-woman work monster. If you think you can do all that, brilliant. But if not, you know, it would be ok just to go and talk to her."

Emily thought she was being kind and it wasn't something she was used to.

"No, I'm not normally like this. It's just that this case has really got to me?"

Emily had other information, of course, from another source, but couldn't say anything about it.

Why don't you give yourself a break? Jim and I were just going to go and call on Edwards. Play it by ear. That's what everyone else will be doing."

"Will it bother you if I do what I suggested? I honestly think I'd prefer to do it that way."

"Ok. But be careful, Emily. If you get too involved there'll be a crash. There always is."

Emily employed her submissive nod yet again.

Back at her desk, there was a message from Keighley. It said that on reflection there was something odd about the crash. The double expletive from the pilot, then silence. "Even in a serious crash, that kind of pattern is highly unusual. We'd normally expect continuing radio contact, even in cases where the pilot isn't sure himself what's going on. I wouldn't make too much of it. There could be a dozen different explanations. But there you go. You asked if there was anything untoward, and on that basis I would have to say yes. Not much. But something."

Emily listened to the message three times. She then logged onto the Financial Times website and searched for Rattigan Industrial & Transport Ltd. She reasoned that it never hurt to read too much or too widely. She researched for almost an hour.

-16-

Bryony Williams wore a padded canvas jacket over a sweat top and jeans. She had shortish hair with a bit of a curl. She was tough, but in the right way. The kind of tough that allowed room for tender. She sat on a low wall that marked the garden of a boarded-up house.

"Busy evening?" Emily asked.

"Not yet."

It was about nine in the evening and the street lamps produced more light than the embers of sunset. Behind them stood a row of houses and in front there was a strip of grass. This had been recently mown and the air smelled of cut grass and river mud.

It was a quiet scene. Pleasant. Except that they were in the heart of the red-light district and, like the stars in the sky above them, the first ladies of the night were beginning to appear. A couple of lads emerged from a pub just up the road, walked passed and whistled at her. She responded with a v - sign and they wandered away.

"You know why I'm here?" Emily asked.

"Yep. Gill said you'd be coming."

Gill Parker was StreetSafe's project co-ordinator. She'd been running the show since 2004. Saint, hero, angel, nutcase. Take your pick. Bryony was hewn from the same stock.

"Stacey Edwards. Gill told me you know her." Emily said.

"Yep. We know Stacey very well. Unfortunately," replied Bryony Williams.

"And you know why we want to talk to her?"

"Not really."

Bryony's tone wasn't exactly hostile, but was certainly not welcoming either. StreetSafe was a charity that handed out soup, condoms, and health advice. They also helped women break the self-destructive merry-go-round of drugs, alcohol and prostitution. They had good relations with the police, but what they did and the actions of the police were aimed in different directions. Enforcing the law was one kind of challenge, but handing out friendship and sympathy was quite another.

Emily said, "Jenna Mancini, drug user and part-time prostitute. Died. Probably killed. Her six-year old daughter was killed too. There's evidence that they were afraid, possibly in hiding, before their death. Stacey Edwards wasn't the killer." Emily went on to tell her about the state of the house and Edwards's prints on the washing-up brush. "It looks likely that Edwards was a friend, trying to help."

"Probably. The women usually stick together." Bryony observed.

Emily was not satisfied and applied a little force.

"Bryony, you need to respect confidences, I know that. But my colleagues want to go in, kick down her door and give her a very uncomfortable interview. The kind of thing that isn't going to help her. It probably won't help us either, or the two dead Mancinis."

"So, what do you want?"

"I want to know about....everything. About Stacey Edwards. About who Mancini might have worked with. Who controls these girls. Who makes money off them. Who might have a reason to kill Mancini."

"You don't want much, then," answered Bryony, with a trace of humour."

The question about who makes money turned out to be the easiest. In the end, everything came down to drugs. Usually class-A. Any money the women made from punters went straight to their dealers.

"What about their pimps? They take a cut, presumably."

"Kind of. Most of the pimps are basically drug dealers. That's how they get the girls to stay. It's a toss-up whether you want to call them pimps or pushers."

"And are these people local or from further away?"

"Mixture. Used to be mostly girls and foreign pimps. Then there were more and more from Eastern Europe. I'd say most of the girls are foreigners now."

"Trafficked?" asked Emily.

"Don't know. What's trafficking? If you get some Albanian girl hooked on heroin and tell her she can earn more money here, she'll probably choose to come. Nobody's putting a gun to her head. Is she trafficked or not? You tell me."

All the time she was talking to Emily Bryony had her eyes on the street. Without a word she suddenly got up and walked a hundred yards and began talking to another woman that Emily had not noticed. She was away for a few minutes before coming back.

"The girls wanted to know who you are. I said you're police liaison."

"Near enough," agreed Emily.

"Yep. You'll need to bugger off in a bit though. You're making them nervous."

"Jenna Mancini?" Emily asked.

"Never met her. Never heard of her. I mean, until I read it in the papers. She wasn't a full-timer. If she had been, we'd have come across her. Not me necessarily, but Gill or one of the others."

"A kind of amateur, then?" Emily ventured.

"Yep. If you like. She was on drugs, you say?"

"Yes, but she was a battler. It was up and down."

"She should have come to us," Bryony said.

"She had Social Services. They thought she was a trier. That's what makes it worse."

Williams nodded. "Domestic abuse?"

"She was single."

"There'll be abuse in the background somewhere. There always is."

Emily hesitated for a second. Jackson's don't mess up message was playing in her head, but she didn't think she was about to say anything wrong.

"Bryony, we've got a hunch, nothing more at the moment, that Mancini might have specialized in what you could call rough sex. Maybe a bit of slapping around, that kind of thing.

"You're talking about violence against women."

"I know, I know. I'm on your side here, Bryony."

"Yep. Could be. Pays more. Dangerous pays more. If she had a child, then in a weird way maybe she thought she was protecting her by working with fewer clients for more pay."

"Would you know which punters enjoy that kind of thing?" Emily asked.

Bryony laughed. "Hell, no. Most of them, I should think."

"Do you recognise either of these men?"

Emily showed her photos of Rattigan and Johnston. The longest of long shots, but you never knew. Williams studied them before handing them back.

"Nope. He looks a nasty one, though," she said. She meant Johnston.

"Yes, he is."

"Don't recognise them. But it's the women we work with, not the men. Why? Who are they?"

Emily gave the names. Jon Johnston, a former police officer and Rattigan, formerly very rich.

She shook her head. "Sorry."

"Nothing at all? Even hearsay, at this stage is useful."

"Rumours are everywhere in this game. Girls who disappear from view have never just moved on. Something dark has always happened to them. There was one woman, I won't say her name, who everyone said had been killed by a couple of your colleagues in the Vice Unit. Then they'd disposed of her body in a warehouse fire, apparently. Chinese whispers. The truth was she'd moved to Birmingham to live with her sister. I got a Christmas card from her."

Emily laughed at that, but there was not much mirth there. She wondered what it must be like to work in such a profession. Where violence does happen and when fear of violence haunts everything you do or say or know. Jenna Mancini may have lived with all that, but she'd wanted better for April.

Williams's eyes were back on the street. A little way up the street one of the girls was talking to a man, before they both walked away, her long white legs catching the dying light.

"I'm seeing Stacey Edwards tomorrow. Is there anything you can tell me about her?" Emily asked.

"Stacey. She's ok actually. Heroin issue, of course. She's been working with us and really wants to get away from this life. She's been helpful. Spreading the word for us. Her problem is getting over her addiction. It's not just a chemical thing for these women. Childhood abuse. Domestic violence by partners and drug pushers. 'Slapping around' by punters. A hostile approach from the police, often as not."

"But she was an evangelist for you," Emily said. "You reckon she'd have been there trying to help Mancini escape?"

"Yep. I do. From what you say, Mancini wasn't as far gone. She stood a better chance. Also…" Her voice trailed off as she wondered whether to complete the thought.

"Yes?"

"Well, I don't know if it helps, but Edwards has a big Anti-immigrant thing. I don't think it's racist, particularly. Her best friend is a West Indian woman. It's the business end of things she doesn't like. She reckons all these women coming in from the Balkans have made it much more dangerous. The drugs are worse, she says. More heroin coming in from Russia. Afghanistan originally, but it comes via Russia. Meantime, the women are made to work harder. Violence has become more common."

Emily listened intently. Not only was she being given details that might move the case on, she was also being handed information of activities on another level. The level for which she had been embedded. The spectre of international activity and the possibility of links to terrorism, maybe.

"From punters?" Emily asked. She needed to be careful; to gradually elicit the material she was seeking, without giving cause for alarm.

"No, from the pimps and pushers. It's all got more organized and nastier. If Mancini had anything to do with the Albanian crews, Stacey would have been doing her best to warn her off."

"We're looking for people who might have known Mancini. Obviously, Stacey Edwards would be one. If you know any others who might have done? Maybe friends of Stacey's?"

Williams considered that request, then shook her head.

"No. Can't help you there. I mean, I know who Stacey hangs out with, but I've got a duty of confidentiality."

"Jenna Mancini is dead. That's why I'm asking."

"And Stacey Edwards is alive. That's why I'm shutting up."

Emily paused. Softly, softly.

"I'm going to show you a phone number," Emily said. "I don't need you to give me a name or address, but can you just tell me if you recognise the number?"

She showed the number that had texted her outside the chip shop that morning.

Bryony Williams searched her own phone contacts. "Yep."

"Would I be right in thinking that the owner of that phone number would be a prostitute who might well have known Jenna Mancini?"

"I don't know if they knew each other, but yes to the first part of the question and quite possibly to the second as well."

"And it's not Stacey Edwards?"

"You're not allowed that question, but no. Not Stacey."

The night had turned black and the bushes were clotted with shadows. Emily was feeling the cold. She was also aware of the night and the danger. She didn't like being there and wanted to leave.

"Good luck, Bryony. Thanks for talking."

"Sorry I couldn't help more."

"You don't know how much you've helped. Sometimes the little things turn out to be the most helpful."

"Hope so," replied Williams, as she rose and got ready to plunge into the fray.

"One last thing," Emily said. "When Mancini died, we were alerted by an anonymous phone call to a police station. But not here in this place. Female caller."

Williams grimaced. "Stacey's sister possibly. Falmouth. If she had been shaken up by something, she'd have gone to Falmouth."

"Thank you. Fantastic. Thank you." Emily was genuinely grateful as they shook hands.

"Just catch the killer who did it." Bryony told her. It wasn't a request; it was a demand.

"I will and you get your girls away from all this," replied Emily, waving her hand at the bushes and the darkness.

"Women. They are women," said Bryony, grinning.

Emily watched as she passed away into the night. Saint, hero, angel, nutcase. She made her way back to her car and clicked the doors locked. Not a precaution she normally took, but she had been unnerved by the lingering, malignant smell of violence.

The plan, so brightly hatched next to Jane Alexander's desk, was to go on to talk to a couple more of the StreetSafe volunteers, but she knew she couldn't face that. She needed to talk to Books. Not just to pass on the titbits she had gleaned that the elite group might be able to use, but simply because she needed to hear his voice, or at the very least, have some contact with the man who was becoming central to her life.

She sent a text. "HEY BOOKS. YOU AROUND? JUST WONDERED. EM.X"

As she started the engine and began to move, her phone pinged.

"CAN BE IF YOU NEED. ARE YOU IN TROUBLE?"

She didn't know what to say to that. Yes, she was in trouble and on the brink of something horrible and terrifying, but wasn't sure what yet. She decided to calm things down.

"NO. DON'T THINK SO. JUST CHECKING IN."

She felt better knowing that he was around if needed. The thought gave her enough comfort to call on another two StreetSafe volunteers. The information they gave filled out Bryony's picture a little, but didn't fundamentally change anything. The thing about Falmouth seemed like a huge piece of information. Even Jackson was going to love her if she had found his anonymous caller.

At ten forty-five she'd finished interviewing and sped home. Her car had a satnav which warned of speed cameras, which was just as well. There was nothing to eat when she got back. She had forgotten to eat and forgotten to shop. She piled fruit and muesli into a bowl, added an energy bar all crumbled up, and ate as if he life depended on it.

Emily turned her attention to typing up her notes and she did so quickly. By a quarter past midnight, she had finished. She closed up. April's face shone out at her.

"We're getting closer, lamb," she told her, before turning off the bedside light and closing her eyes.

-17-
Emily woke up far too early the next day. It was the kind of waking that prohibits any thought of further sleep. She felt the same weird prickling in her body, which was made a little better because she knew Books would be there if needed. She drove into the office, having had breakfast, and walked into yet another briefing. It was Saturday, but the days were all running into each other, as the beast called work ate their weekends and munched overtime. Everyone was tired.

After the briefing, which Emily hardly listened to at all, she went to Stacey Edwards's flat with Jane Alexander. She lived on a rough looking estate. There were blocks of flats on the left, houses on the right. The kind of houses with builder's rubble in the front garden that has been there so long that there were weeds growing in it. Broken fridges and decaying mattresses. The flats were worse.

She had deliberately dressed casually, but Jane Alexander was in a pale green linen suit over a creamy scoop neck top. Her shoes had been chosen to match her suit. She looked completely out of place as nobody there ever dressed like that, not even the social workers.

Edwards lived in a ground-floor flat in one of the blocks. Her doorbell didn't work, but someone clattered down the stairs from the flats higher up and let them into the entrance area. Edwards's front door was a flimsy affair with a polished plywood front. Emily knocked and then Jane knocked. Still nothing.

Emily had managed to persuade Gill Parker from StreetSafe to give her Edwards's mobile number. She called it and heard the ringing from inside the flat. It didn't get answered. The two women looked at each other. At the front of the block there was a parking area with spaces for six cars. Just two were taken, by a silver Skoda and a dark blue Fiat.

Emily called Bryony Williams and asked if she knew whether Stacey Edwards had a car and if so what. It turned out to be the dark blue Fiat.

"Maybe she's popped out to see a friend," said Bryony.

Maybe. The estate didn't look like the popping around sort of place to Emily. Further down the road, a footpath out to the fields was enclosed between spiked railings that were looped with barbed wire. It was that sort of place. Desolate. Bleak. Without hope.

Emily suggested that they wait for half an hour before trying again. Jane nodded and they went back to Jane's car. They sat, mostly in silence. Emily thought it would be a good idea to park a little way away so that it didn't look like they were watching the place, but she decided not to say so. She didn't want to appear bossy.

They waited half an hour. In that time Emily wondered what it would be like to kiss her colleague. She had ventured down that path some time earlier in her young life and found it quite pleasant, but then Books had come into her life and nothing compared.

Eventually, they both got twitchy. Emily tried Edwards's mobile again, but there was still no response. Nothing had been happening at the front door while they had been waiting, and nothing happened when they knocked again. Decision time.

They inspected the flat outside, peering in where they could, but there were heavy nets down over the grimy windows and it was not possible to see much. At the back, they got a clear view into a small kitchen, which looked cleaner than Johnston's but was still hardly a model of its kind. There was a small frosted window which had been left ajar for ventilation. It offered a gap of about six or seven inches if opened to its fullest extent.

It was too small for a normal adult to climb through, but Jane had the same thought as Emily as they looked at each other. Entering premises without permission or a warrant was not to be done lightly. Rules need to exist but that didn't stop them being viewed as a nuisance to the pair. They also couldn't enter without being there to make an arrest or unless they had reasonable grounds to suppose that entry was necessary to save life or prevent serious injury to somebody.

"I'll call one of the StreetSafe people," said Emily.

She called Bryony Williams on her mobile, fishing for her to tell Emily that she was worried about Stacey Edwards.

"Bryony, I need you to tell me that you fear for Stacey Edwards's safety and that you need us to enter her property. I need you to use those exact words."

Bryony thought for a moment and then did so. Jane heard her as well.

Jane nodded and said, "I'll run it past Jackson first."

Permission was given, which also meant they could have a couple of burly officers to smash the front door if they wanted. "

We don't want to wait for that, do we?" Emily asked. It was more of a statement in truth. "I'll be ok. I think."

There was a very rickety picnic table on a paved area at the back. They dragged it under the window. Emily climbed up and the table wobbled alarmingly. She stood there and considered the situation. She was wearing a loose grey cotton skirt, flat shoes and a long-sleeved top. She couldn't see how both the skirt and her were going to negotiate the window together, so she removed it. Jane suggested they wait but Emily's dignity was too far gone to worry about. She opened the window as far as it would go and stuck her head and shoulders through. Inside, there was a toilet, a small basin with a mirror over, and some clutter. She thrashed her legs and squeezed with her arms and was soon balanced on her front in the window aperture. She could see her own red face in the mirror.

She kicked on. Her thighs scraped painfully as they went through the window. She thought she was going to crash down on her head, but didn't. She wasn't sure how she managed it, but she slithered through without calamity. She was in. The front of her thighs were scraped red and angry. Jane poked her skirt through the window and she put it on. She had dust and black mould marks all over her top, and her hair was full of things she didn't want to think about. She washed her hands, and went to let Jane in.

They tried the living room first. Nothing. Or rather, some needles, bits of foil, candle and matches. An old half lemon too. Some of the foil was blackened with candle smoke. Jane and Emily exchanged glances, but they were not there to hunt for drugs.

Then the bedroom. White walls and tarty red curtains. A big purple duvet. Mirror. And Stacey Edwards. Her hands were tied behind her back and there was duct tape over her mouth. No pulse. No breath. Her skin was at room temperature. The only expression in her eyes was no expression at all. Not fear. Not rage. Not anguish. Not love. Not hope.

Jane stepped out and made the call for help. They now needed all the help they could get.

While Jane made the call, Emily sat down on the bed and put her hands on Edwards's stomach. She was fully clothed and her clothes didn't look disordered in any way. Emily didn't know what that meant, but she hoped the obvious had not happened.

Emily had a hundred thoughts going through her head, but one stood out. Jane Alexander and Jim Davis would have gone to interview Stacey Edwards immediately after the briefing. They wouldn't have had her lovely briefing notes and Jim Davis was an awful interviewer. She doubted that Edwards would have said anything to them, but at least she would have been visited by officers before her death. She would have been given a chance, a warning, an escape hatch. Most likely, she wouldn't have taken it. Drug addicted prostitutes with absolutely no self-esteem usually don't.

Emily berated herself. She'd arrived, oh so cleverly, at just the right time to catch Edwards having her morning cornflakes. And found her dead instead. No escape hatch. Just duct tape and ties and, she bet herself a month's salary, a skinful of heroin and a murderer who closed up her nose. The lightest of pressure between finger and thumb. A minute. Two minutes. Five at the most. Then he'd have been on his way, job done as Stacey Edwards's thwarted little soul flew out of the window beyond him.

-18-

At seven-thirty that evening the incident room broke up. Operation Lohan was now in overdrive. When Jenna Mancini died, most officers on the force said, quite correctly, that these things happen when you mix drugs and prostitution. They didn't mean that they should happen, or that it's OK for them to occur, just that they did. The message was simple. Don't take drugs. Don't live that life. Bad stuff happens when you break those simple rules.

But Stacey Edwards's death was no coincidence. Jackson's assumption, which Emily shared, was that the manner of her death was intended to send a signal. It was a murder and not an accidental overdose. Her death wasn't just a one-off. There may well have been others under threat at that very moment. The warning was, 'keep your mouth shut or else.'

As the officers dispersed, Jackson jabbed his finger at Emily and then at his office. His face was craggy and inexpressive. She couldn't read anything there, but she assumed she was in for a rough ride.

"Sit down," he said. "I want some tea. Do you?"

The coffee machine dispensed teas and coffees. For her herbal preference it was necessary to go to one of the kitchenettes and make it yourself. She didn't think she could ask him to do that.

"No, thanks. I try to avoid caffeine," she said.

"No fags, no booze, no caffeine? Are you vegetarian?"

"No, no. I eat meat."

"That's something," he said.

He made a shaggy-eyebrowed look that would have spoken volumes if she'd had the code book.

"You want herbal or something?"

Emily really didn't know how to respond. Her face must have shown her indecision because he solved the problem by opening his door and yelling at someone to bring him tea and "something that tastes like wet hay for this woman here." He slammed the door shut.

"That the first time you've seen a corpse?"

"Yes."

Emily couldn't tell him about her other life in which she'd seen many things.

"Pretty grim, isn't it?"

"I had DS Alexander there. I'd have found it worse without her."

"You did the right thing. I shouldn't have assigned Jim Davis to that interview. You were right to prepare. I think we can take it as read that Stacey Edwards was our anonymous caller."

"We'd have got to her alive if we'd gone straight out."

"Maybe. You don't know that. You might not have found her. You don't know where she was last night. We had no reason to think she was under threat. And even if you had gone out last night, she might still have been killed this morning." He looked for Emily's reaction.

She restricted herself to "I know."

"You need counselling?"

"No. At least, I don't think so."

"It's there if you need it. Just say."

The teas arrived. Hers was camomile with the bag removed, so it had probably had about ten seconds to steep rather than the required five minutes. It tasted to Emily like hot water with a very slight hint of hay. Jackson's order had been obeyed to the letter.

"Go on, then," said Jackson, loudly slurping some tea. "I know you've got a headful of theories and I'm dying to hear them."

"Not theories. Nothing as advanced as that," she said with caution.

"Right. Well, my theory and everyone else's theory pretty much fell apart today. That theory held that some punter killed Jenna Mancini, deliberately or on purpose, and then killed the kid to shut her up. No forethought. No planning. No point. No follow-up. I'd say that theory is pretty much gone."

"I don't have a theory, I really don't," she said.

"But..." he prompted.

"But here are the bits and pieces as I see them. One, Rattigan's card was in that house. That's a hell of a strange place for a rich man's card to be. Two, his wife pretty much told me that he liked rough sex. She obviously didn't share that taste."

"That's still speculation." He put in.

"This is all speculation really. None of this is courtroom evidence."

"Right, but let's go with it. Let's say Rattigan knew Mancini and used to visit her. Somehow or other she got hold of his card." He was entering into the swing now.

Right. Number three, Jon Johnston. Wild speculation, remember," she said again.

"Go on," he encouraged her.

"The thing that was making my head explode with that case was that he seemed to have stolen more money than anybody knew about. I just couldn't work out how he'd bought all the stuff he had."

"That's hardly the point."

"No, I know. We have evidence enough to convict him on a dozen counts of embezzlement, so it was curiosity more than anything that kept me scratching. That' plus a feeling that I'd been doing my sums wrong." She explained.

"But you hadn't."

"No. Or rather I had, because I'd managed to miss the fact that Johnston owned shares in more racehorses than we knew about. He'd taken some very basic steps to disguise his name, that's all. His horses all seemed to be co-owned with Rattigan or his friends. The logical deduction was that Rattigan was paying a bent ex-officer for something. Must have been something big because the payments were big."

"Why didn't you report this earlier?" He asked.

"Um, a few reasons. One, I've only just found out the full picture. Two, I have reported it. It's in my most recent batch of notes and it'll be in my report for Matthews when I present it. But three, it's hard to investigate a crime when you don't know if there's even been a crime, and when we've already got easily enough evidence to bang up Johnston for embezzlement. I thought if I'd come out with it straight, you and Matthews would have told me to forget about it."

"Maybe," he conceded. "And you don't know it was Rattigan making those payments. Could have been anyone."

"Yes, could have been. Except for the coincidence of shared ownership of those horses. And the money. I haven't yet had time to chase up the value of those extra horses, but Johnston's share must have been worth tens of thousands, minimum. You've got to be rich to toss out that kind of money."

"But Rattigan is dead, which rather removes him from the list of suspects."

"Presumed dead. I spoke to the Air Accidents Investigation Branch and asked if there was anything funny about the crash, and the answer was no, not really, well maybe yes a bit."

Jackson considered it for a moment and said, "No. People don't vanish like that. Especially people worth a hundred million or whatever. Unless you've got something else to tell me."

Emily didn't think the chip-shop texts would count, or the look on Johnston's face, or the rust his car had just above the wheel arch or the fact that there was no sheet music for his piano.

"No, I don't think so," she replied.

Emily continued the thought process without verbalizing. Two other things actually, but they were so small they almost didn't count for anything. Number one, Johnston's last extravagant purchase, the conservatory, came fifteen weeks after Rattigan's reported death. Number two, although Rattigan was wealthy by almost any standards, his business had been having a rough time of it. His highest ranking on a sterling rich list came is 2006, when he notched up an estimated value of £91 million. But his businesses were steel and shipping, among the industries worst hit by the recession. At the time of his death, in December 2009, both halves of his company were loss-making and he was seeking to re-schedule some of the debt associated with the steel business. Given the credit markets at the time, that was like asking to be beaten over the head by his creditors and then robbed. After the hurricane had passed, the FT estimated the value of his remaining business at just £22 to £27 million. Would Rattigan have looked at that as a glass half empty because he'd just lost £65 million or half full because he still had £25 million and was still in the game? Would any of it have made him fake a plane crash? And how did any of that connect with murdering Jenna Mancini and her child, and Stacey Edwards? Emma didn't know.

Then another thought bubbled up, and she shared it.

"The StreetSafe people say that Stacey Edwards had a particular hatred for the Balkan types who have been taking over the area's rackets. Her death has an organized crime feel to it, so maybe there's a connection there. And Rattigan's shipping interests were mostly in the Baltic. From Russia to the UK, anyway. Maybe some kind of drugs connections. Who knows? If you did want to smuggle drugs, then owning a shipping line would be a nifty way to do it."

"Seems rather cumbersome, though, doesn't it?" Jackson laughed at Emily in a friendly way. "Go to all the trouble of making yourself a shipping millionaire just so you can run some drugs into the country."

"I know. None of it makes sense."

"OK. Thank you. That's all helpful. Very speculative, but you did warn me. We might get something from forensics on Stacey Edwards.

In the meantime, we need to talk to every prostitute we can find. You getting on all right with Alexander?"

"Yes."

"Then the two of you can stay as a team. I'll see if we can drag some other female officers in to help as well. Jon Johnston. What do you think we should do with him? We could drag him back here and give him the third degree."

"Won't do any good. He told us sod all last time. And it's not as though we can connect him to this inquiry in any meaningful way."

"No."

It was an end-of conversation 'no', that didn't bother to wonder why a certain female colleague currently in the same room woke up at five each morning with a prickling feeling running through her body, like a premonition of murder.

Jackson checked his mug for the third time, only to find it still empty. He banged it down on his desk.

"We forget Rattigan. He's dead. He's not part of this. We forget Johnston. We've got nothing to connect him to it and he'll be a tough sod anyway. As you say, this looks like an organized crime thing. Somewhere out there, there will be people, probably prostitutes, who know what's going on. We find them. We hit the forensics hard. We get our killer. OK?"

"Yes," Emily said. Still no 'Sir'.

She smiled. Her mug was still full. She didn't like watery hay.

"What day is it tomorrow? God, it's Sunday already. You had any time off this week?"

"No."

"Take tomorrow off. Go home. Do whatever you do to relax. Sleep in. If you feel up to coming in on Monday, then it would be helpful. But look after yourself. You need to pace things. Big cases like this, you've got to look after yourself."

Emily nodded as she stood up. His orders were to be obeyed. She smiled to herself as she felt the glow of a lie in with Books and all the naughty things that might entail.

She left Jackson's office and fished out her mobile.

"You at home? I'm on my way. I have a little request for you. Well, it's more of an order from on high really."

She recognized the warm, moist feeling down below and almost ran to her car.

-19-

It was not as hot as it had been. Sometime earlier that afternoon there was breeze from the west and a few sudden, dense showers. Big raindrops hitting the street like a rattle of hail. The clouds had cleared, however, and the rain steamed off. The evening seemed sharper and brighter than earlier.

She jumped into the driver's seat and drove very fast. As soon as she arrived and had parked she jammed the mobile to her ear.

"Now, where was I? Ah, yes. What are you up to?"

"This minute, this evening, or in my life generally?"

"The first two of those."

"I'm talking to you, obviously."

She ignored the witticism and waited for more.

"Apart from that, I'm pouring whisky and settling down to watch a repeat of Morse."

"Which episode and have you seen it before?"

Books told her, and that he hadn't seen it before. Emily proceeded to tell him the plot and outcome in exact detail, despite his protestations.

"Thanks, Emily. You've just freed up my evening."

"Good. That was my intention. I told you, I'm on my way, and I'm not planning on watching TV."

"Ah," came the response. "Where exactly are you?"

"Peering in through the front window. I see the new sofa has arrived."

Startled, he jumped up and almost ran to the front door.

"It's not the best Morse, anyway," Emily said as she walked in. "Saggy middle. I'm knackered."

Books hesitated. "Is that a cry for whisky?" His hands hovered over a bottle and glasses.

She hesitated in turn. She used to avoid alcohol completely. Her head was fragile enough that she thought better of taking anything that might unbalance it.

"Um, too alcoholic. I want something that tastes alcoholic but isn't."

"Gin and tonic, with lots of tonic and just a smell of gin?"

"And ice and lemon. Perfect," she said.

He always hit the spot. It was uncanny, she thought. He asked whether she'd eaten and wasn't surprised that she hadn't. He conjured up spinach and ricotta tortellini, served warm with a splash of olive oil and a bowl of green salad.

"Homemade," he announced. "I've been playing with the new pasta-maker."

I love the English middle classes," she said, "who else has homemade tortellini waiting for waifs and strays?"

"Italians," he ventured.

"Don't quibble," she said, with her mouth full.

She fell silent as she ate and began to think about her wonderful man. He was responsible for bringing her to this point. Others had played their part, but it was Books really. He entered her life when he was in need. He was a petty thief in London and couldn't read. Her father had seen something in him, taken him in and she had spent countless hours teaching him to read. He would never be a great academic, but he had a strength, an inner steel, a resolve that attracted her. He spent time with her and treated her like a human being at a time when she was fragile and pouring more pills down her throat by the day.

She was in the hands of shrinks who seemed to want to deny her any sign of independent thought, movement, emotion or argument. Her father, clever man, saw in Books her path to a meaningful future. He dismissed the doctors as soon as he saw the green shoots.

She spent time with Books. She didn't know how much time, because time was so unclear to her back then. Books was different. He seemed to understand her and made no demands. He, along with her patient father, brought her round. He made her whole again. And, of course, she fell in love with him. And he with her. And, of course, the sex was good as well.

She ate up like a good girl and wiped out his entire stock of tortellini, made a serious dent in his salad reserves and did considerable damage to an apple crumble that she found in the fridge. He put some cheese on a plate. Cheddar and a squishy French one.

They picked away at the cheese, chatted a bit, cuddled on the new sofa and ended up watching the last half hour of Morse. Emily announced all of the essential plot points before they arose and Books rumpled her hair or, if she was being particularly annoying, pulled her ears.

Morse ran out and they segued into Newsnight. Terrorism, mostly, which reminded Emily about her main role in life at the moment. Her silent, undercover role.

She wanted to forget things for a while so she sat up on Books. She could feel him getting hard underneath her. She bounced up and down a bit, just as revenge for his ear pulling. He held her so that she couldn't inflict too much damage, but she noticed he let her bounce a fair bit. Just for the hell of it, she gave a more vigorous bounce, hard enough to make him wince. Time to tease, she decided, gave him an affectionate squeeze and slid off him.

She groped around on the floor for her shoes and toddled off upstairs, treating him to an enticing wiggle as she knew he was looking and would follow.

She sat on the bed and remembered the photos of April. Not images she wanted at that precise moment, but she couldn't fight it. She realised then that all the pictures of April were of the crime scene. April with a smile, but no eyes. Six little dead Aprils, and not a single little live one.

She grinned at herself and felt April grinning with her. Seven grins. She didn't mind the dead. It wasn't them who caused trouble.

-20-

She woke before six am. Far too early. Books slept peacefully beside her. She sneaked downstairs in her dressing gown, found some tea and cereal, and returned to bed. The house was too quiet for her liking, so she went to her car, found a memory stick and whacked it on loudly enough to hear upstairs and continue her breakfast in bed. Sunday morning bliss. Books, music and breakfast in bed.

Eventually she realised that Books was not going to stir anytime soon, so she decided to take a shower. He could always join her if he wished. She hoped he would.

The water was set as hot as she could stand and the water fell like needle sharp rain, heightening her senses, washing away the clutter in her mind. She played the conversation with Jackson in her head. He was right, she knew. Her suspects were one, a dead man, and two, a man who was due to go to jail anyway. Also, of course, she didn't think that either of them had actually killed the Mancinis or Edwards. They were just involved. That meant that as well as having a dead suspect and an about-to-be jailed suspect, she was also missing a crime to connect them to. Strangely, she knew you needed a crime before you can start arresting people, alive or dead!

Her problem was that intuitions like hers were wholly at odds with the way police investigations work. She remembered the old joke about an Irish attempt to climb Everest. It failed because they ran out of scaffolding. The police way was to keep going, pole after pole, clamp after clamp, just plough on. Interviews, statements, DNA tests, prints, millions of bits of data. Thousands of hours of patient grinding analysis. Remorseless, methodical, inevitable. And one day, as frozen fingers haul yet another board into position, the summit is reached. The sunlight comes horizontally. That was how Jackson planned to get his killer and she thought he was right enough.

But would she get hers? She hadn't made any promises to Jackson. When he'd asked her for an old fashioned 'yes', the sort that indicated obedience, she had answered him with a question. She viewed that as giving her a little enterprise on the side. Perhaps, he had even planned it that way and was giving her enough rope. Whatever, she thought, there was no time like the present.

No time except for the present, if it came to that. A frightening thought, if she'd dwelt on it.

She dressed quickly, going for something summery. Too hot for jeans. Mid-twenties and rising. A floaty pinky-beige skirt and a pistachio and coffee striped top. Summer wear. Good mood wear.

She zipped across town and was early enough that teachers, nurses, middle managers and youngish solicitors were still in bed, or yawning their way through toast, or getting ready for a day of marshalling hyperactive kids. The bent policeman at number 27 showed no sign of doing anything at all. The car was there, and its bonnet was cold. There were no lights in the house and no sign of life at all. He was almost certainly snoring away upstairs.

She didn't have a plan. She saw that as a positive as there could be nothing to go wrong. A side passage led to the back garden and she went through, if only to feel less conspicuous. A lady in a garden opposite was putting her washing out. She saw Emily, but didn't say or do anything. No reason why she should, Emily told herself. She didn't look much like a burglar and it was hardly burglar o'clock. The gulls were circling overhead, perhaps forced inland by an impending storm, and looking for something to do. She sat on the back step and waited for the lady to go inside.

Johnston's keys had been bothering her. His house was L-shaped and in the crook of the L was the conservatory. The keys to the conservatory were visible enough in the house but they were equally visible from the garden. A burglar armed with a brick could have easily knocked out a pane of glass, taken the keys and let himself in. Johnston used to be a copper and this was his level of security. That made her think.

She wasn't about to smash any windows, but she'd bet a fair bit of money that Johnston had few friends in this street. Someone to say 'hello' to perhaps, but nobody who would hold a key.

Then there was his kitchen sink. He wasn't slovenly, but he wasn't organized or house-proud. There were beer cans in the kitchen bin. Obviously re-cycling didn't occur to him. She knew he frequented the local pub and that sort of man either needs a wife or a spare key, and he didn't have a wife.

The lady opposite went inside and Emily turned her attention to the back door. The one belonging to the kitchen, not the conservatory. She turned the handle, gently. It was locked.

No flowerpots. A couple of bricks and a few rotted lengths of garden timber, but nothing under those. The doorframe was set into the wall, so there was nothing concealed on top of it or at the sides.

She felt a surge of frustration, but it was quickly replaced by a sense of confidence. She was not wrong, she knew she wasn't. Her reading of Johnston must be correct, there must be a spare key there somewhere. There simply must.

Then she realised. The conservatory was the last thing, not the first. Those keys on the doorframe breached security basics, but he'd hung them at a point when he'd embezzled so much money he must have known he'd be caught. It was a 'what the hell, I don't care', sort of thing and Johnston hadn't always been that way.

She turned around and surveyed the garden. She became Johnston. Just retired from the police force. Honourable career ended by injury. Police pension. Single man. Needs a set of keys handy. She hadn't even completed the thought before she found herself walking over to an old brick-paved area at the back, complete with bench, then the barbecue and the paving area itself. At the side nearest the garden fence, a brick was loose. She teased it out in a crumble of old mortar and a key winked brassily at her from its nest.

-21-

Front door or back door? The key looked like it could fit the back door and it worked first time. She was into the kitchen. Still squalid. The mug that she'd thrown into the bin had been taken out and left on the corner of the sideboard. She dropped it back into the bin to remind him to be more tidy.

Shoes off, and dangling from her hand, she went further into the house. It was still early, not yet seven fifteen. Johnston wasn't an early riser, she thought, but she didn't know how lightly he slept. She would seriously not enjoy him waking up and finding her there. She wasn't exactly frightened, but she recognized the symptoms. Heartbeat. Rapid breathing. An over alert jitteriness. It wasn't good. She wanted to be there, though.

The conservatory was still empty. She had an impulse to lift the piano lid and thrash out a tune to bring some noise into the place. She didn't, of course. She still couldn't see any music and she had a sneaky feeling that he couldn't even play the piano. A music room with no music. A conservatory with nothing to conserve.

The living room looked much the same as last time. The INFORMATION WANTED notice had been folded up and left on the table. She spread it out again to make it easier for him to read and circled the telephone number that people were meant to call if they had information.

In the corner of the room there was a mobile phone charging. Ah! A gift from above. She dropped the phone into her pocket and looked around to see if there was anything else worth taking. There wasn't. No papers. No diary. No address book. The only desk had nothing much on top apart from some computer cables, a note dispenser, a mug of pens, some phone directories. The only drawer was locked.

There was probably a key to the drawer somewhere, there were probably more things to find, but she'd lost her nerve. Her fear had caught up with her properly and she didn't like being there. She didn't want to make a noise and wake the beast. Later in her career, things would be different.

She left as fast and quietly as she could. She locked up and left the key where she'd found it. She didn't feel safe again until she was in her car, and even then she had to drive for ten minutes before playing with her new toy. It had twenty-six numbers in his address book, which she copied into her own. There were no messages in inbox or sent items.

She drove home and made herself some peppermint tea. She jumped back into bed, fully clothed except that she took off her skirt first. Books had gone, but the warmth from his side of the bed indicated that he'd only left recently. She wished he was still there, ready for action.

Never mind, she had twenty-six numbers and a whole day to play with them. She went for the landlines first. She decided to be a flower delivery company sorting out its Monday delivery schedule. She called the first number and got an answerphone. No names. Just "the person you are calling is not available," in a pre-recorded voice. Not helpful. She hung up. The second number was just entered as 'Jane' in Johnston's phone, but the answerphone message referred to 'Jane and Terry'. She made a note but didn't leave a message.

A woman picked up on the third number. Emily went through her spiel. Missing address for the delivery tomorrow. There must be a muddle because she had three deliveries booked for the same address. The woman fell for it and gave Emily her address. Emily asked her to confirm her name "because we just need to know we're delivering to the right person."

There was no logic to it, but the woman gave her name as Laura Hargreaves.

"Thanks, Laura," said Emily. That's fine. I'll probably see you tomorrow, if you're in."

"Oh, thanks so much. I love flowers. I wonder who they're from."

"Well, I'm not allowed to tell you that, but it's a lovely bouquet that they've ordered. What's your favourite colour?"

"Oh, I don't know. Cream probably, in flowers. I love roses, but I love all flowers really."

Emily promised her a huge bouquet of cream roses and hung up. She was enjoying herself now. It felt good to spread a little joy. She made a further twenty-three calls, got through to fourteen people, collected twelve addresses and ten names. She made another round of calls to voicemails and collected another name and address.

She thought to herself that she'd make a good flower delivery person. She credited herself with a lovely telephone manner as well.

She sent a batch of texts to the people she hadn't got through to by then and tootled over to Sainsbury's to stock up for the week. She had a theory that if she bought lots of easy to cook healthy food, then she would start to eat properly. Not quite the proper homemade tortellini version but, hey, she was only a flower girl after all, she told herself. She found a few extras, including one of those little potted begonias that come with their own wickerwork Red Riding Hood basket. It was a bit twee for what she wanted, but it would have to do.

She paid up and tootled home. After putting the shopping away, she made some more calls and prepared a meal for two. It was difficult knowing what to prepare because she was unsure when her guest would be arriving and how hungry he'd be. She settled for a brunchy spread of bagels, cream cheese, smoked salmon and orange juice. She would top up with scrambled eggs if necessary.

She put Paloma Faith on and sung along with her whilst contemplating hoovering. Not now she decided, it would still be there next week.

She waited for enlightenment and, as she did so, she took Johnston's SIM card out of his phone and dropped it into a kettle full of boiling water. She drained the water and popped the SIM card back in the phone. Johnston would need to make good any damage she'd caused, but she excused herself on the grounds that nobody backs up their contacts properly. Also, she reasoned that if the card had now been destroyed she'd probably bought herself a little extra room for manoeuvre.

With regret, she took her pictures of April off the wall and was annoyed to find that the Blu Tack had left marks.

-22-

Johnston arrived at four. She twinkled a wave at him through the window as he pulled up and threw him a reassuring smile. She politely invited him in as he arrived at the front door, but he shouldered past her, smouldering with aggression.

Emily had put his phone on the living room floor, along with the begonia and a little bit of Christmas ribbon. It was her way of thanking him. He took the phone, but left the pot plant. By that time she was in the kitchen putting the kettle on.

"What the hell is this?" he said, standing in the kitchen doorway.

"I'm not sure. I think I'd call it brunch., but I suppose it's more of a brinner by now. I wasn't sure what time you'd be coming. There's scrambled egg, if you're hungry."

He didn't say anything about egg, or whether he'd prefer tea or coffee., so she made coffee, put four teaspoons of instant in the cup and stirred. Peppermint tea for herself.

"You know how people who don't drink coffee always say they love the smell of coffee?" Johnston made no reply and hadn't moved from the doorway. "Well, I don't. I don't like the smell or the taste."

Emily sat down. The kitchen was the nicest room in the house. Not because she'd done anything to make it nice, but because it was reasonably clean and had big French doors onto the garden.

"Help yourself. Tuck in. This is Sainsbury's Taste the Difference Smoked Salmon, but I think they just charge more and you can't actually taste the difference. Or can you?"

Johnston seemed a rather reluctant conversationalist, but he did go to the table, yank out a chair and sit.

"You're a nightmare," he said.

"Oh, these are nicer toasted, aren't they?" She busied herself toasting the bagels. "It's a murder inquiry, you know. Jenna and April Mancini. Stacey Edwards too now as well."

He didn't react to Edwards's name. She hadn't expected him to, but it was worth a try.

"I found her, actually. Climbed in through a window and there she was. Do you want to know how she died?" Johnston made no response, so she told him anyway, making sure she mentioned the cable ties and duct tape. "Obviously no post mortem results yet, but she died the same way as Jenna did. High as a kite. Airways blocked. Finger and thumb. Just like that."

She dropped a bagel on his plate and one on her own. She hadn't eaten since breakfast and was genuinely hungry. She tucked in straight away. Johnston followed suit.

"Did you call anyone?" he asked.

"Yes, Everyone. I thought your mum was nice. She called me love and said 'bless you' twice. I told her that she'd be getting a bunch of tulips tomorrow, so you might want to arrange that."

Johnston opened his mouth. Not to eat, but to say something. There was a depth of calculation in his eyes. She silently urged him to say whatever it was he was contemplating, but he decided against it. He just slapped a chunk of salmon onto a bagel and stood up. Ready to leave.

Emily stood too, in order to see him out. They were standing in the space between the living room and the hall when he turned to her. Half of her thought he was going to say something useful. The other half thought he was going to swear at her. Both were wrong. With almost no warning or back-lift, he hit her open-handed across the face. She was stunned by the force of it. The blow knocked her across the hall and she struck her head on the wall opposite. By the time she'd recovered her wits, she was lying crumpled up on the floor at the foot of the stairs. Johnston towered over her.

He was two miles high and going to kill her.

She didn't do or say anything. She couldn't. Her vision was shot through with bolts of black and red. There was blood in her mouth. Her head felt as though it had been detonated by professionals, then reassembled with sticky tape. She had no idea that one blow could do that. She'd never lacked physical confidence, but she'd never been hit like that. It felt like a brick wall had reached out and whacked her. Her skirt was above her knees and she found her right hand tweaking it down. That was the extent of her resistance. Even her hand felt weak.

That was what it was like. Total surrender. She had not known what it was like before, never knew how total it could be.

Johnston towered over her for another few seconds, then turned on his heels and went. Only when the front door closed did she attempt movement. She kicked her legs out in front of her and arranged herself so that she was sitting on the bottom step. Emily reviewed the damage. The right side of her face, where Johnston had struck her, was moving from numbness and shock to hurting and furious. She poked it gently with her fingertips. Everything was bruised, but not cut or broken. She thought the blood inside her mouth came from her cheek having been slammed against her teeth. There was also a cut on the other side of her head, where she had hit the wall. Her teeth seemed loose, but she thought it was down to shock. Her neck felt painful everywhere, but she thought that was just the combined effect of shock and whiplash. There was a taste in her mouth that she identified as vomit.

She wasn't angry with Johnston. She thought hitting her seemed like a fair enough reaction to the theft of his phone, and she knew he could have done her far more harm. The shock lay in how easily he had hurt her and she was angry at her own feebleness. She stood up, and went to the kitchen to spit some blood into the sink and freshen her tea with hot water.

She was undecided as to what to do next. Eventually she picked her way upstairs and looked at her face in the mirror. The right side was puffy and she saw that her eyes had a dazed look. The world felt tilted and out of kilter. She ran a hot bath and went overboard with the soothing bath salts. She could feel only three things. Numbness, pain and fear. As the numbness began to recede, the other two took over.

Downstairs, on her phone, she could hear the first texts coming in.

-23-

Emily called Books and her father and related the events. Her father told her to stay put and Books did the same. Both promised to be there shortly and she discerned a definite iciness in their voices.

They arrived only minutes apart. Emily filled the intervening time by calling a twenty-four-hour flower delivery outfit and ordering some tulips for Johnston's mother. By the end of that call she had blood in her mouth again.

She spat it out into the kitchen sink on her way to answer the front door. Her father, Frank, swept in and ushered her into the living room. He made her sit down and go through the whole thing from start to finish. Just as she was concluding her story her beloved Books swept in. She could have sworn she had shut and locked the front door, but he appeared nevertheless. He didn't ask her to go through it again.

"I don't need the whole thing, Em. I'll get that from Frank. You should go back with him for tonight. Be looked after. Let your Mum and Dad look after you. Leave this Johnston character to me. He won't bother you again."

He and Frank exchanged glances and Emily caught the implicit messages.

"Don't forget he's the subject of an ongoing police case. I don't want that messed up."

"As I said, leave him to me. He won't bother you again. And the case officers will not even know I've been anywhere near."

Emily knew what that meant and was grateful that she was not named Johnston. More than that, she felt sorry for him, despite what he had inflicted upon her. She had never witnessed Books in full attack mode, but she shuddered at the thought. The fact that her father was willing to leave that side of the affair to Books told its own tale.

They made their way to the family home and there followed an hour or two or family stuff. Her youngest sister, Ant liked it when the whole family were together. There had been developments on the TV in the bedroom front, but Emily couldn't quite make out what they were because everyone was talking and she only had two ears.

Her other sister, Kay, teenaged and all raging hormones, hung around for a while as well. She badgered her father to allow her half a glass of wine, of which she well knew her mother disapproved 'on Sunday, if at all!' She prevailed and, when Mum wasn't looking, it was poured quickly. Kay was dressed casually for her. Leggings. A black sequined top. Bare feet. A long silver necklace but no earrings. She looked gorgeous, as she always did. Long-limbed, silk-skinned and photogenic. She liked being part of things as well, though the teenager in her battled to fight shy of looking too involved. Therefore, she sat side on to the table, listening more than talking running her finger around the rim of her glass, making it ring.

Emily loved being a part of things too. Families are strange affairs, she mused. Somehow her Mum and Dad's genes got sloshed together to create the over-intellectual, fish out of water oddity that was herself, and yet they all got along together. They loved each other. They belonged. That was a rare feeling for Emily and it was the most precious one of all.

Eventually, things broke up. Ant went to bed and Kay slipped up to her room. Mum went to the living room for some TV before bed.

"We'll go through, shall we?"

'Through' meant to her father's lair. It wasn't even in the house, but was a separate studio built on top of what used to be the pool house in the garden, a pool house that was Frank's most prized project, but which had been abandoned after a year passed by with nobody having used it.

'Through' also meant to Dad's world. Out of her mother's much ornamented, endlessly hoovered, precision-arranged utopia. Into Dad's world. A place of giant screen TV's. Huge leather furniture and secrecy.

Her father's conversation slowed and she felt a returning calmness. He talked about the security issues that the public worried about.

Emily knew he was leading up to something and let him get there in his own time.

"Are you worried about something, Emily? If you are, you need to say. Is it getting difficult being embedded in the police? It would be easy to get you withdrawn and no harm would be done. I am told, by various means, that you are doing extremely well and, from our point of view on this side, I'm absolutely confident you will get the results we need."

Emily noted that he had put emphasis on the word 'will.'

"You've already given us valuable details that the team is not working on. But I don't want you taking risks."

Her father let the weight of his words hang between them. The shadows of old arguments crossing their lamp-lit present. His suspicion of the working inadequacies of the police and his anxieties about his daughter's safety and well-being hung between them. He had always been protective of her, just like all fathers, but he knew the increased dangers that came with her work, as well as her illness and afterwards.

He hadn't wanted her to go to Cambridge. For the first few weeks of her first term there, he had dropped in every second or third day, pretending he had business in East Anglia. In the end she had ordered him to desist and not come again until the end of term. Even then, when her life had been put back together again, with no recurrence of the illness, excellent degree, some friends, he felt that a career in the police force was absolutely wrong for her. Besides, he had other plans for her. Plans that could, and now did, involve her in police work whilst allowing him the parental luxury of oversight and care.

He hadn't wanted her to move out, but he'd accepted it and, provided the house she now called her own home. For the first few months he 'popped round' because he was just 'driving past'. She'd had to repeat her Cambridge stance, so that stopped.

The pause compressed the whole debate into a few seconds of silence. It was her father's way that she could always quit her role and come back. Her silence was her way of saying, "thanks, but no thanks." The discussion unfolded in a few heartbeats and ended with a truce.

"You just look after yourself, love. If you need anything, just say."

"I will, don't worry. I've got Books on my side as well and I know we can trust and rely on him."

Her father smiled. He also knew Books could be relied upon. He also knew what Books was doing at that very moment and it made him sigh a very deep sigh.

"I think I'll go to bed. I'm tired. 'Night Dad. And thanks."

-24-

She was late to work, but had slept well and had one of her mother's cooked breakfasts inside her. Kay had worked something close to magic on her bruises with an array of concealers and foundation. There was still puffiness, but at least it wasn't orangey-purple puffiness. It was good enough for Emily.

Ken Hughes, who had taken to noting down the names of officers not present at the morning briefing, saw her coming two hours late to her desk. He started to give her a bollocking, but she whipped out her dental emergency card and played it before he'd really got rolling. He backed down at once.

Other people were being unnaturally nice to her too. It wasn't her grievous dental injuries that were affecting them so, more that she'd found her first corpse two days earlier, which seemed to be an event that apparently entitled her to special treatment. It seemed to her that there was no quicker route to sympathy from workmates than stumbling across a dead body.

It was catch up time. The first twenty-four or forty-eight hours of an inquiry tend to move fast, and the Stacey Edwards arm of Operation Lohan was beginning to crank out data. Meanwhile, most of the people whose DNA placed them at the Mancini house had been interviewed, and the transcripts and summaries were available.

The first two picked up were not very productive in terms of evidence or as possible murderers. The next person to leave DNA at the house, Tony Leonard, was still being interviewed.

Karol Sikorski, whose DNA was also found at the house, had not yet been located. Brydon was leading the hunt for him.

"Any leads?" Emily asked.

He shrugged. "We don't have an address, but we've got some idea who he hangs out with. Not a very nice man, we're guessing."

"Our killer, do you think?"

"Could be. Got to be possible. Organised crime links. He's possessed weapons and he was in the house."

"How about Stacey Edwards? Do we have much on her?"

"Nothing much. Not that they talked about at the briefing anyway. I think they've got you down for digging into her records."

"Oh great. Paperwork."

Emily could predict her findings. Alcoholic and abusive father. Mentally ill mother. Taken into care. Foster homes. Behavioural problems. Difficulties at school. An abortion somewhere along the way. Class A drugs. Prostitution. And, after suitable length of time, death. Another car crash of a life, brutally ended. "I don't know why Jackson always throws the crap at me."

"He doesn't. You're interviewing with Jane Alexander as well. By the way, do you fancy a drink or two after work one day?"

He was not aware of the presence of Books in Emily's life and there was no reason he should have been.

"Maybe. If you're not beating the daylights out of Sikorsky in a cell somewhere."

"Very funny," Brydon replied. "Don't you have to push off and polish your knuckledusters or something?"

He smirked and loped away. Emily recalled that when she'd had her little contretemps with the breast-fondler, she'd managed to break three of his fingers, and followed up by kicking out his kneecap with the toe of her boot. Unfortunately, he'd rolled sideways as he fell, gashing his cheek on the corner of the table. The table corner was sharp and went right through the flesh of his cheek, stopping only when it hit his teeth. Her colleagues loved to remind her of the episode. In the meantime, she had the sweet balm of endless work to keep her cheered and comforted.

Work such as catching up with everything that had been happening over the previous thirty-six hours. Work such as digging into Stacey Edwards' past and getting summaries onto the office system. Work such as checking in with Jane Alexander, and work such as checking her phone numbers.

She had eleven names and addresses from her flower-girl calls. Four of those turned out to be family numbers, one way or another. She didn't know a lot about three of them, but there was a straightforward blokiness about the men who answered, and the names didn't flash up red on the criminal records system. She shelved those.

That left four. All female. There were no vice records on any of them and at least three of the addresses were in areas where she didn't expect to find prostitutes living or working. The fourth address was more marginal, but when she phoned it again she got a brisk no-nonsense voice and the sound of family clamour in the background. She couldn't be certain, but it didn't appear to her that Johnston's phone buddies had much to do with prostitution. That removed one of the easiest possible avenues of research, but there was always room for further thought.

Of the numbers on Johnston's phone there were eight where she couldn't get through to a human being. She sent a text to those.

"MUST MEET ASAP. THIS PHONE MAY BE COMPROMISED. TEXT ME ON NEW NUMBER. BRIAN."

She gave out her own number and had received five texts in return. Of those, four came over as simply baffled.

"IS THIS A WIND UP?" said one typical message.

"SEE YOU DOWN THE PUB. MIKE."

But the last of the five was her prize specimen.

"DON'T EVER CONTACT ME AGAIN. JUST PISS OFF. PISS RIGHT OFF. FLETCH."

Emily loved that message. She liked the fact that it was properly spelled and punctuated. She liked the repetition, which was not elegant but pithy. Best of all though, she loved the "FLETCH." A nickname what was no more than a sawn off surname. She didn't know who it was, or how he or she fitted into the puzzle. She didn't even know if that was one puzzle or two puzzles or maybe even more. She did, however, know that she'd rather lay hands on the enigmatic Fletch than on the darkly menacing Karol Sikorsky.

Just as she was marveling over Fletcher's text, Jane Alexander appeared.

"You ok?"

"Yep. Emergency dentist thing over the weekend. Feels like someone's run over the side of my face."

"God, yes, sorry. That does look sore."

"Oh, you meant..."

"Yes. After Saturday. It was brave of you to go in through the window."

Emily shrugged. "I'm glad you were there."

"Still. You're ok to go out this afternoon? Start after lunch? Two o'clock?"

She agreed. When Jane left, Emily gave Bryony Williams a call. She answered, but there was a din in the background as though about two hundred children were being asked to see how much noise they could make.

"Are you ok to talk?" Emily said.

"Sure. Just give me a sec." A door closed somewhere and the sound level dropped. "Sorry. My day job is teaching art. They'll be ok for a bit anyway."

Emily asked her if they could meet for lunch and they agreed to meet in Boscawen Park at one. That would be useful to Emily because she would be up to date when she went out interviewing with Jane.

Emily poked around on records for any interesting looking Fletchers, but failed to find any who took her fancy. She checked her Johnston case files. She didn't recall any Fletchers there and her memory for such things was normally good, but it seemed an obvious place to look. There was no joy there, though.

She had two hours to find a Fletcher. A maker of arrows. That's what a fletcher is. A missile man. A weapons guy.

She did everything she could to trace him. Databases, newspapers, Google and came up with nothing that made any sense. Her time was up quickly and she ran to the park, getting there just as Bryony Williams arrived.

-25-

The morning started out fine, but the clouds came in from the west on their usual journey eastwards up the length of the west country peninsular. The city felt like what it is: a smear of brick and concrete slotted into the narrow gap between earth and sky, more beautiful than neither. It's the layer where the violence started. They were only a few hundred paces from THAT house and its ghosts were pressing close.

Jane Alexander was her usual brisk, bright, efficient self. Emily felt nothing of the sort as she was still disturbed by recent events. Her neck felt jolted, as though something had been knocked out of place by Johnston's blow and hadn't yet slipped back. But it wasn't so much a physical thing. It was more mental. As though some of her equanimity, her confidence, had been dislodged. She kept remembering, not the actual blow as such, more the state of being in the instant falling. A rag doll useless on the bottom step.

Not a good state to be in.

Not a good state to be in when their third interview of the day started with a dark doorway swinging open and a pale face looming towards them from the darkness beyond. A pale, frightened face.

Ioana Balcescu. A prostitute.

No known link to Jenna Mancini or Stacey Edwards. No known link to organized crime. They only had her data from the records kept as a matter of routine by the Vice Unit. She was dressed in leggings and a loose cotton top. Long, dark hair, not styled or even combed. A thin face, not unattractive. But it wasn't the shape of Balcescu's nose that caught the attention, or whether her lips were full enough. What caught the attention were the dark, purpling bruises around her eyes. The gashed lip and swollen jaw. The way one arm held the other, providing a sling. The caution in every painful step.

Emily found herself staring at her in shock, as though into a mirror. She felt exposed, half expecting Jane to swing around, look her up and down, and say, "I knew it wasn't the dentist."

Jane did no such thing and the moment passed. Balcescu didn't want to talk to them, but they were on her doorstep and she couldn't summon the strength to tell them to get lost. They went through to her front room. There were dirty wine glasses, a tv listings magazine, a gas bill and a portable tv.

Jane Alexander sat on the edge of the couch, as though to have sat back would have transformed her into a drug-addled prostitute. She was dressed the way she always did. Far too classy for her present surroundings. She was far too professional to let it show, but Emily could tell straight away that her colleague was not comfortable. Jane was out of her depth.

When she explained why they were there, her voice was excessively formal, tight and unrelaxed.

Emily stepped in.

"Would you mind, Iona? We've been on the go all afternoon, and if you had a cup of tea, it would be just brilliant."

Emily had noticed that Balkan women fear the police. They don't expect the police to be on their side or to protect them. They often assume jail, prison or extortion to be an outcome of any interaction with police.

"Here, if you show me where the tea things are, we can make it together."

Ioana took her through to the kitchen. Jane remained where she was and Emily hoped she'd poke around, but knew she wouldn't. Ioana stopped at the kitchen door. Emily went in, filled the kettle and popped it on. She found three cups, cleaned them, located tea bags and made tea. There was no herbal, but this was about relaxing Ioana, not drinking tea.

She put her hand up to Ioana's eye and touched it very gently. "Poor you. That looks horrible."

She pulled her head away, but Emily gently persisted. She moved her hand to the woman's side, which flinched from the touch.

"They gave you a really good going over, didn't they?"

No response.

Emily lifted Ioana's top very gently. There were bruises all down her side, front and back.

"My God. You poor love."

She was thin with prominent ribs, like a girl with an eating disorder. When Emily touched one of her ribs where the bruises was at its worst, she winced. A possible fracture.

She put her top down. There was nothing premeditated in her look of sympathy.

"Have you been to a hospital?"

It was a stupid question. Emily knew the answer would be no.

"How do you take your tea, Ioana? How many sugars?"

"One please."

"I'll give you two. You've had a big shock and a big cup of sweet tea will do wonders. It was yesterday they hurt you, wasn't it? Those bruises look horrible."

Ioana didn't answer directly, but adjusted her head in a way that made Emily think she was correct. Emily picked up the cups and they made their way back.

"Now, Ioana, where would you be most comfortable? The big sofa maybe? Jane – this is Jane, by the way. You don't need to call her DS Alexander and you can call me Emily. Jane, I wonder if you could make space." Jane got up, looking awkward, but also relieved that someone else was running things for the moment. "Ioana, why don't you sit here? Or lie, if that's more comfortable. Where does it hurt most? I can fetch you a pillow from upstairs if you'd like. I'll put the tea just here, so you can reach it easily. There, that's better."

After a while Jane got the idea as well and turned from a vaguely scary blonde detective into something a bit more maternal and mumsy. She did mumsy better than Emily, in fact, when she got in the groove. Emily lifted Ioana's top again so Jane could see her injuries. Jane looked on in silence and her face was grim.

"Now, Ioana," said Emily, exchanging glances with Jane and getting her permission to continue. "We're going to ask you a few questions. You don't have to tell us anything at all. You're not under suspicion from us. We're not from immigration, so we're not about to ask to see your visa or your passport or anything like that."

She nodded.

Now, if you'd like us to call you ma'am or Miss Balcescu , then we'll do that, but if you don't mind, I'd prefer to call you Ioana. Such a lovely name. It's the same as Joanna, is it?"

Another micro-nod.

"Now then, we're here because we understand that you may have known Jenna Mancini. Is that right?"

A leading question. Bad practice, but never mind. Ioana nodded.

"Horrible what happened there. I don't know if you knew Stacey Edwards as well, did you?"

No nod this time. A stiffening. Fear.

"Well, you know what, lets' not go into that now. I mean, after what happened last night, there's only so much you want to be reminded of. You're probably scared that if you say too much to us, they'll come back again. Is that what you're scared of?"

"Yes." A firm nod. Still the fear, but at least there was something else in the room.

Emily exchanged glances with Jane. She was meant to be leading the interview, but Jane's glance meant she should continue.

"OK, Ioana, we don't want to get you into trouble, so we're going to make it really easy for you. And I want you to know that we came here in an unmarked car. Do you know what that means? Not a police car with a siren and everything, just a perfectly ordinary car. And we look like two perfectly ordinary people. Nobody knows we're police officers and we're not going to tell anyone either. Do you understand that?"

"Good. And I think you're going to need some help. I think you need to see a doctor." Ioana instantly started to protest and Emily raised her hand to stop her. "I know you won't go to hospital. That's ok. But if we send someone to the house, that'll be all right. We'll do it the same way. An unmarked car. Not a police car. And a doctor just in ordinary clothes. Looking like anyone else. All right?"

"I know you know Bryony Williams. You know who I mean? The StreetSafe lady. Short curly hair." Ioana nodded. The name relaxed her a little. "Now, I saw her this lunchtime. She said to me that she has a programme you can go on to help you deal with the drugs. We know you take heroin – smack – and that's OK. You're not going to get into trouble with us. We just want to help, don't we Jane?" Jane was quick to nod and they again exchanged glances.

"And, Ioana love, what we'd really like to do is take you away from all this. I know that's scary, but it's what we want and it's what Bryony wants. You don't have to say yes now, but just don't say no. We'll take things one tiny step at a time. Do you understand what I mean? One tiny step at a time."

"Yes."

Ioana was half saying that she understood, half saying that she'd sign up for the deal. In a salesman's world it was the moment of maximum reward and maximum vulnerability. Emily moved over to the sofa and put her hand on Ioana's arm. Human contact, without threat, without money, without drugs, without demand. She wondered when Ioana had last felt that.

They fell silent for a moment and there was something precious in that silence.

Finally, "Ioana, you know we need to ask you some questions. I'm sorry, but we do. I don't want you to say anything at all out loud. Just nod or shake your head. If you don't know, raise your eyebrows. Yes, just like that. It'll only take a few minutes. We won't write anything down. We just want to know. Then we'll go again. The next person you'll see will be the doctor. Then maybe Bryony. Are you all right with that? Do you understand what I've said?"

Nod.

"Good. Then let's start."

Jane shifted in her seat. If Emily was interviewing Jane was meant to be note-taking and that had just been ruled out. The note book was on her lap. Time for the first question.

"Did you know Jenna Mancini?"

Nod.

"And little April perhaps?"

Nod. A sideways nod, with a hint of no.

"all right. You didn't particularly know April, but you knew her by sight. Were you there on the night of her murder?"

Shake.

"No, didn't think you were, but it's one of those things we have to ask. My boss would go nuts if I didn't ask it."

Smile.

Emily's hand was still on her arm. She wasn't going to move it unless Ioana did.

"Now, I'm going to ask you if you know various other people. Some of them you will have heard of. Others you won't. Others maybe or maybe not. We'll see. OK?"

She began with names she'd got partly from Bryony Williams and partly from police records. East European girls with an involvement in prostitution. She was betting that Ioana knew a good half of them, and she was right. More than half. She was getting comfortable with the nod/shake thing, which was Emily's main reason for asking.

"OK. We're doing brilliantly. Now some other names. You won't know so many of these. Conway Lloyd."

Puzzlement. Shake.

"Rhys Vaughan."

Shake.

"Jon Johnston."

Shake.

"Tony Leonard."

Shake, but not a very confident one.

"He sells drugs. About Jane's height maybe. Dark hair. Receding hairline. You know, bald."

Emily mimed bald, to help with Ioana's comprehension. She smiled crookedly because the right hand side of her face wasn't doing anything much but causing her pain. Still, she thought, a smile's a smile. It was accompanied by a mini nod, indicating 'sort of.'

"He's not the one we need to worry about, though, is he?"

Shake. A very definite one. Tony Leonard owed Ioana Balcescu a box of chocolates, Emily thought.

"How about Karol Sikorsky?"

Fear. No nod. No shake.

"Was it him who did all this?" Emily indicated her damaged body.

A very slow shake.

"OK. It was one of his friends. Part of his group anyway. That's right, isn't it? Just shake your head if I'm wrong."

No nod. No shake.

But her eyes were telling Emily yes. One of Sikorsky's accomplices. Again, Emily and Jane exchanged glances. They were on the same page.

Emily said, carefully, "Ioana, we think that Karol Sikorsky may be a very bad man. We want to catch him and lock him up. But we need you to help us. I think Karol Sikorsky is part of a group of men who brings girls like you over from Romania and other countries around there. They probably tell you how lovely your life is going to be here, then you find it isn't, but you can't get away. Am I right so far?"

A nod. A good quality, courtroom ready nod.

"Good. Thank you. Now, I think that some of the men get violent. Those men need to be in prison and we want to put them there. So will you do this for me? If you know that Sikorsky is responsible for killing Stacey

Edwards, then please say 'yes.' I don't mean that he necessarily killed her himself, but that he had something to do with it. That he was closely involved. If those things are true, please say 'yes.'"

No nod. No shake. A frozen silence, bigger than the sky, emptier than the ocean. Emily let the silence expand for as long as she could keep it going, before nudging one last time. Now or never.

"If you help us, we can catch him. We can stop him hurting you. We can stop him hurting anyone. Ioana Balcescu, was Karol Sikorsky responsible for the murder of Stacey Edwards?"

"Yes."

"And also for the murders of Jenna and April Mancini?"

"Yes."

"And for injuring you?"

"Yes'"

"Maybe because you knew about him and what he did? Maybe they beat you this badly as a way to warn you to keep silent?"

"Yes'"

It was hardly even correct to describe her answers as words. She moved her lips. Her eyes said yes. Emily didn't even know at the time, and neither did Jane, whether any sound crept into the room. It didn't matter. A loud yes worked just as well as a silent one. Emily noticed that Jane had made notes of her last four questions and the answers. She wanted evidence that could be produced in court. Notes made contemporaneously with the interview. The kind of evidence from which a prosecution could be formed. But she was also conscious of her undertaking to Ioana.

"Now, my colleague here has just made notes. Not the whole interview, just the very last bit. We need that because we want to arrest Sikorsky and put him in prison. For the rest of his life, I hope. Certainly until he's a very old man. But I promised you we wouldn't take notes. If you want us to tear up these notes, we will. You just need to ask us. You need to say it out loud."

A second went by. Two seconds. Five seconds.

Emily felt a huge sense of relief, but she knew Ioana was feeling the exact opposite. She'd be worried she'd just signed her own death warrant, and maybe she had. In the country she was born in, the police did not fill her with confidence. She had to rely on police having discretion, and a clumsy press conference, public statement or a snippet overheard in a pub could be enough to bring the retribution Ioana feared. If they had been seen entering her house, that may have been enough as well.

For a few seconds Emily had the feeling that by answering as she had Ioana was choosing to end her own life. To end it bravely, selflessly, but still to end it, to quit the eternal battle.

Emily felt uncomfortable, but needed to press on.

"Good. Thank you. Now I'll ask one last question before we finish. Can you give me any other names? Friends of Sikorsky? The ones he relies on to do his dirty work. Maybe the men who came here yesterday? If you can give me any names at all, then we can arrest them and send them to jail for a very long time. That's what we want to do. We want to look after you and other people like you. Do you understand?"

A nod, but a frightened one. She didn't want to tell them and she wasn't going to. Her co-operation was almost at an end.

"Can you excuse me for a moment, Ioana? I just need to chat to my colleague. You stay there. Just say if you want anything."

Jan and Emily went into the hall, where they talked rapidly. Jane was worried that the evidence Emily had so carefully collected would be torn to shreds in a court of law, and she was probably right. They agreed that as soon as they stepped outside the house, they would independently make their own notes of the interview and then compare them. Hopefully, they would be very much the same.

The other problem was how much they could expect from continuing. They needed to ask when Ms. Balcescu last saw Jenna Mancini. Also, could she describe her contacts with Karol Sikorsky? She should also be made aware that withholding information in a murder enquiry may be seen as an offence.

Emily said, "should I go in there, one to one, and see if she tells me anything? If we catch the bastards, we could probably coax her into making a statement. If I were her, I wouldn't say a thing as long as they were still out there. For now, I think we'll do better by going softly, softly."

Jane nodded. "OK. I'll see if we can get a doctor over, though. She really needs to go to hospital."

Emily was relieved. She wanted to spend time with Ioana alone, but didn't want to force the issue.

Back inside the room, Emily sat down by Ioana, who looked at her with wide, dark Eastern European eyes. Neither said anything. Emily thought Ioana didn't need a doctor or a pair of intrusive police officers, a time machine would have been more useful. She needed to go back to the age of eight or nine or earlier. Back to being a newborn. She needed different parents, a different upbringing, a different past. She needed to be on a completely different planet in a completely different life. No matter which way Emily read the signs, she knew it would end badly for Ioana.

Through the wall they heard Jane arranging for a doctor and speaking to the office. Planet normal.

"You've done well," Emily told Ioana. "That's Jane sorting out a doctor for you. He'll be here soon."

"Thank you."

"You can trust him. It's safe to let him in."

"OK."

"Is there anything more you can tell me about Karol Sikorsky? Where he lives? Who his friends are? Anything at all?"

She shook her head and looked away from Emily. Enough was enough. Emily wrote her number on her card.

"This is me. My name's Emily. You can call me anytime at all. If you feel up to telling me more, maybe about the men who beat you up, then call me. I'll put it there."

Emily thrust the card under the sofa cushion, so Ioana knew where it was, but it was out of sight of any prying eyes. She didn't want Sikorsky's thugs finding it, for the sake of the health of both of them.

"I'd better go now, "Emily told her. "Do you want anything from the kitchen before I go?"

"No thanks. I'm OK."

"Do you want to see the telly? Here. I'll put it here. "she put the remote control beside Ioana, squatted down and held her hand. "You've done really well. You've been very brave. You've helped a lot of people." She felt a little grip on her hand and smiled. Emily knew that her life hadn't been exactly full with people telling her she'd done well.

Emily then surprised herself.

"Can I ask you one last question? Have you ever heard of a man named Rattigan?"

She wasn't sure what made her ask and she wasn't sure what she expected in return. She hadn't believed that Rattigan was alive. She was fairly sure that he and Johnston were up to something that connected with the Lohan case. Emily realised that she'd asked the question because she wanted to know how the debit card had ended up in Jenna Mancini's squat. Idle curiosity. Something to say.

Ioana tried to pull herself upright from her lying position. Those cracked ribs stopped her and she cried out in pain. Jane had finished her phone calls and popped the door open to see what was happening. That interrupted anything Ioana was about to say. She was silent but her face was shock and fear and distress.

Jane and Emily gaped at each other.

"Can you tell me anything about him? Anything at all?"

The only response was Ioana's staring eyes and a long, swinging headshake. Emily didn't know whether that was a no, a yes, or anything else. In any case, the moment passed and Ioana returned to her own world, remote and uncommunicative.

They said their goodbyes and left.

The street seemed like a different planet. A bit grubby, but normal. The clouds that had bothered Emily earlier were still there, but they felt ordinary and comforting.

"What on earth happened in there?"

"She sat up and hurt herself," Emily lied. "She's upset and frightened.

Jane made no comment and reminded Emily that they needed to get back to the car and write up their notes. A return to the rulebook. Planet normal.

-26-

They had planned two more interviews that day, but postponed them. It seemed more important to deal with the Balcescu one. They drove far enough away to be out of sight of Belcescu's house and sat side by side to write up their notes. The loudest sound was that of pens scratching on paper.

Emily felt frightened by what she'd seen and it made her anxious for comfort. She finished her notes before Jane and sat waiting for her colleague to finish. Jane looked sideways at her and Emily realised that Jane found her intimidating. Not her dress sense, obviously, or her social skills, but Emily was comfortable with words. She could zoom through things like writing notes or summarizing documents in half the time it took most of her colleagues.

Emily felt slightly weird that she was intimidated by Jane at the same time as the feeling was mutual. She wondered why those feelings didn't cancel each other out. She told Jane she needed fresh air. As soon as she swung the car door open, in between pulling the handle and it swinging out to its maximum open position, she realised where she could find Fletcher. It was obvious.

She searched on her mobile and found a number for Rattigan Industrial & Transport. She was put through to a corporate phone centre, and asked for Mr. Fletcher. She was told that there was nobody there at Corporate HQ with that name, but the voice on the other end asked which division was he in. Emily was prepared for that. It seemed to her that scrap metal didn't have much to do with the case, but shipping just might. All those ships coming in from the Baltic could be loaded with Afghan heroin. Enough to keep any number of prostitutes hooked. Drugs and sex. One business, not two.

She asked for the shipping division and was put through.

"Mr. Fletcher, please."

"Just putting you through now. Oh, sorry. Which Fletcher do you want. Huw?"

Emily gambled and said "yes, please."

I'm sorry, Huw Fletcher isn't with us anymore. Is there someone else who can help you?"

"He's not with you? I had a meeting arranged for this coming week. I was just calling to confirm arrangements." Emily put on her best affronted attitude. "What kind of company are you?

"Honestly, I'm afraid we have no idea where he is. He's been away a couple of weeks. But if you want to speak with to one of his colleagues in the scheduling department, I'm sure someone there can help."

Emily couldn't think of anything clever or witty to say, so simply disconnected.

Bingo! She didn't yet know what she had, except that it was something special, something that DCI Jackson really and truly ought to know about, except that she couldn't think of a way to tell him.

She got quietly back into the car and, Jane having finished her notes, they drove back to the office. For a while routine took over. Typing up notes, briefing Hughes as Jackson was out of the office, getting the information onto the system. It was all of the utmost priority because they now had grounds for arresting Karol Sikorsky for the murder of Jenna Edwards. A huge deal. For the first time the case felt on the brink of something. They couldn't arrest anyone without reasonable grounds for suspicion. A DNA sample and criminal record alone did not provide those grounds. Those two things plus Balcescu's evidence did. Once they had an arrest warrant, a search warrant would follow. With luck and a following wind, it was what was needed to crack the case wide open.

At the end of the day, when all was done and up to date, Emily felt the need to go home. To go home to Books. The problem was, she knew he would be dealing with Johnston and didn't want to get involved with that. He would call when that particular nasty was over.

It left her with the prickling feeling again. It was becoming a permanent, but unwanted, guest. She needed to identify it and its source.

It was fear. She felt fear. Worse still, she noticed that when she stamped her feet, she could only dimly feel her toes and heels striking the floor. When she rapped her hand against a kitchen worktop, or pressed it up against the point of a knife, the physical sensations of hardness or sharpness seemed to be coming from a long way away. It was like old news reports conveyed in black and white, or down a crackling phone line. She was becoming numb to herself physically and emotionally, and that was no good at all. It was how it all started. The bad stuff. It was always how it started.

  She didn't mess around. She'd learned not to. She called her Mother and told her she'd be staying another night. She put some bits and pieces in a bag and got ready to go.

  The last thing she did before leaving was to pull out the photos of April. Little April. Little April and her smile and a secret Emily felt too dim to see. She didn't spend too much time with her, though. Sanity didn't lie in that direction, she knew. What she needed was sleep and sanity and at that moment both seemed precarious.

-27-

For two blessed days life went on. Ordinary life. Lots of work. Canteen lunches, office grumbles and intensity. She liked it and felt safe within it.

There was a strong sense that Operation Lohan was making progress. Known associates of Karol Sikorsky had been found and interviewed. They turned out to be the kind of crew not to invite to your daughter's birthday party. Wojciech Kapuscinski was a dangerous character. ABH on record more than once and Emily bet her entire career that would be only the start. His photo and details were on the system. She also read about his firearms conviction. He looked every inch the dutiful foot soldier of organized crime. Tough face, narrow eyes, shaven head, leather jacket. The kind of physique forged by lifting weights and avoiding vegetables. The fat but strong bouncer look.

Brydon and Hughes did that interview but got nothing from it.

"The bugger wouldn't tell us a thing. Didn't expect him to really, except he didn't come up with an alibi and doesn't deny knowing Sikorsky."

Bryon didn't say it, but he didn't need to. Those things don't work because a thug breaks down and confesses something. They work because of pressure being applied. A non-denial here. A piece of CCTV evidence there. A phone call there. Perhaps something new from forensics. Before too long, things get scraped together and there's enough for a charge of some sort. Then the odds start to rebalance. Little extra disclosures appear, scraps of information get released in return for minor favours. Search warrants enable entry to previously closed places. Pressure is ratcheted up and before long a proper leak signals the crack in the dam that will bring the whole edifice tumbling down.

In the meantime, there was an unexpected breakthrough. The Serious Organised Crime Agency provided, on the third time of asking, an address in London where they believed Sikorsky might be found from time to time.

Jackson arranged for Sikorsky's London address to be watched in the hope the man was stupid enough to turn up there. If that failed, he planned to apply for a search warrant and raid the place anyway.

Jackson was pleased with all this because, just after lunch on Tuesday, he sought out Emily and Jane.

"Well done on the Balcescu interview. Good job," he told them.

"Thank you, sir," replied Jane, glowing like somebody had told her she can be form captain. Emily just smiled and avoided the 'sir', yet again.

"Is this one behaving herself?" Jackson asked Jane, leaning his head towards Emily

"Yes, sir. More than that, actually. I thought she was first class with Balcescu. It was Emily who....."

Jane was about to say something nice, but Jackson's earlier instruction that Jane should make the running was knocking around in her head. Emily didn't want him to know that she went off piste, even if it was in a good cause.

"It was me who made the teas. She's milk no sugar and Balcescu's one sugar only. I gave her two, given the circumstances."

Jackson retreated, muttering under his breath. Emily smiled and told Jane that she didn't want Jackson to think she couldn't obey orders. "It's not always my strong suit," she added.

"You don't say," replied Jane.

They returned to work. Lovely work. Tedious, necessary and safe.

That night Emily went home, hoping to find Books in residence. He was, alas, absent. Emily knew he would be working for their elite team doing something important. He might even still be dealing with Johnston. If that was the case, she pitied the poor man. Books was not to be trifled with. He had a gift. A gift that always persuaded others of the error of their ways. His effect on her was quite different, she mused, as she became aware of a familiar warm, damp feeling.

Once again she found the house scarily empty and vulnerable, so she bailed out and spent a happy evening with her family.

Apart from Balcescu, Jane and Emily found nothing useful from their interviews. Three of the girls they'd talked to were reluctant to say more than the bare minimum.

Fletcher bothered her, though. He mattered. Emily just knew he mattered, but she had no way of roping him into the inquiry. He'd left work abruptly enough to puzzle his colleagues, but not puzzled enough to call the police. He sent a possibly suspicious text, which Emily only knew about because she broke into a suspect's house and stole his phone. Even that text was only significant if Johnston was significant as well and, even then, only if Rattigan was. But Rattigan was dead which, in the eyes of her colleagues, meant that he couldn't possibly matter. Emily didn't see it that way, of course. She thought the dead matter just as much as anyone else.

By about halfway through the afternoon those thoughts bothered Emily enough for her to call Bryony Williams.

"Bryony, I need to ask a favour." Straight to business. "Can I ask if you've ever heard of a guy called Huw Fletcher? Some connection with prostitution and/or drugs, but I can't tell you more than that."

"Huw Fletcher? No, I've never heard of him."

"OK, that's fine, but I think he's involved in something nasty to do with the women you try to protect. I can't tell you why, but I've serious reason to think so. Trouble is, I can't reveal the witness who gave me Fletcher's name and I can't introduce Fletcher into the inquiry proper unless I can supply evidence that connects him to it. I want you to be that evidence."

"What do you want me to do?"

"Just say that you've heard rumours from the girls you work with that Huw Fletcher has been involved in sex trafficking and prostitution. You heard the rumours and wanted to pass them on to me."

"Yes, I'm happy to say all that."

"You may, one day, be asked to the same thing in court."

"I understand. That's fine."

"You may find yourself being asked the same questions in the course of a missing person investigation."

"OK." A drawn out OK, that one. "Who's the missing person? Fletcher?"

"Yes."

"All right. Go on, then. In for a penny, in for a pound."

"Bryony, you're a star."

"That's all right. It's not every day I'm asked to fabricate evidence by a police officer."

Emily left the office and went home. Still no Books, but then she spotted it. A small white scrap of paper.

"Meet me at our usual place. I have news!"

The handwriting was not tidy, but she knew immediately it belonged to Books and the onset of feeling a touch isolated was short-lived. She needed his presence and the stability it provided for her. It felt odd to be there. Still not safe, but not as radically threatening as it had been after Johnston's visit. She opened the fridge and was surprised to find it full of food. She forgot that she'd restocked it on Sunday. She went upstairs to change out of her working clothes and prepare herself for whatever her Books had in mind for them.

Then a van pulled up outside and she flooded with fear.

Her knife and hammer were downstairs. She should have brought them up. Her curtains were open and she should have closed them. Simple precautions, trained into her by her father and Books. Simply and carelessly forgotten.

A man got out of the van, walked to the front door and knocked. He looked ordinary. A plumber? Delivery man? Killer? But what do killers look like? What did the man who killed Stacey Edwards look like?

Emily didn't move. She didn't know what to do. The man knocked again and she let the sound echo around in the silence. Then the man walked to his van, and picked up his phone. She could see him, but was careful to step back far enough from her upstairs window that he'd have difficulty seeing her.

Luckily, her window was open a tad. Just four inches to let air in. On the latch with a window lock preventing it from going any further. The gap was sufficient to allow her to hear the man's conversation. Not all of it, but enough. He had a loud voice and was asking for her father.

Fear rushed out again. She was shaky, but moving again. She went downstairs holding both walls as she went, and threw open the door.

"Emily? Your dad sent me. Wanted me to have a look at the alarm and a few bits and pieces."

The world seemed full of people that her father knew. She guessed he must pay a lot of them one way or another, but the relationship never seemed to be about employment, or even much about pay. It was just that if her father asked a favour then it got done. It was just the way it was. 'Your Dad sent me.' Four words that meant your problem was as good as fixed.

"Come in. Sorry, I was upstairs and didn't hear you knock."

It was a feeble excuse, but it didn't need to be any better. The man (Alex someone or other) didn't care. He was inside, taking the front off her burglar alarm, getting her to punch in her access code as he ostentatiously looked away, and then he was off doing tests and checking connections.

He talked all the time. He told her about a big alarm installation job he'd worked on at a local place, the silly things some people did with their access codes. The importance of maintenance.

To begin with she was irritated, but then she realised that he didn't give a monkey's whether he had anyone to talk to or not. He finished with the burglar alarm and was busy polishing away at the Blu-Tack scabs with fine wire wool and white spirit.

"I'll touch these up after. It's going to show otherwise." He said.

"Do want a cup of tea?" Emily offered because it's what you say to workmen.

"White, no sugar please, if you're making it. I've got a cupboard off there. Hinge needed adjusting, it wasn't opening right. It'll be back on in a tick."

Emily made the tea and tried to remember whether she'd noticed any problem with the cupboard door. A little clicky, maybe, on opening. No big deal. Alex was busy with paint pots next, whistling. She preferred his chat to the whistling, so she handed him his tea. She stayed there with him, inviting conversation.

It was like inviting a lecture from a Mormon, a rant from a jihadist. Alex was a whirlwind of chat, the Muhammed Ali of white noise. Gossip, unconnected little snippets, political comment, questions that were asked but invited no answer, all passed his lips in an unending torrent. She said almost nothing and marveled at his ability to blather.

As he put the cupboard door back on, he said something that caught her attention. He'd been moaning about youth gangs in the area, then talked about guns and knives and then, with the sweet inconsistency of his kind, switched the focus of his monologue to the over-regulation of gun clubs.

"People don't want that, do they? That's why you get these places springing up. Unregulated. Not that I should tell you that, seeing you are who you are. There's one place, farmer's turned a barn into a firing range. Nothing dodgy, if you get me, it's just for people who want to have a bit of fun. Handguns, that sort of thing. I think the sheep probably need ear defenders, though."

With that thought his chat streamed off again in a different direction. He moved on to health and safety, fascism, bad things about the government, bad things about the local council. But not for long. The Blu Tack scabs had gone and the cupboard door was back in place. Alex opened and closed the remaining doors to check they were all swinging as they should, and the burglar alarm was as happy as it was ever going to be.

"Sound as a pound," he told her, banging them shut.

He scooped up his stuff and whizzed off.

The house felt weirdly quiet without him. It did also feel a bit safer, though she hadn't thought to worry about the burglar alarm in the first place.

She climbed the stairs, dressed and applied the war paint. Looking at herself in the mirror, she saw what he would see. 'Not bad,' she thought. 'Not gorgeous, but nice. Attractive.' That was all she'd ever hoped to achieve and she liked the way she looked that night.

She skittered out of the house. She still had an undercurrent of anxiety about her physical safety, so she carried a kitchen knife in her clutch bag. She arrived at the wine bar at the same time as Books.

"Bloody hell, Em, you look absolutely smashing."

He would have said that whatever she looked like but the look on his face and the way he kept looking at her told her that he meant it.

"You too, Mr. B.," she said and allowed him to take her inside.

"So what's the news?" she asked. Straight to it. No point in skirting around.

Books smiled and sipped his wine. He treated her to his best loving gaze and whispered, "you'll be pleased to know that Mr. Johnston will not worry you again." He offered no details and continued to look into her eyes. She already knew he always made her feel a certain way, but this seemed special somehow. Nevertheless, she needed details.

"Is that it? No details? Is he in one piece or have you charmed him with the power of your personality?

"Now, come on, Emily, you really do not want to know. He was quite happy to tell me everything, even if he was a little reluctant at first."

"Surely, I deserve more than that," she said, disappointed.

"Look Em., he'll tell you whatever you need to know for the purposes of your investigation quite willingly. Just ask him and mention my name. The stuff he's given me is information I need to deal with together with your father. Nothing to worry about. It has a connection to Operation Lohan, but we'll chase it from our end. It involves a terrorist aspect, as well as the people trafficking, drug running and prostitution angles you're already onto. As soon as I'm able, we'll put it all together. I've been told to leave it at that for your safety. Also, your father is looking after your safety and I have to say, so am I. The work you are doing is absolutely vital to what we are dealing with, and we must not overlap yet."

"Hmm," was all she could muster.

"Let's eat," said Books, in an effort to move the evening on.

The restaurant was close to the wine bar, so they walked. Hand in hand and she felt overwhelmingly safe. When they got there, they had a comedy moment around her chair. She was about to tug it out and sit on it when she realised that Books was wanting to do the gentlemanly thing and pull it out for her, so she could sit down in a ladylike manner. Emily was a bit slow to realise and there was a short tug-of-war with the chair before she came to settle into her best graceful ladylike mode.

He had updated her about work and now the evening was free; cleared just for them. From then on she stuck to the textbook of first dates. There was absolutely no need for it, but she decided to play that game as it felt safe for her. She ran the risk that it could confuse her beloved Books, but what the hell. A little variety and mystery did nobody any harm, she reasoned to herself. Besides, he'd started it with the gentlemanly chair thing.

When the starter came, she told him it was delicious. When the main course came, she told him it was wonderful. They ate from each other's plates and Books told her again that she looked absolutely beautiful. Emily remembered to smile a lot. She could role play with the best of them.

They didn't talk much. Each was wondering how the evening might end, and neither wanted to spoil what could be on the cards. Books had hopes, of course, as every man has had since time began and Emily hoped for the same, but she was in first date role play mode and was enjoying the frisson.

"Tell me, Emily, why did you decide to sign up to what we do? I know your father took on his role from Ray Quinn and bloody good at it he is too. But why you? I don't mean to pry, or touch on sensitive things, but it can't have been easy. I mean, considering your difficulty."

He had addressed the elephant in the room. He hadn't meant to when he planned the evening, but the time just seemed right, to go beneath the surface and find out what really made her tick. He loved her already, but wanted everything.

Emily knew why he was digging and she also knew it had to be talked about sometime, so why not then? A bit more serious than first date rules, but never mind. She laughed nervously.

"If I tell you, you'll think I'm nuts."

He expected her to go ahead and tell him anyway and she wanted to, but she knew enough to take care. She knew she had an illness that meant others could view her as proper nuts, and that made her wary about the reveal.

"I only noticed things weren't right when I was nine or ten and the feeling of giddiness has never left me. My entire name, my world, feels precarious, a conjecture balanced on a riddle. That's why it felt right to become a detective. I've become a practitioner of 'if's. If Rattigan. If Mancini. If Johnston. If poor old Stacey Edwards. A million 'if's, all looking for me to solve them, or at least help to solve them."

Books looked at her with his big serious eyes.

"But I already think you're nuts," he said.

He'd earned a smile, she thought and treated him.

When they left the restaurant, it was not late. Books did the male thing of making the space contain any possibility at all. Had he cottoned on to her first date game, she wondered? Would it be home for eight hours of rowdy and rampant sex? Or a chaste kiss on the cheek and a meaningless promise. She realised he was letting her decide. She thought that a bad idea as first date rules dictate the safe option. Standard Date Girl Operating Procedure dictated bad date equals polite goodbyes, good date equals modest kiss.

As far as she could tell, it had qualified as a good date. Awkward start, but everyone's allowed a ropey opening. After that, she'd had a good time and she thought Books had as well. Despite the intimate questioning about the elephant, she felt good.

They walked and he was smiling at her. She wondered whether it was more like him laughing at her, but dismissed that idea. The air was warm and the streets were relatively quiet, but there was some traffic about. Daylight, or the memory of it, was still alive in the sky. She was feeling a bit spacey, but not necessarily bad spacey. She was pretty sure she could feel her feet when they hit the ground and her heart felt seemed OK, if a little distant.

When they reached a corner, she started to step straight out into the traffic, where a series of fast-moving metal vehicles prepared to flatten her. Books, with surprising deftness, grabbed her and swiveled her so that she stayed on the pavement and avoided being splattered. With equal deftness, he kept his arm on her shoulder as they walked on down the road.

Date Girl was taken aback. She'd been outmanoeuvred, but she quite liked the result. She liked his hand on her. She liked the weight of his arm on her shoulder. All she could think about was his arm on her shoulder and the fading violet sky.

When they got to the car, there was a decision she couldn't avoid, but had already planned for. She turned her back to her car so that she could lean against it. Books was on the case. His mastery of Standard Date Guy Operating Procedure was frighteningly complete. He had a hand behind her back and scooped her towards him for a kiss. A very good one too, Emily thought. Just for a moment her head shut down and feelings took over. Something in her stomach flipped. Her mental health workers all used to be delighted if she had natural, uncomplicated, ordinary human feelings. They put a big fat tick on their clinical interview sheets. Something to boast about as they sipped their coffees at the Annual Psychiatric Conference of Whatever.

She was pleased to have these feelings too, but they weren't simple for her. She knew that too much all at once could flip her fragile little boat and leave her much worse off than before. The whole Lohan thing wasn't much help either. It was a risk factor.

The anxieties she'd had since Johnston walloped her were the same, only more so. Her little boat was in high seas already.

They kissed once more and she felt herself urgent with lust. Tugged by it. Eight hours of rowdy sex felt like a good option at that moment, but she was in control of herself again and knew what she needed to do. After their second kiss, she pulled away, albeit gently.

"My treat next time," she told him.

"There's going to be a next time?"

She nodded. That was an easy one. "Yes. Yes, there will."

Home.

Books had not gone home with her. He said he had business to attend to, and Emily hoped he had merely picked up the vibes and decided to play the long game.

Anxiety at the front door. There was a security light at the front of the house, so she wasn't worried about possible lurkers within. She knew the burglar alarm was now working properly, just as she was perfectly sure it was working perfectly before, but this was a fear that went beyond reason.

She inserted her key, turned it and let herself in. The alarm started blipping at her, as it always did, and she entered her access code to silence it.

House empty. Lights on, as she'd left them. No noise. Nothing untoward.

Her brain was running through the checks, but her heart was racing as though it wasn't too much interested in words from the boss upstairs. She went to close the front door and, as she got there to swing it shut, her toe brushed against something on the floor.

Instant fear. Instant, unreasonable fear. Emily fought down the unreason and made herself look down. It was just a sheet of paper; an advertising flyer or something like it. She closed the door, locked it, checked the lock twice, then bent to pick the paper up.

Not a flyer. It said this: WE KNOW WHERE YOU LIVE. No name. Regular office paper. Ordinary household printer. No need for forensics, because she knew already that there'd be nothing to find.

Her panic was instant and convulsive. She was down on her knees by the door, attempting the same dry-retching that she'd felt after Johnston left. Her clutch bag was well named because she was clutching it obsessively in her right hand, so that she could feel the haft of the knife. She was ready to stab straight through the end of the bag if needed, extravagant silk bow and all.

For ten minutes, fear was two tries and a penalty kick to the good. Emily was yet to get out of her own half. She wanted to call Dad, have him come and rescue her. Call Books, have him come and rescue her. He'd get the best night of his life if he did, she promised to herself. But Dad and Books were stopgaps, she knew. Good for the night. Useless for a lifetime. If she was in the grip of fear, she needed to deal with it herself. And besides, she had a funny feeling that her Father had already helped her.

Checking the door locks again, she went through to the living room and her phone. She called Jon Johnston. His landline, because she'd put his SIM card in the kettle. It rang four times and then he answered.

"Johnston."

"It's Emily"

There was a short pause. She wondered whether he just needed the time to find the right attitude to her. Angry attitude? Slap your head off attitude? No, he opted for a remembering Books attitude. Very wise, she thought.

"Well, how can I help you today?"

"Did your Mum get those tulips? I sent them. I felt bad."

"Yes, she did. Thank you for that."

"Ok....."

Emily didn't know how to answer that. She'd stolen his phone. He'd hit her. She'd bought his mum tulips. It was hard to work out who owed whom what exactly.

"I got a note this evening. Through my letterbox. It said, "WE KNOW WHERE YOU LIVE."

"That's a bit of a cliché, isn't it?"

"I wasn't asking for literary criticism. I know it's a cliché."

"Any case, I do know where you live. You gave me bagels and smoked salmon, remember?"

"It wasn't from you. I know that."

"But you're ringing me up."

"Did you know Huw Fletcher went missing from Rattigan's offices two weeks ago? It's just you had his number on your SIM card."

A long silence. She let it run.

"Listen. None of this has to be your problem. You've got DCI Jackson on the murder enquiry, right? Let him run things. He'll get his man. Forensics. CCTV. All that stuff."

"I know."

"You don't need to do any more."

"Only I already have done, haven't I? Apart from anything else, I've got people sticking threatening notes through my letterbox."

There was a sigh, or not a sigh, maybe an intake of breath, down the other end of the phone.

"Huw Fletcher is an idiot. He's not a dangerous idiot, not dangerous to you, I mean. If you ask me, he's going to be a dead idiot before too long. I didn't give him your address. I did give him your name. Part of explaining that the text you sent didn't come from me. I did use your surname. I did not use your first name. I did say you were police."

Emily ran the same calculation. If Fletcher knew she a cop, he could probably have found her first name by ringing the station switchboard. They certainly wouldn't have given out a home address, but maybe everyone with her name got that message through their letterbox this evening.

"It's the sort of thing that idiots do," says Johnston. "Doesn't mean you need to worry about it."

"I saw a prostitute on Monday. I doubt if you know her. Ioana Balcescu. Someone had beaten her up quite badly. Not a punter having a go. A punishment beating of some sort. She didn't tell us anything at all" – not true, but she wanted to protect her – "but she showed a lot of alarm when it came to a couple of names."

"Oh, yes?"

"Not your name, though I did ask."

"Nice of you."

"De nada. No, the two names that bothered her were Karol Sikorsky..." She left a pause in case Johnston wanted to make a comment, but he didn't, "and Brendan Rattigan."

"Brendan Rattigan is dead. Didn't you know that? Plane crash in the Severn Estuary."

"I know. Seems surprising that he's still terrifying prostitutes."

"Yes, isn't it?"

A long pause. It would have been the end of the call, except neither of was hanging up.

"Do you want a word of advice from somebody who once used to be a half decent policeman?" said Johnston finally.

"I'll take anything going."

"Then stay out of this. There's nothing you can do, and as you already noticed, Brendan Rattigan is perfectly well able to injure people from beyond the grave. Ready and willing. Just stay out of it."

"Have you stayed out of it?"

He laughed. "I used to be a half decent policeman. Doesn't mean I am now."

"And maybe I'm already in it, whatever it is."

"Maybe."

Another beat, then him to her: "Are you all right? After I hit you?"

"Fine. Yes. Don't worry about it."

"I haven't been worrying."

"No, thanks anyway. You've been helpful."

"And Huw Fletcher's an idiot. Trust me."

"I do, weirdly. Can I ask you just one more question? Brendan Rattigan, just how dead exactly would you say he was?"

Johnston laughed. A proper laugh. No disguise or fakery in it. "Well, I wasn't watching at the time, but I'd say he was pretty damn dead. That'd be my guess, anyway."

They wished each other goodnight. Oddly, she found herself trusting Johnston more than not. She didn't know if that was because he was a copper once, and in the end coppers stick together through thick and thin. Or if it was something to do with him hitting her. If that's exorcised something in their dealings with each other.

If the note came from Huw Fletcher, and if Fletcher was a non-dangerous idiot who might be dead soon, then she didn't have more to worry about than before she went out that evening. On the other hand, she honestly didn't know if she was "out of it" or "in it", whatever the "it" might be. And if the real danger came from the possibly dead Brendan Rattigan, then the Johnston-Fletcher axis was by no means the only way in which she might have been stirring up trouble for herself. There were all those calls and texts she'd made to the numbers in Johnston's phonebook. There was her amazing ability to upset Ioana Balsescu by mentioning Rattigan's name. Who knows by what routes word of her activities might not have travelled back to people who might consider her a candidate for a punishment beating or worse?

Not a good thought, that. If those people ever did to her what they did to Ioana, then she wouldn't survive it. She'd be back where she was as a teenager. As good as dead.

The terrors that had so often assailed her nights seemed to be creeping into her waking hours. Against some threats, a paring knife concealed in a blue silk clutch bag is not weaponry enough.

And without considering her actions more than a moment, she was at the door, going out. As she got into the car, she realised she was still in her glad rags, kitten heels and all. Logic suggested going back inside to change, but she always keep a fleece top and hiking boots in the back of her car and just then she preferred to keep moving.

The roads were empty. She'd normally have put her foot down, but bearing in mind where she was going, she was a good girl and stayed within five or ten miles an hour of the speed limit.

She made the turn onto high moorland. No dead miners there, just sheep looming white in the tussocky grass. She stopped at one point to check her position and could hear the wind sighing through the grasses. No cars. No buildings. No people. There were quarries up there somewhere once, but she didn't know where.

She had a sudden worry that she wouldn't find the barn she was looking for. No directions. Driving at night. Her SatNav in the dark as much she was. But then she came to the turn in the hill. There was a little passing place and down a farm track, maybe four hundred yards away, a big white barn with a light over its door. She saw farm machinery and a large concrete yard and not much else, because of the feeble light.

The track was gated, but she thought she'd feel safer walking than driving anyway. She changed her cute little kitten heels for hiking boots and pulled her fleece top over her dress. It was colder up there. Partly the height, partly being out of the city. The sky was half overcast. Some stars, amid long reaches of blackness. The pattern of light revealed the landscape. Orange in the distance towards the town. Virtually nothing when it came to the looming bulk of the moor.

Emily was scared, but it was a good fear. The sort that encourages action, not the sort that encouraged her to kneel by her front door trying to retch up supper. She felt clear and purposeful.

She walked towards the barn. She'd left her knife and clutch bag in the car because they seemed silly out there. She found herself almost enjoying the feeling of exposure.

Once, she heard a sudden movement of feet and her adrenaline responded instantly, but it was only sheep. She could see their thick, stupid, lovable faces peering through the darkness, and walked on.

She reached the concrete yard. There was no one else there. No sound other than those belonging to a farm at night. She didn't know what she expected to find or what she expected to do. There was a big metal sliding door, the sort they have in industrial sheds, but it was closed, and even if it wasn't locked, she wouldn't have known how to pull it back. Beside it, though, there was a smaller door. Human size, not tractor size. She tried it and found it open.

In she went. It was a huge place. Barns are, obviously, but there was something about the huge roof, about the whole vast silent space that altered something in her, whether she liked it or not. She moved forwards, as though tiptoeing through a cathedral.

The place was lit, if that's the right term, by two incandescent bulbs hanging from long cords. They chucked out a hundred watts each, maybe, but in that space and that darkness the light seemed to give up hope before it travelled far. Underneath the near bulb, there were a few bales of straw, marking out a line across the barn. Further on down, beneath the other light, there was a row of paper targets. Human shaped, not target shaped. Picked out in black and white. Black to congratulate you for a chest shot, white to mark you down for a shot to the arm or head.

When she reached the straw bales, she found a handgun there. A cardboard box with bullets lay beside it. She fiddled around with the gun and, feeling like an idiot, adopted the pose. Feet apart. Arms out. Steady gaze. Fire.

Nothing.

She moved the safety catch and repeated the process. This time it fired. The shot was astonishingly loud, reminding her of when Johnston hit her, only the audio equivalent of that. She didn't know if her ears were sensitive, or if it was the sheer volume of silence in the barn that threw her.

As she put the gun down, trembling slightly in her arms, she noticed that there were ear defenders there on the straw as well. She loaded the gun by sliding the magazine out of the handgrip. Closing her eyes and, in the dark, unloading and reloading, she then flipped the safety to off with her thumb. She could probably have been faster, but at least she could do it. On the straw there were four boxes of bullets all told.

She decided that one box could go on practice.

Fire. Fire. Fire.

Close eyes. Turn round. Then whip round to the targets and fire, fire, fire.

There were some 250 bullets or so in the box and she fired about 150 of them. Some of her shots weren't hitting the target, but plenty of others were hitting the white areas: head, hand, groin, leg. But there were plenty hitting black. The target she aimed at didn't have much of a middle by the time she stopped.

Her arms were aching from the effort of holding the gun out, and she put it down, sitting for a rest next to it.

Emily decided to finish firing off the box of ammo, which would leave her with the gun and one more box of bullets. If there were more than 250 people coming to get her, she reasoned, she would just have to take her chances with the paring knife.

She rose and started her routine. Arms together, ignore the ache, feet apart, both eyes open, breathing steady. Fire. Fire. Fire. She did the turning around stuff and then tried shooting one handed. That definitely made accuracy worse, but the target was nevertheless fairly well shredded.

Then as she got ready for another 'close her eyes, turn, fire routine', she suddenly noticed that the door she came in through was open and a man was standing there. Flat cap. Checked shirt under thick farmer tweed. Ageless. Could be thirty. Could be sixty. He was looking straight at her. He inclined his head to acknowledge her presence, but otherwise said and did nothing. For the first time, Emily noticed that up at the other end of the barn, the end that was unlit and in darkness, there were animals stirring. Cattle, she thought. Sheep would be out in the fields. She could dimly see amber eyes gleaming in the darkness. She wondered what the cows made of her shooting. Whether this was something they heard often or almost never.

She pulled her ear defenders off.

"Drop your shoulders," the man told her. "And soft hands. Don't tense up. Ease the trigger. You don't want to jerk it."

"Ok."

"Are you right handed?"

She nodded.

"Then left foot slightly forward. Just slightly. Shoulder's width apart. Select a new target."

She turned back to the gun. The shooting range had lost some of its dimness, now that her eyes were fully adjusted. Feeling the man's eyes on her back, she adopted her stance and shot a magazine of ten bullets in the space of three or four seconds. She tried keeping her shoulders dropped and her hands soft. She'd left the ear defenders off, but this time was expecting the noise and quite liked it. It filled the space.

Emily turned back to the man, who only nodded. She took that as a "go on" and loosed another four magazines. She concentrated on her shoulders and hands, and her accuracy improved. Pleased with herself, she turned back to the man.

"Good enough. Keep your hands soft."

"Thank you."

Another nod. She turned back to the shooting, pulling her ear defenders on this time and went on to finish the box. Soft hands, hard bullets. When she turned back again, the man had gone.

Her arms were properly tired now, but she was happy. She took the gun and two boxes of bullets. It was a slight change of plan, but when Rattigan's army of the undead emerged to snatch her, they would need to number at least 501. Any fewer than that and she'd be ready for them.

On her way out of the barn, she promised the cows that they could get some sleep now. Their breath steamed, but they made no further comment. A hundred amber eyes followed her.

Out in the yard, nothing had changed. No one was present; nothing moved. She walked up the track to her car and drove back the way she'd come. She was thinking about Johnston, Huw Fletcher and Brendan Rattigan.

But mostly, she thought about that kiss with Books. She realised she liked being his girlfriend. The sort who would remember his birthday, act appropriately and think to wear the most expensive knickers on Valentine's Day. She wasn't sure if it was an act she'd be able to pull off, but the idea definitely appealed. She felt giddy at the thought. Vertigious and a familiar warm damp feeling from down south.

And on the last stretch home, she thought about Dad. He must have procured the gun with remarkable speed and stage management. She could ask of course, but that wasn't the way they worked in their secret team. "Don't ask, don't tell" was their policy and she was happy to leave it like that. She also wondered if her Father's feelings around embedding her in the police force were because he had things that she didn't know about. Probably better to not go there and just get on with things.

She got home sometime after two and walked up to her front door with kitten heels and ammo boxes in one hand, gun in the other. For the first time in what felt like an eternity, she didn't feel frightened at all.

-29-

Bedtime. Easier now than it had been recently.

She left the bed where it was and dragged out a futon roll and spare duvet from beneath it. Theoretically, the futon was for guests, athough she couldn't remember any guests having ever actually used it. The futon went on the floor where it couldn't be seen from the door. In the best tradition of these things, she heaped pillows in the bed itself, so it looked like someone was sleeping there. Then she made herself at home on the futon, glass of water and alarm clock near her head, gun loaded and by her hand. She shoved a chair up against the door, which wouldn't stop anyone from getting in, but would make plenty of noise if they did.

She knew all this was over the top, but she felt safe and slept like a puppy, which was all that mattered.

In the morning, the alarm went off too early. She was tired, because she was a good three hours short of what she needed. She didn't care, though because she had at least mastered the art of sleeping in her own home. Also, she hadn't smoked since Saturday, which was good going for her, especially given the way things were with Lohan.

Emily got up and stared out at the place where she lived. She was right at the heart of Planet Normal, even though she was probably it's strangest resident. She didn't care about that. She liked a place where Dads went to work in the morning and people grumbled when the post was late. If Rattigan's army of the undead was out there waiting for her, they were well disguised.

There were some clouds dotting the sky. Those high stately ones that look like ships sailing in from the west. There weren't many of them, though, and the sun was already well into its stride. It was going to be hot.

She drifted downstairs and ate a nectarine straight from the fridge. Made tea. Ate something else, because the good citizens of Planet Normal didn't get by on a single nectarine. She unlocked her garden shed and opened the window because if it was hot outside, the shed could get boiling. It would be too hot even with the window open, but she locked up all the same. She always did.

She had intended to shower, but she had already let too much time drift by. Sharp means sharp. Apart from sniffing her wrists to make sure they didn't smell of the firing range, she did as little as she could. But she had to get dressed. That was easy, normally. Select a bland, appropriate outfit from the array of bland, appropriate outfits she had in her wardrobe. She used to own almost nothing that wasn't black, navy, tan, white, charcoal or a pink so muted that it might as well have been beige. She never thought those colours suited her particularly. She didn't have an opinion on the subject. It was just a question of following the golden rule: observe what others do, then follow suit. A palette of muted classic colours seemed like the safest way to achieve the right effect.

Since Kay turned fourteen or fifteen, however, she'd campaigned to get Emily to liven up her wardrobe. It was still hardly vibrating with life. It still looked something like an exhibition of Next office wear, 2004-10. All the same, she had options now that she wouldn't have had a few years ago. And today she may well be seeing Books. He'd be seeing her. She wanted his eyes on her, and she wanted them to be hungry ones, sexed up and passionate.

She dispensed with her normal functional underwear and put on a bra and knickers from one of the posher M&S ranges. White lace. Summery and sexy. No one but her would see them, but it was a start. And then what? She was indecisive to begin with, then opted for a floaty mint green dress and a linen jacket. Brown strappy sandals. More make-up than she'd usually wear, which wasn't saying a lot.

Emily stared at herself in the mirror. Mirrors tell you nothing you don't already know, huh? This one did. She saw a young woman. Pretty. Tick the box, good solid passing grade, pretty. Also, anxious. She looked a bit like she was off to see the man who might be her future. Good luck sister, but she didn't think she needed it.

Sharp means sharp sent her running from the house. She'd thrown her gun into her handbag, but the boxes of bullets stayed in the house. She drove to work as quickly as the traffic allowed. One speed camera almost caught her, but she was fairly sure she braked in time. The gun was shifted from handbag to glovebox as she entered the car park.

She was there in time to hear the huge overnight news that they'd gone ahead and raided Sikorsky's place in North London. Jackson was in London with DI Hughes. More people were going up now in support. No briefing today, because there was no one to give it and because no one wanted to hear about yesterday when today is where the action is.

It was slightly weird news, and not just for Emily. The office was all at a bit of a loss. The poor guy who had spent a week forlornly combing CCTV footage for anything that might be helpful now faced another day doing just that, well aware that there could be developments up in London that made the whole thing pointless.

Emily was at a loss too. Today was her seeing Books day. Her floaty green dress day. Her day for make-up and girly sandals. She was looking forward to it very much.

She went down the stairs to the print room. Almost no one was going to be using them then, and there were doors at the top and bottom. The door at the top banged and somebody's tread started down. Heavy and light. Heavy because he was a biggish lad, and light because he had a natural athleticism, a bounce that carried through into every movement he made. She knew who it was before he came into view.

"Hey."

Books was on the step above her and she was talking somewhere in the region of his belly button. He came down a step, then hoisted her up to where he'd been standing. They were still not eyeball to eye ball, but were a lot closer.

"Do I see Emily in a dress?" he said. "Have all relevant authorities been notified?"

"And heels," She said. "Look."

He smiled at her. A nice smile, but she knew half his mind was occupied by the clock. He needed to get off to London as soon as he could.

There were still no sounds on the stairs. There was a hum from the print room where one of the machines was doing its thing, but nothing that needed to disturb them.

"I just wanted to tell you I might need to take things slow."

"Ok."

"It's just….things can get a bit crazy in my head, and slow tends to be better than fast."

"Ok."

"I don't want you to think that because I-"

She wasn't sure what she was trying to say, so ended up saying nothing.

"You don't want to think that, although you almost walked out into a line of cars last night, you've got some sort of death wish."

"That's it," she said. "That's exactly what I was trying to say."

For a moment, she thought he was going to kiss her again and she really wanted him to. She felt lust pulling at her like wind. But he didn't. Fortunately for her composure, he bailed out of the kiss and just chucked her under the nose with his index finger.

"Slow is fine," he said.

He was laughing at her again and she realised it was nice being laughed at. Then he was off, up the steps. Heavy and light. Thumping the door at the top open so hard that it whacked against its doorstop. The stairwell echoed with the noise of his departure, a reverberation of wood against metal, then returned to silence. Like he'd never been there, which was what he intended.

He'd gone. To deal with whoever, and whoever that was should be in very great fear right now.

She sat on the step, getting her head into shape again. Her pulse rate was very high, but steady. She counted her breaths, trying to bring her breathing down to a more relaxed range.

She moved her legs and feet, to make sure that she could feel them as normal.

She felt something and thought she knew what it was. But she did the exercise by the book, and the book said she had to run through a range of feelings to find the best available match.

Fear. Anger. Jealousy. Love. Happiness. Disgust. Yearning. Curiosity.

Love.

She felt the feelings, piece by miraculous piece. "Is this what humans feel like when they are getting ready to fall in love"? she wondered.

She rose from her step and walked slowly back upstairs to her desk. This was what humans feel like. This was what it felt to be normal.

There was a voicemail from Jane Alexander. Her boy was ill and she'd been unable to arrange alternative childcare, so she was stuck at home. She told Emily to call her if necessary. In the meantime, though, her interviews for the day were probably off, unless she could find a DS who would interview prostitutes with her, which, given the recent news, she probably couldn't. Jackson and Hughes and pretty much everyone who counted were out of the office and wouldn't want to be contacted.

She had a stack of various tedious paperwork-type jobs to do, but few of them were urgent. Over the other side of the office, a couple of DCs were making piles of empty coffee cups and trying to knock them over by throwing a soft indoor rugby ball at them. There were yells of laughter when they succeeded and more yells when they failed. She sometimes thought it must be a lot easier to be a man.

Emily pulled out the notes she'd made on all those Social Services files. April and Jenna. Stacey Edwards.

There were a million points of comparison between their stories, but there were bound to be. It isn't any old person who becomes a prostitute. It's the messed up ones. Broken homes, muddled childhoods, some disastrously wrong steps in adolescence. Jenna and Stacey both ended up in care because their parents were crazy, sick, violent or useless. In effect they never knew their parents. The state took over. What kind of person could go through all that and not end up a bit crazed themselves?

That was part of what hooked Emily about Jenna and April. Jenna had a crap life and she fought to give her kid a better one. She failed and yet it wasn't the failure that captured her but the depth of her trying.

Inevitably, Emily had the photos of April up onscreen as she reviewed all this. The interesting dead ones, not the dull toffee-apple ones. It wasn't quite true that April was trying to tell her something. It would be more accurate to say that she already knew it – whatever 'it' was – and April's job was to remind her. Emily couldn't figure it out, though. She stared away from her desk out to the boys fooling around with the rugby ball.

She should be doing other things, she thought.

In London, they were searching Karol Sikorsky's house. Last night Books kissed her, and today he almost kissed her again. In the glovebox of her car she had a gun and at home she had 490 bullets. The rest were already in the gun.

She was thinking those thoughts when she got up to make some tea and a phone started ringing. It wasn't on her desk but, since there was no one else around, she picked it up.

It was Jackson. "Who's that? Emily?"

"That's right."

"Listen. We're in the house here in London and we've come across about a kilo of what we're pretty sure is heroin. It's going straight to the lab."

"Ok, so you want me to get on to the lab here...."

"Yeah. Let's see if we can make a connection between stuff we've got here and stuff elsewhere."

"And the names we already have? You want me to start seeing if we can connect them to the drugs?"

"Precisely. And listen. I want as many warrants as I can get. Everybody you can think of. Also, do you think there's any chance that your prostitute...."

"Ioana Balcescu..."

"Right, any chance that she'd broaden her evidence? Name more names?"

"I don't know. I can try. But if we're right, then any number of prostitutes might be able to testify against these guys."

"Anything you can get on them. Minor stuff. That's fine. We just need enough to justify an arrest and a search warrant. I want to start interviewing with a charge sheet behind us."

"I'll get onto it right away."

"Take my name in vain if you need to. Don't let things get held up for lack of resources."

"I won't."

"Ok. Good. Any problems just shout. Any breakthroughs, tell me right away."

"Will do." She still couldn't manage "sir."

Jackson had rung off before she could have said it anyway. For a moment, she forgot why she was at a strange desk and then remembered her tea. She decided against making any.

She called the lab straight away and let them know about the developments up in London. The London lab would liaise with their own lab in any event, but it never hurt to let both groups know that they were breathing down their necks.

She called Jane Alexander and told her that she might want to get herself into the office, childcare crisis or no. Jane thought about it briefly, then said, "I'll see what I can do as soon as I can."

Emily called Ioana Balcescu, but didn't even get through to a voice-mail. She was doubtful that she would give anything further anyway, though she'd keep trying.

She bumped into Mervyn Rogers who was one of the officers who interviewed people in the early stages of the investigation.

"Jackson wants to pull all the suspects, however weak we may think a connection is, and give them the third degree. Tell them we can connect them to a major drugs ring in London, plus the murder of the two Mancinis and Stacey Edwards. Terrify them, basically."

Rogers grinned. It was the sort of assignment he'd relish. She was aware of having added a little salt to Jackson's instructions, but if there was a breach of procedure, it was Emily's, not Jackson's.

"Start with Leonard. Hit him hard and early. His career and character suggests him being a bit-part player, which means he's more likely to crack under pressure. I'll start making some calls. See if I can get anyone to name him as a dealer."

Back to her desk. She had a distinct feeling this involved more than drugs and needed to let Books and Dad know. She thought the drugs were a means to an end. Money making to fund more dangerous activities. Terrorism even. She called her Father on her mobile when she knew there was nobody within earshot and brought him up to speed. She gave him names. Men and women. She realised they would be visited by her lovely Books and would not enjoy the experience, but that was their problem, not hers.

"Thanks, Em. Not a word to anybody. I'll get onto it. Books may be occupied for a while but we'll keep you informed. Be careful. Walls have ears and we don't know the extent of all this yet."

"I will. Love you, Dad."

Her next call was Bryony Wiliams at StreetSafe. It got voicemail and Emily didn't leave a message. She called Gill Parker instead, and got through. She told her where things were and what she wanted from her.

She sounded doubtful. "I can ask around if you like' Let you know if any of our women respond to the names you've given me."

"That's no use to us, Gill, sorry. That's hearsay, and we're in a place where we need more than that. We need grounds to make arrests. That means reasonable suspicion, and that means specific, named women supplying on the record statements about crimes they have witnessed. We don't need to go public with anything. We just need material to put in front of a magistrate."

She wondered whether Books would get to them before her more official approach bore fruit.

Gill started to list all the reasons why she couldn't do what Emily wanted. She spoke as though she's swallowed some social workers' dictionary of psychobabble. Every third word was something like 'support', 'facilitate' or 'empowerment'. It was the sort of thing that made Emily come over all Tourette's on people. It was why she'd called first. She pointed out to Gill that it was hard to help sex workers challenge their negative self-imaging patterns when the sex worker in question was comatose with heroin, had duct tape over her mouth and is having her nostrils squeezed shut by some sex-driven arsehole. She was being good so didn't use that last word, tempted though she was.

Gill told her that she'd "forum the issue with colleagues" tonight. Emily reminded her that so far two prostitutes have been killed, another one badly beaten up and that there may well be others that nobody knew about yet.

"This comes from the very top here, Gill. We need maximum co-operation. There'll be a shit storm if we don't get it."

She hung up after Gill told her she would see what she could do. Emily smiled as she pictured her having a little visit from Books. She certainly wouldn't be just having a 'forum with colleagues' after that.

Emily called Jane Alexander again. She sounded stressed and said that she could be ready at three and work through into the evening. Emily began making calls to line up interviews. Phone numbers that were on their own database. Others that she had coaxed from different sources. Mostly she got through to voicemail, but she did get one girl – Kyra - who seemed to think that a police interview would be brilliant fun. She was probably off her head on smack, but they arranged meet her and 'the girls' in a house later that evening.

Result. Emily hoped Kyra stayed high, because she'd be more forthcoming that way. She sent a text Jane to let her know the place and time, and grabbed the landline again ready to make further calls.

But she didn't do it. She couldn't. She couldn't let go of the Huw Fletcher thing, and that meant she couldn't persuade herself to do the things that Jackson would want her to do in the way he'd want her to do them. She did try though, she really did. She had the phone in her hand, trying to will herself into making those other calls, and couldn't quite do it. Instead she called Rattigan's shipping division and asked to be put through to Huw Fletcher. There was the same rigmarole as before, except that this time she asked to speak to a colleague – Andy Watson – and told him who she was.

"How can I help?"

Good, polite start.

"I'm pursuing an inquiry that may involve Mr. Fletcher, and I understand that he's been missing for some time now."

"That's correct. It would have been two, two and a half weeks since we've seen him."

"And you've reported him missing?"

"No, I....No, we haven't."

"You have tried to contact him on his usual numbers?"

"Um, yes. Landline and mobile. Also e-mail. He's got the facility to check in from home."

"And no response?"

"No."

"So a man has been missing for two and a half weeks without explanation. You've not been getting any response to your attempts to communicate with him. And you haven't troubled to notify the authorities. Is that correct?"

Big gulp down the other end of the phone. Emily loved the ability to intimidate. She was learning the art of being threatening without making threats and she loved it. Books had a degree in it. It's what's not said that gets them. Their imagination runs wild and Books just added to it until breaking point was reached. There are times, however, when psychology is not enough. She hadn't yet witnessed him being physically intimidating and she didn't think she wanted to. The thought terrified her, so what it did to the person on the receiving end she could not begin to imagine. Her Father, Frank, had once told her that Books was better at both methods than him at his age and only Sir Ray Quinn was better. Quite an accolade. The founder of their elite and highly secret little group. Now retired and living somewhere on Exmoor, still giving considered advice behind the scenes when necessary. You never completely retire from such work.

"Yes, that's correct," Watson said, bringing her back to the present.

"If you want, you can make a formal report of his disappearance now. We need a report from a member of the public to start up a missing person inquiry."

"Yes. Yes, ok. I'm happy to do that."

"Good. There's some paperwork I need to run through, then. I'll come over and see you. Be with you in about half an hour."

She finished the call and added some notes to Watch. Good police procedure. 'Following a tip off from Bryony Williams, a prostitute outreach worker, I make a call to investigate Huw Fletcher. I discover Fletcher is missing. I consider that fact relevant to Lohan. I determine to pursue enquiries on the ground.' Jackson wouldn't like it because she was not making tea and taking notes, but he would like it when he understood she was on to something. That was her reasoning anyway.

She was about to click goodbye to her little dead April onscreen, but instead of closing down she brought up an image of Brendan Rattigan. The dead face of a dead man, or just possibly the living face of a living one. There'd have been a time in her life when she couldn't have handled that ambiguity at all, but right then it didn't seem to bother her much. Indeed, she quite liked it. There was something boring about people only ever being one thing or the other.

"I'm coming to get you," she told him.

He sneered at her, but that wasn't going to stop her coming.

-30-

Up close, Falmouth is a town with an authentic maritime history. It bustles with seagulls, cranes, fishing boats, pubs, restaurants and seawater.

Rattigan's offices were in a low-rent estate on the edge of town. The grass around the car park was in need of local authority attention. Car windscreens caught the sun and threw it at her over the tarmac. Over the other side of the road was a field, proudly offering land for sale.

Rattigan's building had corrugated metal sides, painted a colour somewhere between grey and blue. A sign gave the company name and nothing else. No frills. Not many of his millions were spent there. At reception, she was whizzed straight through to a conference room. Did she want tea? Coffee? Sparkling water? Coke? A girl with the expression of a calf asked her these things, as though the provision of fluid was guaranteed to deflect the wrath of the CID. Emily unsettled her by saying no to everything. Before long, Andy Watson appeared, two of his male colleagues and a secretary. They were all anxious. The men slid business cards at her.

She started out hard-faced and tough, and information flowed like sweet wine at a hen party. Huw Fletcher was last seen on 21st May, when he'd put in a full day at the office.

He did not appear for work on the 24th. Or the 25th. Or any day that week. His secretary – Joan, the one in the room now – called his mobile number and landline, and left messages. An email was also sent. Emily was offered a copy, which she said would be nice and the email was promptly brought. She took a minute or so to read it, even though it was just two lines long and of no interest at all, but silence is frightening to the frightened, so she created plenty of it. She was interested in the dates, though. The Mancinis were found dead on the Sunday night – the 23rd – but had been killed late on Friday or in the early hours of Saturday. The timing of Fletcher's disappearance could be just coincidental, but as far as she was concerned, the coincidence was reassuring.

"The email you sent. Obviously, that means that Mr. Fletcher has remote access to his emails.

"Yes."

"No doubt we'll be able to tell if they're being opened."

Emily didn't chase that one. She left it hanging. A little present. "What date did you leave those messages?"

The secretary, Joan, said, "I sent the email on the 27th. That would be the Thursday. I think I called and left messages that day as well. Landline and mobile."

She recorded the date in her notebook. Slowly. Silently.

"Can you give me all the contact information you have for him, please?"

"Yes, yes, of course." Joan rushed out of the room to oblige and Emily turned to the men.

"Which one of you is Fletcher's manager?"

The middle man, Jim Hughes, said it was him. He looked like a fat man who'd lost weight. Either that or he was issued with skin that came two sizes too large. He'd got dark hair and almost Mediterranean colouring.

"Is it normal for your employees to go AWOL in this way?"

"No. Not normal. No."

"I can understand that on the Monday, you weren't too concerned. One day is just one day. But by Wednesday or Thursday of that week, you must have had real concerns."

"Yes."

"Yes, but you didn't do anything or tell anyone?"

Hughes was less worried by Emily's act than anyone else present, but he was careful to be helpful too.

"We sent someone round -Andy, it was you, in fact, wasn't it? – round to his house to see if he was there. No sign of anyone. No car. We assumed he'd just taken off."

"You didn't attempt to contact his family?"

"Family? He's unmarried. Lives alone."

That was news to her, but she hid it. "I mean parents. Other relations."

Hughes raised his hands. "We don't have any contact details for his family. I don't even know where they are."

Joan came back into the room with a datasheet on Huw Fletcher. An address, among other things. She took it without saying thanks, but asked her to leave new messages on all Fletcher's lines, including his email. Emily told her to say that a missing persons' inquiry was being set up and could Mr. Fletcher please make urgent contact? She left the standard 0800 number.

She turned her attention to Hughes.

"So weeks pass, you don't tell anyone. Why not?"

A short pause as he composed himself. He was a shrewd one was Mr. Hughes.

"Why not? That's a fair question, and I'm slightly embarrassed now about the answer. But here it is. When Huw worked here, and when Mr. Rattigan was still alive, the two of them had an unusually close relationship. They used to fish together. Deep sea fishing, not standing on a riverbank. Huw used to come and go, keep his own hours, do his own thing, really. Back then, if he was away for a week, that was that. He wouldn't necessarily tell me in advance, but he always came back. To begin with, I used to try and keep him in line, but if he was off with Mr. Rattigan or going about Mr. Rattigan's business, then I was hardly going to have much luck doing that. So I suppose it just developed really."

"Deep sea fishing? Overseas or…..?"

"Don't know. I suppose I…"

"You suppose?"

"Well, I always assumed it must be local. He never looked like he'd seen the sun."

"And after Mr. Rattigan's death?"

"The same. He went away a bit less. Maybe every month for several days, and we just counted it as holiday or sick leave. I imagined he was doing jobs or something for the family. Shouldn't be done on company time, in all honesty, but…"

"And on this occasion, 24th May, and since then, you thought it was just more of the same?"

"I suppose. Truth is, I don't like working that way. If he was gone, then so much the better. And if he'd come back, I'd have sacked him. Now that Mr. Rattigan's not with us, I don't have to make the same allowances."

"You have no idea of what he might have been doing for Mr. Rattigan or the family?"

"No."

"Did he have any special areas of expertise? Any special skills?"

"No."

"Was he good at his job? Or rather, precisely what was his job? What did he do for you?"

"Shipping management. Managing schedules. Sorting out bookings for shippers. Locating containers that have gone missing. Chasing up customs problems. Boring stuff really, unless you're in business. Huw was fine at it, but nothing special."

"Did he look after any particular sector, or do you all do everything?"

Hughes looked at Watson and the other man, who'd hardly spoken. "We all do everything, I suppose. Andy and Jason here deal more with Scandinavia, maybe. Huw handled most of the cargoes coming out of Kaliningrad, and some of the ones of Petersburg. But any of us do what needs to be done."

"And you're always based here? Or you need to go out to the Baltic?"

"From time to time, yes. Mostly it's phone and email stuff, but it always helps to know the client. Andy was in Stockholm last week, and Jason, you'll be in Gdansk – what - the week after?"

"So Fletcher would have gone to Russia occasionally? St. Petersburg and Kaliningrad?"

"Yes. And sometimes, maybe a bit longer ago now, he'd have spent as much time in Sweden as in Russia. That's what you get if you get work for a Baltic shipping line."

Emily asked other questions and the answers weren't too illuminating. What goods do they transport? All sorts. Pulp and paper. Ores. Containers. Vehicles. Some petrochemicals. Anything.

Fletcher wasn't known to have a drink problem. Ditto drugs. No financial problems. No health issues. She filled out the pre-printed MisPer form. She also asked for a photo and they said they'd email it over.

"Did you like him? Did you people socialize with him?"

Everyone looked at everyone else, but it was Hughes who said, "Not much. We felt he was taking liberties. I was looking forward to him coming back here so I could fire him."

Emily left the office. In the car park, she called through to the office with Fletcher's address and asked for a car registration. They came back with the details, and she asked them to put the registration plate on the wanted list. If Fletcher was in his car and driving around, then he'd be detected by the first camera or police car that he passed.

But Emily didn't think he was driving around. She headed back to her car and called those prostitutes for whom she had phone numbers. Most didn't answer. One did and didn't want to talk. Another one did and said grudgingly that she didn't mind seeing Jane and Emily later on that afternoon. There were other calls she could have made, but she decided to leave them for later. At least she'd tried.

She drove around till she found a place that sold her some food.

It was forty minutes since she'd left Rattigan Transport. Not quite enough, maybe, so she drove around pointlessly for another fifteen minutes, before heading up to Fletcher's house. Nice enough place. Modern houses, double-glazed and comfortable. Speed bumps in the road and cars neat in their driveways.

Nothing remarkable about any of it, the house or the street, except that there was an unloved dark blue Toyota Yaris parked up in front of Fletcher's address, window wound down, and Jon Johnston's darkly haired arm beating time to some inaudible music.

She wasn't surprised to see him. She didn't altogether know what the dark lines were that connected Rattigan, Fletcher and Johnston, though she had her my ideas. She didn't know that Johnston had been good at protecting himself. Not the embezzlement stuff. He stole stupid amounts and in stupid ways because some part of him wanted to get caught and punished, but he kept well clear of the bad stuff. She was pretty sure he had ways of watching Fletcher's emails or phone messages, or at the very least of keeping himself informed if the police started to get on to Fletcher's trail. That was why she was so explicit about getting Joan the secretary to leave a message for

Fletcher on every phone and email address she had, and also why she wanted her to give Emily's name.

She wasn't sure that any of that brought Johnston, or what she'd do if it didn't. But she didn't have to worry about that. There he was.

Johnston got out of the Yaris and leaned up against it, waiting for her.

"Well, well," he said.

"Good morning, Mr. Johnston."

"The home of the mysterious Mr. Fletcher."

"The mysterious and missing Mr. Fletcher."

Johnston checked the road. No other cars. No other coppers.

"No search warrant."

"Correct. We're making preliminary enquiries about a reported missing person. If you have any information that might be related to the matter, I'd ask you to disclose it in full."

"No. No information."

He got a key out of his pocket. A brass Yale key, which he held up twinkling in the half-sunlight.

"I want you to know that I have nothing to do with any of this. I made some money that I should not have made. I did not report some of the things I should have reported. I messed up. But I didn't mess up the way he messed up." He jabbed an index finger towards the home of Huw Fletcher. "I'm not that sort of idiot, and I'm not that sort of bastard."

Emily reached for the key.

He held it away from her, polished it in a handkerchief to remove prints and sweat, then held it out. She took it.

"Time to find out what kind of idiot you aren't," she said.

Johnston nodded. She was expecting him to move, but he didn't, he just kept leaning up against the Yaris and half-smiling down at her.

"You're going in there alone?"

"To begin with, yes. Since I am alone."

"You know, when I was a young officer, wet behind the ears, that's what I'd have done too."

"Junior officers are required to use their initiative in confronting unforeseen situations," Emily agreed. She didn't know why she'd started speaking like a textbook to Johnston of all people. Maybe because it felt strange to be speaking to him like that. Last time she'd seen him, he'd practically knocked her head off, a thought that made her step back a little.

"You like me. You know that? You're like me and you'll end up like me."

"Maybe."

"Not maybe. Definitely."

"Can you even play the piano?"

"No. Not a single bloody note. Always thought I'd like to, but I get a brand new piano in the house and I never touch it."

"That is like me," she nodded. "That would be just like me."

His half-smile extended into a three-quarters one, held for about three-quarters of a second, then vanished. He gave her a half-salute, slid back into the Yaris and drove off, slowly because of the speed bumps.

The street was empty and silent. The sunlight occupied the empty space like an invading army. There was just Emily, a house and a key. Her gun was in the car, but it could stay right where it was. Whatever was in the house wasn't about to start a fight, or at least she hoped it wasn't.

She approached the door, inserted the key, turned the lock. She felt a kind of amazement when the lock turned. It was like turning the page in a fairy story and finding that the story still continues exactly as before. At some point, this particular tale had to come to an end.

The house was ……just a house. There were probably twenty other houses on the same street that were exactly like it, near as dammit. No corpses. No emaciated figures of runaway shipping managers chained to radiators. No weapons. No stashes of drugs. No heroin injecting prostitutes or little girls damaged beyond repair.

She tiptoed around the house, shrinking from its accumulated silence. She'd taken her jacket off, and wrapped it around her hand whenever she touched or shifted objects.

She didn't like being there. She thought Jon Johnston was right. She'd got more of him in her than she cared to admit, but she wished she was more like Books.

In the bedroom, there was a big double bed, neatly made with white sheets and a mauve duvet cover. In the bathroom, just one toothbrush. All the toiletries were male. In the living room, three fat black flies were buzzing against the window pane, whilst a dozen of their comrades lay dead beneath them.

In the kitchen, she opened cupboards and drawers, and in the place where tea towels and place mats were kept, there was also cash. Fifty pound notes. Thick rolls of them. Held together with rubber bands. The drawer below held bin liners and kitchen foil, and even more bundles of notes. These ones were stacked up against the back of the drawer, making multiple rows. A little paper wall of cash. With one finger, and still through her jacket, she rifled one of the bundles. Fifties all the way down.

She didn't like being there at all. She didn't like being Johnston. She wanted to go back to plan A, which was to put more time and effort into being Books' girlfriend. To experiment with her putative new citizenship of Planet Normal.

She closed the drawer and left the house. The lock clicked shut behind her. She found an old terracotta flowerpot in the garden and stowed Johnston's key underneath it.

Back in her car, she found she was sweating and cold at the same time. She tried to go back to that feeling she had with Books. That feeling of being somewhere close to love and happiness. Living next door to the sunshine twins. She couldn't find them anywhere now. When she stamped her legs, she could hardly feel her feet when they hit the floor.

Emily called the station. It was all she could do and she felt relieved when the silence ended.

-31-

The day went crazy and the craziness kept her sane. As far as anyone else was concerned, there was no real connection between Huw Fletcher and Operation Lohan, so she shouldn't even have been there. But since she was there, she stuck around.

The first thing that happened, impressively fast she had to say, was that a squad car turned up. Two officers in uniform. Emily identified herself and told them that she was following up a minor lead from another case. She reported the essence of her conversation with Fletcher's workmates and showed them the key that she'd 'found' under the flowerpot.

"Have you checked with the neighbours?"

"Yes," Emily told them, having managed to remember to do that just a few minutes ago. "Most people are out. The one couple I could find to speak to haven't seen the individual for several weeks."

The officer she was speaking to, an intelligent sergeant who looked like he enjoyed his pie and mash, called the office on his radio. He needed approval to enter the property, and soon secured it. He took the key and went to the door, rang the bell and then knocked. A crashingly loud knock, from the lion's head knocker that was probably Huw Fletcher's pride and joy.

For a moment, Emily had this insane feeling that Huw Fletcher would just come to the door. She realised she didn't know what he looked like. She imagined a slightly podgy forty something with receding hair and ill-fitting jeans. She imagined him opening the door, bewildered by the police car on his driveway, the uniforms at his door. She imagined everyone turning slowly to look at her, the girl with a gun in her glovebox and a head full of make-believe.

A long drawn out comedy moment that would take a good deal of explanation. But it didn't happen. Nothing did. No one came to the door. The sergeant and his colleague used the key to enter the house and Emily followed them because it seemed silly not to. They peered into the living room, the kitchen, the bedroom, the spare room. They opened cupboards, looked under beds. No Huw Fletcher. No nothing.

The sergeant said, "Let's check the fridge. See if there's milk there."

Emily thought, 'God bless you, Sarge. You're an honour and ornament to your force.' They trooped into the kitchen and the sergeant opened the fridge. His buddy opened a couple of kitchen cupboards and, because there was nothing else to do, Emily opened the drawers.

The sergeant didn't find any fresh milk. His buddy didn't find anything he didn't expect to find, but Emily came across all the cash, just where she last saw it.

"Bloody hell," she said, stepping rapidly backwards. "Look at that."

The sergeant looked and said, "bloody hell," too. He got down, pulled stuff out of the drawers and took a proper look at the cash. She thought that each bundle contained Fifty notes. Fifty fifties, making "£2,500 in each. And dozens of bundles, dozens of them. There was upwards of £100,000 there lying around with the kitchen foil and the spare tea towels.

They pulled rapidly out of the house. The house wasn't a crime scene exactly, but it was pretty clear that the forensics boys would wAnt to have a look over it. The sergeant was on the radio back to base, non-stop. A DI came racing up.

Emily's role had suddenly become rather more delicate. Everyone was staring at her. The newly arrived DI, named Luke Axelsen, got her into his car.

"OK. Shoot. What do you know?"

"Not much. Really not much."

"Good start."

But she told him, about Bryony Williams and other things.

"That was yesterday? That doesn't seem like a very urgent follow-up."

"No, it wasn't. Williams didn't really believe the rumours. She only told me because I asked. It was a low-priority lead. When I called Rattigan Transport this morning and confirmed that the guy had gone missing, it became a little higher priority."

He bit his lower lip. Thinking. He was thinking that he didn't want to hand this case over. He wanted to keep this as his case.

"For what it's worth," she said helpfully, "I don't think that we've got enough to match this case to Lohan. It's still only hearsay."

He was happy to hear that. Emily was covering up her other suspicions about links to more serious activities. Terrorism and much more. Suspicions she needed to keep to herself, and make sure Dad and Books were the only people she confided in.

And then the craziness really got going. Axelsen assembled a team to investigate Fletcher's disappearance. He briefed the team, then got her to brief them on her angle. Emily kept it short and sweet, which was pretty much all she had to offer anyway. She was asked where she thought the money came from, and replied that she didn't know. Drugs. Prostitutes. Both. Embezzlement. God only knows. "Just keep us in the loop on anything at all you come across. We'll do the same for you."

All this ate a couple of hours and more. Emily was hungry again, but couldn't find anything that looked edible. She texted Books, but didn't know what to say. Eventually she just wrote 'HOPE ALL'S GOING WELL. SEE

YOU SOON. EM. XX.' She liked those Xs. They meant something.

She called Jackson, because she reckoned she ought to let him know what was going on, but got straight through to his voicemail. She left a raggedy kind of message for him. She wasn't good with voicemails. They squeezed out all her natural charm and wit.

Then she didn't know what to do. She wanted to get seconded to the Fletcher inquiry, but it would take Jackson to sort that out. Plus, she was meant to be back at the station on patrol with Jane Alexander. Because she didn't know what else to do, she started driving back. It bothered her somehow that something so large, so deep-bellied and dark, as the ocean that surrounds the South West peninsular should be so good at hiding from view as she drove. The Atlantic Ocean; the world's biggest graveyard.

She thought about Johnston. Not so much how he intercepted those Fletcher messages, more why he came at all. Why help her out? Why give her a key? She thought the honourable Jon Johnston wanted to do something to redeem the screw-up. She wanted to dislike the man, but couldn't quite bring herself to do it. Too much of her in him.

She drove thinking about all that, driving in the slow lane with Radio Two shoving a Britpop retrospective at her, when she got a call on her mobile. She made a mess of the hands-free system and then got it right, and when she did, Dennis Jackson's voice came crashing out of the Peugeot's very capable sound system.

"Emily, what the hell is going on?"

Because of the almost surround sound speakers, it sounds like the universe was asking her that question. God coming through in quadrophonic, bass booster set at full.

"I've no idea," she said, with a fair degree of truth, but she gave him the bits and pieces she had. A conversation with Bryony Williams. A phone call. "It all developed from there."

"Is this another of your solo efforts?"

"Sort of, I suppose. It wasn't meant to be."

"Because I don't like solo flyers on my inquiries. I especially don't like it – in fact, I bloody hate it – when I've given specific instructions earlier in the day to get moving with the main line of enquiry into a murder investigation."

"Yes."

Without adding the 'sir', she told him what she'd done on that front so far. The calls to the lab. To Bryony. To Gill Parker. To Jane Alexander. The chat with Mervyn Rogers. Her first effort to arrange further interviews with prostitutes. She'd managed quite a lot, in fact, and Jackson sounded somewhat mollified.

"And Rogers is on the case is he?"

"I think he's beating the shit out of Tony Leonard right now," Emily said, wondering if she was being impertinent or simply in tune with the boss's mood.

"Yes, I hope he bloody is." The sound system went quiet for a moment, which meant either that God was thinking or she'd lost reception. But it was the former, because God came back again. "Do you know how much money they've found in that house? So far, I mean. They're still pulling up the floorboards."

"No."

"Two hundred and twenty grand so far. One fifty in the kitchen. More in the bathroom. Axelsen just told me."

Emily didn't know what to say, so stayed silent.

Jackson didn't know what to say either, so he was silent a moment or two longer, before saying, "Right. In the meantime, I want you doing what I asked you to do. That means chasing the frigging lab to make sure they don't forget about our bloody heroin matches. It means working with DS Alexander to get statements from those sex workers of yours. It means finding a way to get ourselves some search warrants for premises that may well have links to the Lohan killings."

"Yes," Emily said. They were not her sex workers, but she let that pass.

She didn't say it out loud, because she didn't think she needed to, but she had just obtained police access to premises that contained evidence strongly suggestive of serious crime. Jackson's thoughts were running along the same lines because the next thing that boomed out of the loudspeakers was, "You think it's a drug connection? That's what you're saying?"

"Fletcher worked in shipping. Arranging cargoes out of the Baltic. Mostly Russia. He went away on numerous long trips. Plus the cash. Sikorsky has a pile of heroin in London. Fletcher has a pile of cash as well. If there are drugs around, there has to be money as well, and maybe we've just found it. Plus, most heroin comes from Afghanistan, which means that the Russian transport route could make sense. It's all circumstantial, but the connections are there."

"And you managed to uncover the connection thanks to some community worker passing on some hearsay conspiracy bollocks from a prostitute, who's probably high as a kite when she says it."

"Well, there was a missing person. And one who does connect, even if only remotely, to the Mancini house."

"Very bloody remotely." Another long pause. "Listen, are you driving?"

"Yes. M4 going back to the station.

"Ok. Pull off when you can and give me a call back."

God rang off without waiting for an acknowledgement.

Emily carried on driving, thinking at the same time. If only Jackson knew just how far her thinking had gone. She'd made connections in her head. All those he listed, plus more. Drugs, prostitution, money laundering, Russia, Afghanistan, Romania, trafficking, corruption, and she thought it was all a huge cover for terrorism and impending ISIS action in this country. The perfect storm. The bad guys at long last getting their act together and co-operating to stage a massive event.

She passed a few places that would have been perfect to pull up in, but she wanted time to think; to order her own thoughts. She called her Father and relayed everything before she put in the call to Jackson.

"Ok. Look. I told you not to piss around with me. I told you to do what you were told to do, when you were told to do it and with no bollocksing around. And you can't do that, can you? You just can't bloody do it."

Part of her wanted to pick a fight. Actually, she had done everything she'd been told to and she'd done it fast and fine. She'd just done some other stuff as well. Oh, yes, and by the way, she'd obtained access to premises with almost 220 grand of almost certainly illegally procured cash and had launched a Missing Persons inquiry into the likeliest target.

But she didn't say that. She just sat mute as Jackson lobbed rockets at her.

"Emily, what made you chase after Fletcher? Don't tell me it was hearsay conspiracy crap, because I won't believe you?"

"It was a bit to do with that, but there is another part that I can't tell you about. Sorry."

"It's not your father, is it?"

"No, nothing to do with him. I made a promise to someone and I have to keep it."

How much did Jackson know about her father and their secret world? Had he just let slip, deliberately, that he knows? There's a pause. Crackle on the line. Microwave radiation from the beginning of the universe.

"I would love to give you a formal warning. I really would."

Obviously something was holding him back. She thought that it must be Dad. It must be that he has sought and received guidance as to how best to get results from her. In other words, let her run. Let her be and see what she came up with, but maintain control outwardly for the sake of all the others on the case. Did he know about Books? Emily wouldn't go there, if he didn't. "I can't work the way your Dad works. It pains me to say it, really pains me, but much as I would like to give you a bollocking for this, I can't quite do it. I've checked with Alexander and Rogers and the lab, and they tell me you've been on the case. And you did find two hundred grand in drugs money."

"Thank you."

Yes, thank you. You noticed. Hallelujah.

"But you're not off the hook. I'm not sure if you're the kind of detective we can use. You're either very good or absolutely terrible, or a bit of both. And I can't use terrible. Do you understand?"

Emily could almost hear the others listening in and only just managing to control their laughter. This was for their benefit. And his own, of course.

"I understand."

"Ok. Now, if I asked you what you wanted to do next, interview with Jane Alexander or attach yourself to this current inquiry, what would you tell me?"

"I'd like to do both. As much as I can. I think Jane and I are working well with our prostitutes, but I don't think we should lose sight of the Fletcher angle.

"You'll manage to do both, will you?

"I'm not sure. Working with prostitutes is an afternoon or evening thing anyway. I could split my days and do half on each."

Ok. Fine. Don't kill yourself, but a little bit of self-harm where you're concerned, would do me fine. I'll call Axelsen and let him know to expect you. Don't get yourself into any trouble with him, because if you do, I will murder you. Literally murder you. And no flying solo again with me, ever, under any circumstances Is that clear?

"Yes."

"Ok."
Jackson rang off. Emily knew he'd ranted to save face. She thought it must have been a difficult balancing act for him.

-32-

Six days slid by almost unnoticed. Dark fish in an urban canal. Sleep and Emily weren't the best of friends. She was averaging four or five hours a night, and that only with the futon and gun arrangement. It wasn't the regular way to get some kip, she knew that, but had given up on being Little Miss Regular a long time back. She was tired all the time and not eating properly, but she was surviving. She was getting by. When she woke up at dawn, she drank tea and read in bed. It wasn't sleep but it was not a bad substitute. It was all she had anyway.

Her mornings were spent at the station. They had taken over a chunk of the Rattigan Transport building and their little team worked out of a conference room there. It smelled of warm laptops, copier paper and male sweat. Hers too, for all she knew. The air con was another area where Rattigan seemed to have saved his pennies.

And the stuff she learned. Stuff she never even knew existed. Like, for example, deep-sea fishing off British coastal waters. That image you have of it – all Hemingway, and bulging forearms, and Floridian sunshine, and marlins dangling from the scales -all that is bollocks. In British waters, the sort that Brendan Rattigan and his best buddy Huw Fletcher used to fish in, you don't get marlin. You don't get tuna. You don't get fish that you want to hang from scales and show your friends in the pub.

You get cod. You get whiting. You get herring. Turbot. Small cold fish swimming around in small cold seas. Grey waves and rain. It was a sport for blokes who brought tea with them in flasks and boasted about how bad the weather was.

That morning her first phone call was fielded by Miss Titanium again. Emily told her who she was. She was icy with her. Hostile. She didn't say anything she shouldn't, but that was what you got from paying top dollar for your support staff. Even their hostility was classy.

"Look," Emily said, "I'm very sorry to have caused an upset last time. The inquiry was important and the question did need addressing."

"Maybe so."

"I don't need to bother Mrs. Rattigan this time, but perhaps I can ask you a number of simple questions. Just three. Literally."

"Very well."

"First, have you ever heard of a man called Huw Fletcher? A colleague or friend of Mr. Rattigan's, perhaps?"

"No never."

"Have you ever heard of a man called Jon Johnston?"

"No."

"OK. Last question. A certain person currently under investigation claims to have been deep-sea fishing with Mr. Rattigan. Not just once, but many times. Days on end sometimes. In the UK, probably. Or starting from here. So, the Irish Sea, the North Atlantic. Perhaps the North Sea or the Baltic."

She hadn't even finished before Titanium interrupted. "No. Your information is incorrect. I've never heard of the late Mr. Rattigan showing any interest in fishing at all. He didn't even fish on the river outside the house here. I can't imagine anything he would have liked to do less. Will that be all?"

She had a nasty edge of triumph in her voice and obviously wanted Emily to believe that she'd messed up, got it wrong and were idiots.

Emily replied, very warmly, "that's exceptionally helpful. No interest in fishing at all? Excellent. Thank you very much." She intended to offend and annoy her, and hung up satisfied at a job well done.

But that was a highlight. For the rest of the time, they were simply sifting through heaps of tedious data. Vessels and routes handled by Rattigan Transport. Logistical issues. Client contacts. Bills of lading. Customs dues. Bonded warehouses. Emails. Phone logs. Bank statements.

Nobody seemed to know what they were looking for. They all assumed they'd know it when they saw it, except that Emily didn't think they would. It was either under their noses already or not there at all. They got everybody together and pressed them to supply any photos they had of nights out with clients or any other images they had of Huw Fletcher's contacts. Most of them had nothing at all, but Andy Watson turned out to have a fair few on his phone, and they started collecting names and images. They could check the names against the criminal records system, show the images to prostitutes and the people from StreetSafe. It all felt like fishing in the dark. The cold, rainy dark.

Those were her mornings.

The afternoons were more or less the polar opposite of all that. Or not afternoons, exactly, but early evenings. Usually, by about two in the afternoon, she was back at the station, catching up on paperwork for an hour or so, then at three having a briefing with Jane Alexander. Not on Sunday, of course. She more or less took that day off, and Saturday was a half-day, though she was too shattered to relax. But apart from those breaks that didn't feel like breaks, they pushed on, talking to as many prostitutes as possible, trying to gain their trust, trying to find Jackson an angle that would break the case open.

To begin with their technique was simple. They brought as many prostitutes as they could together in one place. They used their own homes or flats and bribed them with cakes and chocolates. Then they showed them photos.

Loads of them. Photos of the victims: Jenna, April, Stacey Edwards, Ioana Balcescu. Photos of anybody associated with the crime scene or the primary suspects. Any CCTV images that seemed relevant for some reason. Photos from the Fletcher inquiry, Russian shipping clients that just might have had a drugs connection somewhere along the line. Piles and piles of photos.

It didn't work. The first couple of days they got exactly nowhere. Kyra, who had been so stupidly free on the phone with Emily, clammed up completely when she understood what was wanted. The other girls were sullen. As soon as they were shown photos that were really meaningful they just stopped talking. They ate their cake, chain-smoked and squirmed under questioning like teenagers at a family do. Jane got tart and police-officerish with them, and the mood deteriorated completely.

After two days of that, at Emily's suggestion, they tried another tack. They printed off bundles of celebrity photos from the Internet. Film stars, TV actors, singers and added in photos of people who were only celebrities in Romania, Poland or the Balkans. Photos that would get the East European girls chattering.

And chatter they did. The conversation flowed. They mixed up all the photos so there was no particular order to them, and the girls were vastly more talkative. Then when they showed them the Tony Leonard photo, two of the girls reported that he had dealt them drugs in the recent past. The photos of Sikorsky and Kapuscinski made them clam up, but even then their clamming up was significant – a sign that they knew things they didn't want to say, not just a general protest against having police officers in their living room.

As they got out of the house that evening, Jane Alexander was vertiginous with pleasure, doing a little dance of triumph down the pavement, a slim blonde Ginger Rogers waltzing to the river.

"That was brilliant," she said. "That was probably the best thing that's happened to me since being in the CID."

She phoned Jackson on his mobile, getting him at home. She told him that we had reasonable suspicion to arrest Tony Leonard for drugs offences, and enough grounds to apply for a warrant to search his house.

She listened a bit to whatever Jackson had to say. "Yes," she said. "Yes...yes." With each new yes, she tried to curl her hair back behind her listening ear, only to lean forward again, causing the hair to fall forwards. When she got off the phone, she did another side-shuffle, fist-pumpy thing of pleasure.

"Jackson's going to arrange a dawn raid. Apparently, the London lab has just confirmed that the London heroin matches the samples found at Allinson Street. This could be it. It could be the thing that breaks the case open."

Because Jane was obviously so pleased Emily allowed herself to do a high five with her. She felt an idiot doing it, but she liked Jane in Ginger Rogers mode. She did not, however, think that raiding Leonard's house would give them what they needed.

Sure enough, Jackson organized a raid and started to rip Leonard's house to shreds. Emily didn't hear all the details, but she bet the lads involved loved it. Mervyn Rogers was assigned to do the interviewing and he'd love it. He did a good tough interview and Leonard would be a soft target. There was a decent chance that Leonard would say something to implicate Sikorksy.

Meantime, Jane and Emily kept their noses to the grindstone. A grindstone that turned and brought them nothing further, beyond bloody faces.

Sikorsky was still out there. So was Fletcher. So was Jon Johnston, who probably knew how the whole thing stitched together, keeping his mouth shut as people died.

-33-

Emily stopped knowing who she was and by Thursday, she felt ragged. She'd had her worst night yet. Three scant hours of sleep. Mint tea in bed, energy bars and Amy Winehouse singing to her from downstairs.

She thought about Books. On her weekend off they met again. In the same place as before. All very middle class. She dressed nicely and washed her hair just for him. She was girlish and supple and appreciative and not tough. And he took control.

"Em, are you sleeping properly?"

"No."

"Do you get bad dreams at all?"

"No."

"But it's this case., isn't it? It's getting to you."

"I suppose. Everyone's telling me that."

"But no bad dreams?"

She shook her head. "None that' I'd count".

He nodded, and then took her to a pizza place. She asked for salad, and he countermanded her, adding a pizza and dough balls and large orange juice to her order. He made sure she ate it too, bossing her into eating the bits she wanted to leave.

In the end, she just let him boss her. She forgot to smile lots and ask questions, but was fairly sure she didn't say anything offensive either. When she'd eaten as much as she could, he called for the bill and drove her home.

"Don't worry, Em. Whatever this is will soon be over. And there's no rush. With us I mean. We'll just take it slow. OK?"

She nodded. She believed him, and they kissed. She couldn't really feel the kiss, but at that time she wasn't feeling anything much. When Books left she went to bed with mint tea, and her gun lying flat on her stomach. It was is the only thing she could feel and she didn't let go of it all the time she was there. .

At eight thirty, Amy Winehouse had fallen silent. Gone back to black. Emily called Axelsen and told him that she wasn't feeling well and wouldn't be coming over that morning. He was fine with that. Emily didn't think he wanted her on his team anyway.

Sikorsky still hadn't been found.

Under questioning from Rogers and gang, Tony Leonard had admitted to dealing drugs. Drugs that he bought from Sikorsky. He knew Kapuscinski by sight, but nothing more.

Emily felt increasingly detached from herself, from the inquiry, from Books, from everything. Because she knew that she needed human contact when in this state, she played everything according to the book. Called her mum and chatted with her. Called Bev, chatted with her. Called Books, got his voicemail, didn't leave a message but sent a text instead.

She called Jane, who was in the office, and told her she was taking the morning off. She told Emily not to worry. "You really need it." She told Emily that she had more interviews set up for that night, but "only come in if you feel you can. You need some rest."

Neither of them knew what to call the prostitutes. They called themselves 'girls', which seemed patronizing. They mostly called them 'prostitutes', which seemed derogatory. Gill Parker always referred to them as the 'sex-worker community', which made them sound like a cross between an important export industry and a bunch of special-need kids. Which, to Emily, at least had the virtue of accuracy.

At midday, Emily realised she hadn't really eaten anything. She took the gun off her belly, put some clothes on and skedaddled out in search of something like food. She went to a sandwich shop up by the Aldi at the top end of the road. It was a rubbish shop, but at least she knew her way there, and she got the dozy shop assistant to put some gloopy tuna-sweetcorn mix into an ageing baguette. She completed the concoction with a lettuce leaf that was brown along the edges. But it was food.

She sat outside in the sunshine to eat it. On a bit of grass opposite the Aldi, she checked her phone and found a message from Books. She'd forgotten that he was back up in London, and his text said, "PROBABLY STILL BE HERE

TOMORROW. SEE YOU AS SOON AS I CAN. X".

She sat there staring at the message, reading all sorts of things into it, but pleased that he'd ended it with a kiss.

She couldn't put the phone away. She went on chewing her baguette, which wasn't too bad in the mouth, but then turned to something like decorator's caulk in the belly. She was right to take the morning off, but was feeling a little lost, missing the banter of colleagues.

She made further progress with the baguette, but the blunt pointy end had an armour plating that she couldn't penetrate. She scooped out the last bit of tuna with her fingers, swallowed that and chucked everything else away.

Then, she hesitated no longer, licked the tuna gloop off her fingers and sent a text. To Lev. Her contact, not Dad's contact. Her own personal helper of last resort. A wanderer on the dark side.

"IF YOU'RE AROUND, I'D LIKE TO SEE YOU. EM."

Before she got back into the house, she got a reply.

"TONIGHT."

She felt relief. Lev was coming. Everything was going to be ok.

That evening with Jane, they were sitting with five prostitutes in a bedsit. Photos. Chocolate cake. Net curtains in the windows and carpet down to the warp. The battery had been pulled out of the smoke alarm, because it kept going off otherwise. A pink lace top hung over the bedside lamp, because the whole place risked looking too classy without it.

Silly girls swapping clothes and comparing underwear and giggling at the photo of George Clooney and not telling them anything that would allow them to save them from whichever bastard was going around murdering their friends.

Emily lost it. Jayne had shoved the photo of Kapuscinski at them, and they were wanting to move quickly onto another image. She shouted, really shouted. These things aren't just a question of volume, they're a question of energy too. Of really meaning it. And she really meant it.

"Don't touch that!" She shouted at the girl, Luljeta, who was about to toss the photo to one side. "Don't you dare touch that! You know this man, don't you? Look at me. Look at me. You know this man, don't you? Yes or no? Don't lie."

She was terrified. The room, including Jane Alexander in her powder-blue linen dress next to Emily on the sofa, was utterly silent. And Luljeta nodded.

"Yes."

"What's his name? Give me his name."

Luljeta paused, trying to be tactical, but Emily was too angry for tactics. She opened her mouth ready to yell again, but Lujeta pre-empted her, with a voice that was tiny but truthful.

"Wojtek. Polish guy."

"Surname?"

Luljeta shrugged, but that was probably real. She probably didn't know.

"Kapuscinski, yes? Is that correct?"

"Yes, I think."

"And what do you know about him? I need to know everything. Not just, Juljeta. All of you."

It took time, and Emily had to yell twice more, but they got it. Kapuscinski was one of Sikorsky's thugs. Sikorsky was reputed to have organised and maybe committed the Mancini and Edwards killings. All that much was hearsay. No search warrants for hearsay. But then Jayney, one of the local girls, pulled up her top. She was bruised yellow and purple. Horrendous and not just fists either. It looked like boots to Emily, and maybe a stick or iron bar or something as well.

"That was him," she said. She was crying as she said it and pointing to the photo of Kapuscinksi. "He's who Sikorsky mostly uses. He said that I'd been buying from someone else, but I hadn't. I just haven't been using as much recently. I had flu and wasn't working, but he didn't believe me. He just came in and ....."

She continued.

Jane's perfect-policewoman mode was called for now. Her pencil was flicking across the pages of her notebook, prompting names and dates and times and places. Jayney's admission triggered something similar from Luljeta, and further confessions followed. Accusations, in fact, but they felt and sounded like confessions. By the time it was over, they had material evidence not just on Sikorsky, but on Kapuscinski, a Russian called Yuri and someone else called Dimi.

Arrests to make. Warrants to obtain.

Jane took about two hours to get through the evidence that came tumbling out. Emily didn't participate much. She felt drained and empty. She knew she ought to have been taking notes to supplement Jane's, but she couldn't. She couldn't pretend to. Jayney had her top down by then, but Emily saw straight through it. All these girls looked naked to her now. Little bodies, covered with bruises. Bruises that existed only in the past or in the future, or in the past and the future, for the other girls here. Bruises that would go on existing, go on multiplying, no matter what bunch of arseholes was controlling the drugs trade, because whenever young women sell their bodies for sex, there will be leather-jacketed men to make sure that the profits end up in other hands, other fists.

Twice, as Jane was doing her stuff, Emily put her hands up to her eyes. She wanted to see if she could feel any tears. She couldn't, but Emily didn't know whether she had to make a physical check to be sure. Even if there weren't any at that moment, but she had a feeling inside that might be the sort of thing that normally went with crying. She didn't know, though. She wasn't the best person to ask.

She would like to kill Sikorsky and Kapuscinski and Fletcher and Yuri Someone and Dimi Whoever. And then, after having done all that, she would like to resurrect the drowned and fish eaten Rattigan from the deep, so that she could kill him too.

She let Jane finish doing her stuff and sat next to her in a daze, pleased she was there.

When they emerged onto the street, it was 9.00 p.m. Jane had magicked a navy blue cardigan from somewhere and put it on. Emily was wearing a white top, but she wasn't cold, or not cold in that way.

"Are you OK?"

"Yes."

Jane brandished her notebook. "I'll deal with this, if you like. Jackson will want to know."

Emily nodded. Yes. Jackson would want to know. He'd got what he wanted.

"If you want to....I mean, if you want to tell Jackson with me, then you should."

Emily was puzzled by that. She didn't understand and must have said something to indicate her puzzlement, because Jane explained.

"I'll tell him anyway. That it was you who did that in there. I don't know how you knew to do that, but it worked all right. I'll make sure that Jackson knows that."

Emily shook her head. She didn't know to do anything. She just did it.

"I lost it, Jane. That's all. I couldn't stand those girls keeping their mouths shut any more. I just lost it."

"You'll be ok?"

"Yes." Everyone was asking Emily that at the moment. "I think I'll go home. Is that ok? Sorry to leave you with all the follow – up."

"You go home."

The sky above was that mid-blue of summer evenings, neither light nor dark. The streets were blinking on, but they were not needed, not yet. The house behind them was quiet. The little Edwardian street was mostly quiet too. At the bottom end of the road, the river filed past, holding its silence. A river insect, confused by the lamplight, ended up fluttering around in her hair. Jane reached for it and released it.

"Thanks," she said.

She smiled at Emily, tidied her hair back into place where she and the insect ruffled it, then said, "drive safely."

Emily nodded and did just that. Sober and safe and under the speed limit. It's not what she wanted, though. Some part of her wanted the exact opposite. It would be like a two-hour drive on empty roads and no speed cameras. She didn't get it, but she did home in one piece.

There was a ready meal in the freezer and she microwaved it from frozen. It was icy in the middle when she ate it, but at least she ate it.

She had a hot bath. She considered putting some music on, but couldn't think of anything that would alter anything, so just left the silence. When she got out of the bath, she didn't put on office clothes again. Lev was due soon and he wasn't an office-clothes kind of guy. She settled on jeans, gym shoes and a T-shirt.

Then Books called from London. He had just heard the news Jane brought in to the station. Huge excitement, apparently. He wanted to talk all about it, but she closed him off. Emily moved the conversation on because she felt they had spent enough time talking about work things in their lives, so instead they talked rubbish. Nice, affectionate, directionless rubbish, for twenty minutes. Then he yawned and she told him he should go to bed.

"See you soon, Em."

"Yes, see you soon. I'm missing you."

"Likewise. Look after yourself."

Emily had an image of him making love to her on the living room floor. Urgent and intense. Not too many words. Not too gentle or solicitous. A lovemaking that leaves marks. She wondered if that was how ordinary people have sex. They said goodbye.

She wanted to snooze but couldn't because her adrenaline was up and she didn't know when Lev would be coming. She never did, except that it would be far too late. Not a morning person, was Lev.

She had the TV on. There was a black and white film on. It involved violence against women, so she watched with the sound turned off and even then all she could see was Jayney's bruises. She shouldn't have even been watching it really. Sometime after midnight, she started to doze, and then heard a car engine coming to a halt outside the house and caught a couple of headlamps shutting off.

Emily got her bag, checked the gun and went to the door.

-34-

Lev looked like he always looked, which is to say like not much. Old jeans, a much-washed sweatshirt, trainers. Not a big man, maybe five foot eight, something like that, and not particularly broad. Lean and muscled in his leanness, the way you might expect an ocean sailor or a mountain climber to be. Dark hair, always a bit too long and never very combed. Ambiguous skin that could place him anywhere in the arc that runs from Spain through to Kazakhstan and beyond, though she was sure he wasn't Spanish. His age was similarly indeterminate. She used to think he was about her own age when she first met him, a little older, perhaps, but not much. Then she realised from one or two snippets he'd let slip about his past that he was a fair bit older. He could be anywhere between thirty and almost fifty. Emily honestly couldn't narrow it more than that. The one thing to be noticed about Lev, or more accurately, something not noticed, was the way he moved. It was something only noticed afterwards. Catlike. That would be the normal term, but she imagined that whoever first developed that queen of clichés never spent much time looking at cats, who are always licking their ears and other bits or finding new ways to scratch themselves. That wasn't Lev at all. He was still mostly, but there was a poise in his stillness, a potential for sudden flowing action, which meant that his stillness had more motion in it that anyone else's movement. More motion and more violence.

"Hey, Em," he said, light pouring outward from the hall and his eyes already checking the space behind.

"Lev. Hi. Come on in."

They didn't kiss or shake hands. Emily didn't know why not, but she felt it was hard to know what social rules to apply when in his presence.

She let him stalk around the house for a bit without saying anything. His normal procedure when he visited. Doors, windows, exits. Hiding places. Blind spots. Potential weapons. Her kitchen morphed into a kind of conservatory at the back, which meant a large area of glass opening onto the dark garden beyond. Lev fiddled around until he found the switch for the security light, which bathed the back garden in 150 watts of halogen happiness. He left it on. He took a chair and sat down and his inspection was of her now.

"What's up?"

"Nothing much. Just wanted to see you."

"Sure."

"Do you want something. Tea? Coffee? Alcohol?"

"Are you still growing?"

"Yes."

"Then I don't want tea, coffee or alcohol."

Emily laughed, stood up and got the keys. She unlocked the French doors and Lev stepped out into the garden, instantly assessing the air and peering over fences. She fiddled around with the padlock on the shed and got it open.

There wasn't much inside, because she didn't like gardening. A lawnmower and a hoe, and she'd never used the hoe. And there was the bench with the grow lamps and her plants. The poor dears had been much too hot recently, she thought, but they were doing alright. She had brought the seeds home from India when she was there on holiday once as a student, before sniffer dogs ruled the airports. The current plants were their daughter and granddaughters. She checked the plants were watered, but otherwise left them alone. She'd more or less given up smoking resin, but did dry the leaves in her oven and then kept bags of them under lock and key in the shed. She took one good -sized bag and locked up again.

She rolled a joint in the kitchen, but decided she wanted tea as well, so got Lev to put the kettle on. He wandered through to the living room to flick through her music, making clucking sounds of disapproval, before finding something by Shostakovich. Before long the air filled with dark-toned Russian pessimism, played out on the bassoon and a sea of violins.

"In 1948, did you know, Shostakovich used to sleep outside his apartment by the lift shaft?"

"No, Lev. Amazingly enough I didn't know that."

"His work had been denounced. Denounced for the second time. First time was in the 1930s."

"Well, I can see why that would drive anyone to sleep by the lift shaft."

"He thinks he is going to be arrested and he doesn't want the police to disturb the family."

The joint was ready. She never smoked tobacco.

She made peppermint tea for herself and dug out some chocolates. Lev sorted himself out, so she left him to it. He made black tea, noxiously strong, found a smaller jug of hot water and took some raspberry conserve from the cupboard. Slightly mouldy conserve, to judge by the way he scowled and dolloped a few blobs down the sink before going over to the table. She sat there, smoking, drinking tea and eating chocolate, while Lev smoked, mixed jam, tea and hot water in his cup and drank it.

"So. What's up?"

She shook her head. Not because there wasn't anything to say, but because she didn't know what order to say anything in. Maybe it didn't matter. She started randomly.

"I've got a gun."

"Here? In the house?"

She fetched her bag and gave him the gun. Emily watched as he became all Lev-like with it, as she knew he would. He pulled back the slide to see if there was a bullet chambered, which there wasn't. He pulled out the magazine to see if it was loaded, which it wasn't. Checked the safety. Checked the sights. Checked the feel and heft of it. With magazine out and no bullet in the chamber, he took aim and fired. First statistically, still seated and at a fictive, motionless target. Then moving. Him, the gun, the imaginary target.

"It's a good gun. Have you fired it?"

"Yes. On a shooting range. I learned to keep my shoulders down and soft hands."

She showed him.

"Good. The grip is OK? You've got small hands.

"It's fine I think. It's a small gun."

"Tak."

Tak, she happened to know is Polish for 'yes'. She was also fairly sure that Lev wasn't Polish. Then again, she wasn't exactly sure what he was, and when he inserted foreign words into his English, she was pretty certain that they came from half a dozen different languages, maybe more.

"You have done any real shooting?"

"No."

"That's why you called me?"

"I suppose. I don't know."

"You are under threat?"
"No. I don't know. Maybe."
"That's not a very logical answer for a Cambridge girl."
"No one has threatened me. Not exactly. One man hit me, but that was different."
"Hit you? How? What happened?"
She told him. Not the edited highlights, the full version. Lev needed them to act it out, so he could visualize where she had been standing, where Johnston was standing, where she landed and what happened next.
"You didn't strike him?"
"No."
"But you're on the steps, there, in that position?"
Lev had got her to adopt the exact position that she was in after Johnston hit her. Arse on the bottom step. Legs out. Head and torso slumped against the wall. It felt freaky to her, being there. Frightening. Lev wasn't Johnston. Not as tall or powerful, but from down there on the floor any man looked two miles high.
"Yes. This position. I told you already."
"And this man. What was his name?"
"Johnston. Jon Johnston. He's not such a bad person really. I might even like him.
"So Johnston. I'm Johnston. I'm in the right place?"
"Yes. No. A bit closer and nearer to the wall. Yes, there. About there."

Emily was really uneasy now. Johnston was dark. Lev was dark. Same place. Same posture. Because the hall light was behind Lev's head, he could have been Johnston.

"Ok. I'm Johnston. I've just hit you. You're wearing what?"

"What? A skirt. It was a summer's day, Lev. I was wearing a skirt, Ok?"

"No. I don't care about that. Your shoes. What kind of shoes?"

"Flats."

"I don't know what that is, flats. Did they have a sole, anything heavy?"

"No, Lev. I don't live in a war zone. I'm a girl. And it was a summer's day."

"Ok. So no shoes. You can strike the knee. Do it."

"Lev, I've got a gun now. Johnston hit me once and buggered off. I didn't need to strike him. He just let himself out of the front door and drove away."

"So it was tactical, you are saying? You chose not to strike?"

"No, it wasn't like that."

"I'm Johnston. I hit you once. I'm going to hit you again. Maybe I'm going to kill you. Maybe play around a little first. Yes. Then kill you. Probably that. Play around first.".

He made the tiniest movement towards her. There was something menacing in him, the light behind his head, the way his voice tightened, the way he was holding himself. She was in terror now. She felt just like she had back on the step with Johnston. A body memory, perhaps, but no less terrifying for that.

"Play with you, then kill you."

Lev moved fractionally closer.

And then some instinct took over in her. A fighting one. A killing one.

She lashed out with her uppermost leg, her right one. She aimed for his kneecap and caught it cleanly. Lev spilled over backwards, and she followed through with a hard stamp down his testicles, mashing down on them twice with her heel, then got poised to start kicking him in the windpipe until she'd shattered his larynx and his windpipe and the poor sod would be on his knees choking for breath and pleading for mercy and ready to feel the smash of her kneecap in his face.

"Good. Really good."

Lev never let her really hurt him. He lifted his knee at the last possible second, so she caught him on the upper calf. As for the testicle stamp, he caught her leg with both hands and took the weight off it as it came down, shifting it sideways onto his thigh as he did so.

But she wasn't there. She was not in the world that Lev was in. Unarmed combat practice. Everything a series of moves and countermoves. She was panting, partly from the exertion, but mostly because of a flood of feelings that she didn't recognise. She didn't even really feel them as feelings at all. She just felt spacey and out of her body and like she wanted to kick Lev's windpipe until he was breathing through the toe of her shoe.

She knew he was talking to her and she had trouble focusing on his words. She did her best. He repeated himself.

"You were scared? At the time it happened, you were scared?"

"No. It was beyond that. Terrified. I felt helpless."

"But you weren't helpless. You could have disabled him. Like just now."

"I know. But I wasn't in that headspace then."

"No one ever is when it happens. You have to find a way to be there like this."

Lev snapped his fingers. Then, because Shostakovich was doing something that made Lev happy, he raised a finger for a moment's silent appreciation and they listened to violins and oboes for a while.

They went back to the kitchen as he needed tea with jam.

"The other situation you were in. Not recently. Last year or whenever. When you hurt the guy."

"We've been through that."

"So we go through it again. You've only been in two situations, right? We need to understand how you react."

"Ok, in one situation, I beat the guy up. In the other I let him knock me over and then I was so terrified I didn't know what to do next."

"Fine. So we go back to the first one. We play it out again."

Emily didn't know why she got Lev involved in things sometimes. He never let go of them. Then again, that was exactly why she got him involved.

"I'm here. Wet behind the ears, writing in my notebook. You're standing up, wandering around. I'm not feeling anything weird going on. Then you step behind me. Not that side. This side. You reach down and fondle my breast."

Lev reached down and put his hand on her breast. There was nothing tentative about his touch. There was no apology and nothing seedy. For Lev, it was just about realism.

"Ready?" I asked.

Needlessly. Lev was always ready. He still had his hand on her breast.

"Ready," he said.

Then she moved. As near as possible to the way it happened. Chair back. Slam her hand upwards to catch his jaw. She felt Lev jerk back in an imitation of pain and surprise. That pulled his fondling hand away from her breast, giving her room to grab his fingers and yank back against his line of motion. That's what broke the guy's fingers, when it happened for real. She was standing now and able to kick out at the kneecap. Lev was big on kneecaps. She knew that if she was in a fight with anyone, then she was going to lose if it lasted for more than a few seconds. Likewise, if anyone could get hold of her, they'd be far too powerful for her. Kneecaps and, to a lesser extent, testicles represented her principal means of immobilizing an opponent. For that reason, most of the instructions that she'd done with Lev had focused on those fine body parts.

This time, once she'd caught his kneecap in a nice clean blow, he stopped.

"I fall now, right?"

"Yes. Kind of sideways and down. That way, yes."

"But there was more, no?"

"The guy was rolling as he fell. I shoved him against the table. An instinct thing. But I pushed quite hard and the corner penetrated his cheek. There was a lot of blood."

"And then?"

"The fight was over. He had three broken fingers and a dislocated kneecap. Plus, he was whimpering like a six-year-old and there was blood bubbling out through a hole in his cheek."

"Ok, but then he's on the floor here. How had he fallen? This way? Like this?"

"Yes, like that. No, legs apart a bit more. Yes. Exactly like that."

"And then?"

"Lev, this was the very first time it had happened, Ok? I wasn't in an ordinary state of mind."

"Of course you weren't. This was fight."

That was a big theme of Lev's. The reason why he taught Krav Maga. The reason why the Israeli Special Forces developed the technique in the first place. Fights – real fights – don't happen on tatami mats. They don't start with people bowing to each other and sprinkling water from brass bowls. They start in pubs, in alleyways, in places you don't want to fight. They make use of whatever weapons come to hand. They don't have rules. They don't let you submit gracefully and make a respectful bow to the person who felled you.

Krav Maga is strictly real world. Functional. In Krav Maga, you don't get instructors saying things like, 'And if your assailant comes at you with a sword...' It's all about making use of what you've got. Low risk, efficient manoeuvres. Proceeding as rapidly as possible from defence to attack. Maximum violence, maximum disablement. Fast, nasty, decisive.

At Hendon, when she was undergoing police training, they learned a set of techniques that were more jujitsu based. Useful enough and quite pretty. But she was way ahead of them. She'd been working on Krav Maga with Lev since Cambridge, and her own training at Hendon was to avoid revealing how much she really knew. She passed that course with the lowest grade possible. Petite, bookish, geeky Emily. No one expected anything else. Perfect cover.

"Ok," she said, because she knew Lev wouldn't let go of this until she told him. "I just stood over this guy and kicked between his legs until I could hardly feel my toes."

"He was disabled?"

"One burst testicle. Everything else was patched up ok."

"And your employers. You got into trouble for this?"

"Yes. Some. More than I wanted. But everyone believed me when I said that he'd started it. I told them that I was frightened. I said he went on trying to grab me and I used reasonable force in self defence."

Lev, whose sense of humour was mostly buried as deep as an Iranian centrifuge, found this funny and repeated it twice. But that exhausted his supply of mirth and he turned to other things. He checked for tea, found that everything had gone cold and Shostakovich had gone silent. He found more music to put on and reboiled the kettle.

"Not frightened, I think. Trauma."

He said 'trauma' with one of his non-standard pronunciations. "Trow-ma."

"Good heavens. Why would that be? Someone slaps me across the hallway in my own house and I'm frightened. How strange."

"Not then. When the guy grabs your breast."

"That wasn't exactly traumatic. I just overreacted."

"Exactly. And why did you?"

"Why did I? Lev, I'm not you. You've spent half your life training for these situations. I haven't."

He shook his head. "Ok. I know what inexperience looks like. I train people. I know. This is not like inexperience. This is trauma. Sometimes it makes you too frightened to move. Other times it makes you go crazy. When we were there in the hallway, practicing just now, and you decided not to be frightened, you were crazy inside. We were only practicing, but you were crazy inside. I could feel it."

"You scared me. You did it deliberately. Johnston didn't say the things you said."

"So? It was only words, and these were pretend words as well. You have the trauma inside you. That's why I find it so easily."

Emily was angry with all this. She didn't know exactly why she had asked Lev to come. Or rather, she knew ever since getting the gun that she should get some instruction from Lev on how to use it. He had a contempt for firing ranges. That's not where pistols are fired for real. He'd want her to practice with a gun the way they practiced Krav Maga. Tired. In bad light. With movement. Swinging lights. Running. Moving targets. Too much else going on. Noise. The whole business about soft hands, lowered shoulders, left foot forwards was so much hooey. Something to worry about on a firing range and nowhere else on earth.

But bloody typical Lev, he never operated to her agenda, only ever to his own. And right then his agenda was inventing some rubbish theory about her past.

"Lev, when I was a teenager I had a breakdown. A really big, really bad, really serious breakdown. Stuff you wouldn't understand. If you want to call that a trauma, then fine. It was a trauma. But if you're trying to imply that there was anything else, then you're wrong. Just plain wrong. I've never been raped. Until that idiot, no one ever touched me inappropriately. I've got a sane, stable, loving family. I'd never even been in a fight until I started getting lessons from you."

"You have breakdown? When?"

"When I was sixteen. It lasted until I was eighteen."

"And at Cambridge, when I met you, you were how old?"

"Nineteen. I was still in recovery. I still am. I guess I always will be."

She met Lev at Cambridge. He was newly arrived in England and was making some money teaching combat techniques to students. Emily signed up with him. She didn't know why then. Didn't know why now. She hadn't tried to analyse it. She just felt safer knowing she could take care of herself if she had to.

"And you don't tell me about this breakdown until now?"

"I don't tell anyone, Lev. I never tell people."

"Ok. So let me get this picture. You're happy little Emily, wandering through life, then in walks this great big breakdown for no reason at all. And when breakdown is gone, and you are in bad situation, you are either crazy woman or too frightened to move. So why would I think trauma?"

Silence. Or at least, silence between them. Violins from next door.

Lev realized that the kettle had boiled and made more tea for himself. He raised his eyebrows to ask if Emily wanted any. She said no, but changed her mind. What she really wanted was alcohol, which obliterated her mind much better than anything else, but which she hardly ever touched because she'd had some very bad experiences with it. University does that to many people. Times when she almost felt her illness back again, creeping into her bones and grinning at her like a gap-toothed skeleton. That's why she was a dope-smoking teetotaler, or near as dammit.

"Maybe the breakdown was the trauma," she added. "For two years, I didn't know if I was alive or dead. You can't know what it's like. You couldn't do."

Wrong thing to say. Wrong thing to say to Lev.

He sucked some more jam off his spoon and took a swallow of tea. Then he crouched down opposite her chair. Made her look into his eyes. Brown and fathomless. As deep as history. As empty as bones.

"For two years, I was in Grozny. Grozny, Chechnya. The Russians were there. Also rebels. Bandits. Jihadists. Mercenaries. Spies. Every evil on earth was there. With guns. I was there because....doesn't matter. I stay because there is a lady and a little boy I care for very much. For almost two years. Because of who I was, everyone wants me, nobody trusts me, there is...shit, Emily. There is shit. Every day. Friends are killed. Sometimes friends are killers. Every kind of bad thing that can happen is happening, and this is normal. This is how it is. Am I alive, or am I dead? I don't know. For two years, I don't know. Not only me, but everyone in Grozny. Everyone in Chechnya. I know what it's like, Emily, I know."

Emily waved her hands in a gesture of pardon-seeking. "Sorry, Lev. Sorry. So maybe you do know. Maybe your thing was worse, even. But mine was different. I wasn't in Grozny, I was here at home. And the shit wasn't happening outside, it was happening inside. It just came and took me over."

Lev nodded. "Trauma."

"From nowhere. Trauma from outer space," She argued back.

"You sleep ok?"

"Yes. Like a baby. Better since I got the gun."

"And before?"

"Before that, sometimes ok, sometimes not."

"Dreams?"

"I never dream." And that was true. She never dreamt except sometimes when she woke up in blank terror and had no idea what she was terrified of. Nights with gaping horror in the middle of them and no reason why. A skull grinning in the dark. Nights when she had all too little difficulty in identifying her emotions.

"Fear? You get frightened sometimes for no reason?"

She was about to tell him about those nights of terror, but then stopped. She remembered that prickly feeling she could never quite place. It had become worse recently, but she'd had it, or something like it, for as long as she could remember. Maybe fear was the right name for it. Maybe that feeling was fear.

She said, "Maybe," and instantly knew that to be wrong. That feeling *was* fear, and she'd had it all of her life. So she corrected herself. "Yes. Not maybe. Yes."

Lev nodded. "Trauma. You have trauma. What's it called? Soldiers come home with it."

"PTSD. Post-traumatic stress disorder."

"Da. That. PTSD. You have that."
They left it there.

She couldn't argue any more. Her family home was as safe and protected as you could ever ask for. She wasn't even bullied at school, for heaven's sake. Except she knew he was right. She had trauma in her bones and she'd never be at peace until she dealt with it.

She stood up. She was far too tired. Lev was sitting and she rubbed the back of his neck and for a minute there was nothing else. Emily massaging, him leaning into it. Violins.

She wondered how old he was, what else he'd seen. They knew nothing about each other, not really.

"Thanks, Lev. Are you staying? I'm off to bed. The keys are there if you want them."

She showed him the keys to the garden shed. There was an even chance that he'd stay all night, smoking dope and listening to Shostakovich. There was an equal chance that he'd be gone in the morning. She didn't know what their relationship was. It wasn't like friendship. Not in any normal way. But then they were both freaks. Emily because of her head and Lev because of his history.

"Goodnight, Emily."

The gun was still on the kitchen table and he pushed it towards her. He knew she'd be sleeping with it.

"If you get into a situation, remember you have trauma. Your instinct will tell you to do too much or too little. Both are bad. Use your head, not this."

He pointed to his heart.

She nodded. She knew what he meant, and had a slogan for it.

"To hell with feelings, trust reason," She said.

He grinned and repeated it. He liked that.

-35-

She was too tired. Much too tired. She slept decently because of Lev, but even so she was late to bed and her alarm blitzed her awake at seven fifteen. Five hours sleep, not even, and that was her best night for a while. She blinked herself into wakefulness. She was still on the futon, not the bed. Her hand found the gun before it found the alarm clock.

She went to take a shower. Lev was sleeping on the upstairs landing. She didn't know why he chose there, but he'd have had some reason. He woke up as she went past, or at least opened his eyes. With Lev, you could never really tell what was awake and what was asleep. She went back to her bedroom for a pillow and gave him that, though there was an entire bed in the spare room if he'd wanted it, then she went to shower. Even after the shower, her face looked tired. She chose soft, comfortable clothes and went downstairs.

After eating something she went into work. Not because she wanted to, or because she cared about any of it. Just because it was what she knew to do. She knew she'd been a bit odd lately, more odd than usual, but she could feel that something had intensified overnight. It was because of Lev. Him and his theories about trauma.

'Trow-ma'. Hers or his? Maybe he's no longer able to tell the difference. She wondered what he was doing in Chechnya. A bad place to be.

As she drove to the station she banged her palms on the steering wheel, pressed down into her toes. She could feel her body, but only dimly. Through anaesthetic. Layers of padding.

Eight thirty, sharp. Jackson gave the morning briefing. He was in a crumpled shirt, no tie, no jacket. He'd been up all night and was looking tired but happy.

"We'll keep this short," he said. "Most of you know the important stuff anyway. Last night two officers obtained evidence that three men, currently identified as Wojciech Kapuscinski, Yuri Petrov and a third man known for the moment only as Dmitri, have committed serious assaults on local sex workers. One local woman, Jayne Armitage, exhibited signs of an extremely serious beating, which is a grave offence in its own right, but as you all know, we believe these men are connected to Karol Sikorsky and quite likely also to the Operation Lohan murders, which still represents our prime focus.

Overnight, we've succeeded in arresting Kapuscinski and Petrov. They are being interrogated now. They shared a flat and we've got forensics crawling all over it right now. The flat is a proper mess, which is a good thing, because it increases the likelihood that we find something of value. No definite news yet, but we're right on top of it.

I also want to say that this enquiry owes a lot to Emily and Jane. It's not easy getting these street workers to talk. They achieved it. Many would have failed. Well done."

He was going to continue, but was interrupted by a round of clapping. Jane wasn't even there. She had a late night last night and she had family to manage. Emily didn't know what to do or feel, so just sat there looking like an idiot. A task she performed with considerable ease.

Jackson continued.

"When Petrov was arrested, he had a little black address book with 'KS' in Cyrillic inside. The initials are assumed to refer to Karol Sikorsky and the house in question is under surveillance. If there's no movement at the house within twenty-four hours, a warrant will be applied for and the house searched. Meantime, CCTV has placed Sikorsky and Mancini together on the street. Mobile phone records have established that Sikorsky was in the relevant areas for all three incidents under investigation: the Mancinis, Edwards and Balcescu. We've sent an officer to Ioana Balcescu to see if she'll be willing to give us a formal statement."

Emily felt a bit weird about all this. The inquiry was moving rapidly towards a close.

"Perhaps Sikorsky is already back in Poland or Russia or wherever he comes from, but if he isn't then it's very likely that he'll be arrested. Ports and airports have been watched since we got the DNA sample. In any case, Kapuscinski, Petrov and Leonard are all now under arrest for provable offences. Once we've done the forensic work on the properties associated with them, it's highly likely we'll be able to put together a case for murder too."

The mood around the room was jubilant. Good old Jackson. Old reliable. All they needed now was Sikorsky and everyone's joy would be complete.

Emily thought of Ioana's battered body. Of Jayney's bruises. Of Stacey Edwards's corpse. April's little head. Images she needed to avoid. She wasn't feeling well.

Jackson ended the briefing with a request for questions or any further points worth communicating.

Emily wanted to stick her hand up. She wanted to say that they had not mentioned that a man went missing leaving a huge amount in cash, and that she had looked into Charlotte Rattigan's eyes. That her husband had a predilection for street girls. She wanted to say all sorts of things but she couldn't because she was the only person in the room who seemed to care about those things. She'd have been like the cartoons on the back page of the newspaper. The funnies at the end of the news bulletin. 'And in other news…' That would have been her. The pet rabbit who got stuck up a tree. The cat who did a You Tube dance with the dog. She kept schtum.

The briefing broke up. Everyone felt that success was imminent. They were about to get the killer. Job done. Beers all round. Not quite, because the office comedy act, little old Emily, didn't drink beer. Not a real police officer, see, but they were proud of their efforts to increase diversity. They hired all sorts these days and still caught the bad guys.

Emil smiled inwardly. If only they knew. Her cover had been perfect. Nobody had an inkling. Just as well because she knew that this case was far from completion. And she had the lovely Books. Head and shoulders better than the rest of them put together.

Bev Rowland sought Emily out, worried that she was looking ill. She had a face as round as the moon, only kinder and more talkative. She started to fuss and cluck Emily into well-being, but the latter was not fussable today. Emily told her that she was going to catch up on a few emails, then take off. They agreed to rendezvous for tea once they'd checked their emails, and Emily wandered upstairs.

A mistake. Hughes caught her at her desk. A trap. A Hughesian trap. He said something about timesheets and interview notes, but she didn't really listen. It wasn't his case anyway. Lohan belonged to Jackson. Johnston belonged to Matthews. Fletcher belonged to Axelsen. When Emily tuned in again, Hughes was saying something about the Stacey Edwards post mortem. He was saying that because she'd done a good job with the last one, she could do this one too. Go along on Monday afternoon, to take notes as Hughes and Dr. Aiden Price sought to bore the pants off each other in what would surely be a world-class boring match. It would be a tense affair, but Emily's money was on Price.

She'd forgotten that there would be a post mortem for Edwards. There had to be, of course, but she just hadn't thought about it. She said, "Yes, fine. That's fine," but she couldn't work out what she felt about seeing Edwards again, because she couldn't figure out much about anything. She went on saying 'yes' whenever there was a gap and eventually even Hughes had enough and went away again. She looked at her emails for twenty minutes, but couldn't work out what she was doing with them. She drank some peppermint tea and managed a half-sensible conversation with Bev before heading out.

The team at Rattigan Transport had shrunk to just two, and neither of them was on the case full time. They had a house full of money, a missing person, but no actual honest-to-God crime. There'd be more urgency about this if there were a proper crime. She thought she should have stuck a dead body in Fletcher's bathroom before calling in the uniforms.

She made her way to the conference room and the computer that had been allocated to her. The girl who had the expression of a calf got her some undrinkable tea in a plastic cup that buckled when Emily tried to pick it up.

Once settled at her desk, fog claimed her again.

She recalled going for a walk on Exmoor with her aunt Gwyn. It started out misty but pleasant, the collies racing ahead of them through the bracken, a little frost, a nice day. Then the mist thickened, as though the light had hardened, or grown more dense. And then the world was gone. Vanished into the silence and the cold. The collies still came and went. Emily didn't think they had a problem. But they were suddenly wanderers on the void. Gwyn had known this place all her life and even so they were forced to feel their way until a hedge stopped them, and then they kept it on their right until at last they came across the gate and the lane by which they had entered. Had they somehow missed that gate, Emily thought they could have been wandering there forever.

It was like that today, only without the collies and aunt Gwyn and that blessed gate. Axelsen was around more often today than he had been. He was in and out, keeping an eye on things. She listened to him assigning her a task and nodded her agreement. Two hours later she had sheet of doodles and was trying to remembering what she was meant to be doing.

Axelsen thought she was taking the piss and so did the others on the team. She apologized and promised to do better.

As soon as she had done that, they got off her case, but the fog immediately descended again. She couldn't remember what she'd said five minutes before.

Cod, whiting, herring, turbot.

What about halibut? What's a halibut? Some kind of flatfish, she thought. Google told her that you can catch halibut in the North Atlantic. It told her that for six months, the halibut has eyes on both sides of its body and swims in the normal fishy way. Then, after six months, one eye migrates to the opposite side, the fish rotates 90 degrees in the water, and it spends the rest of its life with both eyes staring up at the roof of the sea, and no way of looking down at all. A fish with vertigo.

She couldn't see Rattigan wanting to catch halibut.

Every time Fletcher went off on a 'fishing trip', there was a Rattigan ship coming in from the Baltic. Usually Kaliningrad, sometimes Petersburg. That would be a more impressive fact if Rattigan didn't operate a fleet of such ships.

Kaliningrad. Major exports: Russian gangsterism, Afghan heroin, criminality that combines capitalist organization with Russian murderousness. Best of both worlds.

She forgot what Axelsen had told her to do, so instead she called all the fishing vessels available for charter on the south coast. She asked them if it would be possible to see their log, when, for how long and where they were going. Most of them said yes. A couple said that should be fine but they'd need to refer it elsewhere in their corporate structures. One skipper hung up when she told him who she was. A little further digging told her that the hanger-up had a criminal conviction for armed robbery and another for GBH.

Emily told all this to Axelsen the next time he visited.

"Do you think Rattigan went with Fletcher?"

"No."

"So why would either of them want to charter a fishing boat?"

"I don't know."

"You're remembering that Rattigan owns an entire fleet of ships? That if he wanted a boat, he could buy one? That Fletcher's day job was arranging charters for Rattigan's fleet?"

"And that Rattigan has been dead for almost a year?"

"Yes."

"So, do you think maybe all this is a red herring?"

"A red halibut maybe."

Emily laughed. She laughed a lot because she thought it was funny. Axelsen didn't, so she shut up.

"Have you got that list I asked for?"

She scrunched her eyes up and start to give that question some serious thought, but then the fog crept in again and answers didn't seem to arrive. She couldn't remember what list he wanted.

She wondered if he'd be interested in hearing about halibut instead, but there was a look on his face that suggested not, so she said nothing, which was a pity, because they're interesting fish. Halibut have white bellies, so from below they look like the ocean floor. A light and a dark side. And the light side travels blind.

"Are you feeling Ok? You don't look well."

"I don't feel well."

"You weren't in an accident or something?"

She shook her head. She didn't remember the day going terribly well, but she would have remembered that, surely.

"You look like someone in shock. Why don't you go home, get some rest, take it easy over the weekend? You're no bloody use to me at all the way you are now."

She nodded and tried to look wise, as though they were making a tough judgement call together and after due consideration she'd come down in favour of his assessment.

"I'll go home. Yes. Good idea. Sorry."

She wasn't sure why she was saying sorry, except that 'no bloody use' is a phrase she'd heard before, and not in a good way. Emily sat at her desk to clear her things, and Axelsen marched off to catch criminals and make the world a better place.

Before she left, though, she typed into Google and got up a Wikipedia page. It offered her three alternatives:
- Shock (circulatory), a circulatory medical condition
- Acute stress reaction, often termed 'shock' by laypersons, a psychological condition in response to terrifying events
- Post-traumatic stress disorder, a long term complication of acute stress reaction.

It took her some time to understand this. It took her some time to discover all those interesting things about halibut too. But she didn't have circulatory shock. That was something you got in hospitals and had nothing to do with her.

PTSD. That's what Lev told her she had, but that's a long term thing. A continuing response to something that happened way back.

Acute stress reaction was more interesting, though. 'often termed "shock" by laypersons.' It was a bit harsh to call DI Axelsen a layperson. He was a detective inspector for heaven's sake, but layperson or not, maybe he was on to something. Here's what Wikipedia says about it:

Acute Stress Reaction (also called acute stress disorder, psychological shock, mental shock or, simply, shock) is a psychological condition arising in response to a terrifying or traumatic event.

A bit further on, she learned what her symptoms were meant to be:

Common symptoms sufferers of acute stress disorder experience are: numbing; detachment; derealisation; depersonalization or dissociative amnesia; continued re-experiencing of the event by such ways as thoughts, dreams and flashbacks.

Numbing? Tick. Yes, got that. Detachment? Yep, that too. Derealisation? Not too sure what that is, but if it's what it sounds like, then she had it. Depersonalisation or dissociative amnesia? Yes, got that big time and, back in the day, used to have it mega big time. World class depersonaliser, she was. Never beaten, seldom matched. But then there was that last bit. Continued re-experiencing of the event by such ways as thoughts, dreams and flashbacks. No. What event? She tried to find something on Wikipedia that told her what event she was meant to be experiencing, but couldn't find anything. But what about her night-time terrors? The gaping horror at midnight? The skull grinning in the dark? Did those things count as dreams or flashbacks?

If they did, then she ticked every box. Ticked 'em big. Ticked 'em good.

But what was the event? There wasn't any event. Lev thought there was and layperson Axelsen thinks there was, but there wasn't. There just wasn't.

It was odd, Emily reflected. Even in her dazed state, she knew it was odd. When she first got ill, there was this big investigation into why. What made it happen? Her condition was something that safely brought up teenagers weren't meant to get. It made no sense. Psychiatrists pushed and prodded and Social Services tried to foist their crappy little theories onto her poor old mum and dad. No one got anywhere. There was no explanation that made sense, so the whole question – certainly in her mind and, she thought, in everyone else's too – got shoved aside. Her illness was just one of those things. No more logic than an earthquake. Wrong place, wrong time, tough luck.

And now, when she least expected it, Lev and Axelsen were telling her to think again. Continued re-experiencing of the event. There wasn't an event, but Lev and Axelsen and Wikipedia all begged to differ.

Next to her the phone rang. One of her teammates picked it up. There was a muttered conversation, which she didn't follow, because she was hot on the pursuit of knowledge and couldn't concern herself with trifles. The phone conversation ended. The teammate approached.

"That was Axelsen calling to check you'd gone."

"Ah, yes."

"I'll take you to your car, shall I? You'll be all right driving?"

Emily nodded. Very meek. Very submissive. She was led out to the car park and drive home so carefully that she was honked at for doing forty in the slow lane.

-36-

She reached the house vaguely expectant, but there was nothing there. Lev had gone, as anticipated and there were no messages or texts.

The kitchen was tidy, which was Lev's doing rather than hers. He'd left a note for her on the counter, though. "to hell with feelings, trust reason." A very good slogan indeed, though she did say so herself.

She started to apply it. First, the whole issue about shock. Clearly, she ticked most of the boxes for PTSD. Pretty clearly, she was looking and acting like someone in the grip of major – league shock right now, this minute. At the same time, however, she was missing the most single most crucial ingredient in the formula, a 'terrifying or traumatic event.' That was a puzzle, but not one that needed to be solved right away. She decided to leave it.

Next, she needed to find some way to lessen the symptoms. She was not managing them well and she knew how dark they could get. She made a list of her standard techniques for dealing with head – craziness:
1/. Smoke a joint, 2/. Bury myself in work, 3/. Go to stay with Mum and Dad, 4/. Breathing exercises etc.

She immediately crossed item one. She'd smoked too much lately and it only helped when her problems were mild to moderate.

Right then, they were moderate to bad, with the course set for hard to severe.

Item two was likewise forced to bite the dust. She'd just been sent home. Everyone on Lohan was looking at her strangely and telling her to go home. She had no work to bury herself in. And the work wasn't helping.

Item three was more interesting. It would probably work. Not straight away, but give it a few days and she'd be right as rain. But it felt like a backward step. A palliative, not a cure. She decided to leave that one aside and come back to it if there was an emergency.

Number four was like a pair of sensible shoes or a high fibre cereal. Good for you, but sinfully dull. All the same, four was a good one. She would come back to it shortly.

Floating around, though, was a possible number five. Making love. She'd not had many lovers. A couple of spottily awkward students, ickily overeager to get into bed with anything in a skirt. One chap after Cambridge. A nice chap. Runs a bookshop now. No charisma. Safe.

And now Books. Part of her wanted to go rushing off to Books. Get him into bed. Make love urgently. Use him. But she wanted to do things right with him. She wanted to learn the art of being a girlfriend. A proper one. A permanent, stable one, for whom lovemaking was about nothing more than making love. Simply that. Not a sort of self - medication.

She made a cup of tea and spent forty minutes doing exercises. Breathing first. In, two, three, four, five. Out, two, three, four, five. When she'd done fifteen minutes of that, she started her bodywork. Moved her arms. Moved her legs. Felt them as she moved them. Stamped on the floor to see if she could feel down to her feet.

What next, she wondered? What should she do next? What did she want? Nothing came to her, so she got out her paper again and wrote, WHAT DO I CARE ABOUT?

Almost immediately, she wrote in capitals, APRIL MANCINI. Emily moved her pen, ready to add further names to the list. Jenna Mancini. Stacey Edwards. Ioana Balcescu. The names of the victims. And maybe there were other things, other people she wanted to find out about. Rattigan. Fletcher. Johnston. Sikorsky. But her pen didn't move. APRIL MANCINI. That was who she cared about. She was all Emily cared about. The toffee-apple kid.

With a sudden awful rush, she realised that she'd forgotten her funeral. She had promised to go to it, even promised to tell the nice lady – Amanda, she thought it was – who'd phoned the helpline early on and started crying when she told her how Jenna and April died. She was going to come to the funeral too.

She phoned the office, but couldn't find anyone there who knew or cared. She phoned the hospital too. Ditto. But she was not on maximum power, so she was probably asking the wrong people in the wrong way. Instead, she phoned Bev Rowland. She didn't know, but promised to find out, and sure enough called her back in ten minutes. The funeral was going to be on Tuesday, the day after the post mortem. Unless something unexpected cropped up at the mortuary on Monday, Stacey Edwards and Jenna and April Mancini would all be cremated the following day.

She thanked Bev and put the phone down. She felt instantly more human. She knew what she was doing now. She needed to arrange a proper funeral for April. She didn't know why, but felt the need not just for herself, but, more importantly, because April needed her to.

She phoned her school and insisted on being put through to the Headteacher. She encountered a bit of resistance from a pointlessly obstructive receptionist, but her juices were flowing now and she was getting harder to resist. She bulldozed her way through to the Headteacher and told her that April's entire class needed to come to the funeral. She told Emily that their lessons had already been planned, so Emily told her that someone dropped a sink on April's head and she wasn't lucky enough to have any lessons. The Headteacher told her, tartly, that the crematorium was too far from the school and it was too late to organize transport. Emily conceded that was absolutely fair enough, and asked her when she wanted transport and how many kids were in April's class? Ten minutes later, Emily called back, having hired a coach to pick up the children. The Headteacher, now backed into a corner, conceded less than graciously and even thanked Emily.

Emily's speed was picking up. Next stop, neighbours at the estate where Jenna used to live. She got a local print shop to print 500 flyers. Nothing much. Just typed details about the funeral arrangements and at the bottom a request for information: JENNA AND APRIL MANCINI WERE MURDERED. CALL IN CONFIDENCE. That and her phone number.

She drove to the estate and found a couple of kids mooning around on bikes. She offered them fifty quid to distribute her flyers to every house and flat on the estate. Twenty up front. Thirty when they finished. She told them she'd check three random doors to ensure they had done the job properly. They had a brief discussion, then agreed. Emily stuck around for just long enough to check that the flyers were entering some letterboxes, and then hurried off.

There was a 'drug users' drop-in-centre that Jenna used to use. Emily went there to get them to put up a notice. A helpful woman serving teas said that she would email a few people who might be interested. Emily asked her if she knew any women's centres that might be interested in knowing about the funeral. That proved a success as well.

She called Amanda, the lady who'd cried, and told her when the funeral would be. Amanda cried again, promised to be there and said she would phone some of the other mothers.

Back to the estate and the kids were still shoving flyers through letterboxes. Emily gave them the fifty quid. She asked them if they wanted another fifty quid for doing the same further up the road, around Stacey Edwards's old stomping ground. They looked at her as if she was mad, but Emily took that as an agreement. She phoned the print shop again and got them to run off more flyers, with Stacey Edwards's name in place of Jenna and April's. She told the kids where they could pick up the flyers and told them to call her when they'd finished. The kids pedaled off, delighted at her inability to drive a decent bargain.

What else? Flowers. Music. She called the crematorium and asked what they did for music. She stressed that she didn't want tapes, or any old recording. She wanted an organist. She wanted a choir. She wanted a parade of trumpeters. for God's sake. After a bit of discussion, it seemed that she could get a string quartet and a solo vocalist for £400. That seemed steep to her, but she said, yes. She did ask about the trumpeter, but they were out of stock, alas.

She had the conversation as she was driving. Not on the hands free but just juggling the phone, the steering wheel and the gearstick. She knew that was wrong, but excused herself by the conviction that it helped build concentration and did wonders for the coordination. Like rubbing your tummy and patting your head at the same time, only harder.

She arrived at the market as it was closing. A clutter of stalls housed in a palace and it was like some entrepreneurial refugees had got stuck in a Victorian railway terminus and set up shop there. Stallholders were taking down their sports shirts, their ethnic jewellery, pulling shutters down over veg boxes and bookstands. There was a pleasant end of day mood. A box of red apples being flogged off cheap.

Emily ran around looking for a flower stall, found one and asked the bloke in green wellies how much for his flowers. He looked at her as if she was barking. He pointed to the buckets of flowers. Each one had its own blackboard on a spike, with prices chalked on each board. She looked at him like he was barking. She didn't want one stupid bouquet, she wanted his flowers. She wanted the shop.

Once she'd managed to explain this, he asked if she was serious, then quoted a price of

500 quid. Emily had a feeling she could get them for a lot less, but didn't want April to think she was tight, so agreed. She asked if he could help get the flowers into her car and wanted the buckets as well. He, in turn, agreed, which proved to be a bad move on his part, because her lovely car wasn't really the acres of boot space sort of car and it took half an hour of careful wiggling to get everything inside.

She got a call from the bike kids and went to pay them, before going home to make further progress.

She made some more calls. The church in whose parish Jenna Mancini was found dead. Ditto the one in the part of town where she used to live. Ditto Stacey Edwards's old parish. She spoke to the vicars. One of them agreed to say a blessing. He seemed a good soul, and even said he knew a trumpeter. Lord bless the man. He gave Emily a phone number, and two minutes later, she had her trumpeter. She asked for something triumphant rather than funereal. He then went on to waive any fee, so she told him that he was her new favourite trumpeter.

She called a couple of newspapers and placed funeral notices, making sure she got all the bits and bobs. Extra words, bold type, boxes.

She was wondering what she could do next when the phone rang. It was Books. He said the station was going full pelt on Lohan and the forensics on the Kapuscinski house looked positive. Emily didn't care about that and said so.

"Listen, I've got the day off tomorrow," he said, "I thought maybe we could..."

"Yes."

"You don't know what I was going to say?"

"I was going to say maybe we could spend some time together."

"Yes."

"I'll call you tomorrow morning, then. We could go somewhere."

That sounded like a man plan to Emily. 'We could go somewhere.' Gosh, the imagination! But she didn't argue. A man plan was good enough for her. They rang off.

She was slowing down now, tired, but in a good way. She needed to get an early night so she could catch up on some sleep, but there were things to do first.

She made up some bouquets. She wasn't the world's best bouquet maker, but she didn't need to be. She made about twenty, tied them with kitchen string and dropped them on the passenger seat of the car. In each bouquet, she put a handwritten note: "*Most of all, I would like it if you came to the funeral. But I am also a police officer. If you want to tell me anything at all about Rattigan, Fletcher, Kapuscinksi, Petrov or Sikorsky, then please call me, in total confidence, on the number below. Very many thanks."*

She knew it was a bit early for things to be really busy, but she drove to where Friday night custom could get crazy. The girls were out already, hunting for custom. She knew a lot of them now and some of them even liked her.

One bouquet at a time, she approached. With each girl, she explained who she was and why she was there. She was a friend of Jenna Mancini's. Also of Stacey Edwards. It was their funeral on Tuesday and she wanted people to know. She also wanted to give out flowers.

She met Kyra, the stupid cow who gave Jane and her nothing at all that first time they met. She was wearing platform shoes with a five-inch heel. She was absurdly happy to see Emily, which meant nothing about Emily, but everything about how recently Kyra had taken smack.

"Flowers? For me?" she asked.

"For you. Or for you to bring along to the funeral to place on the coffins. I don't mind. Either way, the flowers are to commemorate the women who died. And Jenna had a little girl, so the flowers are for her too. She was six years old and her name was April."

Kyra looked at her as though she was crazy, but she took the flowers. It was the same with the other girls she met. They thought she was nuts, but Emily told them that she would see them at the crematorium on Tuesday.

It took her four hours to hand out most of her bouquets. She was beginning to sway with tiredness when she heard a familiar voice from behind. Bryony Williams. Equipped with her ciggy, her canvas jacket and her messy hair. And a bouquet wielding prostitute who Emily vaguely recognised. Alta, possibly.

"I heard someone was doling these out," said Bryony, indicating the flowers. "Though it might be you."

She grinned. "Three more to go and I'm done for the evening."

Bryony said she would do them. Emily told her about the notes she had put inside and she nodded approvingly.

"Where did you get the flowers?" she asked.

She bought the shop, she told her. She explained that she wanted people to come to the funeral. She didn't know why it felt important, but she thought it was because Jenna and April and Stacey had such unnoticed lives. She wanted them to go out in a blaze of glory and told Bryony about the trumpeter and the coachload of schoolchildren.

She gave Emily a hug, hard and long. When she came away, her cheeks were wet. Emily envied her for her tears. She wondered what they felt like. She wondered if they hurt.

-37-

Saturday.

Books called her at eleven and she was ready for him, give or take. It was another proper summer's day, a hot one. She'd tried on four different outfits and ended up with a pistachio and coffee striped top that she wore the day Johnston hit her, a long skirt and flat shoes. She looked nice, she thought.

When he called, she was amazingly nervous. She thought he was too. They started out very awkwardly but gradually shook free of it. He'd told her to bring her swimming costume. She told him that she bet he'd got white legs and burned after ten minutes in the sun. She didn't own a swimming costume, so she chose a bikini that gave her more cleavage, which pleased her and, she hoped, him. She wore that under her clothes.

They talked to each other on hands-free, comparing notes on the density of the traffic as they closed in on each other. They agreed not to talk about work. The awkwardness was evaporating in the heat.

He arrived first and told her which café he was in. He suggested they treated it as a blind date, as if they'd never met before. "Might be fun," he said.

Fifty yards away from the café she had to stop and collect herself. She was nervous but ok. No depersonalisation. She spent a moment texting Bryony, and told her that she was on a date and didn't want to be disturbed. She told Bryony to spend as much money as she wanted and that she would pay. That left Emily with a stackload of flowers to deal with, but she'd just take them to the funeral with her.

Then, as she moved closer to the café, she saw Books at table. White parasol flapping in the sea breeze. Shadows jumping to avoid the sunshine. He was nervous too, and she realised that was because he cared. Cared about her. She felt a wave of pleasure at the thought and wondered what she had done to be so lucky?

He saw her almost as she was close to him. They played their blind date game for a bit, which definitely helped to deal with the nerves. Emily felt awkward, but Books accepted it in a way that made it seem endearing, not edge of breakdown weird.

Books did have white legs, she noted, and she bet he'd burn before the day ended. In the sunlight, his hair looked properly blond, not just sandy.

They had lunch and walked along the beach. He swam. Emily sort of swam. They splashed each other. She tried to duck him under and failed totally, until he laughed at her and performed a huge pretend drowning act. Then he picked her up and dropped her in. She shrieked, but liked the way her body felt in his arms. When she'd been duly ducked, they stood up and he kissed her. She felt Comrade Lust tugging at her again, but they were taking things slowly. After all, why rush?

When they tired, which came fairly early in Emily's case, they drove back to her house. She cooked spaghetti Bolognese and they ate it with a bottle of extremely cheap red wine that had been knocking around for such contingencies. She only took a token sip, but Books manfully disposed of half the bottle.

When the Bolognese was done, Books washed up. Emily was meant to dry, or do something, but she just watched him. The way his hair was speckled and had tiny salt crystals glittering close to the scalp.

She kissed his neck and asked if he was all right to go off home. She was trying to be sensible, knowing that she needed to take it all slowly and in a Date Girl way, that she wasn't ready for sex quite yet.

He didn't take it that way.

"Not exactly," he said, with exaggerated patience. "No. not unless you've got me a special licence to drive with raised blood alcohol levels."

She stared at him. Was he serious? He'd had half a bottle of wine and wouldn't even drive for a few minutes?

For a second, maybe ten seconds, she was genuinely panicked. She thought it was some kind of ruse on his part to get into her knickers. Her panic was temporary, but immediate and all-consuming. Comrade Lust was nowhere to be seen. It was as though her reason had been taken over by a troop of Methodist grandmams, wagging their fingers at her and declaiming, 'they only want one thing you know.'

She didn't know what look she had on her face, or what she said or did, but Books saved her embarrassment.

"Hey, hey, hey, it's ok. I can't drive, but I can order a taxi."

He phoned for one, ostentatiously, calming her down. When the cab firm asked what time he wanted to be picked up, he asked, "we've got time for coffee, haven't we?" The Methodist grandmams went into overdrive, chorusing about the double entendre in the word 'coffee', but she was already calming down and told the grandmamas to shut up. Books ordered the cab for half an hour's time.

She made coffee for him, peppermint tea for herself.

"Sorry," she said, "I'm not very good at this."

There was a question on his face, which she answered. "I'm not a virgin, but...I'm not very experienced." She thought about that answer and realised that was the truth but not the whole truth. "Also, I'm an idiot."

"Duly noted."

"You do know that I'm not quite like you, don't you? That I'm a bit strange?"

He made a joke. Deflected.

Emily persisted. "No really. It matters. I'm not like you. If that's a problem, then....I don't know. But you need to understand that. Sometimes I'll go to places that you've never been. I might need your help."

He looked her, but she couldn't interpret the look on his face. He said, "well, if you do, just ask," which sounded like the right thing to say, but somehow wasn't.

She didn't quite know what the best thing to say was, so she said what was almost certainly the wrong thing.

"And I'm not a big one for rules. I don't get on with them very well."

"I'm a police officer, Emily, so are you.

"Yes, but...."

"Rules are our business."

"I know..." but the gun. The grass. The thing I'm planning for Monday. The thing I'm planning for later in the week." The list of possible buts was long and getting longer. She didn't finish her sentence and didn't push the point. Another rule of hers, 'always, always put off till tomorrow anything that doesn't have to be done today.' She didn't apply that to work, but used it for pretty much anything in her personal life.

For their last twenty minutes, they cuddled together on the sofa. Emily was impressed. Books was a good kisser. A broader repertoire than you'd guess. He was good on the passionate knee-wobblers, but he also had a good range of nibbly, nuzzly, intimate, flirty kisses too. She wondered again what she'd done to be so lucky. As she was wondering, her phone bleeped the arrival of a text. It was Bryony telling her that she was giving out flowers and notes like crazy. HAVE A GOOD TIME. YOU DESERVE IT. The text ended on a non-work note.

"Anything important? Asked Books
"No."

They went on cuddling until the taxi came and it was time to see him off at the door. She felt like a true citizen of Planet Normal. She was going to be a girlfriend. This man was going to be her boyfriend. They were both police officers. Except they were much, much more than that.

Once the taxi left, she didn't close the front door right away. She held on to it, that feeling. She was showing the world how happy and normal she was.

-38-

Sunday was a nothing day. Emily pretended to clean and failed to go to the gym. She also forgot to eat anything much, so she went to Mum and Dad's for tea and end up staying until ten. She talked to Books twice on the phone, but they didn't see each other. 'Slowly does it', she told herself. Her Father smiled a knowing smile as he overheard them.

The next morning, Monday, was another one of those weird ones. She went into work bang on time, no foginess, no shock, and found that the case had once again moved on. Over the weekend, they kept an eye on what they believed to be Sikorsky's address. After no sign of any movement they launched a massive dawn raid and searched the place. A massive SOCO type operation, the biggest yet by all accounts. Office rumour said that forensics had taken some clothes and thought they had a blood splash on a trouser leg. If the blood was April Mancini's, then Sikorsky was inching ever closer to a life sentence. Better still, and unbelievably, the address had yielded a roll of duct tape and some cable ties from a DIY shop. Both used, though still in the original shopping bag with the receipt. Rumour had it that the cut end of the duct tape in Edwards's flat matched the roll in Sikorsky's bag. Emily was amazed by the stupidity of most criminals. Stupid and lucky. They'd have a hell of a job convicting them otherwise.

All they needed now was Sikorsky himself. The prosecution case felt largely complete. But a case isn't much use without a criminal to convict. To get as far as they had without getting their hands on the probable killer felt frustrating, to say the least. The betting around the coffee machine was that Sikorsky was already in Poland or Russia. If the former, then they had a twenty or thirty percent chance of getting him, because the Poles aren't too corrupt and because they're EU members who try to behave themselves. If he was in Russia, then they were pretty much buggered.

Most reckoned he was in Russia and Emily was inclined to agree.

Meantime, Axelsen's effort seemed to be winding down. Traces of cocaine had been found in both Fletcher's home and in a desk drawer. They already knew, from Emily's interview with Charlotte Rattigan, that the big man used to take the odd bit of coke when he was still alive, so the ruling assumption was that Fletcher was dealing. That was where his cash came from. Some drug world problem made him do a runner. He might be in another country or dead. Whatever it was, it must have been a pretty urgent problem to make him leave 200 grand in cash lying around. As for the whole Rattigan fishing trip thing, it was being assumed that Rattigan and Fletcher were coke buddies. Fletcher got a kick out of hanging out with criminals. Stranger things have happened.

Because it was all go on Lohan, because Axelsen wasn't exactly desperate to have her back and because Jackson and Hughes both had other things on their minds, no one really cared what she did.

Just as well because she was busy with funeral stuff and wanted to save her energies. She'd already called a journalist at the local paper and told him about this people power demonstration of solidarity that was expected at the crematorium. Because bugger all happens on a Sunday, which means they're always desperate for material to fill the paper on a Monday, they had the whole front page of the newspaper: 'Hundreds Expected at Dead Girl's Funeral." Gill Parker of StreetSafe was quoted as saying that the funeral was expected to show the town's opposition to violence against women. A rent a quote local pop star was reported as saying much the same thing, and implied that she was intending to be there herself.

Emily spent some time on Facebook groups and other women's group things, getting the word out. She called the coach company and asked them if they could provide more transport if need be. Business is business, so they said ok. Then she called eight Headteachers of schools close to April's. She told them that there was a big kids' movement wanting to protest against violence. She told them that transport was arranged and paid for, so they just needed to call the coach company to arrange pick up times. Six of the eight sounded really interested. Emily knew the newspaper headline helped. Maybe the pop star too. She called crematorium and told them to expect 800. She called another flower place and told them to send £1,000 worth of flowers.

All the time she was making calls, she had April's little dead face up on her screen. "we're doing good, kid," she said to her. April smiled at Emily. 'She's never had a funeral before, so she's looking forward to this one, and quite right too', Emily mused.

She was doing all this when she spotted Books drifting over. He smiled at her and sat on the corner of her desk. Nothing unusual. They hadn't talked about it much, but neither of them wanted the office to know about their relationship, so they played it cool. Only a lift of the eyebrow as he sat indicated that he quite liked the way he'd spent Saturday. She wrinkled her eyes back at him, to indicate the same thing. If truth be told, she felt a little odd about the way they had finished. That thing about rules. Was that really Books telling her that he was going to have a problem with little things like the odd speeding ticket or unlicensed gun? She was hoping for more give and take than that. But still, no need to worry about that now. Always put off till tomorrow...

"What was it again?" he said. "Bastard, thieving, wish he'd go and top himself Johnston? That was your phrase, I think."

"Drown," I said. "It was drown himself."

"He's just come in downstairs. Wants to plead guilty apparently."

"Does he? Ha!" Some noise like that anyway. Not a real word. She was trying to work out what this meant, and got up to go, grabbing her bag and a book from her desk drawer.

"I'll see you again, will I?" said Books, who didn't want her to rush off.

"Yes. Not this evening. I can't do this evening. I've got family coming round for dinner. The day after tomorrow? Are you free?

"I am, yes. Subject to operational requirements."

"Then subject to operational requirements, you've got yourself a date."

She rushed off downstairs.

If you want to plead guilty, you notify the court, not the police station. If Johnston came here, it was to send her a message. Then she remembered that Books had already had a quiet word about hitting her, pointing out the error of his ways. Her Books. Looking after her; handing Johnston to her on a plate. Subtle or what?

She wasted a minute or two trying to find out where he was and discovered that he'd come in, spoken briefly to the duty officer, then walked out again.

Emily went outside. Which way? If he wanted to see her, he'd make himself easy to find. She found him in Boscawen Park. No kites today, she noticed. He was drinking from a paper cup. He had a brown paper bag next to him, with another coffee cup in it.

"For you," he said, passing it over. "I forgot you don't drink coffee."

"That's ok. Thank you."

Now they were there, she didn't know what to say, so opted for silence. It seemed to her that the ball was in his court anyway.

"I saw the thing in the paper this morning," he said.

"That's people power for you."

"Yeah. And a little birdie tells me that the good folks of this place have got Fletcher nailed as a coke dealer."

"What are you going to do?"

Emily shrugged. She wasn't very focused on Fletcher at the moment. April had most of her attention. Still, a civil question deserves a civil answer, as her granny used to say.

"Don't know. Find him. Catch him. Arrest him. Prosecute him. You might be cellmates, you never know."

"I doubt it. I've got a lawyer who's very sympathetic. Police hero wounded in the line of duty. Lots of flashbacks. Difficult stuff psychologically. Poor lad needs a bit of support, but doesn't get it. Goes off the rails. Feels awful. I'm going to try to cry on the witness stand, but I don't know how that'll come off."

"You'll be wonderful I'm sure."

"What do you reckon? A year? Maybe out in six months. Worst case scenario. An open prison too, probably."

Emily didn't say anything to that and for a while they just sat in silence, letting the wind comb through the park, looking for answers. It was Johnston who broke the silence.

"He might be dead already. Hard to arrest a dead man."

"Oh, I don't know. At least they don't run." Johnston knew more about this than she did, and most of what she knew was supposition. "Can I just check a couple of things with you? First, has Fletcher really been as stupid as I think he has?"

"Oh, yes."

"And he's as dangerous as I think he is? Dangerous on his own, I mean?"

"On his own, he's about as dangerous as my old nan. Not even. My nan had more balls than he does. Or did. Whichever."

Emily nodded. Good. It was nice to have those things confirmed.

Johnston asked, "Do you know where he is?"

"No, not exactly, but out west somewhere. Why? Do you know?"

"Not exactly, but you've got it about right. I know it's right on the coast, like even a minute's walk away. That's all I know."

"You've never been?"

"Not my cup of tea, any of that. I didn't want to see it."

"You had his key. His phone number. You could check his emails."

"Listen, he wanted me involved. I totally refused. He gave me cash, his phone details, his email passwords, his bloody door key. He begged."

"You kept the cash, though."

"That bloody conservatory. I don't even like the bugger."

The bugger that was purchased fifteen weeks after Rattigan's death. Money that had come from Fletcher, not Rattigan.

"It wouldn't look good in court."

"Emily, none of it would look good in court. But I didn't help them. Either of them."

She raised her eyebrows at that. She didn't believe him.

"Listen, forget courts. Just you and me."

She nodded. "Ok."

"It started as pure chance. I saw some idiot drive his Aston and I was interested to see what kind of idiot stepped out. It was Rattigan. I recognized him. Talked to one or two of the girls. I found out everything and he knew I'd found out. I think it could even have been Mancini who told him."

"So you started to blackmail him? It wasn't operational advice; it was just blackmail?" Somehow that felt worse.

"Not really. That's the stupid thing. It was hardly even that. Rich bastard knows I know and starts giving me money. He invites me to the racecourse. We find we actually like each other. Rich bastard, corrupt copper."

"But you weren't corrupt. Or hadn't been."

Up until that point, they hadn't really been looking at each other. They'd been staring out at the park, letting the world spin on its axis, doing what it does. But now Johnston wanted her gaze as well as her attention. He touched her on the shoulder and got her to look at him. Emily investigated his features more carefully that she'd done before. The tough cop act was only half of Johnston, maybe less. The bigger chunk of him was more solemn, more thoughtful.

"You're right. I'd been a good cop. That thing about crying on the stand, it's not all bollocks. I did feel cut off from the police service, as it happens. One moment, I was the bee's knees, the kipper's knickers. Medals from Her Maj and letters of commendation from the home secretary. Next thing, It's just a monthly pension and invites to the annual police dinner. I was disorientated for a while. Rattigan felt like a way out."

"A way out...." She began, but Johnston stopped her.

"I know. People died. Don't think I don't know. That's why I did what I did. A cry for help. Isn't that pathetic? I've turned into the sort of person I used to hate."

She didn't answer or push the point. Johnston's immortal soul was not her concern.

The wind travelled inland from the sea, hurrying up from the south. Rushing about, confused by the city, peering in every nook and cranny, rustling leaves, moving picnic blankets, blowing up skirts and dresses. A wicked wind, a restless wind.

"Then Rattigan dies."

"Yes. I thought that was it, and so it was really. Fletcher, well, he was just as much of an arsehole, but he wasn't fun to hang around with."

"But?"

"But nothing. He wanted in. He thought I'd jump at the chance. But I didn't. I've only been into his house once and that was to tell him he was an idiot."

"Did you hit him?"

"No. Wish I had though."

"Me too."

There was more she wanted to ask, but Johnston touched her arm and pointed.

"See that man there?"

It was a man in a suit. Forty something. Pleased with himself.

"Ivor Harris," he told her. "Ivor Harris, MP. A Tory."

She shrugged. "The Conservative Party is legal, you know."

"You want to know his first name? It's Piers. Posh Piers. He changed to his middle name because he thought it would attract more votes."

"So, that's allowed too."

"Best buddies with Rattigan. Coke snorters. And he knew. Not the whole thing, maybe, but he knew enough."

"You don't know that."

She wondered for a second how Johnston knew that posh Piers would come a wandering by, then realised that he didn't. This park was a favourite stomping ground of the local powerful. You probably couldn't spend an hour or two here and not find someone who used to hang out with Rattigan.

"I do know that. Rattigan couldn't get high without boasting about it. And Ivor bloody Harris is an MP. Bloody Johnston is a criminal."

"Same difference."

He laughed. "Yeah, fair enough." He let that comment die away, then added another. "Do you want to know how much personal income tax Rattigan paid?"

"I didn't, but I do now."

"Nineteen per cent in the UK. Nothing at all overseas. And most of his income came from overseas. He probably averaged under ten per cent in taxes. Because he's rich and has clever lawyers. Rattigan, Ivor Harris's buddy."

"Yeah, but it's better, isn't it? Being like us, I mean. Ordinary work, ordinary money, ordinary tax."

Johnston laughed. "Ordinary criminal, ordinary jail time."

"Yes, that too. Even that."

He'd finished his coffee and scrunched up the cup.

"Weird thing is, I'm a bit scared of prison. I didn't think I would be."

"You'll be ok."

"I know."

"I'll visit you, if you like."

"Would you? Really?

She nodded. "If you like."

"I would like. Yes. I would.

The more she knew Johnston, the more she liked him, despite all that he'd done and not done. They sat on the bench and stared out into the park. Harris had gone from view.

"Here, I've got something for you."

She gave him the book that she'd taken from her desk drawer before coming out. It's 'My First Book of Piano Classics.'

"I didn't know if you were into classics more or pop stuff. I thought maybe the classics."

He was touched. Genuinely moved. She'd only got the book on the off chance. She'd intended to post it, but hadn't got around to it.

"Thanks, Emily. I'll let you know how I get on."

"I'll want a recital."

He nodded. They were in silence for a moment, but he knew what she was about to ask.

"Fletcher. That place, where is he now?"

She nodded. "Yes?"

"It's a white house or shack or something. A little tower or something. I only saw a photo once, and I didn't look for long. But I know it's white and close to a beach."

"Mooring?"

"I don't know, I just don't know."

"You had a sailing club t-shirt on the time I came to your house."

"Did I? Never been sailing, though. I haven't been there."

"Ok." She believed him.

"I'll come with you, if you like. I'm not much use for most things, but I know how to hit people."

Emily laughed out loud at that. She didn't tell him that she'd practiced stamping his testicles to pulp, or that she had a certain Books in reserve. She doubted he would have forgotten his encounter with her precious Books.

"I'll be ok. A girl's gotta do what a girl's gotta do. And it's only one man, isn't it? One man that your old nan could take out."

"You hope."

She stood up and chucked her still full coffee cup into a bin.

Johnston nodded farewell. When she left him, he was still on the bench, the book open in front of him, his fingers practicing movements on an invisible keyboard.

-39-

The mortuary visit with DI Hughes wasn't as much fun as the one with DCI Jackson. Hughes and Price did have a boring contest, and Hughes came out of it much better than she'd expected. Price scored heavily with his torrents of uninteresting detail, but Hughes countered with that depressive hostile thing he did, an adaptable technique and one that really worked for him. In the end, she couldn't call a winner. There was no knockout, and the judges would have to make a decision on points.

By the time they were done, she'd filled twenty-one pages of her notebook. She was rustling like taffeta, just like the first time.

The room they were in contained Stacey Edwards on a proper bench, and the two Mancinis on gurneys They were only wheeled in there so Price could make one or two points of comparison between the corpses. They were all due to be burned tomorrow. Released up through a chimney into the sky. The weather forecast was to be like today. Windy, dry. hot, overcast. A good day to be burned, she reckoned. The wind would give little April her freedom at last. Freedom and light.

Finally, neither Price nor Hughes could think of anything else worth saying. They covered the bodies and left the room.

Emily looked down at her watch.

"Gosh, is that the time?" There was a big hospital clock on the wall that confirmed it. Six o'clock, near as dammit. "I'm meeting someone. Thank you so much, Dr. Price." He got a handshake, then to Hughes, "if it's ok, I'll touch base with you tomorrow. I'll have my notes typed up first thing."

"That's fine. See you tomorrow."

She rushed off to the women's changing area, gown flapping, boots galumphing. Behind her, the men strolled through to their section, still talking.

Her heart was doing a thousand beats a minute. She yanked off her gown. Her fingers were trembling so much it was actually hard for her to undo it properly and she ended up just ripping it off. Kicked her boots off, slipped on her shoes and edged back towards reception, listening. The men were in their changing area.

There was a security button by the main exit. She pressed and the door clicked open. She then let it slam shut. The sound echoed for a moment off bare walls and the polished hospital floor.

For just a second, her heart switched off and she had a moment of something that passed for clarity

Apart from anything else, there was a certainty in her bones that said, 'this is your opportunity. Use it. Use it now. It's never coming back.'

Quietly now, she slipped off her shoes and walked back to the Ladies' in her stockinged feet. She turned off the light, making sure that the switch didn't click. The room was bare and empty. Nothing to see.

It wasn't too late to reverse course, she knew that. Free will was offering her escape routes with every second that passed and she didn't take any of them. Her heart was still beating too fast, but she felt strangely calm. She opened the cleaning cupboard door, walked inside and pulled the door gently shut.

There was a bucket there and she sat on it. She was in the dark. Hidden. Invisible. Forgotten. She waited.

Noises from outside. Mostly hospital ones. The ventilation system. A window cord tapped in a draught. An electronic beeping from some machine somewhere. The little clicks and creaks of any large building.

And then she heard Hughes and Price walk back out into the reception area. A short pause. Keys. Some muttered conversation, then the click of the front door. The slam of it closing. The turn of the lock. Two pairs of footsteps walking away.

Now it really was too late. Escape routes were well and truly sealed off. She was incredulous at what she'd just done, but was partly incredulous because she didn't regret it at all. Her decision felt entirely right. She felt intoxicated by the simplicity of it all.

For about an hour she didn't move. Bum on a cleaning bucket in a cupboard outside a silent changing room. She didn't even allow herself to shift her weight around or stretch out her legs.

Then she did. Jackson and Price weren't coming back. She very much doubted if hospital security patrolled there at night. The dead aren't known for their rowdiness, and presumably the point of those lock down security procedures is to make sure that what she'd just done can't possibly happen.

She was alone in the mortuary. Alone with the dead.

She assumed that Price had locked the exit and that she was stuck there for the night. She didn't think she'd ever been so excited, so happily excited, in her life. She let some more time pass, taking things slow. No need to rush.

Then finally, she wandered out into the reception area. She poked the rubbery looking plant with her finger to check that it was real, and it was. There were a few odds and ends on the reception desk and she moved them around just to feel her own presence there a little more. There were no security cameras in the ceiling, no nothing. She didn't expect they anticipated much movement from the residents.

She suddenly became aware of being a bit cold. She was wearing a dark skirt, tights, white shirt and a jacket. For obvious reasons, mortuaries are kept on the cool side and it wasn't going to get any warmer overnight. She put on the low healed office shoes that she was wearing earlier, to keep her feet off the floor.

There was something weird about being so formally dressed, given the circumstances.

She wandered about a little more, and tried couple of the internal doors. They all opened easily. Why wouldn't they? The entrance was locked and the place was empty.

In the women's toilets, she put the lights back on and stared at herself in the mirror. Short dark hair. Low key make-up. Dutiful, efficient little face. She could never work out if she looked like herself or if she looked nothing at all like herself. She didn't know. She ran hot water over her hands, then wet her hair, spiking it up, the punk look. More her, or less her? she wondered. She didn't know, but left it spiked.

She was nervous now, really nervous, but she knew what happened next.

She dried her hands, turned off the lights and walked calmly over to Suite 2, where the bodies of Stacey Edwards and the two Mancinis lay. The door was closed, but she knew it wasn't locked from having tested it earlier. She paused for just a moment, not gathering strength, but, well, pausing. If she were the praying kind, which she wasn't, then that was a praying moment. She didn't rush in. She was about to put her hand to the door when she found herself checking that her shirt was tucked in and not rumpled. Had to look smart now.

She went inside. Outside, it was starting to get dark and the room was full of shadows.

An evening room. She didn't put the light on or uncover the corpses. She moved around slowly.

There were two workbenches, a 'dry' area for papers and such like, and a 'wet' area for organs, innards and other delights. The anglepoise lamp. Some wall charts. Not much. The room had its share of hospital noises, but it was the quietest place she'd ever been. The most peaceful.

Emily said hello to Stacey Edwards first. She looked much the same as she did when Emily first saw her. No duct tape. No cable ties. But equally dead. She held her hand for a while and stroked her hair. She had no reason for doing so, as it wasn't why she was there. But she felt it would be wrong to leave her out just because she didn't feel a connection to her. This was the last night of her stay on earth. She'd be joining April and Jenna in the winds tomorrow.

"You'll be all right, love," Emily told her.

She didn't react to that and Emily conceded that she couldn't blame her, given the circumstances.

"You were brave. Did you know that? It was because of you that this whole thing came out. You did a good job. You did your bit."

Then Emily shifted across the room, to the side of Jenna Mancini's gurney. Not a good word, that. Gurney. Clumpy and undignified like orthopaedic shoes. They were only on gurneys because they've already been sliced and diced. They were moved in there as accessories to the Price -Hughes bore fest. No point in moving them back anywhere. Not tonight, their last on earth.

Emily decided that for her, for tonight, for Jenna and April, those gurneys would be their biers. They could lie in state like a medieval queen and her young princess.

She unshrouded Jenna. Top to toe. She folded the cloth up and left it on the dry workbench. The room was dark enough now that most colour had gone. Jenna's hair still looked coppery, but so dark that it was hard to tell any more. It was wonderfully soft and long. Emily had never had long hair, not at least not since she was eight or nine.

There was a circular wound at the back of her head where Price would have sawn through the skull so he could remove the brain for analysis. He was a tidy worker and the join was a neat one. Feeling naughty now, she lifted away the trapdoor of bone and felt inside. Emptiness. There was something wonderfully liberating about the feeling. To be so dead that your skull is actually void, now there's a trick most corpses don't manage to pull off. She allowed her fingers to roam the cavity.

She didn't cut herself off from herself, the way she normally would. She had all night, so she allowed herself to explore. The skull felt like the largest thing in the universe, containing galaxies. She let her fingers drift among the stars, enjoying the space and silence. When she finally fitted the skull back together again, it closed with a hollow clop.

Jenna's expression hadn't changed at all. It was hard to say what her face was communicating. Release, she supposed. That would be the normal thing to say, but then again she was aware that her citizenship of Planet Normal was on temporary hold while certain irregularities with her papers were investigated. Actually, she didn't think 'release' was correct. She didn't look like it was more than that, purer. It was as though death had perfected Jenna, brought her to the best possible version of herself, untouched by life's misfortunes and untouchable now and forever.

She ran her right hand down her body to her feet. All her internal organs had been removed, weighed, measured, analysed. Sometimes they are returned to the body. Other times they're disposed of and the body is packed with cheap fillers. They use pipe insulation for bones, for example. But her skin felt wonderful. It was partly the cold, she supposed. Cold skin always feels smoother, but the truth was that Jenna Mancini was a pretty woman with good skin, and she wasn't all that far from being a real beauty.

Emily pushed gently down on her feet, so they were pointing like a dancer's, not stuck out at ninety degrees like a policeman's. Her fingers could almost completely close around her ankle, whereas Emily was an inch away from being able to the same with her own. She wondered what Mancini could have been with a better start in life. A nursery school worker. A secretary. Strange things to think about when she was lying cold and naked in front of her, and when she knew the commercial uses that nakedness was once put.

"Who killed you, Jenna Mancini? Was it Karol Sikorsky?" Emily asked her softly.

She didn't answer.

"We're going to get him. We're going get to everyone who ever hurt you."

She still said nothing.

"You did your best, I know that. You always did your best."

Emily had an impulse to cover her again, but realised that the dead don't care. Their nudity is as neutral to them as pale blue hospital cloth and white gauze.

She unwrapped April.

Her little body ended at the nose. No eyes. No forehead. No empty cavity in the skull. But she had her lovely little smiling mouth, her skinny little kid's frame, and a hand that happened to lie outstretched towards Emily. She held it, for long enough so that her skin cooled down and April's warmed up. They were the same temperature now and it felt to Emily like they knew each other; old friends.

"And who killed you little April?"

She didn't reply.

Emily was born in April too. Perhaps they had the same birthday.

She smiled at Emily. She liked that.

"You worried about your mum, didn't you? It wasn't easy being you. But you know, she did her best. You did your best. And there's absolutely nothing in the world to worry about now."

Not for them and not for Emily. She wasn't sure how long she stayed with them, but the room was totally dark now with just a little violet light coming from the lamps in the car park outside.

She'd got stiff, so she paced around a bit. She explored the rest of the mortuary. There were three other cadavers that she could find. One old man, a real character by the looks of him. Emily named him 'Good Time Charlie', and he flirted outrageously back at her. Then an obese fifty something man. She didn't get on with him at all, and didn't even give him a name. He wasn't sorry to see her go. Last up was a lovely silver haired woman, naked as the moon and grinning upwards at the ceiling as they sat and chatted. Emily liked her best of all, but it was Jenna and April who'd brought her there and so it was back to them she went.

Emily pulled April's bier over to Jenna's, so she could sit with the mother and hold the daughter's hand. She started telling April a bedtime story. They enjoyed the story to begin with, but then they preferred silence and they sat, the three of them, not talking but feeling happy together.

April was Jenna's daughter.

That was what April was trying to tell her all the time and Emily had only just twigged. April was Jenna's daughter. Jenna herself never really knew her mother, because she was taken into care from an early age. Same thing with Stacey Edwards.

But Jenna stayed close. She did what she could. She wanted to be April's mum and did all she could to be the best one she could possibly be. And April appreciated her mother's efforts. April was Jenna's daughter. Same genes, same blood.

That's what April was trying to tell her.

Emily would have laughed at the simplicity of it all, only this was a night for silence, so her laughter was silent too. One more thing for her to do list.

Emily was as happy then as she'd ever been. Everything was going to be all right.

After some time, she felt tired, so she butted the two biers against each other and lay down in the middle to sleep. She slept holding April's hand and with her face against Jenna's enviable copper hair. They slept the sleep of the dead.

-40-
It was just after dawn. Emily was as stiff as a board and as cold as last night's tea. Jenna and April were doing just fine. They were probably laughing at Emily. She shoved the two gurneys back into their proper positions and re-covered the corpses. She gave each of them a kiss before leaving. Jenna on her forehead, April on what there was left of her cheek. Stacey got a smacker too.

"Goodnight, ladies. Goodnight, sweet ladies. Good night. Goodnight."

She gave them a blast from Hamlet, just so they knew they'd spent the night with a girl who knew her Shakespeare, then pulled her attention back to the escaping train wreck that threatened to undo not just her career but everything she'd sought to build over the last few years.

This problem had only just occurred to her. It didn't once enter her thoughts when she pulled her disappearing stint in the Ladies' last night. It didn't really occur to her when she was planning this particular escapade.

She tried the main exit door, but it was locked, as expected. There was a fire exit, but it had a big green sign telling her that the handle was alarmed and she decided not to risk it.

She really wasn't the climbing out of windows sort, but there wasn't much else available. Jenna and April's window was small, high, and she couldn't see anything to help her on the outside. Then she remembered the viewing room, and thank God, it had a decent sized window and the inestimable blessing of the catering facility roof. She threw her bag outside, which sort of committed her to following it. She wondered what to do about her shoes as they weren't made for climbing out of second floor windows. She took them off and they followed the bag outside. Then her jacket. It was in the way, but she also didn't want to ruin it. She wondered if there was any one in the catering building and whether they'd noticed that someone was chucking their wardrobe down on top of it.

Emily stood on the chair that she'd pulled over to the window and tried to clamber on out. Her skirt was not designed for vigorous athletic activity, but she decided that climbing naked out of a mortuary was worse than climbing out clothed, no matter how undignified. So she tucked her skirt into her tights and bundled herself out. She hurt her thigh on the window catch as she climbed climb out, then her upper arms on the lip of the window as she dropped down. Her left ankle hurt too. She was really, really not cut out for this kind of thing.

Skirt out from tights. Jacket on. Shoes on. Handbag gathered tidily under an arm. She pasted her hair down, but knew it wouldn't look right without a shower. Still, she looked thoroughly respectable she thought, apart from the fact that she was standing on the roof of the mortuary's catering facility at five in the morning. There were a few people floating around but they were mostly support staff types who didn't care whether there was a mad woman on top of their building or not.

She probed around for a while, looking for a way down. Alas, nobody thought to provide her with a ladder, so she ended up hanging off a drainpipe, dropping a few feet to the ground and hurting her ankle for a second time, only worse.

She sat among the pile of bin bags for a few minutes swearing until she felt better. Then she hobbled over to her car and blipped it open. Where to now? Her first instinct was home to Mum and Dad. They were only a few minutes away, and Mum was always up ridiculously early. She started driving that way, but no more than thirty seconds later she changed her mind and set course for home. Her home.

She was wildly happy. Huge ocean waves of happiness come crashing down around her. Last night was great, but it was peaceful. This morning was great. She wanted to honk her horn, kiss strangers, drive at a hundred miles an hour and shower the world with roses.

She put the soft top down, drove too fast and played music at maximum volume. She couldn't stop smiling and didn't even try.

-41-

The funeral was a hundred million times better than she expected. There were so many people there that the crematorium couldn't accommodate them. Most of the service was held outside and amplified on loudspeakers. Probably eighty per cent of those present were schoolkids, there only because their schools decided to make a statement, but Emily didn't care. Schoolkids are the perfect audience anyway. The ones April would care most about. The trumpeter was fantastic. The string quartet was a bit too polite and quiet to make much of an impact, but April and Jenna and Stacey must have been flabbergasted to find themselves with a string quartet at all. The solo vocalist was much better. Apart from Emily's, there wasn't a dry eye in the house. The rent a quote pop star did turn up. She read a sentimental poem badly and everyone cried. There were heaps of flowers too. She didn't know if they were all hers, but she didn't care. They all had petals, and that's the way April and Emily liked them.

A conveyor belt took the coffins out of the room where the service took place and off to the furnace. Red curtains divided one side from the other. When April's tiny coffin went sailing down the conveyor belt to the curtains, everyone in the entire building started clapping. Emily thought some of the schoolkids started it, because they didn't know what they were meant to do, but felt they had to do something. Anyway whoever started it, it was the right thing to do and it only took a moment for everyone, inside and outside, to be clapping and clapping hard.

She thought it was possible that she was the only one not to have tears in her eyes. Most people present actually had tears running down their cheeks.

She wondered what it was like. Mostly though she was with April on her last journey. Into the fire. Up the chimney. Into the wind. She was happy now. Her and Jenna. Stacey Edwards too, she expected. They were all happy now. Happy ever after.

-42-

After the funeral, a couple of things.

Books was there. Emily didn't know how he knew she cared, because she hadn't made a song and dance about it. He didn't come close to her at the service itself, because he wanted to give her space. But as everyone spilled out of the crematorium itself into the flower-beddy bit outside, he came up and squeezed her arm.

"You ok?"

"Yes."

"That was quite a send-off."

"Yes."

"Must have taken a fair bit of organization on someone's part."

She smiled at him. "Yes."

They chatted a bit longer, and she noticed that Books was taut about something. Was he angry? Angry with her? She didn't know. If he was, she didn't know why. But it wasn't the place to ask him, so they said a few more things to each other, feeling strained, then said they had to rush off to something else. Which in his case was probably true. They still had a date for the following night, theoretically. Whatever it as, it would come out when it was ready.

More important, though – more important for Emily anyway – was something that Bryony Williams had for her. She was there, of course. No black for her. Rainbow top and big chunky beads. The kind of thing Emily would look awful in. She gave Emily a huge hug and told her she was fantastic.

"Good trumpeter," Emily said. "He wouldn't even charge me."

"I should bloody well hope not."

Bryony went on to say how much she liked the poem and how well she thought the pop star read it. Emily agreed because she didn't want to spoil the mood. Bryony said something about it looking good on television, and Emily was confused because she didn't know anything about TV, but sure enough there was a camera and a sound man up in a gallery at the back. She spotted them packing up their stuff and leaving.

"And I brought you this," Bryony went on.

She held up a sheet of paper. One of Emily's notes. Nothing on it, other than her handwriting.

As she started to look puzzled, Bryony switched the paper around. On the back, someone had written, *'Try the old lighthouse. Kill the bastards.'*

Bryony explained, "you know that bag I carry around with me when I'm on patrol? Soup, condoms and health leaflets. That's what it's full of normally. When I was unpacking it on Sunday night, I found this inside. I don't know who put it there or when. I don't know what it means."

The old lighthouse.

Emily knew what it meant. She needed to spend some time with Google Earth and Postcode Finder to get a location, but that was just a question of time. She realised she was grinning like an idiot.

"You look like you've got what you were looking for," said Bryony.

"The last twenty-four hours," Emily said, "have been the best of my entire life."

-43-

Morning.

Just a week or two away from the longest day of the year. The merry old sun nosed above the rooftops just after four, but the sky was full of light and emptiness long before that. Emily was awake by about three thirty, having only got to sleep sometime after midnight.

She put some music on downstairs, found some food and rolled herself a joint. She lay in bed listening to music, eating and smoking. She handled her gun with eyes shut. Safety on, safety off. Magazine in, magazine out. Reload the magazine. She liked the way the bullets clipped in. It was neat, precise and metallic. Reliable and with a purpose.

She thought about April's funeral. Little April, blind and dead, now free to take the next steps on her journey, whatever they may be. Already her connection with Emily was looser. Looser in a good way. She had told Emily the thing she needed. A thing so laughable in its simplicity that she couldn't believe it took her so long to notice it. She knew she could be a total idiot at times, but quite liked that. She preferred people who aren't too simple.

By four thirty she was restless. There was no need to wait for anything, so she got up, showered and dressed. Boots, trousers, top, denim jacket. An impulse took her to the mirror and she rubbed styling gel through her hair, spiking it up. Then make-up. Red lips, killer eyes. Tooled up and ready to motor.

She was in the car and driving by a quarter past five. There was rain due later, but the day opened fine and bright. It felt like it was on parade for a morning inspection. Shadows ruled out on roads and pavements with stencil edged accuracy. Lawns mown. Cars all present and correct. Nothing moved except Emily.

She was flying west, the sun at her back. Music loud, energy bar, handcuffs, gun, ammo and phone on the passenger seat. Her car's shadow flew along the road in front of her and she flew after it, trying to race the turning world. She passed the turn where she and Books had been for their day out. The sea lay somnolent and glittering, watching her as she drove. It was not impressed.

Eventually she drove more slowly as she hit unfamiliar lanes. Cows on the road. Just been milked and on their way to pasture. A farm worker with a hazel switch and a collie walked behind the cows, nudging them back into their field, then raised a hand at her as she passed. Emily waved back and drove on.

Sea on every side now, except her back. Straight ahead, her target. A nowhere place in a nowhere land. An old lighthouse that lights nothing and protects no one.

Not just an old lighthouse, but The Old Lighthouse. And it was white. She knew that from photos. It was hard to access and remote.

Until she got there, she couldn't be entirely certain, but every possible indication was pointing to the same location.

This was the tip of infinity, the edge of oblivion.

It was seven fifteen and Emily was ready.

-44-

A mile or so away from her destination, she parked up. The verge was so thick with tall stalks of cow parsley that she had to mow a swathe through them to get off the road. All their pretty white decapitated heads. Gulls wheeled above her, and the sea chuckled at her presumption.

Gun. Phone. Handcuffs. A pocketful of ammo. She didn't need anything else. With a bit of luck, she would only need the cuffs and the phone. She checked it for signal and was relieved to see that it was running at full strength.

Emily walked slowly towards the lighthouse, cutting through the fields, and navigating by feel. It wasn't hard. She aimed for the sea, and the sea was all around her. A couple of wheat fields first, the crop just starting to show the first hints of gold. Sea breeze. Gorse and broom blazed yellow in the hedges. Then a field of sheep and her view of the lighthouse.

It was a smaller building than she'd constructed in her head. A stubby little tower, disused and doing nothing. A low building beneath it, almost barrel shaped against the slope. A door, with half a dozen stone steps running up to it. Two windows that she could see. Maybe more that she couldn't. A dirt parking area with a Land Rover, nothing else. There was a barbed wire fence around the property and a locked gate, but nothing impenetrable. More of a warning to tourists to keep their distance than anything else.

She was relieved to see just the one car. Two would have scared her. But then she saw something that she didn't like at all.

Along the coast, maybe four hundred yards along, there was a boat moored offshore. A blue boat with a dirty white stripe along the side. Martyn Roberts's boat, if the image on his website was to be trusted.

The only charter boat captain who didn't want her to check his sailing log. He who had hung up when she was at Rattigan Transport, making enquiries. The ex-con.

As she watched, a rubber dinghy chugged out from the shore. It was hard to tell from this distance, but it looked like there were three figures on board. Hard to tell, but she thought that two of them were male, one female.

She felt unprepared. An amateur.

She felt the same way as when she saw Lev fight for real. Still practice fights – she'd never seen him try to hurt anyone – but fights where he was up against someone with almost his own level of training and ability. She realised when she watched those things that she was a million miles from being ready for serious conflict. She realised how vulnerable she truly was.

She should have brought binoculars. She should have been there two or three hours ago. She should have come with Lev or Books or both of them. She should have forced a meeting with DCI Jackson and insisted on him sending a full armed response unit to the scene and threatened to resign if he refused.

She could have even done that now. Call Jackson, tell him where she was., tell him what she thought was going on. Tell him that she needed helicopters and divers and marksmen and vehicles there in an instant. But those things could not be there in an instant. All that was there was Emily and there was no time to lose.

She took the gun out of her pocket and started running.

She was running fast through the sheep field. Then there was another field, along slope of cropped grass and lichened stone, running down to the sea's edge and the lighthouse. The windows were angled away from her direction of approach. The door didn't open. She hoped that nobody would walk around the side of the building.

Fifty yards from the lighthouse, she stopped. Heart yammering, blood racing. This was it. What Lev prepared her for.

You never get a fight where or when you want it. You never get the fight you prepared for. You only get the fight when it reaches out for you. And that moment was now. Battle music.

She let her pulse rate slow, then scaled the locked gate and walked purposefully towards the lighthouse door. She kept her eyes on the door. Every five paces, she swept her gaze round everything else. The little dinghy had reached the boat. There was nothing stirring in the car park. There was a little shack housing a wood pile and some basic tools. There was no one moving to either side or behind her. The sun and the sea were her audience. Seagulls yelled their disapproval.

She arrived at the base of the stone steps. She couldn't tell if the door was locked. There was no sound from anywhere, except the sea, sky and gulls.

If the door was locked, she would shoot the lock out, she decided. If the door was unlocked, she'd sweep it open with her left hand and have her gun up and ready in her right. She visualized both motions, then ascended the steps.

She was there in an instant. Time seemed to move in jerks. Quantum jumps from one state to another, no smooth passage in between. She was at the door. Ready. Go.

Her left hand tried the catch. It was free. She swept the door open. Gun up and ready top fire. Heart in her mouth was an understatement. Heart somewhere through the top of her head and thumping around in the ceiling joists was more accurate.

But there was no threat inside the room. Just horror.

Huw Fletcher was there all right. The man she wanted to catch. Alive and catchable.

He wasn't going to offer much resistance either. Not the way he was then. Poor old Fletcher was in a state of disassembly. He lay against the wall, mute, unmoving, eyes staring through Emily and beyond into the ruins of his future. On the floor next to him lay the fingers of his right hand. His ears. His tongue. Blood leaked from between his legs, from his mouth, arm and the side of his head. He was alive, but the loss of blood may yet collect his soul, she thought.

She didn't feel sorry for him. She felt a fierce rage, made fiercer by coming face to face with its target. These were strong feelings, but they were hers and they were human. They belonged to her and she wasn't afraid.

She said nothing to Fletcher. She did nothing to help him. She cared about him not at all.

Treading around the pools and splashes of blood, careful not to make a footprint, she made for the flight of steps heading down to the cellar.

Emily had her gun in a double grip now, but it had become part of her. An instinct. A single being. She was Lev and her name was vengeance. What lay below was worse, she knew it, than anything that lay bleeding above. She kicked open the door and swept the room through the sight of her gun.

She had found what she'd come for.

-45-

And what she found was horror. A horror beyond description. A horror that she knew, even before her gun sight had finished sweeping the room, would last the rest of her days. Time's ruinous fingers may, one day, muddle and obscure this moment, but what had been done there could never be set to rights, could never be undone.

What she saw were four women. They were naked, except for long T-shirts, white once but grubby now. Each of the women was chained by her ankle to one of a number of iron hoops set into the wall. The floor was covered in straw. Lots of it, like a freshly prepared cow barn. Except none of it was fresh. Buckets steamed in a corner under a tiny window. The women were dirty. Their hair was rank and uncombed. They were all too thin. All bruised, some nastily. They had the string eyes of people who are shocked beyond shocked. And steaming high on heroin to boot. There were ten iron hoops altogether. Six of them were empty.

She took it all in and, in a movement as natural and spontaneous as drawing breath, vomited. A single reflexive gag. Just one. Time was moving ahead with its jerky quantum beat and the reflex that made her retch was already jerking away from her into the past.

So, she thought, it's got to be like this, has it? She had to deal not just with Fletcher but with all Sikorsky's ugly buddies too. So be it. Let them all come. It is what it is and she was ready. She just hoped Roberts's shitty little trawler wasn't full yet. If it was, then she would forever hate herself for arriving too late.

It was one of those situations, one of those blessed situations, where for once her instincts moved faster and more wisely than her brain.

Before she knew it, she was signalling 'shush' to the women, but she doubted if any of them spoke much English. She started ripping off her own clothes as fast as she could, hurling them into the angle of the cellar door where they couldn't be seen from the stairs. There was a stack of more dirty white T-shirts in the corner of the room, piled on top of some army-surplus grey blankets. She took one of the shirts and put it on. She hated the feel of it, the way it made a slave of her, but in that place slaves were invisible, and invisibility was her friend.

She frisked her own clothes to grab the ammo from the jacket pocket, then decided she needed her boots and put them on again. There were only ten bullets in her gun. If it came to unarmed combat, she'd be more effective if she could kick.

Emily made for the corner of the room. There was a single bulb in the centre of the ceiling, but it didn't cast much light in her corner. She lay down, covering her booted feet with a blanket.

She made the 'shush' signal hard and aggressively to the women, two of whom had started talking rapidly in what she thought may have been Romanian. They didn't stop talking, but then she aimed her gun at their heads and they did. They were still staring at her and she tried to gesture at them to look away.

She lay there in the straw, in the pit created by Rattigan.

A place for him to bring girls from Eastern Europe. A place to get them high on heroin, to rape them, abuse them, half starve them, knock them around, until they dropped dead or until he decided he wanted a fresh supply. Rattigan and whichever of his buddies happened to amuse themselves the same way.

She didn't know if Fletcher shared the same tastes, or if he was just happy. Rattigan's fixer who made it all happen. She guessed a bit of both, but Fletcher was only ever really the ops man. The guy who got the girls onto the ships, then off again. A shipping guy. The logistics man.

Then Rattigan dropped into the sea. Properly dead. No messing around. A common or garden plane crash. And, with the boss's body still bouncing around on the sea floor, the idiot Fletcher, a pygmy who mistook himself for a giant, decided to go it alone. Presumably there were clients who Rattigan chose to bill. Perhaps they chose to pay. Perhaps Fletcher thought this was a business venture he could expand.

A mistake. The worst mistake of his life. A mistake that had currently cost him his ears, tongue, and fingers, not to mention the blood blackening the floorboards upstairs. Did Fletcher decide to keep the Rattigan name? quite possibly. Balcescu reacted to Rattigan as though he were alive. Perhaps Fletcher pretended that the boss had faked his own death, was still alive and operating. Or maybe Balcescu was just behind the times. Either way, her reaction was one of the clues that led Emily to that place.

Anyway, for a while Fletcher made some money. The business worked. But if you want to play hardball with Russian gangsters, you've got to be as tough and as hard and as ruthless as them. Rattigan was. He had the cash. More than that, he had the ability, the charisma, the swaggering drive, the aggression. Fletcher was a pygmy waddling around in the clothes of a giant. Before too long, he tripped over his own hem and his nice Russian friends took advantage. Probably they didn't like someone making a fool of them. More than likely they thought that if Fletcher had an operation that was making money for him, it would make even more money for them. They decided to march in, take over Fletcher's turf, tighten up.

Jenna Mancini was the first victim. That debit card of Rattigan's. Once upon a time he told her more than he should have done, but let her live. Jenna, foolish girl, said more than she should have done to her friend Stacey Edwards and word got back to the lads from Russia. She got to hear that she was in danger. Escaped to her squat, but she needed to be in a different continent. A different street wouldn't do. The people hunting her tracked her down and killed her. April too, for no reason beyond ensuring that her little six-year-old mouth held its silence. No doubt Sikorsky was the killer, but he was just a hired man, the small fry. The Mancini case, for Emily, was never about Sikorsky.

The same thing with Stacey Edwards. She spoke too much. Threw accusations around. Made a noise. Sikorsky visited her too. Killed her in a way that sent out a signal. The sort of signal that the Russian boys were so good at sending. Silence or else.

Emily had worked it out, even though she knew DCI Jackson would certainly have told her it was mostly speculation, but she knew you can't always reach the truth without a little wild surmise along the way. Perhaps the exact story would prove to be slightly different in minor respects, but she would bet her life that she'd got the gist of it. More than likely, the full details would never emerge. They usually didn't.

But she hadn't reckoned on this particular endgame. It hadn't occurred to her that the clean-up would extend out there. She hadn't guessed they might be this effective and this ruthless. She hadn't thought laterally enough, because she thought the pygmy Fletcher would represent her opposition.

More fool her. But you live and learn as they say. Of course, it might be 'die and learn' in this particular instance, but there were worse things than being dead, as she knew better than most.

She wriggled down into the straw and felt the prickle of its cut ends through her T-shirt. Straw against her breasts, thighs and tummy. You couldn't live like this and not become half beast. Kept alive so a bunch of rich men could abuse you, beat you, then dump your body out at sea when they were done. It would be hard to stay human, living like that, dying like that.

The room was silent now. The two Romanians had ceased their chatter.

The gulls outside were inaudible. There was just the tick of straw settling down and possibly, unless it was her imagination, the drip of Fletcher's blood from upstairs.

She remembered the targets at the firing range. Black and white. Black to congratulate her for a chest shot. White to mark her down for a shot anywhere else. She imagined her targets. Imagined their black centres. Brought to mind all the bull's eyes she'd scored, at longer range and in worse light conditions.

Once again, she was ready. She was perfectly still and perfectly ready.

-46-

It took longer than she thought. Longer than she wanted. Perhaps her perceptions of time were altered. Perhaps they were taking their boat out into the Irish Sea before coming back there. Or perhaps something else. Maybe something obvious, like stopping for tea, or having a bite to eat. Must take it out of you, after all, slicing off Fletcher's body parts, hauling women onto the handy little motorboat. A comrade must want a bit to eat after all that work. Black tea and jam.

She didn't know how long it was, but she guessed and hour, before she heard boots on the step outside, the door opening and voices.

Voices and laughter. She didn't recognise the words, but guessed from the tone that they were talking to Fletcher. Laughing at him.

She hoped so. She hoped Fletcher was still alive. She wanted him alive, and mute, and crippled, and behind bars for the rest of a very long life. He deserved no mercy.

Then the boots and the voices came downstairs.

Emily's heart rate didn't change. There was no separation between her and her feelings. For once in her life, she had no difficulty at all in feeling alive, in feeling the way a human is meant to feel. It was crazy, but she felt at peace. Integrated.

They were still talking as they came down the steps. Stone steps with stone wall on either side and a cellar all of stone as well. The sound of those voices was tubular, echoey. Hard to gauge how distant they were.

She had face pressed down into the straw. To these men, one more slave woman was just a counting error. But her rock-chick make up would give her away and she wanted that moment to be as late as possible, so she deliberately deprived herself of a full view.

She assumed there were two men. The two she'd seen taking the girl onto Roberts's boat, now come back to collect the next one.

She waited for both men to fully enter the cellar. If they'd noticed that there were the wrong number of women there, they hadn't yet shown any sign of it. The man in front had a leather jacket on over a white T-shirt. The one behind was shorter and she didn't see him properly. They were killers. Russian killers. Sikorsky's chums there to complete their business.

Emily moved. Still lying prone, she swept her gun out in front of her. Aimed up, at the first man's chest. Not black on white the way it was at the firing range. There, the man's T-shirt was the target and at that range she could not possibly miss.

She fired.

She couldn't even hear the shot. Her senses were leaping way ahead of her brain. They were telling her what she needed to know and what she didn't. The concussion of the shot was irrelevant. All that mattered was that it was a perfect bull's eye. A chest shot. Lethal.

The man went down, and she was leaping up, firing as she moved. The second man was moving too, jumping back to the cellar steps. Her first shot missed altogether. Her second shot hit him in the hip. The third in the leg.

If she had wanted to fire that third shot into the chest, she could have done. But she didn't. She wanted there to be nothing swift about the way that justice claimed those men. The first man had to die. There was no other practical solution. The second one had his hip smashed and his thigh pulverized. He wasn't going anywhere.

And, fool that she was, she thought she was done. That was where Lev would be still moving. Reloading. Keeping the initiative. That was where she was thinking, thank God I'm finished.

And she almost was.

Mr. Russian the Third came plunging down the stairs, a gun in his hand, aiming to kill her. He only didn't because he was temporarily confused. He must have come down expecting a man, or at the very least someone with proper clothes on. All he found were five half-naked women, and it took him a second too long to work out which of them had been shooting up his buddies.

He shot. Emily shot.

The air was ablaze with sound. So loud that she registered the concussion more than the noise itself. As if some natural disaster were translated into sound and compressed into this narrow gap of time and space.

She didn't even know what was happening. Didn't know until the hammer of her gun clicked and clicked on emptiness. She didn't know until she noticed that the man she was shooting at had a smashed hand, a smashed shoulder and a pair of bullet wounds that straddled the gap between his lung and his kidney. He wasn't shooting. He wasn't standing. He wasn't even moving much, unless you counted his good hand, which kept touching different parts of his body and coming away crimson and horrified.

All the time Emily was shooting, she thought he was shooting back at her. She had to check her own body, by eye and by hand, to convince herself she hadn't been hit. She realised that, thanks to her tiny advantage, her having enjoyed a clear target and him being confused by a choice of five, he never even got a shot away. She was standing over him as she worked it all out, watching blood jet from his belly, pulsing in time with his heart.

But her brain was starting to engage properly now. Her moment of triumph was over and there were steps up above her just now, running hard out of the lighthouse.

She snapped handcuffs over the two wounded men, cuffing them to each other. She tried to reload her gun, but her hands were shaking so much she couldn't do anything right. Instead, she grabbed the Russian's gun, which lay useless on the floor, and then she was up and out of the lighthouse. She ran past Fletcher, down the steps and out of the house, through the gate, which had been unlocked and was swinging open.

It was the cliff path she was after.

She didn't run hard. She wasn't sprinting. She wasn't in good enough shape to run at maximum pelt and then be useful for anything afterwards. A couple of times, when the view widened, she saw a man running ahead of her. Jeans and a T-shirt. He couldn't have a gun, she thought, or he wouldn't be running.

The ground underfoot was Ok. It was dry enough and there was a proper path. But it was not even. Rocks protruded. There was churned ground where puddles once lay. Gorse roots and sudden twists. She needed to keep her eyes on the path in front of her, so she was able to look ahead less than she wanted.

Then she came around a bend and face to face with the man. Waiting for her.

He had no gun, but he had an axe. Snatched from the wood-pile at the lighthouse, Emily guessed.

She raised her gun and fired. Nothing happened. There was no bullet in the chamber, so she pulled the trigger again and still nothing happened. Apart from pulling the trigger, she had no idea what she was meant to do. If she'd had more time, she would have sat down with the gun on her lap and worked it out. But she had no time. She knew and the man knew it. She threw the gun far back into the field behind her, depriving her opponent of a weapon that he presumably did know how to use, but it wasn't much of a victory at that stage.

The man grinned. He wasn't even swift or oblique in his triumph. He was thinking, 'I've got the bitch and I can take my time. Take my time and enjoy it.'

He drew the axe back. It was a long handled thing, not a hatchet. Its head and shaft were grey-brown, a tone equidistant between wood and rust. The sun lay behind the man and the axe, so he was just a silhouette and his shadow etched its double on the grass.

Emily suddenly realised that it was Sikorsky. He hadn't escaped. He wasn't in Poland or Russia. He was there, completing his assignment.

She thought she was stupid, but he was worse.

Something Lev taught her. A distrust of long handled weapons. They feel good in the hand, but they take too long to swing. You expose yourself as you swing them. Too easy to evade, and, especially for her. Small fighters lack power, but they move faster. At that moment, Emily knew she wanted speed rather than power.

She gave Sikorsky his moment. The axehead up in the sun. The semi naked woman in front of him. A lovely day for murder.

"Zdravstvuite, Karol," she said, pleasantly.

He swung. His movement was over-signalled. Too big and too slow. Emily moved to one side, deflecting the axe shaft with an arm. At the same time, she kicked hard at his shin. As hard as she could. As hard as she'd ever kicked.

It wasn't the best move in the world. A good kick at a knee cap has more scope to disable. But right then she was in risk minimization mode. The boots she was wearing were adapted for her by Lev himself. Steel tipped. Nasty.

The Russian discovered the meaning of pain and for a second or two was out of action with it.

All the time in the world.

Another hard kick to his other shin brought him to his knees. As he came down, his chin came towards her and that got a hammering as well. He was on the ground moaning now, so she kicked him once more on the side of his head. A really hard one. Steel toecap connected with the bone. His head jerked back and a spray of blood droplets made patterns in the sunlight.

She could imagine Lev congratulating her for that one.

Sikorsky jerked spasmodically and lay still. Not dead, because he was still breathing, but there were blood bubbles on the corner of his mouth.

She wasn't sure what to do now. She didn't have her handcuffs with her. Her phone was back at the lighthouse. The guy was hurt, but he'd recover. She couldn't afford to let him get to the boat.

She peered over the edge of the cliff. She wasn't brilliant with heights, but she wasn't awful, and in any case these were special circumstances. The cliff wasn't all that high, maybe fifty feet, and it rolled down at seventy degree or so to the vertical. Good enough.

She gave Sikorsky another good kick in the head. No point in taking chances. Then bundled him over the edge. All a bit improvised, but improvisation was her strong suit. He rolled down like a sack of potatoes wrapped in a carpet. He bounced lifelessly, like a punctured football. She couldn't see the base of the cliff, so she didn't know what happened at the bottom. She couldn't even hear anything. Half deaf from the gunfire earlier, she couldn't even hear the waves.

She was tired now. Unbelievably thirsty.

She trudged into the field behind and found the gun. There was a slide on the barrel, and she knew it wouldn't take long to work out.

The journey back to the lighthouse seemed like a hundred miles and felt every inch of it. Despite her T-shirt, she felt completely naked. She didn't like violence, but she'd learned it, studied its dark and unpredictable arts. What she'd just done revolted her. What had happened there was revolting.

When she got back to the lighthouse, she couldn't go in straight away. To the house of horror. Fletcher's mute, repulsive eyes.

For a minute or two, she sat on the stone steps and just let herself be. She wasn't consciously practicing her breathing, but these things had become part of her now, and she did it without noticing sometimes. Her pulse rate slowed and she felt calmer. She noticed what an extraordinarily beautiful day it was. What a beautiful place. Cropped grass, lichened stone and the endless cerulean sea.

Since parking her car on the verge above the lighthouse, there had been no barrier between her and her feelings. None at all. She had never been herself as much as that for so long.

Then she dragged herself inside. That dark interior, home to so much cruelty. Fletcher was alive but unconscious. The bleeding seemed to have stopped, so she decided not to move him. She didn't trust herself to make good decisions then. Better to get the professionals to look after things. She went downstairs, picking her way over the two semi-conscious men and avoiding the dead one.

The women stared at her. They didn't know they'd been saved. Maybe they didn't know they'd been about to be killed. In any case, given what they'd been through, their salvation was a good way off. They may never find it. Jenna Mancini never did. Stacey Edwards never did. It's no good living in a world at peace if your own head is at war with itself.

She couldn't find the keys to unlock the women, and in any case that was not a priority. She checked the two handcuffed men. They weren't in good shape, but they were alive and she didn't feel like giving them first aid. She found her clothes and phone. There was no signal in the cellar, so she walked back outside to the steps and called Jackson.

He started to give her a bollocking for going AWOL and she interrupted to tell him where she was and what she'd found. She told him there was one man dead and four others who might or might not be dead by the time help arrived. She also told him about the boat.

"There's at least one woman on it. I'd guess more. Maybe as many as six. I'm pretty certain they were going to be taken out into the Irish Sea and thrown overboard. You need a helicopter from above, and divers ready for an instantaneous rescue job if whoever is on board tries to dump the evidence. And if you can find some snipers from anywhere, you might want to take them."

Jackson, bless the man, took her at face value. He believed her. He told her to stay on the line. She could hear him barking orders, using his landline, getting the clean-up operation mobilized. Every now and then he checked in with Emily. Precise location of the vessel. Identifying marks. Number of men guessed to be onboard. She didn't have an answer for that one, but it couldn't be many.

It was easy for her now. Someone else was making decisions, getting the job done. She unzipped her boots and took them off. The little stone steps made something of a suntrap. A nice place to lie around, but she got dressed properly. Trouser. Top. Boots. She remembered about the ammo in her jacket pocket and took it out. She popped back inside and left it on the table in the upstairs room. She gave it a quick polish in the lining of her jacket to remove some of her prints and sweat.

She left the Russian's gun next to the ammo. She was gunless now. Fully clothed, yet she felt naked. Too naked. Bracing herself one last time against the horror, she went back inside and retrieved the gun. She sniffed it. It hadn't been fired that day. Chances were, it hadn't been fired in any place that would give the ballistics people the opportunity to get the measure of it. These days, guns are one use only affairs. Used once, then ditched. The throwaway society.

The Russian gun was bigger than hers, but not too big. Not unusably big. She quite liked the heft of it, the greater weight, the absence of compromise. A gun for grown-ups.

She wondered what to do with it. Hand it over to the good folk who were about to arrive? Keep it for herself? That was the answer her instinct preferred. She liked having a gun. She slept better for it. She felt more complete owning a weapon and knowing how to shoot it. But it had been a big day and these questions felt bigger than she wanted to address right now.

In the field above the lighthouse, there was a little stone sheepfold. An old one, set down and into the hill. She went to the shed with the woodpile, rooted around and found an old fertilizer sack. She wrapped the gun in it, then jogged up the hill to the sheepfold and stowed the gun in its fertilizer sack somewhere down in the rocks at the back. She could just about see where she'd hidden it, but it looked like an old bit of dirty plastic. A good place for a gun to be.

She was just walking down the hill when she heard a helicopter coming over and spied two boats skimming over the waves. The helicopter had its side door open and two rifle bearing snipers were looking out.

Good work Jackson. Fast work too. Behind her she heard sirens. Police cars. Ambulances. Big men who knew how to deal with the mess she'd helped create. She welcomed their arrival. By the time they came, she was sitting on the stone steps, shaking and shaking and shaking.

-47-
Emily was thinking that one of the very best things about this country is the quality of its coppers. She knew there is the odd rogue, of course, and more than a few idiots, but she was content to contemplate such thoughts as Jackson made her drink milky, sweet chocolate at a café. He'd ordered her beans on toast because he thought she needed to eat. She gave it her best shot.

"Four women on board," he told her, then paused. "I don't know if you want to hear this now, but given what you've already seen today, I suppose you may as well know."

She nodded.

"Four women. None of them English speakers. Duct tape over their mouths. Hands cable-tied behind them and breeze blocks chained to their ankles. They were just going to take them out to sea."

"I know."

"Can you imagine it?"

DCI Jackson, he of the bushy eyebrows and the growly demeanour, couldn't complete his sentence. He didn't need to. Emily knew what he was going to say and she knew how he felt.

She thought she felt the same. Almost. She didn't have tears at her disposal, of course, or that easy familiarity with her own feelings that Jackson had. But still. The glass wall between her and her feeling had got thinner these last few weeks. At times it hadn't even been there at all. She hadn't been normal, but was closer to normal than she'd been since before she got ill. She could tell how DCI Jackson felt and thought she felt something almost similar. The feeling was a sad one, but nothing was as bad as not feeling anything at all.

She felt so proud of herself for being there, sharing the same emotional space as Jackson, that part of her wanted to laugh for happiness. She didn't, though, as it would spoil the mood.

"It wouldn't have been the first time," she said. "I think Roberts was doing the same work old work for new customers."

"Yes. I agree. I'm sure you're right."

Emily made a face and tried to eat some beans. They seemed like heavy going, so she drank some hot chocolate instead. Jackson asked the waitress to bring another. Emily wanted to object, but knew that he'd do it anyway. She only stopped shaking about ten minutes ago.

"I expect one day you'll want to tell me how you knew to go looking in a remote lighthouse. You'll probably also want to tell me how come you decided it was good idea to storm in there yourself instead of asking me to supply the required resources."

"First question: I had a tip off," Emily said. "Conspiracy hearsay bollocks from a prostitute. As for why I didn't tell you, well, you'd have told me it was conspiracy hearsay bollocks. Unwarranted speculation. And I don't blame you. Would you even have got a search warrant?"

"Emily, you are one of my officers. I won't say you're the easiest person I've ever managed, but you're still one of mine. You could have got yourself killed today and it's my responsibility to make sure that doesn't happen."

There was a pause and she left it, and wondered what he would say if he knew even half the truth about her and her real role.

"Bloody hell, Emily, you seem to have looked after yourself all right."

He shook his head instead of continuing, but she got the gist. How come a will-o'-the-wisp thing like Emily ended up wreaking so much destruction? When the cavalry did come charging over the hill to rescue her, she was so grateful for their arrival and in such a state of shock that it took her about forty minutes to remember that she'd found Sikorsky, the one that everyone had been looking for. When she remembered, and started trying to tell people about it, and how she'd tipped him over a cliff, they assumed she was blathering nonsense. Eventually, she got so fed up with being patted on the head and patronized that she managed to grab a couple of people and lead them down the cliff path to the spot. Since there was an axe sticking out of the gorse just where she'd told them it would be, and a spray of blood on the path where she'd kicked his head in, they had to take her seriously. It took them fifty minutes to reach the base of the cliff, because they had to get the RAF chopper to fly out some ropes and tackle, and when they did, they found Sikorsky, battered but alive, on the rocks at the bottom.

"I guess I must have learned something at Hendon after all," she suggested.

"You know there's going to be an inquiry here? A massive one. Blow by blow forensics, the whole works. Don't get me wrong. I think you did a good job today. If you'd killed all of them it wouldn't bother me. But when a police officer discharges a firearm...."

"I know."

"There has to be an inquiry. And when there's a dead man and three others seriously injured...."

"I know."

"Sikorsky is in intensive care. Injuries to the skull as well as half the bones in his body. I don't know if..."

She didn't care whether the vermin lived or not.

"You fired in self defence."

Half statement, half question, but not one she disagreed with. "Yes."

"That first shot, the man you killed, was fired from a distance. There are no powder marks, and the entry wound was very clean.

There's no sign that any of those coming at you discharged a firearm."

"They'd have killed me. They'd have killed me the same way they were about to kill all those women."

"Emily, this isn't a bollocking. You won't get one from me about this. For a change. But you're going to be asked a lot of questions. You'll need some answers."

"To be honest. I've no idea what happened. I'm more of a logic type than an action type. The whole thing's one big blur really."

The waitress came with hot chocolate and gave it to her. There was something maternal in the way she handed it over. Or rather, it was as though Emily was special needs and she was looking at Jackson to check that she was doing the right thing. He nodded her brusquely away. He'd not done with Emily yet.

"One big blur. That's cute, but..."

"I think there must have been a gun on the table when I came in. I picked it up. I knew I was in a dangerous situation."

"Ok. You wanted to deny firearms to the suspects you were there to apprehend. Good. Then you went downstairs to pursue your investigations further."

She stared at Jackson. Her brain wasn't working too well and it had to turn over a couple of times, like a car starting in the cold, before she got what he was doing. He was giving her the lines. Rehearsing her.

"Yes. I went downstairs to pursue my investigations further. I sought to liberate the women I found, but they were secured with chains."

Jackson nodded. She was doing well. "And you weren't able to call for help, because...."

"Because of the women on the boat. If Sikorsky's men had heard police sirens, the women could have been tossed overboard immediately. I had to let those men come to me, so I could, um...."

"Arrest them," suggested Jackson.

"Exactly. So I could arrest them."

"When they entered the cellar, I expect you identified yourself and gave them an opportunity to surrender their weapons."

Emily stared at him. He really meant it? She went though it in her head. 'Hello, you must be the Russian Gangsters. I'm Emily, just about the lowest ranking police officer that exists. Following budgetary cutbacks, I'm all that's left of our armed response unit and, in the spirit of community togetherness, I'd very much appreciate it if you could lay down your weapons and turn yourselves in. Maybe we could all tidy up the place afterwards.'

Jackson held her gaze without a flicker.

"I expect you shouted, "Police," or, "Drop your weapons," or something like that."

"Police, I probably shouted police."

"Good. You shouted, 'police'," says Jackson, neatly excising her 'probably'. He continued, "They raised their weapons, clearly intending to fire."

"Yes." That bit was true.

"And in the subsequent firefight, you killed one, disabled two and all without any of them getting a shot away."

"That's the blurry bit."

"Then you beat Sikorsky to a pulp and throw him off a cliff?"

"Not throw. It was more of a roly-poly thing."

"Ok. You rolled him off a cliff, because of a continuing desire to protect the women on the boat. Correct?"

"Correct."

"As soon as the threats were secured, you made contact with me, and we come in to apprehend Roberts and secure the vessel."

Emily nodded.

"At least you left something for us to do." Jackson laughed into his coffee. "And by the way, I think you're right. I think if you'd come to me with hearsay and speculation and no grounds for a search warrant. I'd have told you to go away."

"I thought I'd find Fletcher. Maybe some women. I had no idea the Russians would be there. If I had, I wouldn't have gone. And I was confident that I'd be able to handle Fletcher on my own."

"I'll say so. Bloody carnage it was in there. Carnage." He chuckled for a while, then changed the subject. "Jenna Mancini. Do you reckon she was taken there and got away? Or found out some other way?"

"I'm totally guessing now," I said, "but I'm pretty sure the lighthouse was only used for imported goods. I think Rattigan must have had sex with Mancini at some point, perhaps several points, but in whatever place she normally serviced clients. He'd have been high. Talked too much. Maybe he even liked her. The honest truth is, I think he liked her. He wouldn't have told her otherwise. He must have dropped that debit card in her flat and she kept it as a souvenir. Her client, the millionaire."

"Or kept it for its blackmail potential."

"Or thought about buying stuff on it, before losing her nerve. Could have been anything,"

"Pity he's not alive," said Jackson. "It would be nice to send him to jail, wouldn't it?"

"Yes. Yes, it really would."

Emily tried another forkful of beans, but they were not going anywhere and Jackson moved her plate so she stopped annoying him by pretending to eat things that were never going to end up eaten.

"Emily, if anything like this happens again, tell me first. If you've got some conspiracy hearsay bollocks again that you believe in, tell me and I'll believe it too. No more solo flights on my watch, ever, for any reason, ever. Do you understand?"

"Yes."

"But well done. I don't know how many rules you broke today, and I hope to God I never find out, but you saved some lives. You won't get any crap from me about that. Well done."

She ought to have said something in response, but couldn't think of anything straight away. Then Jackson's mobile chirped and he answered it. He was giving someone directions to the café. Emily tuned out. She wasn't feeling quite herself. She thought she needed to go home and lie down. She thought she probably shouldn't drive too fast on the way. She was feeling a bit too sleepy to go fast.

A moment later, Jackson straightened.

"Well, well. Look who it is. Your ride home."

She looked. It was Books. He was looking for her and his face was full of emotion. Jackson took her car keys, promised to get her car back and slotted her into Books's car.

"Are you ok, love?"

"Did you just call me 'love'?"

"Yes."

"Then I'm ok. I'm definitely really fine."

The rain that the weatherman had promised had ridden in from the west. It was one of those rainstorms where huge raindrops whack down on the windscreen, where the road is sheeted in water and even with the wipers on full frantic speed, it was hard to see more than a dozen or so yards ahead. But she didn't care. She was half asleep. Safe and sound. And Books had called her 'love.'

-48-

It was a day and a half later and she was on leave. As much as she wanted. Her only jobs were to eat and sleep and get herself in shape again. Jackson's orders.

Every now and again, someone from the investigation team came along wanting to ask her something about something, and she answered as best she could. There were things she couldn't tell them and things that she couldn't or didn't want to, so she told them the first set of things and withheld the second. Strictly speaking, in fact, there were two investigations. One was the culmination of Lohan, the other was the IPCC inquiry, which had to take place. She wasn't in trouble, exactly, but Jackson had done well to rehearse her.

She stumbled her way through without making a hash of anything. Shock was her excuse, and it was more than an excuse anyway. She had it. Proper shock. 'Traumatic or terrifying event' and all. It was nice to have a textbook case of the syndrome for a change. She recognized that Lev was right and Axelsen was right. She had lived with something like shock for as long as she could remember. She couldn't remember ever having lived without it. So to have it now, in a proper setting and with as much support as she could ask for, was something of a relief. It felt like another part of her descent to Planet Normal. At least this time she had a reason for feeling weird.

At five o'clock Books arrived. He had a couple of grocery bags – chocolate for her and beer for him, ready meals for them both – and bounced over. She was on the sofa, under a duvet, watching kids' tv and enjoying it. There was a story on about a podgy hedgehog who was too fat to curl up into a ball, and she found she genuinely wanted to know what happened.

But she was a grown up and she'd been doing almost nothing all day. She switched off and they kissed.

His range of kisses went on impressing her. Right then he was scoring high in the tender-kiss department: 5.8s and 5.9s every one of them.

They chatted for a while. He told her how Lohan was going. Not really an investigation now. More like a massive clean-up operation. Given what they came across, no magistrate was going to refuse Jackson warrants to search whatever the heck he wanted to. There was a huge forensics operation at the lighthouse. The emphasis was on identifying any punters who may have used it and left a genetic trace of themselves there. Miss Titanium's kingdom was being turned over too. There was almost certainly nothing there, but it amused her to think how she was not going to like it. She hoped she knew she was responsible. Charlotte Rattigan she felt sorry for though. She was not her sort of woman, but she was just another injured party. A long list.

As for the women from the lighthouse, they were being given one-to-one rehab care. Bryony was one of those involved. The women were being shown photos and asked to identify any men who may have abused them. It was going to be a lengthy process. Lots of photos, lots of questions.

Emily had told the team that she knew for a fact that Ivor Harris, MP, was one of the men involved. That was a lie. Emily believed Johnston when he said that Harris would have known about Rattigan's little hobby. Knew about it and kept silent. But neither Johnston nor Emily had any way to know whether Harris was more personally involved, and Emily only handed over Harris's name because she wanted to frighten him and mess up his life as much as possible. If they could find a connection between any of Rattigan's other friends and the lighthouse, then so much the better. Ditto any connection between any of Rattigan's other friends and the lighthouse. Emily wanted everyone who ever set foot in that place without reporting it to the police to do time in jail for the rest of their lives.

Nor did she absolve Johnston. His silence was as lethal as everyone else's. Sins of omission looked prettier, but they still meant duct tape and breeze blocks out in the Irish Sea. Only two things made Johnston any better than the rest. The first was that he swore to her that he knew about the sex trafficking. The violent sex. The slapping around and worse. He said he didn't know the rest. She believed him. Second, at least he nudged her to the right answers. Of all those involved, he was the only one who had tried to do something.

If the current investigation uncovered Johnston's role and jailed him for it, over and above what he got for the embezzlement, then she'd be pleased. That would be the right outcome. Deserved.

But she wouldn't make it happen. Johnston helped her and she wouldn't repay him by grassing on him.

Books and Emily chatted and sometimes just fell silent. They hadn't yet made love, though they were getting closer. She didn't want to make love from a state of shock. They didn't. So they kissed and cuddled and chatted, but as time went on, she noticed that he was starting to get a little taut. Like he was after the funeral.

She asked him what was bothering him. He said nothing, but she knew otherwise. Whatever it was, it would be better to get it off his chest.

Deep breath. Sigh. He got up and paced around.

He was a restless sort. A Labrador retriever. He just couldn't sit still. They both started talking at the same time.

"Look, Em, I don't want to...."

"Did you have any dogs when you were a kid?"

She was the girl, so her question trumped his, but she let hers pass and waited for him.

"Look, it's a stupid thing, but it's been bothering me. That night, Monday, before the funeral. We were going to see each other, but you said you couldn't because you had family over. I thought I'd give you a ring, see if you felt like me popping round afterwards. Just for a quick drink or whatever. No answer from your landline. I was in the area anyway. I probably shouldn't but I came past your house. Lights off, no car. No people. No nothing.

Now I was worried. I don't know why. I'm not normally the jealous type. Not paranoid. But I felt worried. I know you'd been at the mortuary with Hughes, and I just went over there. I don't know why really. Like I say, it's not like me. But there was your car. In the middle of the bloody car park. A long way from any damn family party. And a long time after you'd finished with Hughes."

He wound up. He was embarrassed at having pried, but he also needed an answer. Deserved one.

Her first instinct was to fob him off. Create a story. Make something up. She was supple and inventive and could do that easily. But Books was now her boyfriend and therefore deserved better. It was time for explanations.

She didn't know where to start. She was scared of saying anything at all. She found herself alone with the truth and unsure what to do with it. She could just try speaking it, the naked truth, and trust that Books would not be freaked. She could do that. She could do it now. Unsure of herself, she started out gently.

"As a teenager, I was ill. You know that?"

He nodded. He did. Everyone did.

"Do you know? I don't know if anyone knows what I was ill with. I don't know what the office gossip is."

"There's no gossip, Em. I've always assumed it was some kind of breakdown. It's not my business and it's in the past now anyway."

She smiled at that. "In the past." That was what healthy people say about things and there was no one in the world healthier that Books.

"Do you want to sit?" she said. "It's hard to talk to someone marching around like this."

He sat down opposite her. Old face, serious face.

"Thanks. Yes. Some kind of breakdown, that's correct. The breakdown was a special sort of breakdown. Special enough that it gets its own name. Cotard's. Dr. Jules Cotard. Le delire de negation. Cotard's Syndrome.

Books stared at her, sombre and without judgement. She knew he didn't know what she was talking about, but she was getting there. This was very hard.

"It's a syndrome that sounds funny to the outsider, not funny at all to those who have it. It's a delusional state. It's much more than a breakdown. I was properly, properly delusional. A crazy."

Books nodded. Not scared. Not judgemental. She knew that if she nudged him, he'd repeat that thing about it all being in the past, but she wanted to keep talking before she lost her nerve.

"And the reason why Dr. Jules Cotard got to put his name to this particular syndrome was its oddity. In a mild form, patients suffer from despair and self-loathing, but my form wasn't mild. Not mild at all. I had the full monty. In a severe state, patients hold the delusional belief that they don't exist, that their body is empty or putrefying."

She wanted to stop there, but when she checked Books's face, she could tell he hadn't got it. No normal person would get it from what she'd just said. Deep breath. 'Say it, Emily, say it out loud. Say it to the good man sitting opposite you. Tell him everything and trust that things will be all right.' The voice inside her head. And she did.

"Books, for two years, I thought I was dead."

A pause. A long, long pause.

Time enough for her to worry that she now had an ex-boyfriend. That she was being marched to the nearest rocket station on Planet Normal and was about to be blasted back into the orbit from whence she came. It felt like neither of them had blinked for an eternity.

"And that's what you're telling me? That's where you were that night? In the mortuary?"

She nodded. "With Jenna and April mostly. The Mancinis. And Stacey Edwards actually. In the autopsy suite."

He reached over to her. They were both on the sofa now, Emily leaning against one arm, Books leaning against the other, feet and legs intermingled in the middle. He took hold of her hand and started talking to her in the voice that people reserve for the genuinely nuts.

She interrupted him as he got to the 'it's ok' bit. His mistake was inevitable, of course. Anyone would make it, but the wrongness of it made her laugh.

"No, no. I'm not feeling crazy. I know what craziness is like and this wasn't like it at all. I've seldom felt so alive."

That was her logic. To her, it made sense, but her skills at regular human logic had never been that brilliant and that evening her compass was all askew.

"You spent the night with three corpses, all murdered, and...."

She put up a hand. Time to stop this. "Books, I'm going to need to ask you for some understanding. Sorry, but hear me out. Ever since I made my recovery, well it's not even like that. Cotard's is something that recedes, it never really goes away. Not that I'd admit that to my shrink, mind you. But it's there. I always know that I could one day go into it again. I've been afraid of it every hour of every day since getting better."

"Your shrink. You still...?"

"Not really. With a case like mine, there's a consultant assigned to me, in case stuff happens. I'm meant to go in for a chat every now and then, but I don't. Haven't been for years."

"And that night. In the mortuary...?"

"That night wasn't really a thought-out thing, it was more of an impulse thing. I just felt I needed to be with some dead people. It wasn't just the Mancini's, it was the others there as well. You know, to you, they're dead. They're alien. It actually bothers you that their hearts aren't beating and that their organs are mostly missing. To me, they're just people. They're dead people, but I've been dead myself and I find them pleasant company. Easy, contented, pleasant. If I'm honest, I find them easier to get on with than the living. I know that sounds strange to you, but you're not like me. No one is."

"There's nothing....? Jesus, Em, whether it's true or not, please tell me that there's nothing funny in all this, is there?"

She gawped at him. She didn't know what he meant, so she tried to guess what an ordinary decent human would ask in a moment like this. Then she got it. "Anything sexual? Is that what you were going to say?"

He nodded, pleased that she hadn't make him come out with the words.

"Nothing even a tiny, weeny, remotest bit like sexual. Dead people aren't interested in sex. That's not a joke. We're not. I mean, I wasn't when I was ill as a teenager and they're not now. They're just....they're just dead."

"Ok. Let me get this straight. Stop me if I get it wrong."

She agreed. The mood was getting lighter. She wasn't thinking very clearly, but she knew she'd said the worst thing. The big thing, the Cotard's thing, and Books hadn't leaped up off the sofa. He was still there. Still with her. He hadn't given up. That didn't mean she was in the clear, she knew that, but the worst thing that could have happened hadn't.

She listened to Books's attempt to summarise her summary.

"Once upon a time, there was a doctor. Dr. Cotard," he began.

"Correct."

"He gave his name to Cotard's syndrome."

"Bang on."

"For two years, you were unfortunate enough to suffer from the aforementioned syndrome."

"Two-ish. Dead people aren't all that concerned about time."

"Ok, so about two. Then you got better. Or better-ish."

"I did."

"A few panic attacks, maybe? But nothing you couldn't handle."

"Correct." Not quite correct actually. The first three years or so after 'recovery' were awful. Those years at Cambridge were the worst, with the ghost of her own death peering at her through every gloomy window. She didn't even like thinking about them. They felt worse, in a weird way, than the two years of Cotard's itself.

"Then you find yourself on police business in a mortuary."

"With DI Hughes engaged on Operation Lohan."

"Quite so. And....I don't know. Help me out on this bit. You needed to be with some dead people. Why?"

"I don't know. If I knew, I'd tell you. I think it's because I felt safe enough. I felt sufficiently alive that I could dare to be with the dead. Does that make sense? I was alive, they were dead, we spent some time together. And I felt fine. For the first time since I was fourteen or fifteen, my Cotard's wasn't anywhere to be seen. It was gone."

Emily suddenly noticed that Books's face was full of emotion. There was more emotion there than she had feelings herself.

"That's amazing, Em. If that's true, that's bloody brilliant."

"I don't know if it's true. Like I say, it hasn't gone. I don't think it ever will."

"Well, don't bloody spoil it now. You had me going there."

"It was a good night, it really was."

He nodded. How many in the world could hear all this and be as accepting of it? Outside her family and mental health workers, Books was the first person she had ever talked to about her illness.

"What was it like, Em? How can anyone think they're dead?"

"I can't really tell you. I suppose I had thoughts. My brain was still able to function. But I don't think I had any feelings. No emotions. I couldn't really feel pain. Human touch was a bit funny for me. Numb or something. It never really felt like anything. So what was I meant to think? In a weird way, believing myself to be dead wasn't so far wrong. I mean, I wasn't alive. Not really. Not the way you are now."

Books took it all in.

"Well, bugger me," he said at last.

She took his forearm and bit it, hard enough to leave a mark.

"Dying is when you can't feel that?"

He bit her arm, but gently. Something that had been between them slid away so completely that, for both of them, it was hard to remember what it ever felt like. Books's face looked two shades brighter. Emily felt different herself, and the cuddles turned into foreplay, and the foreplay turned into lovemaking. Making. Love.

They didn't make love on the floor, they used the sofa. And it was not bitey-passionate and wordless as she'd imagined it could be, but it was tender, committed and heartfelt. It was perfect for the moment.

She'd spoken the truth and they were making love. She'd spoken the truth about her illness and they were lying on her sofa making love. She could not believe her good fortune.

When they were done, they laughed and ate ready meals. Books drank beer and Emily sipped miniscule amounts from his can. They cuddled, mostly without words, for half an hour or more. Books was lovely, but she could also see that he was taken aback by her Cotard's. She didn't blame him. Anyone would be. It's not a small deal for anyone. It probably didn't help him to remember that two days ago, his new girlfriend killed one person and made a real mess of three others. That wasn't your classic feminine love gambit.

"Books," she said, "I think maybe you need an evening off. Time to yourself. Think about everything. It's a lot to take in. I know that and it's ok."

He started to protest, but she wasn't having it and he pretty soon saw that what she was saying made sense. He was nice about the way he did it, but he was happy enough to leave.

She saw him to the door.

There was one more thing that she thought about saying. She almost said it to him on the front doorstep. But she didn't. Only when he was in his car, and waving at her, and off down the road and out of sight, did she let herself say it.

"And, my dear Books, there is one other thing. I think it's possible that I'm falling in love with you."

That sounded so good, she said it again.

"I'm falling in love with you." The nicest words on Planet Normal.

-49-

Emily's to do list was not quite done. Almost, but not quite. One more call to make. Mum and Dad were both at home and she told her mother three times that she'd already eaten, then drove on round.

A strange feeling, this. There had been so many varieties of strange over the last few weeks, but this was a whole new one. Anticipation. That's what shrinks would call it when working through their list of feelings. Anticipation, Emily. You are thinking forward to an event in your future. You aren't yet sure how that event will turn out. There is a range of possible outcomes. Some good, some bad, some mixed. The feeling associated with that state is called 'Anticipation'.

She tried to review things. For the last few weeks she'd been working on a case where a little six-tear-old girl had her head smashed in by one of those monster Belfast sinks. You know the sort. You may even have one in your kitchen. The rustic look. Expensive. Anyway, this girl had the top of her head obliterated by a large chunk of kitchen ceramics, leaving just her little mouth to smile at Emily. And smile she did. For most of the last three weeks, She'd had that little girl's picture up on her wall or on her screensaver, or both. Haunted her, you could say, only it was a very nice haunting. She liked it. Invited it, in fact. And just to be clear, it was the dead girl who haunted her. She was afraid to say it, but the live one never interested her all that much. Now, she felt like the little dead girl had something to teach her and she just wasn't getting it, so she decided to spend a night with her in the mortuary. She spent the night with her and her mother, who was dead as well. She learned something very interesting. Something that she needed to discuss with her parents. In a funny way, she thought that conversation may alter the entire way she viewed her own personal history. Possibly in a good way. Possibly not. There may well be a mixed outcome. So she had a feeling inside her now and she thought she wanted to call it Anticipation.

All this was just as it used to be when talking to the doctors. She also used to freak them out without having any idea of what she was doing to make it happen. She often used to end those sessions with the doctor telling me that her medication needed to be 'adjusted' in order to make her more comfortable. Roughly translated that meant they were going to increase the dosage of whatever she was on to make themselves feel more comfortable. At least once, and maybe more than once, she ended up being 'restrained' by two burly psychiatric nurses as the doctor administered a sedative by injection. The funny thing was, you'd think that someone would go into mental health because they enjoyed working with the mentally ill, but she realised that wasn't it at all. Most of them, apart from the actual saints, seemed to have entered the profession because they hated mental illness. Hated it and wanted to punish it.

Once she'd worked all this out she used to go into those sessions and deliberately mess with their heads. Yank their chains. She'd say outrageous stuff that would upset them, but at the same time be careful not to say or do nothing that would allow them to get out their needles or prescription pads. She started to get legalistic on them as well. Researched her rights under the law and started to challenge them about whether something they wanted to do was legitimate under whatever paragraph of the Mental Health Act. She was bolshie and argumentative.

Her father never had a brilliant relationship with authority figures either, so he loved to join in. She bonded more closely with him because of that.

Yet, she had to say those doctors gave her something. Concepts and techniques she still used today.

She drove up outside her parents' house and braked to a halt. Selected neutral. Engaged handbrake. Ignition off. Listened to the engine die. Breathed in and out a few times and repeated. Anticipation.

-50-

Mum said, "I didn't cook, because I know you said you'd eaten, so I just thought I'd put out a few bits, in case you wanted to pick."

Sausages, potato salad, tomatoes, lettuce, coleslaw, salamis, cold ham, French rolls, cheese, pickles and bottled beer.

Dad looked at the spread and his eyes widened. Kay and Ant arrived to share the feast. Everyone present had already eaten, but Mum was the only one not to pick her way through a whole lot more. Before too long, Kay got half a chocolate cake from the fridge, and she and Ant started to mine into its defences and soon left it pretty much ruined. Everyone talked about their own thing, and nobody cared much that no one was listening too closely.

The clock ticked to nine. Ant's bedtime, and the signal for Mum to settle down with her box set.

Emily said, "Mum, Dad, do you think I can have a chat with you?"

Kay's eyes widened. Whatever it was, she wanted to be part of this, but Emily told her it was private, if she didn't mind. She did mind, but not so much that couldn't be persuaded to go to her bedroom, and spend the next two hours talking to her friends by phone, text and other means.

That left Emily, Mum and Dad alone in the kitchen. They'd clearly moved into some new social-emotional territory and Mum's instincts were slightly confused. For her, any new territory of this sort needed to be marked by the production of something edible, but they'd all just gorged ourselves on a second supper and even Mum couldn't quite bring herself to do the same all over again. She compromised by making tea. Dad rushed off to get port, whisky, brandy, Cointreau and some noxious looking Italian liqueur the name of which he couldn't pronounce and which he couldn't wait to try out on someone. Since he knew Emily was practically tea-total, that person was unlikely to be her, but he liked creating a show anyway. And the glasses looked nice.

Eventually the chatter was over. Mum and Emily shared herbal tea. Dad had a mug of builder's tea alongside a tiny glass of that Italian stuff.

Emily fetched a photo from the hallway next door. A recent one of all of them.

"I think it's time we came clean with each other. Time you came clean with me. It's ok. I'm ready for it. Really. I'd prefer it."

They looked at each other. They were worried, but she was pretty sure they knew what she was talking about. She saw that she needed to nudge a bit more.

"I've been spending some time with this little girl I came across because of work. The cutest little thing, a real smasher. Anyway, I came to realise that she had something. She was her mother's daughter. That sounds so stupid, doesn't it? But the mother had this unbelievably troubled life. I won't go into it all, but it wasn't easy. And she made huge efforts to keep her daughter with her. The authorities wanted to take the little girl into care, but the mother always fought back. She wanted her daughter to have a better life than she did. In the end, she wasn't entirely successful, but she tried. She gave it her all.

Anyway, as time went by, I felt increasingly sure that this little girl had something to teach me. Something really obvious, as it turned out. I felt the little girl was telling me that I wasn't my mother's daughter. Nor my father's. That little girl had a terribly difficult life, but all the same she had one thing that I didn't."

She held up the photo.

Dad was tall. Mum was tall. Kay was tall, slim and gorgeous. Ant was racing upwards. And that left Emily. The over intelligent, fish out of water.

"It's so obvious really. I'm not like you at all. Not physically, and not in so many other ways too. Don't get me wrong. I love you both so much, and Kay and Ant. This family is by far the best thing that ever happened to me. But I need to know where I came from. Maybe I wasn't ready before. But I am now. I'd like to know."

She didn't say it, and wouldn't, but there was more to her intuition than April's insistent hints. It was the thing that Lev said as well. And Axelsen and Wikipedia.

She'd been in shock for most of her life. She'd ticked almost every box. Indeed, if you think of her Cotard's as being simply the most extreme, the most extravagant form of depersonalization going, then you could argue she'd also suffered from the most extreme, the most extravagant form of shock going. When it came to her mental life, she'd seldom done things by half.

The only problem with this hypothesis was the single box left unticked. The one that absolutely had to be ticked. The event. The traumatic or terrifying event. The event that never happened.

What she'd said to Lev was true. She knew that her family was safe. No physical or sexual abuse. No alcoholism. No hint of divorce. Very few marital arguments. No threat from outside. No dodgy uncles. No assaults on her from strangers. No family could have been safer. Dad's money, his energy, his reputation were walls thicker than concrete. Any hypothetical evil-doers would have preferred to mess with virtually anybody else rather than make an enemy of her Dad. There was almost nothing he couldn't get done if he minded. All her life, she'd been as safe as anyone can wish to be. All her life, for as far back as she could remember.

And, of course, his role with the nation's elite little band made things doubly safe for Emily. And now, deeply and anonymously, embedded into the police for Operation Lohan and what had sprouted from it, she'd taken the first steps to becoming part of that scene. Books was a real bonus, of course. And so was love for anybody outside her family. And she knew she was in love.

But traumatic events can reach far back into the past. Further than childhood. Further than memory. What happened in the first year or two of her life? Why could she recall her childhood only through a fog of forgetting? Why did her Cotard's stalk out of nowhere to ruin her teenage years? Why did she sometimes wake with night terrors so vivid that she was drenched in sweat and lie, lights on, awake and staring, through the rest of the night, sooner than risk going back to whatever it was that visited her in her dreams?

She didn't say these things out loud, and she would never say them to these two people who had loved her so dearly, but it was time for answers and they knew it.

They looked across the table at each other. Dad put his hand on Mum's and rubbed it briefly. Then he got up.

"One moment, love."

He left the room and Mum and Emily were left alone with the ticking clock. A ticking clock in a silent room. She smiled at Emily. A brave, uncertain smile and Emily smiled back. She felt ok. The anticipation she felt before had quietened down. She wasn't quite sure what she felt now. Or to be precise, she was in touch with the feeling, but didn't have a word for it. It was like a melting inside. It was not a bad feeling. She didn't mind it. She just didn't know what it was. She didn't think that even her doctors could give this one a name.

Dad returned and he was carrying things. A photo and an old plastic shopping bag. He sat at the table, smiled at Emily and Mum and then back at Emily. The clock ticked too loudly in the silence. They were all nervous. It was as though the room itself, the empty space, the entire house was in a state of anticipation. The doctors would probably have told her off for saying that. They'd say that empty space can't have feelings. But they'd never sat as she was doing now. They'd never known what it was like for the whole of one's life to sit trembling on the cusp.

Dad showed her the photo, passed it over. It was a photo of Emily aged about two and a half. Pink dress. White bow. Tidy hair. Shy smile. A small white teddy bear. She'd never seen this photo before, but she recognized the car she was sitting in. It was Dad's old Jaguar convertible. The roof was down. The day looked reasonably sunny. She couldn't see enough of the street to tell where it was. She had no reason to think there was anything odd about the photo at all.

"Emily, love. That photo was taken with this camera here."

He took it from the bag and passed it across the table. A small brown camera in a leather case, with a leather neck strap attached. It looked reasonably old.

"And we found the camera the same day as we found you. We'd just gone to church and when we came out, there was the car, just as we'd left it, only with a little miracle inside. You. We came out and there you were. Sitting in our car with this camera around your neck. When we had the film inside the camera developed, there was just this photo. A photo of you. There was not note, no nothing. Just this amazing little girl in the back of our car."

Emily heard all this. It made no sense at all and it made perfect sense at one and the same time. It was like that moment in a theatre where one stage set is revolving in from the left as the last one is disappearing on the right. You see both things at the same time. See them in their entirety. Understand them. But you also know that one thing is replacing the other. That the thing is about to disappear, never to show itself again.

"You say you found me? You just came out and you found me?"

"Yes. Your Mum and I wanted children. We love the little bleeders, don't we, Kath? But we'd had troubles conceiving. I don't know why. The two girls upstairs both arrived in the ordinary manner. But anyway. We came out of the church. We'd have been praying about it. We always did. And there you were. Thank you, Jesus. The answer to our prayers. Honestly. Our own little miracle. And not even the crying, puking sort. The Good Lord had got you through all that, sent you to us clean and sweet and nice to meet. Even your own little teddy bear."

"Of course…" Mum said, uncomfortable with Dad's implication that they just drove off with me.

"Yes. Your Mum's right. We had to tell someone, so we did. If your real Mum and Dad had shown up, we'd have handed you over. We wouldn't have liked it. Wouldn't have wanted to. We fell in love with you straight away. I mean, the very instant. But we'd have done right by you. If your Mum and Dad had come looking for you, we'd have handed you straight back."

Mum then started to tell her more. The adoption process. How it was "you know, a bit complicated, what with your father and all."

An understatement, Emily thought. Dad's reputation was such that the adoption authorities would have been loath to hand a child over just like that. But then again, when her Dad wanted something he generally managed to get it. By hook or by crook.

Emily was listening to Mum talking, but she wasn't interested in the adoption process. She was interested in herself.

"How old was I?"

Dad shrugged. "No one knows. At the time, we guessed, maybe two and a half. We were just going by height, but you've never been the tallest lass, have you love, so maybe we were a bit out. Perhaps you were older."

"Didn't you ask me?"

"Oh, love. We asked you everything. Where your Mum and Dad were. Where you lived. What your name was. How old you were. Everything."

"And"?

"Nothing. You wouldn't speak for eighteen months. You understood things all right. You were a sharp little thing even then. And we had you tested and poked at and all that. They couldn't find anything wrong with you. Not a sausage. And then one day, you just started speaking. You said, "Mum, can I have some more cheese, please?"

Something inside Emily had changed. The scene shift was complete. She couldn't see or feel the old world any more. This new world was now hers. It made no sense. It raised a million questions. About who she was, where she came from, how she came to be in Dad's car, why she couldn't speak or wouldn't. About those two or three missing years. About what happened in that time that stored up such trouble for her future life.

And yet all of that didn't matter, or not this minute it didn't.

Dad took the last few things out of his bag. The pink dress with the white bow. The teddy bear. A hair grip. A pair or shiny black shoes with some white knee socks tucked into them. He passed them over the table to her.

Emily's past. Her mysterious past. The only clues she had. And even as she buried her head to smell the dress, she knew that those things didn't matter either. What mattered now was what was happening inside her. An old barrier had gone. Vanished. It had been extinguished.

And then she knew. She knew what was happening. These were tears and she was crying.

It wasn't a painful sensation, as she always thought it must be. It felt like the purest form of expression of feeling that it is possible to have. And the feeling mixed everything up together. Happiness. Sadness. Relief. Sorrow. Love. A mixture of things no psychiatrist ever felt. It was the most wonderful mixture in the world.

She put her hands to her face again and again. Tears were coursing down her cheeks, splashing off her chin, tickling the side of her nose, running off her hands.

These were tears and she was crying. She was Emily. Paid up citizen of Planet Normal.

-51-

What would it cost?" she had asked herself at the outset, "to give a girl back her life? The girl who couldn't tremble because she came without a name, looking for meaning and something, somebody to hold her together."

She understood now that Love had caught these fragments, swirled them through the winds of night and delivered. Love had delivered her a special family. Her saviour. Her redemption. It was also in the process of delivering Books. Her very own Books. Her own choice of love.

These were the first stones in her new jar. The search was almost over, and yet it was only just beginning.

L - #0122 - 200521 - C0 - 210/148/24 - PB - DID3093407